Winter's Orphan

Katie Flynn is the pen name of the much-loved writer, Judy Turner, who published over ninety novels in her lifetime. Judy's unique stories were inspired by hearing family recollections of life in Liverpool during the early twentieth century, and her books went on to sell more than eight million copies. Judy passed away in January 2019, aged eighty-two.

The legacy of Katie Flynn lives on through her daughter, Holly Flynn, who continues to write under the Katie Flynn name. Holly worked as an assistant to her mother for many years and together they co-authored a number of Katie Flynn novels.

Holly lives in the north east of Wales with her husband Simon and their two children. When she's not writing she enjoys walking her two lurchers, Tara and Sparky, in the surrounding countryside, and cooking forbidden foods such as pies, cakes and puddings! She looks forward to sharing many more Katie Flynn stories, which she and her mother devised together, with readers in the years to come.

Keep up to date with all her latest news on Facebook: Katie Flynn Author

Also available by Katie Flynn

Available by Katie Flynn writing as Judith Saxton

KATIE FLYNN

Winter's Orphan

PENGUIN BOOKS

PENGUIN BOOKS

UK | USA | Canada | Ireland | Australia
India | New Zealand | South Africa

Penguin Books is part of the Penguin Random House group of companies
whose addresses can be found at global.penguinrandomhouse.com

First published by Century in 2023
Published in Penguin Books 2023
001

Copyright © Katie Flynn, 2023

The moral right of the author has been asserted

Typeset in 10.3 pt/14.15 pt Palatino LT Pro
Printed and bound in Great Britain by Clays Ltd, Elcograf S.p.A.

The authorised representative in the EEA is Penguin Random House Ireland,
Morrison Chambers, 32 Nassau Street, Dublin D02 YH68

A CIP catalogue record for this book is available from the British Library

ISBN: 978-1-804-94243-7

www.greenpenguin.co.uk

Penguin Random House is committed to a
sustainable future for our business, our readers
and our planet. This book is made from Forest
Stewardship Council® certified paper.

To our darling Snoopy who will never be forgotten

Prologue

Libby Gilbert spluttered as the icy water of the River Thames gushed into her open mouth. As the murky liquid slid down her throat, her outstretched arms floundered above her head in a desperate attempt to find something to hold on to, but the current was too powerful, and the banks of the Thames slipped past her fingers before she could find a purchase. As her head sank below the water, Libby felt sure that her time was up, until she heard a large splash and a hand with a vice-like grip grabbed hold of her. Fearful that the hand might belong to her aggressor, she tried to fight it off, but its owner was too strong, and within seconds it had hauled her onto the bank.

Gasping for breath, she looked up at her saviour, but instead of locking eyes with a man hell-bent on revenge, she found herself gazing at a young man with curly dark hair and green eyes which twinkled kindly.

Seeing the anxiety in her face, her saviour took a step back, his hands held up in a submissive gesture. 'It's all right, Treacle. Jack Durning ain't gonna hurt yer.' Seeing a cut above her eye, he leaned forward with his hand outstretched. 'You appear to have taken a lump out of yer noggin.'

As she scrambled to her feet, she attempted to scrape her hair, now plastered to her face, away from her eyes. Speaking through chattering teeth, she mumbled her appreciation. 'Thanks for rescuin' me, Jack, but I'm all right.'

Jack eyed her studiously, his face full of concern. 'Pardon me for sayin', but you don't look it.'

She followed his gaze from her soaking wet frock, torn and muddy, to her bare feet, which were covered in cuts and bruises. 'I've lost me shoes,' she said. It was a fib, but she'd rather he believed she'd lost them in the water than explain why she had been running through the streets of London without any.

To her relief, Jack jerked his head in the direction of the river. 'I expect they came off when you went in the water, but you can't walk round barefoot—' He was interrupted by the distant thrum of heavy bombers making their way towards them, and held his hand out to her. 'C'mon, we'd best get us to safety before it's too late.'

Scared that her aggressor might still be nearby, she shook her head. 'Don't worry about me, I'll be fine.' She took a step forward and yelped as one of the many cuts on the soles of her feet hit the cobbled road.

Jack strode towards her in a no-nonsense manner, and scooped her up into his arms. 'Sorry, miss, but I wouldn't consider meself to be much of a gent if I left you in this state, with the Luftwaffe droppin' bombs willy-nilly.'

Ordinarily, Libby would've objected to such an assumption of authority, but she knew that he was right. If she didn't get to a shelter soon, her assailant – wherever he might be – could prove to be the least of her problems. With tears slowly trickling down her cheeks, she felt Jack's arms tighten around her as he quickened his pace.

Ducking through the doorway of one of London's many public shelters, Jack ignored the ARP warden, who'd given a short exclamation on seeing the two of them soaked to the skin, and took Libby to the back of the shelter to sit her down on one of the benches that lined the walls. 'Wait there, miss, whilst I get you a dry blanket.'

'My name's Libby,' mumbled Libby as she hugged her knees close to her chest. Glancing up at him through wet black lashes, she saw that he was smiling kindly at her.

'Right you are, Libby. I'll just have a quick word with me dad – he's the one what's mindin' the door – but I'll be right back after that.'

As more people entered the shelter Libby kept her head down in case any of them turned out to be the man from whom she had been trying to escape. Watching from under downturned lids, she could see Jack talking quietly to the warden, who kept throwing her sidelong glances. It was obvious that they were discussing her, and it seemed that Jack was having to reassure his father about her. *He knows*, Libby told herself, *he can tell just by lookin' at me, and he must be tellin' Jack that he doesn't want someone like me in the shelter*. At last Jack broke away from his father, and Libby watched as he took a couple of blankets from under one of the benches and made his way towards her. She thanked him for the blankets and proceeded to wrap one of them around her, making sure she kept a small peephole so that she could see who was entering the shelter.

Hoping to learn something about the dark-haired beauty whom he had just rescued from the Thames, Jack tried to engage her in conversation. 'Me dad was wonderin' what you were doin' in the river in the depths of winter?' Anxious that he should not appear too nosy, he winked at her before continuing in a

3

light-hearted fashion, 'Surely you must've realised it's not safe to go swimmin' durin' an air raid?'

She was about to reply when the curtain flap covering the door opened, and the man from whom Libby had been fleeing entered. Her heart in her mouth, she watched as he scanned the room, and feeling trapped like a rat she turned pleading eyes to Jack. 'Please don't let him see me.'

In answer, Jack settled down on the bench next to her and slid his arm around her shoulders, pulling her into his chest. 'Don't you worry yer head none. If he says owt, I'll say you're with me.'

Libby whispered, 'Thank you,' whilst keeping a keen eye on the mutton-chopped man in his mid-sixties who was now sitting heavily on the bench nearest the door. Scratching his throat, his eyes travelled over the occupants of the shelter before settling on Libby, and Jack felt her stiffen under his gaze. Sensing her fear, he coughed into his fist before addressing the individual by way of explanation. 'Me girlfriend's scared of the bombs, and who can blame her?'

The man gave a small grunt as his eyes flickered to Jack. Apparently losing interest, he drew a watch from his pocket, flipped the case open, then closed it again before pushing the watch back into his trousers.

Jack's father, Gordon, took the seat opposite the man. He had no idea why his son was choosing to make up lies, but he knew it must have something to do with the girl. Keen to keep the older man's attention away from Jack and Libby, he said in a conversational tone, 'I was hopin' we'd seen the last of the Jerries for one night.'

The man pulled a disgruntled face. 'Not with my luck.'

Gordon eyed him inquisitively. 'Oh?'

The man glanced back in Libby's direction. 'I got robbed by some tart, just as the first siren sounded.'

4

Huddling closer to Jack, Libby whispered, 'I didn't mean to.'

Keeping his arm firmly around her, Jack pulled a disbelieving face. 'She must've been pretty feisty to get the better of a gentleman like yerself! Or did she pick yer pocket?'

The man started to shake his head before changing his mind and nodding instead. 'Dirty little bilge rat 'ad it away on 'er toes before you could say "knife!"' His eyes narrowed. 'I chased 'er as far as the docks, but I lost sight of 'er after that.'

Gordon tore his gaze away from Libby, hoping the older man would do the same. 'Some things are more important than money. You should be grateful you got in here before they started droppin' bombs.'

'I'll wring 'er flamin' neck if I get me 'ands on 'er,' the older man growled. He turned his attention away from Gordon, back to Libby. 'Pretendin' to be all nice, then runnin' off with me money. There's a name for women like that.'

Not wanting to hear what might come out of the man's mouth next, Jack tried to change the course of the conversation. 'Maybe she was desperate.'

The man spluttered indignantly. 'What the 'ell do you mean by that?'

Gordon, who was keen to keep things from getting too heated, cut in swiftly. 'The lad didn't mean anythin' by it. He was only suggestin' that she nicked yer money out of desperation.'

'I couldn't give a toss how desperate she was,' grumbled the older man. 'You don't rob someone before . . .'

Jack stared at him. 'Before what?'

Having said more than he'd intended, the man brought the conversation to a close. 'What's important is she took what wasn't 'ers to take, and if I find the filthy little wretch, I'll take what I'm owed.'

Libby turned tear-brimmed eyes to Jack. 'It's not how it sounds . . .' she whispered.

He gave her shoulders a reassuring squeeze, before hissing, 'Wait until they sound the all-clear; you can speak freely then.'

Libby lowered her head. Speaking freely wasn't going to be easy – not considering everything she'd just been through.

Chapter One

Libby took a large bite of her apple as she made her way from her parents' furniture and bric-a-brac stall in Petticoat Lane to the house they rented on Whitechapel Road. Britain had been at war with the Germans for the best part of a year, though they'd seen little sign of action as yet, and with people christening it the phoney war Libby and her parents were beginning to think that Hitler wasn't going to bother attacking north of the English Channel.

'They bit off more'n they could chew in the first lot,' her father Reggie had assured her. 'They won't make the same mistake twice!'

Libby's mother, Orla, was quick to agree with her husband. 'He tries bombin' us and it'll be the biggest mistake of his life. Us Brits won't roll over like the rest of 'em.'

Libby had eyed her parents dubiously. 'What about Dunkirk?'

'We rescued our boys—' Orla had begun proudly, before being interrupted by her daughter.

'They shouldn't have needed rescuin'.' Then, hesitant in case she might upset her parents, Libby continued candidly, 'We might not have rolled over, but we did run away . . .'

Reggie scowled at his daughter from over the top of his newspaper. 'We didn't run away.' Disappearing behind the pages again, he continued stiffly, 'It was a tactical manoeuvre so that we could regroup.'

That conversation had taken place several weeks earlier, and as there was still no sign of Hitler's invading Britain, Libby had begun to think that her parents had been right.

Now, as she turned off Middlesex Street onto Goulston Street, she nearly collided with Mrs Fortescue, who lived on the same street.

The old woman grinned toothily. 'Hello, Libby luv. You on yer way home?'

'I certainly am, Mrs F.,' said Libby pleasantly.

'I hope Pete's not packed up for the evenin',' said Mrs Fortescue. 'I forgot to get carrots when I went shoppin' earlier.'

'He's still there,' Libby assured her. 'You know Pete, he won't call it a day until the streets are deserted!'

It was the last week of her summer holidays, and Libby was going to miss the camaraderie of the other traders. She simply adored market life; so much so, she had even suggested to her father that she might pack school in so that she could help him out permanently, but Reggie had been adamant that he wanted better for his daughter.

'Me and yer mum work hard to make sure you have a good future, and that you don't have to stand behind a market stall in all weathers,' had been his reply. 'You may think it's fun in the summertime, when the sun's shinin', but I've noticed you're not so keen come Christmas when the snow's thick on the ground.'

'But trading's in me blood,' Libby had insisted.

'Only cos you know no different,' retorted Reggie. 'If you get yerself a decent education, you'll be able to work yerself out of this hellhole, maybe even meet a decent man whilst you're about it.'

Libby wrinkled the side of her nose in a reproving fashion. 'If a penpusher is your idea of a decent man, they're nowt but stuck up snobs, who wouldn't look twice at a girl like me.'

'They would if you had yerself a good job, though,' Reggie pointed out.

'This *is* a good job,' argued Libby. 'Everythin' we own has been paid for by the sweat of our brow, if that ain't decent I don't know what is.' She held up a finger as her father tried to object. 'It's better than bein' a landlord. They've got loads of money, and they mix in higher circles than what we do, but you wouldn't want me to marry one of them, would you?'

Reggie knew that his daughter was referring to their own landlord, with whom he'd had many an argument regarding the lack of repairs to the property they rented. 'You marry the like of him and you'll be puttin' me in an early grave,' he muttered, 'pompous, stuck up . . .'

Having proved her point, Libby pressed on. 'Supposin' I get meself a job in some swanky office, and by some miracle the boss's son proposes to me; what do you think his parents would say when they find out who I am, and where I'm from? Not to mention the fact that my folks work down Petticoat Lane.'

'Middlesex Street,' sniffed Reggie, but Orla was quick to intervene.

'It'll always be Petticoat Lane to them that know it.'

'Because they steal yer petticoat down one end and sell it back to you the other,' giggled Libby, much to her father's annoyance.

'Maybe a long time ago, but that's not been the case for years,' he said, somewhat woodenly.

Orla frowned at her husband. 'In Liverpool they call a spade a spade.'

'Well, you're not in Liverpool any more,' said Reggie, adding, 'and you needn't pretend that all Scousers are saints.'

'I'm not sayin' they are,' Orla protested. 'What I was *trying* to say is we are what we are, and Libby's right, we shouldn't try to be any different.'

Reggie scowled at his wife. 'Whose side are you on?'

'Ours,' cried Orla. 'You, me and Libby.' She held up her hands in a placating fashion. 'I know you want what's best for Libby, as do I, but tryin' to force her to be summat she ain't isn't the way to do it.'

'Then what's the point in us workin' all the hours God sends?'

'To own our own home,' said Orla. 'Somewhere we don't have to live in permanent fear that the landlord's goin' to chuck us out cos he's havin' a bad day.'

Libby tagged on to her mother's line of thought. 'We could even own our own shop,' she said excitedly. 'Just think, Dad, no more standin' on the streets whilst the heavens throw what they may at you.'

Up until that point Reggie had been adamant that he was in the right, but he found the idea of running his own shop most appealing. He rubbed his chin thoughtfully. 'A shop, you say?'

Libby's eyes twinkled as she spoke. 'That'd be one in the eye for Mr Gibbs, don't you think?'

'It'd be more expensive than a stall, but if we could get a flat above a shop that would be two birds, one stone . . .' He paused. 'But we'd never be able to afford anythin' in London, mind you.'

'If we had our own shop we could go anywhere,' said Libby. She turned to her mother. 'Was it expensive to live in Liverpool?'

Her mother spoke vehemently. 'I am *not* going back to Liverpool.'

Libby's enthusiasm left her. 'Why not? I thought you loved it there.'

Orla eyed her daughter irritably. 'I did, but . . .' She turned beseeching eyes to her husband, who came to her rescue.

'We're not going back to Liverpool. Now let that be an end to the matter.'

Disappointed that her mother refused to go back to the city of her birth, Libby was quick to come up with an alternative. 'We could move to Ireland. That way me and Emma could stay together!'

Her father pulled a rueful face. 'Sorry, luv, no can do. Emma's family are Irish, so it's different for them.'

Libby glanced in her mother's direction. 'But Mum's Irish . . .'

Orla laughed. 'Your grandparents are Irish, but not me. I was born in Liverpool.'

Determined to find an answer, Libby turned to her father. 'So, how about Norwich? That's where Grandma and Grandpa Gilbert came from.'

Reggie appeared deep in thought as he perused the possibilities. Norwich would certainly be a lot cheaper than London, and with his knowledge of the area . . . He reached a conclusion. 'I s'pose it couldn't harm to make a few enquiries.'

Orla sank slowly on to her husband's lap. 'It would be wonderful to move away from London, Reg. And seein' as we've been savin' our money, I should think we'd soon have enough to put down as a deposit.'

'We'll have even more once we've sold the business,' said Reggie, who was beginning to get into the swing of things. 'That's got to be worth a bob or two.' He snapped his fingers. 'I could sell it to our Tony.'

Orla's mood changed instantly, something which could be seen by her reproving face. 'Couldn't you find someone else?'

'I know you don't like him,' said Reggie, 'but he's always been keen to get his hands on the stall, and I know he'd give us a good price.'

'No, he wouldn't,' said Orla tartly, 'he'd guilt you into letting him have it for half the price, and even then he'd want to pay in instalments. And we'd not receive another penny, once we moved, cos he knows there's bugger all you could do about it once you're out of London.'

Reggie rolled his eyes. 'You make our Tony sound like a spiv.'

'He is!' cried Libby, much to the amusement of her mother. 'Little Millie Dowling's mum said he sold her a half leg of lamb last week, and you can only get stuff like that off the spivs . . .'

Reggie's eyes boggled. 'For Gawd's sake, don't you go repeatin' that to anyone else, or we'll have the Bluebottles buzzin' round, wantin' to check our stock.'

Orla shot her husband a chiding glance. 'The scuffers can come around all they want, cos we ain't got nothin' to hide . . .' Her voice faded when she saw the dark look in her husband's eyes. 'Oh Reggie . . .'

Placing a hand over his forehead, Reggie barked at Libby to go to her room, but Libby wasn't going anywhere. 'I'm sixteen. You can't send me to my room.'

'I can jolly well do as I please,' snapped Reggie, but Libby was resolute.

'I need to know if I'm handlin' dodgy goods, so that I don't slip up should the Bluebottles come sniffin' . . .'

Reggie rested his chin on steepled fingers whilst speaking in a slow, deliberate fashion. 'It's not illegal, as per se; and seein' as how everyone needs a sneaky snifter to keep their pecker up, I don't see the harm . . .'

Her eyes widening, Orla interrupted her husband without apology. 'You're selling hard *liquor*?'

Reggie winked, tapping the side of his nose in a conspiratorial fashion. 'Nope, I'm sellin' vases . . .' he hesitated before adding, 'very expensive vases.'

Orla held her hand up, silencing her husband. 'I don't want to know, but I will say this: whatever you've got you can get rid of it. I will *not* see my husband go down for dealin' on the black market. We'd never live it down if the neighbours found out.'

Reggie mugged sheepishly. 'It's the neighbours what are buyin' it.'

Libby burst into laughter, before hastily pinching her nose in a bid to stifle her mirth. Orla shot her daughter a chiding glance before turning her attention back to her husband. 'Our Libby needs a good role model, so that she doesn't end up acting like her father.' Muttering 'God help me' beneath her breath, she left the room to put the kettle on.

Libby made sure that her mother was out of earshot before pulling the door to the kitchen to. Settling into the fireside chair opposite her father's, she asked the question uppermost in her thoughts. 'Why doesn't Mum want to go back to Liverpool?'

Reggie lowered his voice, keeping an eye on the kitchen door. 'Families,' he said simply. 'Yer mother doesn't exactly see eye to eye with hers.'

'Why not?'

Reggie smoothed his hair down. 'Gawd knows. Your grandparents were very strict, but it didn't seem to be a problem until you came along. That's when everythin' changed, next thing I knew we was movin' to London.'

'But there must've been a reason?'

He shrugged. 'If there is, then I don't know about it. I've tried askin' but yer mother sends me off with a flea in me ear.'

'I know we don't see much of them – in fact I can't remember ever seein' my aunt,' Libby considered, 'but I thought that it was mainly down to the distance.'

Reggie leaned forward, keen to not be overheard by his wife. 'Families are strange things; you've only got to see what yer mum's like with yer uncle.'

'There's no love lost there,' agreed Libby, adding, 'although it does seem a tad rich that Mum doesn't tar you with the same brush as Uncle Tony, considerin' you're both sellin' stuff you oughtn't.'

'That's because she loves me,' chuckled Reggie.

'She doesn't love Uncle Tony, then?'

Reggie emitted a strange gurgling noise from the back of his throat. 'Most definitely not, which is why she doesn't want him to have the stall.'

'Do you think she'll change her mind?'

Reggie's eyes widened. 'I think she'd sooner sell it to Hitler.'

Libby giggled. 'She must really hate Uncle Tony.'

'It started when we first moved to London,' mused Reggie. 'I'm not sure what happened to change things, but they haven't really spoken since then. I know from the way she's fallen out with her own family that there's no talkin' to her once she's made her mind up about summat, so I left her get on with it.'

Libby narrowed her eyes as she gazed at her father. 'I find it hard to imagine Mum fallin' out with anyone. She's so easy-goin'.'

'I know, but like they say, you can't choose yer family, and for whatever reason, yer mum's not keen on hers.'

'It's a shame, considering he's yer only brother, but maybe it explains why he's a bit standoffish with me . . .'

She stopped speaking as her father cut across her. 'He is? I never knew that.'

'Oh, yes. I suppose he tars me with the same brush as Mum, which is daft, because I don't hold anythin' against him.'

Annoyed, Reggie spoke through thinned lips. 'He's old enough to know better, but havin' said that, maybe havin' no kiddies of his own means he's never really grown up, which could be another reason as to why yer mother's taken against him.'

'Maybe,' said Libby, 'but even so, I'd rather we sold it to Uncle Tony, cos at least we'd be keepin' it in the family.'

'My thoughts precisely,' said Reggie. 'All we have to do now is persuade yer mother.'

NOVEMBER 1940

For the past three months, the city of London had been under attack from the Luftwaffe, and they were showing no sign of letting up. After careful deliberation regarding the pros and cons of a new life in Norwich, Libby's parents had come to the conclusion that they needed to get out of London as soon as possible, and, whilst previously reluctant to do so, Orla had agreed to selling the market stall to Tony if it meant they could get away sooner.

'He'll use it as a cover to sell black market goods,' she warned her husband as they started the tedious task of packing their possessions into boxes. 'Everyone'll know that yer brother . . .'

'Has kept up the family tradition,' said Reggie, as he examined a teapot which his wife was insisting they took.

Orla tutted her disapproval. 'You make it sound like it's acceptable!'

Reggie placed the teapot down before sliding his arms around his wife's waist and resting his chin on her shoulder. 'I'm only doing . . .' he started, before correcting himself, *'we're* only doing what hundreds of others do.'

'And if hundreds of others jumped off a cliff, would you do that too?' chided Orla. Reggie chuckled, much to her annoyance. 'It's not funny, Reggie! If you get caught . . .'

'Only I won't,' Reggie insisted. 'Because when we get to Norwich, I shall do everythin' by the book.'

'Good,' replied his wife, adding somewhat sullenly, 'and it better stay that way.'

He kissed the top of her head before turning his attention back to the tea set. 'But just so we're clear, do you honestly think the likes of Mrs Winthorpe would turn her nose up at a punnet of grapes, if offered?'

Orla imagined the other woman in her mind's eye. She would walk down the middle of the market, holier than thou, but word had it her stockings were made from wartime silk. 'Possibly not,' she conceded reluctantly.

'Definitely not,' said Reggie. 'She might be married to the church warden, but she ain't no angel.'

'I can't wait for us to move in,' said Libby. She had been looking at the photograph of the small flat they would be occupying in Elm Hill.

'Fingers crossed it will be a lot safer there than it is here,' said Orla. 'From what I've heard they've not been bombed since the summer.'

'So, what's happening with the stuff from the stall? Surely we aren't takin' it with us?'

Reggie gazed at the boxes by his feet. 'Gawd no. I've agreed to sell the remainin' stock to our Tony.'

Orla sniffed her contempt. 'I hope to goodness people don't associate us with him.'

'That's the whole point in him buyin' the business,' said Reggie. 'Anyone can get a stallholder's permit, but it takes a long time to build a good reputation.'

'And ours will be in tethers by the time *he's* finished with it,' said Orla through pursed lips.

'Will it matter, if we're not coming back?' asked Reggie reasonably.

'Yes! Because that snooty Winthorpe woman will tell everyone "I told you so".'

Reggie chuckled knowingly. 'Not if she wants a slice of the action, she won't.'

'I'm with Dad,' said Libby. 'It shouldn't bother you what other people think, especially when it's highly likely you're never going to see any of them again.'

'I know it shouldn't, but the thought of them thinkin' we're like him gets my dander up.'

'No one likes being judged, love,' Reggie assured her, 'and you shouldn't respect the opinions of those that do it. Cos *you* don't do that to anyone else, certainly not our Tony . . .' He put his tongue into his cheek as a giggle escaped Libby's lips.

Orla shot him a chiding glance before breaking into reluctant laughter. 'It's hard not to judge someone who behaves as badly as he does.'

'We're goin' to be in Norwich just in time for Christmas,' said Libby. 'It'll be a new start, in a new city, with a shop of our very own.'

'Onwards and upwards,' agreed Reggie. He turned to his wife, who was placing newspaper in between the plates she was stacking. 'You'll be so busy with the shop you won't have time to worry about what folks here are saying, and to be honest I don't think this lot'll give us a second thought once we're gone.'

Libby agreed with her father wholeheartedly. 'I know you may not approve, Mum, but Dad's right. The locals won't give a monkey's that we've gone; all they'll care about is whether they can still get the stuff off Uncle Tony the same way as they did Dad.'

Orla glanced at her husband. 'Has yer brother signed the agreement yet?'

Reggie rubbed the back of his neck with the palm of his hand. 'I'm going to take it over later.'

Orla counted to three before responding. 'You shouldn't be so trusting. The longer you leave it the more Tony'll try to use it as leverage to get the price down.'

'Not that you're judging him of course,' chuckled Reggie. He packed the last of the tea set into the box and rubbed his hands together. 'That's me done for today. I'm off to pay the deposit to the solicitors.'

Orla pulled a grim face. 'It seems wrong to me that we're paying for the new place when yer brother hasn't paid us for the business yet.'

Reggie swung his coat around his shoulders and kissed his wife on the cheek. 'You worry about getting our crockery to Norwich in one piece, and leave the rest to me.'

Libby waited until her father had left the room before turning to her mother. 'I know I don't know Uncle Tony that well, but I trust Dad, and if Dad says Uncle Tony'll pay, then I believe him.'

'Yer father doesn't know what his brother's really like,' said Orla guardedly. 'If he did, he'd not be so trusting.'

'Dad's not stupid . . .' Libby began, but was interrupted by her mother.

'I know he's not, love, and even though he sometimes trades in stuff he shouldn't, deep down he's honest, which is more than I can say for yer uncle. The only reason why I'm goin' ahead with yer father's plans is so that we can get away from Tony and start afresh.'

Libby began wrapping the candle holders in newspaper. 'Why do you take against Uncle Tony so, when Dad's not much better?'

Orla pushed her hands through her hair. 'It's just different.'

Libby pulled a face. 'How?'

Orla placed three plates aside for their use. 'We'll need these for our supper.'

With her mother drawing a line under the conversation, Libby turned her thoughts to what her uncle could have done or said to upset her so, but the only explanation she could come up with was that Orla must secretly blame her brother-in-law for leading her husband astray. But if that was the case, then why not just say so? Unwilling to let the matter rest, she said, 'If you really think Uncle Tony's goin' to diddle Dad out of his money, then I think one of us should have a word with him, and seein' as you won't, I will.'

Orla breathed in sharply. 'No! Yer father would go spare if he thought we'd approached his brother behind his back!'

Libby stared at her mother with deep curiosity. 'But if Dad continues to bury his head in the sand, and you truly believe Tony can't be trusted . . .'

Orla covered her face with her hands. 'Don't listen to me. We can't go rockin' the boat now, not when we're so close to leaving.'

'We've still got two weeks to sell the business, and I reckon there'd be a few on the market that would jump at the chance of buyin' a thrivin' concern like ours, especially with our prime spot.'

Orla heaved a weary sigh. 'Yer father would have kittens if he knew you were goin' to confront his brother. Please, luv, just leave it. Two weeks and London will be nowt but a distant memory.'

It was their final day on the market and Libby was taking an inventory of the remaining stock whilst her parents packed the last of their belongings into the removal van.

As she wrote *Queen Anne chairs x 2* a voice called out from behind her. 'I can't believe you're gonna be movin' before us!'

Libby abandoned her pad and pencil to take her oldest friend in a firm embrace. 'I ain't half gonna miss you, Emma Bagshaw,' she sniffed. 'I wish we were goin' to Ireland with you.'

Emma pulled a rueful face. 'Me too! That bloomin' Hitler's got a lot to answer for.'

Libby turned her attention to a potential customer who was eyeing up a bow-fronted writing table. 'My 'ubby reckons it'll all be over come the new year,' said the older woman informatively.

Emma tutted beneath her breath. 'So we could be movin' all the way to Ireland for nowt?'

The woman spoke from over her shoulder as she slowly sauntered towards the next stall. 'I wouldn't say that. After all, you've only got to be unlucky once.'

Emma rolled her eyes. 'Blimey! She's a ray of sunshine.'

Libby gave a half-shoulder shrug. 'She's right, though. Look at poor Steph and her family.'

Emma drew the sign of the cross over her chest. 'Wrong place at the wrong time.'

'Which is why our parents want to move us far away from London,' said Libby plainly.

Emma gazed thoughtfully after the woman moving along the stalls. 'Do you think her hubby's right?'

'I hope so,' replied Libby, 'but my parents didn't think the Krauts would bother crossin' the Channel, so who knows?'

Emma sank down into one of the winged-back armchairs. 'Do you think you'll move back to London when all this is over?'

Even though Emma's question had come as a surprise, Libby thought she knew the answer. 'Not if the shop's a roaring success; and I know it will be with Dad at the helm. What about you?'

Emma rolled her eyes. 'I hope so—' Her words were cut short by the all too familiar sound of the air-raid siren. 'Oh lawks, not again!'

Abandoning the stall, the girls hurried to the nearest public shelter. Craning her neck, Libby hoped to catch sight of her parents, but it had been a busy morning down the market, and as a result the shelter was now jam-packed with shoppers who'd been hoping to grab themselves a bargain.

When the girls had found a place to sit at the back, Emma turned to Libby. 'What a way to spend yer last day.'

'The way things have been lately, I'd have been more surprised had the sirens not sounded,' Libby said glumly.

'It's becomin' the norm,' agreed Emma. 'That's why Dad says we're to sleep in our clothes; it's one less thing to do when Moanin' Minnie goes off at some ungodly hour.'

Libby lowered her voice so that others couldn't hear what she was about to say. 'The sooner we get out of London the better. It's rotten that we won't be together, but I'd rather you were safe.'

'You too,' agreed Emma. She tucked her arm through Libby's. 'Do you suppose we might be able to visit each other?'

Libby looked downcast. 'Sorry, Em, but I can't see them lettin' us get the ferry across to Ireland.'

'Me neither,' said Emma sadly, 'but we can always write, and with our new lives we shan't be short of things to say.' She brightened. 'Has the shop got a 'phone?'

'I dunno. I suppose it could do.' Libby thought about it for a moment before adding, 'Gosh! That'd be summat, wouldn't it? Havin' our very own 'phone.'

Emma waved to her parents, who had just entered the shelter along with her little sister, Cathy. Spotting his daughter, Daniel Bagshaw made his way through the crowd.

He greeted the girls, his features stern. 'We've had a change of plan.'

Emma and Libby exchanged worried glances.

'We're leavin' for Ireland on the next train.' He lifted a suitcase to show his daughter. 'Yer mother's packed the essentials.'

Emma gaped at her father. 'But what about the rest of our things?'

'We can buy new when we get settled—'

Emma cut her father short. 'Did Mum pack our photos?'

'Some of them,' said Daniel, 'but not all. We can't take everything, and I'm not wastin' another moment.' He lowered his voice. 'We've been lucky so far, but our luck might not hold out for much longer.'

Hearing his words, Libby felt her stomach drop. She stood on tiptoe, searching for her parents. 'Have you seen me mum and dad, Mr Bagshaw?'

Daniel tried to turn, to see if he could see the Gilberts, but there were too many people in the shelter. 'We're packed in like sardines; all I can see is heads.'

Libby crossed her fingers, and saw that Emma was doing the same. 'I expect they'll be at the front,' said Emma. She slipped her hand into Libby's. 'You'll probably see them when they sound the all-clear.'

'I hope so, but there's that many people in here . . .'

Emma gave Libby's fingers a reassuring squeeze. 'I'll help you look.'

'You will not,' said Emma's father stiffly. 'I told you; we're on the first train out of here, and I meant it.'

Emma folded her arms defensively. 'You don't know how long we're goin' to be in here. It could be hours!'

He shrugged. 'I couldn't give a monkey's how long we're in here for; as soon as them sirens sound, we're gettin' the first train out.'

As her eyes settled on the suitcase Emma looked up sharply. 'Please tell me you've packed the address book?'

He patted the pocket of his jacket. 'Safe and sound.'

'Good! I wouldn't want to lose Libby's new address.'

As she spoke, a sickening thud shook the shelter, and the occupants stared nervously upwards as dirt and grit sifted through the planked ceiling like small waterfalls.

Libby turned round to Emma's father. 'What the hell was that?' she asked in a frightened voice.

The woman who had been admiring the bow-fronted writing table spoke before anyone else had a chance. 'It was a bomb. Bloody close too, if I'm any judge.'

Libby felt a sense of panic rise within her as she began to look round desperately for her parents. 'Mum? Dad?'

Eager to help, Daniel turned to the man standing next to him. 'Libby Gilbert's lookin' for her mum and dad. Pass it round.' But with more bombs falling the shelter fell silent, save for the whispered prayers of those nearby.

Emma had turned pale. The girls had been in many shelters but they'd never experienced bombs falling quite as close as this. 'Are we safe in here?'

Daniel averted his gaze. 'Safe as houses.'

Hearing a murmur of voices, Libby tilted her head to see if it was something to do with her parents, but it was just the sound of people singing 'Amazing Grace'. With all hope of finding her parents safe in the shelter temporarily lost, Libby and Emma joined in, only falling silent if a bomb fell too close.

Libby couldn't be sure how long the air raid had gone on, but to her it felt like hours. As soon as the all-clear sounded, the shelter began to empty, and Libby could hear the exclamations of those who saw the devastation for the first time.

'We're lucky to be alive,' said Emma, as they emerged into the street.

Cathy joined the girls, hugging Libby round the middle. 'Mum says we've got to say cheerio, cos we's off to the station.'

Libby kissed the top of the little girl's blonde curly hair. 'Look after yer big sister for me, won't you?'

'Course I will,' chirruped Cathy, before running back to her mother, who was striding towards Libby. Taking her daughter's friend in a warm embrace, she whispered, 'Good luck, Libby. Let us know how you go, and for goodness' sake, don't waste any time leavin'.'

Libby felt a tear track down her cheek. 'Will do.'

Daniel ruffled the top of Libby's hair. 'Look after yerself, kiddo.'

Emma threw her arms around Libby's neck. Speaking between loud sobs, she bubbled, 'I ain't half gonna miss you, Libby Gilbert.'

Holding her friend tight, Libby's voice quavered as she tried to hold it together. 'Write as soon as you get to yer new home, and I'll do the same.'

Tears cascaded down Emma's cheeks as her father led her away by the hand. 'I will. Goodbye, Libby.'

Wiping the tears from her cheeks, Libby waved farewell before hurrying off to find her parents. Stopping strangers who were passing by, she asked them if they'd seen Orla or Reggie Gilbert, but with no news to impart they would apologise before hastening off to find loved ones of their own.

With many buildings lying in ruins, Libby was finding it difficult to get her bearings, so she stopped and scanned the area to see if she could spot anything familiar. Deep in concentration, she jumped as a hand came down on her shoulder, and a familiar voice broke through her thoughts. 'Libby?'

Turning, Libby found herself face to face with her next-door neighbour, Ethel. 'I can't find me mum and dad. Have you seen them?'

Ethel's lips parted. 'Weren't they down the market with you?'

'No. They stayed behind to pack the van.' Seeing the look of dismay on her neighbour's face, she swallowed. 'Why are you lookin' at me like that?'

Ethel was wringing her hands. 'Do you think they could've gone to a different shelter?'

'They might've been in the one we were in . . .' began Libby, but Ethel was quick to dash her hopes.

'Me and my Larry were two of the last ones in. We did hear a whisper that someone was searching for the Gilberts; I take it that was you?'

Libby spoke slowly. 'So, word did get round.'

Ethel squeezed Libby's hand. 'Indeed. I'm afraid they definitely weren't in the same shelter as the rest of us.'

Libby looked towards Whitechapel Road. 'If they were sheltering somewhere else, then surely they'd be home by now?'

Ethel averted her gaze as tears began to form. Speaking in choked tones, she gazed into thin air. 'I'm afraid you ain't got a home, not any more.'

Libby stared at the older woman, her eyes widening. 'No!'

A tear trickled down Ethel's cheek. 'Ours too.'

Desperate to come up with a reason for her parents not to have been home when the bombs dropped, a sudden thought entered her mind. 'Did you see the van?'

Ethel thought hard before answering. She knew that Libby was referring to the removal van which had been parked in front of the Gilberts' house since early that morning. A vision of the road outside the two former houses entered her mind, and there wasn't a van in the picture. 'No, the van's gone, but I don't know when it went.'

Relief swept Libby's face. 'If the van's not there, then neither are they.'

Ethel puffed her cheeks out. 'Thank goodness for that, cos there ain't nothin' left of yer old house, mine neither.' She smiled encouragingly. 'It seems as though you're movin' in the nick of time.'

'Not a moment too soon,' agreed Libby. Thanking Ethel for her reassuring information, she headed off towards her old home at a trot. She had no idea where her parents were, but she assumed they'd make their way back to the house eventually and wait for her there.

As she rounded the corner of Whitechapel Road, she could see why Ethel had looked at her aghast. Where there once stood her family home, there was now a heap of bricks and rubble. Grateful that her parents had left before the bomb fell, she pushed her way through the people who had gathered to stare in horror at the scene of destruction before them.

'Bloody hell,' she said softly. 'Thank God they weren't in.'

A man tilted his head to face her. 'Libby!'

'It's all right, Mr Coppack. My parents went away in the van before the bomb hit. Good job, an' all.'

Mr Coppack exchanged nervous glances with several of the group. 'But it wasn't yer parents that moved the van . . . Mrs Fortescue said it was someone else.'

Libby gawped at him. 'Who?'

Mrs Fortescue shuffled into view. 'Tall, dark-haired, with a moustache. He reminded me a little bit of yer father, only skinnier.'

'Sounds like my uncle,' said Libby. 'He must've been with them when the siren sounded.'

Mrs Fortescue glanced nervously at Mr Coppack before turning her attention back to Libby. 'But if that's the case, why weren't they in the van with him?'

Libby tilted her head to one side. 'Are you *sure* they weren't?'

'As eggs is eggs,' confirmed the older woman. 'He was on his tod.'

Without warning, Libby dashed across the rubble, half sliding, half falling as the bricks gave way beneath her feet, yelling from the top of her lungs as she went: 'Mum! Dad! Where are you?'

A small cascade of broken bricks came tumbling down as she made her way haphazardly across the debris. An ARP warden who had been standing nearby shouted for her to stop, but Libby blundered on, tears blinding her progress. Desperate to find her parents alive and well, she fell to her knees and began throwing bricks over her shoulder as she tried in vain to clear a space. She hadn't got far when she was detained by a couple of wardens, who grabbed her roughly by the arms and dragged her to safety. The warden who had first yelled at her to stop was eyeing her sternly.

'I understand that you're worried, miss, but we have to tread careful in case we make things worse than they already are.'

Libby stared at him in tearful disbelief. 'How the hell could we make it any worse?'

He pushed his cap to the back of his head. 'Movin' stuff round willy-nilly could create a further collapse, burying anyone inside.'

'Then why on earth didn't you say so from the start?'

'We did, only you weren't for listening.' He waved over a woman from the Women's Voluntary Service. 'Can you take care of Miss . . .'

'Gilbert,' Libby choked.

'. . . Miss Gilbert, and see she gets a cup of hot, sweet tea?'

The woman placed a comforting arm around Libby's shoulders. 'Come with me, luvvy, and let the men do their job.'

In shocked silence, Libby allowed the woman to walk her away. What on earth had she been thinking of? She knew full well that it was dangerous to go clambering over bombed buildings. Inside the WVS van, she took a cup of tea from one of the women and placed it to her lips; blowing gently, she gazed into space as she took the tiniest of sips. According to Mrs Fortescue, the man who'd moved the van sounded very much like her uncle, but if that were the case, where had he taken it and why? She wondered whether her father could have asked him to drive for some reason, and her parents had been in the back, but she quickly discarded the idea. The van had three seats, so there was no reason for them to ride in the back; besides which, her father would surely have been the one behind the wheel. She glanced across to Mrs Fortescue, who was chatting to a passer-by. Could she have been mistaken? Again, Libby dismissed the thought without hesitation. The van wasn't there, so someone must have moved it, and whilst Mrs Fortescue might've been mistaken about the driver, surely to goodness she'd have seen Orla in the passenger seat?

Libby continued to mull these thoughts over, each time coming to the same conclusion. Her uncle must have moved the van, for what reason she had yet to fathom, but no doubt she'd get to the bottom of that sooner or later. Leaving the van, she wandered back to Mrs Fortescue, tapped her on the shoulder, and stared somewhat woodenly at the woman who turned to greet her.

'Are you certain my parents weren't in the van? Only the man you described sounds ever so like my uncle, and it would be helpful for the rescuers to know if my parents are safe in his house.'

Mrs Fortescue spoke ruefully. 'I only seen him.'

Libby mulled over the possibilities out loud. 'Dad did say he wasn't going to take everything to Norwich, because Uncle Tony wanted Grandma's old sideboard, even though it's a bit rickety.' She brightened as she recalled an image of her mother grasping the sideboard, which had threatened to part company with its legs when they had tried to move it out of the hall. 'That must be it! My uncle must have driven, whilst Mum and Dad held the sideboard steady in the back!' Breathing a huge sigh of relief, she took the plump Mrs Fortescue in a tight embrace. 'Thanks, Mrs F. I was really worried for a minute there, but this makes perfect sense.' She turned and waved to the warden. 'It's all right. My parents are with my dad's brother.'

The warden cupped his hand around his ear and shouted for Libby to repeat herself, which she did, but still unable to hear he had begun to walk towards her when there was a cry of alarm from the men who were sifting through the rubble. He held up a finger, indicating that he'd be with her shortly, and turned back to join them.

Libby stood on tiptoe as she tried to see what was going on. 'Do you think they've broken through?' She grimaced. 'I feel guilty seeing them risk their necks for an empty house. Do you think I should say summat?'

Mrs Fortescue had been watching the men with a keen interest. From what she could see it very much looked as though they'd found something. She placed a hand on Libby's wrist. 'Hold on a mo, luv.'

Libby glanced down at Mrs Fortescue's hand, then to her face, which was etched with deep concern. 'Why are you lookin' so worried? We know there's no one in there,' Libby insisted, adding, 'They've probably found a cat.'

One of the men carefully made his way into the hole, whilst the warden Libby had been talking to turned to look back at her, grim-faced.

Libby turned to Mrs Fortescue, her eyes widening. 'Why's he looking at me like that?'

Releasing her hold on Libby's wrist, Mrs Fortescue took her hand instead. 'I dunno about you, but I could with a cuppa.'

'I've just had one, but you go if you like,' said Libby, who couldn't fathom why the older woman wanted a cup of tea now of all times.

Mrs Fortescue turned pleading eyes to Libby. 'Please come with me. It does you no good to stand here worryin' . . .'

Libby's face grew stern. 'Only I'm not standin' here worryin', because I know my parents are safe and sound at my uncle's.'

Mrs Fortescue had been present during several rescues, and she knew the routine all too well. If the wardens had found someone alive, then they'd be calling for help, in the form of more hands and an ambulance. If they'd found an unexploded bomb or a gas leak, they'd be telling everyone to stand back.

It was only when they'd found bodies that things went quiet. Desperate now, she tugged Libby's hand. 'I dare say they are, but why haven't they come back to let you know that they're all right?'

Libby rolled her eyes. 'Whitechapel Road wasn't the only street that got bombed! You've seen what it's like: roads blocked, burst mains, not to mention fires. It'd be a miracle if they could get here.'

Mrs Fortescue gazed at her quizzically as she tried to recall something that Libby had mentioned earlier. It hadn't sat right with Mrs Fortescue at the time, and she now knew why. 'Only yer uncle didn't take the van until *after* the all-clear sounded. If he could get here, so could they.'

Libby gawped at her, before reaching a conclusion. 'Well, that's it then! It couldn't have been him. There's no way he would've driven off with the van if he thought his brother's family might be trapped inside the house! They probably think that I'm down the market.'

Mrs Fortescue was about to say that she thought this unlikely when she saw men carrying two stretchers along with a couple of black blankets over to where they'd been searching. A horrible feeling rose in her throat as she turned to Libby, who was also staring at the scene, her lips parting slowly.

Her mind racing, Libby was trying to come up with feasible reasons for the stretchers. She momentarily clasped at the idea it could be her neighbours, before remembering she had spoken to Ethel a few minutes ago. She had just begun to toy with the idea that someone might've been trying to loot the house during the raid when the warden came over. Removing his cap, he turned the brim through his fingers.

'Sorry, miss, there's no easy way to say this, but I think we might've found yer parents.'

Libby stared through him. 'No, you haven't,' she said sternly. 'Because my parents are with my uncle. I know how it must look, but you're wrong.'

He ran his tongue over his lip in a nervous fashion. 'I sincerely hope you're right, but either way, we need you – or someone who knew yer parents – to make an identification.'

Libby looked to Mrs Fortescue. She would have asked the older woman to carry out the task in a heartbeat if she hadn't known she wouldn't trust anyone's opinion but her own. She turned hollow eyes to the warden. 'I'll do it.'

He gestured for her to follow him. 'Come with me.'

Libby followed the warden to the back of a van where they waited for the men to arrive. As they stood, it began to occur to Libby that she was about to see a dead body – she corrected herself: two dead bodies – for the first time in her life. She might be keen to prove that it wasn't her parents who lay beneath the blankets, but how would she feel seeing a stranger or a neighbour lying dead to the world? She had begun to think that she was making a mistake in agreeing to identify the bodies when the men carried the stretchers towards the van.

Taking a deep breath, Libby caught the warden's attention. 'I'm sorry, but I don't think I can do this. Not because I think it's my parents, because I don't, but . . .' She fell silent.

The warden held up his hand, indicating she needn't go any further. 'Is there anyone else you can think of?'

Libby turned to indicate Mrs Fortescue. 'The woman I was talking to over there. Not only does she know my parents, but she's a neighbour of ours, so if it's anybody local, she should know.'

The man walked off to fetch Mrs Fortescue, and Libby waited for them to come back. In the meantime, the men bearing the stretchers arrived at the van, and placed them down on the ground. To Libby's horror, the arm of one of the bodies slipped out from the beneath the blanket. It was covered in brick dust and blood, but Libby couldn't stop her eyes from travelling down to the fingers. Feeling the air rush to her head, she saw her father's signet ring before everything went black, and Libby collapsed where she stood.

Tony Gilbert stared blankly at the road ahead of him. He had gone to visit his brother in order to see if he could persuade him into letting him pay for the business in instalments. Reggie had welcomed him in with open arms, but Orla had made herself scarce, claiming she needed to check that they hadn't left anything behind.

'I swear I'll have the money to you in the next couple of months,' pleaded Tony. 'You know things are tight at the minute. But as soon as I get started on the stall, I can pay you what I owe. I can't say fairer than that.'

Reggie had heaved a weary sigh. 'If I agree I may as well be handin' you the business on a plate, cos we both know I'll never see my money once I've signed on the dotted line.'

Glancing to where Orla had been standing, Tony tutted beneath his breath. 'Sounds like someone's been whisperin' in yer shell-like.'

Reggie shrugged. 'It's not just my business though, is it, Tony? If you don't cough up, it's not just me that'll suffer.'

'I know, which is why I swear to pay you every last penny, even if it takes me a while.'

Reggie hesitated as his wife came back into the room. 'I'm sorry, Tony, but our mind's made up. If you've not got the money, we'll have to sell it to someone who has.'

Tony started to laugh, but stopped when he saw the look of determination on his brother's face. 'Surely you can't be serious?'

Orla joined Reggie, sliding her hand into his. 'Like Reggie said, it's not just him that'll suffer if you don't stay true to yer word.' She gave him a sidelong glance from under her lashes. 'Surely you wouldn't see yer niece go short?'

Tony stared at her, his jaw flinching. 'Are you bleedin' jokin'? Cos if you are, I don't find it funny.'

Reggie scowled at Tony. 'Don't have a go at Orla, she's only lookin' out for our Libby.'

Tony rolled his tongue around the inside of his mouth. 'Do you know what? Forget it! I don't know why I bleedin' bother.' He looked directly at Orla. 'It's a good job I know how to keep me gob shut.'

Reggie gave his brother a warning glance. 'I think it's best if you leave.'

'Aye,' said Tony bitterly, 'cos I'm the black sheep of the family, which is pretty rich considerin' Orla's folks want nowt to do with her.'

Her cheeks blooming, she lowered her gaze to the bare boards that ran between them. 'I never claimed to be a saint.'

Tony laughed sarcastically. 'You could've fooled me, swannin' round like butter wouldn't melt.'

Enraged by his brother's behaviour, Reggie stepped forward, only to be detained by Orla's outstretched arm. 'Don't, Reg. He's not worth it.'

'I want to know what he means!' Reggie seethed.

Tony prodded himself in the chest. 'That I'm not the only black sheep of the family, that's what.'

'Black sheep?' barked Reggie. 'You don't even act like you're a part of our family. It's you what's pushin' everyone else away, not vice versa. Even our Libby's noticed.'

Tony shot him a withering look. 'You haven't got a bleedin' clue, have you?'

Infuriated by Tony's refusal to take responsibility for his behaviour, Reggie launched himself at his brother, and the pair fell to the floor, Reggie's arms whirling like windmills whilst Tony did his best to fight him off. It was only Orla's pleas that caused Reggie to break away.

Standing up, Tony straightened his jacket with one hand, whilst wiping his bloodied lip with the other. Casting Orla a look of pure hatred, he muttered, 'You make me sick.' He was turning to leave when he saw his brother rush at him from the corner of his eye. Quick to defend himself, Tony punched Reggie, sending him scuttling backwards, and without further ado ran out of the house, just as the air-raid siren split the air. He was running for cover when the first bomb hit. Turning, he stared in horror as the house next door to Reggie's crumpled, taking Reggie's with it. He leaned against the van as his knees began to buckle. Crying out, he took in the full devastation before him, only coming out of his trance when accosted by an ARP warden.

'What on earth do you think you're doin'?' barked the warden.

Tony stared at him. His eyes widening, he pointed towards the house. 'M – my . . .'

The warden grabbed Tony by the shoulder of his jacket, and dragged him to the relative safety of an Anderson shelter. 'Get in there.'

Tony sank down onto one of the benches, whilst the enormity of what happened flooded over him. *But for the grace of God, you'd have been in that house,* Tony told himself. His thoughts turned to Libby, who would come home to find her parents most probably dead. *She ain't your responsibility*, Tony told himself, *and it'd be best for her if we kept it that way.*

When the all-clear sounded, Tony went straight to the house to see if by some miracle Reggie had made it out alive. But one look at the remains was enough for him to know that no one could've survived. Leaning against the van, he lit a cigarette as he processed his lucky escape.

The warden who'd dragged Tony to the shelter wandered over. 'I can understand that you wanted to move yer van before it got damaged, but you're safer in a shelter than you are on four wheels.'

Tony was about to say that the van wasn't his when a thought entered his mind. Orla had been checking to make sure they'd got everything out of the house, which meant that everything they owned, including the deeds to the business, must be packed in the van. With his brother gone, no one could prove that Reggie hadn't signed the papers prior to the explosion. He looked back at the warden. 'Thanks, mate. We don't always think with a clear head, do we, but I'll move it now so it's not in the way.'

Praying that his brother would've left the keys in the van, he was relieved to see them in the ignition, and the crank handle under the seat. Telling himself that he was doing the right thing by keeping the business in the family, rather than giving it to a young chit of a girl who'd probably run it into the ground, Tony quickly climbed into the van and drove away without so much as a backward glance.

Now, as he continued, he comforted himself with the knowledge that whilst his last interaction with his brother may have been regrettable, things would've been far worse had he truly spoken his mind.

Libby heard the sound of lowered voices as she slowly came to. Peering out through slitted eyes, she could just make out the nicotine-yellow ceiling above her. Wherever she was, it couldn't be home, because no one in her family smoked.

The plump face of Mrs Fortescue suddenly appeared above her, startling her. 'How are you feelin', ducky? Would you like a nice hot cuppa?'

Libby raised her head a little, but the searing pain that shot through her skull caused her to rethink. Gingerly placing a hand to her head, she looked at Mrs Fortescue with alarm. 'Why's my head bandaged?'

Mrs Fortescue gave her a grim smile. 'You didn't half go down with a whack – cracked yer head open like an egg, so you did, and you've been out like a light ever since. Luckily for you an off-duty doctor treated the wound, so you'll be good as new in no time.'

Gingerly laying her head back onto the pillow, Libby wondered how she'd come to fall, until a vague memory replayed in her mind's eye. She remembered the air raid, and that Emma and her family were heading to Ireland earlier than planned, but nothing after that. She hesitated as another image flashed before her eyes, and then, the colour draining from her face, she recalled the whole nightmare. Only how it could be true, when some of it seemed to make no sense, especially the part where her uncle came for the van *after* the bombing. Her mother may not get on with her brother-in-law, but it would be ludicrous to suggest that he'd driven off with the van without checking on her parents; so much so that Libby could only come up with one explanation. She turned to Mrs Fortescue.

'I've had the most terrible nightmare . . .' As she started to explain, Mrs Fortescue laid a kind hand on her forearm.

'I'm sorry, Libby, but that weren't no nightmare.'

Libby sat up so sharply she caused Mrs Fortescue to cry out. 'Careful! Or you'll be on the floor again.'

Swinging her legs out of the bed, Libby looked round for her jacket and shoes. 'If you expect me to lie here while my parents go out of their minds with worry . . .'

Hearing the commotion, the ARP warden knocked briefly against the door before entering. 'Can I be of assistance?'

Libby shot Mrs Fortescue a reproving glance. 'Yes! You can tell Mrs Fortescue that while I may have let me imagination run away with me earlier I'm fine now.'

The warden closed the door gently, whilst indicating that Libby should sit back down. 'I realise it must have come as one hell of a shock.'

'A shock?' echoed Libby. 'Too right it has. I didn't even see . . .'

The warden cut across her. 'I know you didn't, but Mrs Fortescue did, and I'm afraid . . .'

Unable to bear the thought that the older woman might be right, Libby pointed an accusing finger at her neighbour. 'She doesn't know what she's talkin' about. She wanted it to be me parents before you'd even found anyone.'

Mrs Fortescue let out a gasp. 'Oh, Libby luv, I know you must be upset, but I didn't want it to be true, honest to God I didn't.'

Seeing the tears brimming in the other woman's eyes, Libby hastily apologised, before speaking to the warden in hushed tones. 'I didn't mean to be cruel, but she's old, and has probably confused my parents with someone else.'

The warden turned to Mrs Fortescue. 'Can you leave us for a minute?' The older woman dabbed her eyes with a handkerchief before quietly slipping out of the room, and the warden gestured for Libby to sit down. He waited for her to do so before speaking his thoughts. 'You might not remember, but the fellers what brought the bodies out said you fainted when you saw your dad's signet ring?'

Libby shrugged as the memory of the image entered her mind. 'Lots of people have signet rings. I dare say one looks very much like another.'

Kneeling down on his haunches, the warden made sure he had her full attention before speaking. 'True, which is why I don't think you're goin' to believe anyone until you've seen for yerself.'

'Would you? If someone told you that yer parents had died?'

'Maybe, maybe not. But either way, I don't think I'd have spoken to that poor old lady the way you did, especially when she's been kind enough to let us use her house. Whether you believe her to be wrong or not, that was totally unnecessary, not to mention hurtful.'

Libby's cheeks coloured. She wasn't proud of the way she'd spoken to Mrs Fortescue, but she was desperate to prove the woman wrong, and making unkind accusations had been her only defence. She glanced at the warden through her lashes. 'I know, which is why I apologised . . .'

'By sayin' she was gettin' mixed up?'

Libby closed her eyes. 'It's all I've got, because if that ain't true . . .'

He indicated a door across the corridor. 'Look, luv, as it stands we're havin' to use every vehicle at our disposal to ferry the injured to hospital. Mrs Fortescue has let us use her bedroom until summat suitable becomes available.'

Libby's stomach lurched unpleasantly as she stared at the closed door. 'You mean they're in there?' she asked in horrified tones.

The warden got to his feet. 'Are you ready?'

'I'll never be ready,' said Libby, her voice barely above a whisper. 'But there ain't no sense in draggin' this out any further than need be.'

When Libby entered the room, she tried to avoid looking directly at the bodies laid out on the bed. It was only when the warden cleared his throat that she glanced fleetingly at her parents. Sobbing, she collapsed to her knees as the enormity of the reality left her overwhelmed with grief.

The warden hastened to her side. 'C'mon, luv, let's get you out of here.'

Allowing him to help her up, she shook her head. 'Not until I've said goodbye.' Walking unsteadily, she wiped away tears with the back of her hands before tentatively kissing her father, then her mother, on the forehead. 'Look after each other,' she whispered, 'and don't worry about me. I can look after meself.' She wanted to stay in the room so that she could be close to them, but the warden was gesturing for her to join him outside.

'You can see them again, luv, but right now we need to move them from here, whilst there's a car free.'

Whispering 'I love you,' Libby took one last look at her parents before joining the warden in the hallway, where a couple of men were waiting to take them to a car which was parked outside. 'At least they were together at the end,' she said, her voice quavering as she spoke.

Having been one of the first on the scene, the warden knew first hand that Libby's father's body had lain across his wife's, as though trying to protect her. He said as much to Libby, hoping that it might bring some sense of comfort, and she blinked the tears from her lashes. 'He was always protecting her. I've never known a couple to be as much in love as my parents.'

When the warden and Libby entered the parlour, Mrs Fortescue rose to her feet, and Libby sank into her arms, apologising profusely for her harsh words, in between heartfelt sobs.

Mrs Fortescue's lips trembled as she smoothed Libby's hair. 'Don't you worry yer head none. That's all forgotten about.' She blinked back the tears which continued to form. 'You're welcome to stay with me until the end of the week. After that I'm goin' to be movin' to Scarborough to live with my daughter and her family.' She shrugged helplessly. 'I wish I could do more, but Mr Gibbs has already arranged for someone to move in the day I move out.'

'Thanks for the offer, but I shall stay with my uncle,' said Libby. A look of uncertainty crossed her face as she remembered Mrs Fortescue's recollection of events. 'Seeing as it can't have been him who took the van, I wonder who did?'

'Scum, that's who,' said Mrs Fortescue bitterly. 'Lord only knows there's plenty of them around.'

Libby's face clouded as the penny dropped. 'You mean they robbed us?'

The warden pulled a rueful face. 'I'm afraid burglary is rife durin' air raids.'

'Well, they aren't goin' to get away with it, cos I'm goin' straight to the Bluebottles, and when they find the feller who took our things I hope they bloody well hang him!' snapped Libby.

'I doubt they'll be able to find out who nicked yer stuff,' said Mrs Fortescue in a matter-of-fact tone of voice. 'You saw what it was like, complete and utter mayhem. No one will think twice about seein' someone drive off in a van, not when there's so much else goin' on. By all means go to the police, but please don't pin yer hopes on findin' the culprit.'

Libby set off for the nearest station, only to find that Mrs Fortescue had been right. The police made a note of the van's description, and the company her father had hired it from, before regretfully informing her that there was little to no hope of recovering her belongings, let alone finding out who'd taken them.

'They'll be the other side of the country by now, if not further,' said one of the constables. 'These fellers know what they're doin' and they don't hang about. Sorry, miss.'

'But you will keep an ear to the ground?' asked Libby hopefully. 'It's not about the furniture, but the memories. That van had all our photographs and keepsakes tucked away. I've got nowt to remember my parents by, save for the memories in me head.'

The constable twinkled at her sympathetically. 'Be thankful no one can take those away from you. And rest assured, if anythin' should turn up, I'll make sure that you're the first to know!'

Only after he had driven well away from the city, and prying eyes, did Tony feel confident enough to pull over into a secluded lay-by, hidden by a large blackthorn hedge. Applying the handbrake, he turned the engine off and walked round to the back to open the tailgate, where his attention was immediately drawn to the briefcase which stood amongst the suitcases. He grasped the case and flipped the catch. Pulling out a sheaf of papers, he began to hurriedly search through until he found the one he had been looking for. His eyes danced as he read the agreement between himself and his brother that, once signed, would ensure the business was his.

He breathed the word 'Bingo!' before carefully folding the paper and placing it in his pocket. He then continued to search the case until he found the contract between Reggie and the solicitors acting on his behalf, and quickly scanned each page until he got to the one bearing Reggie's signature. Congratulating himself on a job well done, he closed the back of the van and climbed into the driver's seat. He was heading for a house where he knew no questions would be asked and the contents of the van would be sold off at an auction far from London, the proceeds being split sixty forty. He'd use his share of the money to pay someone to forge Reggie's signature on the agreement, and the business would be his.

Chapter Two

It was the morning after the devastating attack, and Libby was sitting at Mrs Fortescue's kitchen table nursing a cup of tea which was rapidly growing cold. She had gone to her uncle's place the previous evening, but none of the people he shared the house with seemed to know where he was, or what time he'd be back. Knowing the sorts of rackets her parents believed him to be up to, Libby knew better than to ask questions, so she had decided to leave things until the following morning, when she hoped she would have a better chance of tracking him down without interrupting his activities – whatever they might be.

She had gone to bed that night with a heavy heart, expecting that she would cry herself to sleep, but she hadn't slept a wink all night. All she did was go through the whys and wherefores of the previous day. She'd lost count of the number of times she'd wished that they'd left London earlier, or that her parents had joined her on the stall where they would have been safe. True, they'd still have lost their belongings to the thieving scum who'd driven off with them, but at least they'd be alive, and they could always start afresh.

Exhausted, Libby knuckled her eyes whilst stifling a yawn. She knew she had to make a start on things sooner rather than later, but the prospect of having to relay the events of the previous day to her uncle was filling her with dread. It was bad enough going through it the first time, without having to watch her uncle crumble as he learned of his brother's fate.

Seeing that Libby had hardly touched her tea, Mrs Fortescue came bustling over. 'Another cuppa, dear? That one must be stone cold by now.'

Libby handed the cup over. 'No thanks, Mrs F. I feel as though I've drunk enough tea to sink a ship.'

'What about summat to eat then?' suggested the older woman. 'A round of toast, or perhaps a nice bit of porridge?'

The thought of food turning her stomach, Libby held up a hand. 'I'm really not hungry.'

'What did yer mother used to make you?' ventured Mrs Fortescue. 'I don't mind givin' anythin' a go.'

Libby looked up from her lap, her eyes welling with tears, and spoke softly. 'Mum used to do us kippers at Christmas, cos Dad loved them, but they always had too many bones in for me, so I had porridge.'

Mrs Fortescue sat down opposite her. 'You can't beat a nice pair of kippers for yer brekker,' she said kindly. 'What did she used to give you on a normal day?'

Libby dabbed her eyes with the hanky she had pulled from her dress pocket. 'Marmalade or jam on toast, and if she had any we'd have crumpets with lashings of butter, so thick you'd have to lick it from your fingers afterwards.' Her face crumpled. 'I wish she was here now.'

Mrs Fortescue shuffled forward in her seat and clasped Libby's hand in hers. 'I know you do, luv.' She hesitated. 'I'm goin' to have a word with the neighbours to see if anyone's got any spare clothes that you can have, seein' as some swine nicked all yours.'

'Thanks, Mrs F. I don't know what I'd've done without you.'

Mrs Fortescue patted the back of Libby's hand. 'You're welcome, sweetheart. I wish I could do more to help.' She paused.

'What time are you goin' to go and see yer uncle? I don't mind comin' with you, if you'd like me to?'

Libby curled her fingers inside Mrs Fortescue's. 'Thanks, but I've got to start doin' stuff on my own.' She heaved a sigh. 'I need to see the solicitors, to see if I can get back the deposit my father put down on the flat in Norwich. I dare say we'll've kissed our first month's rent goodbye on the shop, but there's not a lot I can do about that. I've also got to get down to the stall and see if Mr Filmer will give me time to sort things out.'

'Who's Mr Filmer when he's at home?'

'He's in charge of the market,' Libby told her.

Mrs Fortescue cupped Libby's cheek in the palm of her hand. 'Dear lord, you've got a lot on yer plate.'

Libby stood up, swayed, and sat back down sharply.

Mrs Fortescue wagged a reproving finger. 'You might not feel hungry, but you're goin' to need all the energy you can get, so it's toast for you, my girl, whether you like it or not! Yer parents would never forgive me if I let you go off on an empty stomach.'

Despite not feeling hungry, Libby obligingly ate the slice of toast and blackberry jam, if only to please her host. Breakfast eaten, she pushed her arms into the sleeves of her coat. 'Thanks for lookin' after me, Mrs F. I think I needed that.'

'You're welcome, dear. I'll be doin' a nice bit of tripe for tea, say six-ish?'

Libby felt herself going green around the gills, but her parents had brought her up to be well-mannered so she replied pleasantly, 'that'll be grand.' Buttoning her coat, she headed out of the house, wondering whether she could come up with an excuse to get out of eating tripe. An image of her mother sprang to mind, wrinkling her nose in disgust as she cut a slab of tripe into slices.

'You eat what you want, Reggie Gilbert, but that don't mean me and Libby have to do the same,' she had said firmly.

'You know me, Orla,' her father had replied. 'I'd eat a manky 'orse if it come with chips.'

Much to her mother's disapproval, this expression had become one of her father's favourites since the outbreak of war.

'I'll thank you not to compare my cooking to a manky horse!' Orla had snapped, as her husband roared with laughter.

Libby stopped walking as she tried to banish the tears which were threatening to form. *You can't keep cryin'*, she told herself, *you've got too much to do, and now you're on yer own you can't afford to let others see yer vulnerability*. Yet with no money she knew that vulnerable was exactly what she was, but all that would change once she got the money back from the solicitors. She felt her tummy jolt unpleasantly. She had no idea whether they were obliged to return her father's deposit, but hoped fervently that they'd take pity on her plight and hand the money back. As she continued to walk, she mulled over what she should do first. As her uncle was her father's brother, he should be told before anyone else, but she didn't want to face that just yet. She turned her thoughts to the solicitors. They had her father's deposit on the property in Norwich, and without that money she had nothing. Having made up her mind, she headed for the solicitors' office on Butler Street. Thankful that her father had seen fit to discuss the ins and outs of his transactions with his family, Libby quickly located the correct premises, only to emerge a few minutes later feeling all but broken.

Her father's solicitor had been apologetic, saying he wished there was something he could do to help, but the money had already been transferred, and would act as compensation for the owner who would otherwise have to face losing a month's rent whilst he sought another lessee. Libby had begged him to reconsider and show some compassion, but her words had fallen on deaf, if sympathetic, ears.

Standing with her back to the solicitors' office, Libby took a couple of breaths before heading off to see her Uncle Tony. She had no idea where he'd be, but she was sure someone on the market might know, and she could inform Mr Filmer that she would open up the Gilberts' stall the very next day whilst she was about it.

She had barely stepped foot in the market before being waylaid by concerned stallholders all wanting to give their condolences, as well as offers of help. Thanking them for their kind words, she soon tracked down Mr Filmer, who removed his cap and held it between the tips of his fingers. Flashing her a fleeting if rather awkward grimace, he attempted to speak, cleared his throat and tried again. ''Ello, Libby. I'm ever so sorry to hear about yer parents. It's a dreadful thing to 'ave 'appened. If there's anything I can do, please don't hesitate to ask.'

Libby thanked him, before adding, 'My parents always spoke highly of you, and I know they'll appreciate you helping me to keep their business up and runnin'.' Seeing that he was about to say something, she continued in haste, 'I know we weren't meant to be here, but obviously that's all changed now.'

Mr Filmer shot her a surprised look. 'But what about yer uncle?'

Supposing that Mr Filmer probably knew of Tony's intention to buy the business off her father, she brought him up to speed. 'My uncle never got to sign the papers, which is just as well given the circumstances.'

He jerked the corner of his bottom lip downwards. 'I'm afraid there seems to 'ave been a misunderstanding.'

Libby stared at him in shocked disbelief. 'You can't have rented our pitch out already!'

His cheeks burning with embarrassment, he leaned forward and lowered his voice. 'As you already know, no one owns a pitch, and it takes years of trading to establish a trusted business.'

Annoyed that he had gone behind her back, Libby scowled at the market inspector. 'What's that got to do with the price of fish? You *knew* I'd lost my parents, so you must've realised I'd need the stall . . .' Her voice faded as a thought entered her mind. Petticoat Lane might not be the dodgy place where the upper classes once feared to tread, but there were still hooky deals and backhanders going on. 'Don't tell me – you've given our pitch away for a backhander! Who did you give it to and what did you do with the remainin' stock?' Without waiting for a response, she marched between the rows of stalls, keeping her eyes peeled until she saw the sign for Gilberts Furniture and Bric-a-Brac above her parents' stall.

Grief and anger swelling within her chest, Libby broke into a run. Skidding to a halt, she grabbed the market trader by his elbow and spun him round so that she could give him an earful, then reeled back in shock. 'Uncle Tony!'

Snatching his elbow out of her hand, he glared at her. 'Who the bloody hell did you expect me to be?'

She gaped at him. 'I dunno. My brain's not exactly functioning very well at the moment.' She averted her eyes from his gaze before looking back guiltily. 'I did try to find you yesterday, so that I could tell you what happened, but no one knew where you were.'

Tony stared at her for a moment or so before replying. 'So, it was you who called by. The fellers did mention summat about a young woman lookin' for me.' He paused. 'Sorry to hear about yer parents.'

'I'm not the only one who suffered a loss,' said Libby. 'Dad was your brother.'

Tony looked down at the ground below the stall, hoping that Libby wouldn't see the sickly colour his cheeks had turned. Praying that she would leave, he glanced back up, and saw Mr Filmer approaching them. 'Was there anythin' else?' he said quickly.

Uncertain as to what he meant, Libby pressed on. 'I appreciate you keepin' the stall goin'. It was very kind of you.'

Wishing fervently that the market inspector would sling his hook, Tony turned his back on the older man, indicating that Libby should join him around his side of the stall. Once he was satisfied that they were out of earshot, he spoke hurriedly in an effort to keep the conversation as short as possible. He had no idea whether Libby knew the sale hadn't gone through or not, so he decided to prey on her vulnerability and use the confusion that she must have suffered over the last twenty-four hours to his advantage. 'You do remember that your father sold me the stall?'

Libby felt as though the bottom had dropped out of her stomach. 'When?'

'Yesterday,' said Tony, removing his cap, 'moments before tragedy struck.'

Libby stared at her uncle to see if she could spot the mildest hint of deception, but his face remained impassive. Perhaps realising that she didn't quite trust him, Tony produced the paperwork from his back trouser pocket and held it out for her to see.

Taking the agreement, Libby briefly glanced over it, her eyes lingering on her father's signature on the bottom of the last page. She looked at the date, which confirmed that the documents had indeed been signed the previous day. Handing them back, she felt her bottom lip tremble. 'I see. I didn't realise . . .' She hesitated. 'I'm takin' it you gave Dad—'

'Cash,' said Tony quickly.

Not quite out of earshot as Tony would've liked, Mr Filmer gave a disapproving huff. 'I wish I had that kind of money to hand.'

Libby eyed her uncle questioningly. 'I thought you were makin' a payment plan? Dad said—'

He cut her off once again. The last thing he wanted was for Libby and the inspector to work out that he was lying. 'I was, but then I won the money,' he said, adding, 'fair and square.'

Mr Filmer's jaw dropped. 'Where on earth did you win that kind of money?'

Tony felt his cheeks begin to redden. 'The gee-gees, over at Newmarket. I had a hundred to one on an outsider, and it come rompin' 'ome in first place.'

'Cor blimey! Some people have all the luck!' exclaimed Mr Filmer, before remembering who he was with. He mumbled a hasty apology to Libby, but she was staring fixedly at her uncle. Was he telling the truth? It seemed a tad coincidental that he'd managed to win enough money to pay his brother as well as seal the deal before the bomb hit. Not only that, but Tony seemed to be having enormous difficulty in making eye contact with either herself or Mr Filmer, although being of a shady nature Tony was always looking guilty over something or other. As she mulled these thoughts over, another more pressing one entered her mind. 'So, where's the money?'

Tony shrugged, but beads of sweat were beginning to prick his brow. 'Yer father had it.'

'And all this happened moments before the explosion?'

Tony pulled a rueful face, whilst keeping his eyes lowered. 'I wasn't even a street away when it hit.'

Libby tried to envisage the scene in her mind. 'So, you'd only just left the house?'

'Luckily.'

Libby remained silent as she mulled this over. Something about her uncle's scenario didn't sit right. Her mother was paranoid when it came to air-raid warnings. Determined that the Luftwaffe were aiming for their house, and their house alone, she would be first out of the door, yelling to Libby and her father that they'd be brown bread if they didn't get a move on. Libby said as much to Tony, adding, 'So why hadn't she left?'

Tony stared at her, the colour draining from his face. If he were to say that Orla hadn't been worried by the siren, Libby would know that he was lying. Thinking on his feet, he came out with words so terrible he couldn't even look at Libby as they left his lips.

'They were waiting for you.'

Libby stared at him in horror. 'For me? Why on earth would they do that?'

'When the sirens went off yer mum wanted to leave immediately, to get as far away from London as possible. She thought you'd come home as soon as you heard them.'

Libby rocked slightly on her heels. 'Are you sayin' it's my fault that my parents are dead?'

Tony's face fell. He'd wanted to give an explanation, not point the finger of blame. 'No!'

'Then what are you sayin'?' asked Libby. Her voice growing hoarse, she pressed on. 'Because that's how it looks to me!'

Having come too far in the lie to turn back, Tony carried on doggedly. 'Yer mum shouldn't have refused to leave,' he said. 'I begged her to listen, but she was determined you'd be there any second. I'm sorry, Libby, but I wasn't goin' to hang around to see if she were right.' He heaved a sigh. 'Maybe I should've stayed longer, tried harder.'

Mr Filmer patted Tony's shoulder. 'Don't worry yer 'ead. We all have regrets – coulda, woulda, shoulda, as me old ma used to say.'

Libby spoke hollowly. 'It didn't occur to me to go home. I just headed for the nearest shelter, but I suppose in Mum's mind we would've been driving away to safety.' She fell silent, envisaging the moment Tony handed the money over. 'The money must still be in the house. Dad kept all his money in his wallet . . .'

Tony had agreed with her before he could stop himself. 'Didn't anyone mention it?'

'No, but maybe they've not . . .' She fell quiet. She had been in the same room as her father. Had his wallet been on him all that time? 'I'll have to ask the undertakers . . .' She swallowed as a lump formed in her throat. 'Sorry. I still can't quite come to terms with everythin'.'

Tony laid his hand on her shoulder. 'Would you like me to ask?'

'No!' said Libby; so quickly she startled Mr Filmer. Realising she had spoken too hastily, she continued more placidly. 'It's all right. I've got to call in at the undertakers, so I'll ask then.'

Mr Filmer lowered his gaze. 'I know you probably don't want to think about these things, but do you know where you're going to live?'

Libby shot Tony a sidelong glance, noting as she did so that he was quick to lower his head and avert his gaze. His actions showed that he didn't want her living with him, and quite frankly she was glad. Whilst she had no reason to disbelieve her uncle, she still couldn't help but think that things had fallen into Tony's lap at a time when there was no one to tell otherwise. She looked to Mr Filmer. 'I'm staying with Mrs Fortescue until the end of the week, but I'm sure I'll find somewhere after that.'

Mr Filmer looked at Tony pointedly, but eager to avoid any awkward requests the other man turned his attention to a customer who was inspecting a teapot. He'd never had any intention of offering Libby a place to live, but certainly not now he'd inadvertently made her feel responsible for the death of her own parents. Mr Filmer turned back to Libby. 'I guess it's true what they say.'

Libby gave him an astute glance. 'That you can't choose yer family?'

'Indeed. And whilst I never had yer uncle down as the compassionate sort, I did hope he might be different given the circumstances.'

'We don't really have much to do with each other,' said Libby as she and the market inspector began to walk back along the stalls. 'He's not what you'd call a family man.'

Mr Filmer stopped walking as they neared the start of the market. 'Are you goin' to be all right?'

She gazed steadily at him. 'I will be, cos I've got no choice.' She gave a short, mirthless laugh. 'I've got too much on my mind to be grievin'; I don't know whether that's a good thing or not?'

He adjusted the scarf around his neck as a sharp chill entered the air. 'We each cope in our own way. I . . .' He paused momentarily as he rethought his words. He had been about to say 'I hope you have a good Christmas', but that obviously wasn't going to be the case for poor Libby. He continued on a different tack. 'I hope you get things sorted. If you let me know the date of the funeral, I shall make sure that word gets passed around.' He jerked his head in Tony's direction. 'Maybe I'm wrong, but I don't think we can rely on yer uncle.'

She sighed resignedly. 'I'm afraid you're probably right. Thanks for all yer help. I'll call by as soon as I've set a date.'

As she walked away, Libby wondered just how she would cope visiting the funeral parlour. They'd want money, but . . . she suddenly remembered the cash her uncle had supposedly given her father. If he was telling the truth, that amount of unclaimed money could prove to be very tempting to the wrong individual. Hastening, she broke into a trot. The thought of someone stealing from her father whilst he was no longer able to defend himself was more than she could bear, and with that thought uppermost in her mind, she began to run.

Reaching the funeral parlour, Libby caught her breath, entered the building and waited for one of the directors to appear. A young man with black hair, thick with Brylcreem, came out from the curtained-off area and stepped forward, adjusting his tie. 'Good morning, and welcome to Roberts Brothers. How may I help you?'

Libby quickly explained who she was, and the reason for her visit. 'Has anyone been through my dad's things?'

Looking slightly perplexed the man pulled a face. 'Sorry, what things?'

'His wallet,' said Libby. 'He always had it on him; it would've been in his back pocket.'

'I wasn't here when they brought yer parents through; if you'd like to take a seat, I'll ask Mr Roberts.'

Libby took the seat which the undertaker had indicated. Keeping the fingers crossed on both hands, she waited with bated breath for him to reappear.

He came back through to the front, with the wallet in hand. 'Is this the one?'

Blowing a sigh of relief, Libby took the wallet and opened it. She stared at the loose change, before looking back at the undertaker. 'Where's the money?'

He looked at her in alarm. 'What money?'

'The money my uncle gave him. It was on him when – when . . .' Her breathing had got so fast, she began to feel light-headed. Sitting back down on the chair, she took a few deep breaths before calming down. 'Who's had access to my parents?'

The man was looking nervously from her to the room he'd just come from. 'Only the people who work here, and I can *assure* you . . .'

'What about before they came here?'

'Yer parents were picked up from a Mrs Fortescue's house,' the man explained. 'So maybe someone there?'

Libby quickly dismissed this. 'There's only me and Mrs Fortescue in the house.'

The man went to speak, but changed his mind.

Libby narrowed her eyes. 'What?'

He shrugged before saying reluctantly, 'I was goin' to say the rescuers or the wardens, but I really can't see—'

Libby jumped up, startling the undertaker. 'Of course! Thanks for yer help.' She was just about to leave when the undertaker coughed into his fist.

'Would now be a convenient time to discuss yer parents' funeral?'

Libby tutted beneath her breath. She knew he wouldn't like her answer, but there was no point in lying. 'Not if you want money, because I haven't got any, or not yet anyway.'

He eyed her in a somewhat condescending fashion. 'I see.'

Libby placed her hand on the door handle to leave, but she wasn't about to let this man make presumptions about her parents. 'No, you don't. My parents were leaving London for a new start in Norwich. All our things were packed into a van ready to go, and my father spent just about every penny he owned on the first month's rent of the flat and shop we were taking over. So, you don't see anythin' further than the end of yer own nose.'

He held up his hands in a placating fashion. 'I'm not here to judge.'

'Really? You should try tellin' yer face that.' Storming out of the parlour, she took care to slam the door behind her, causing the bell to ring alarmingly. *How dare he assume I was goin' to try and get out of payin' for their funeral by pulling the old "I've lost me wallet" stunt*, Libby thought to herself. *I hate it when people judge you unfairly, and whilst I probably don't look my best at the moment –* she glanced down at the clothes she had slept in *– that's no reason for him to cast aspersions.*

Such was her annoyance, it hardly took her any time to arrive back at her parents' former home, where she quickly sought out the warden from the day before. Waving to get his attention, she waited for him to join her.

'How're you bearin' up?' he asked, climbing over the debris.

'Rubbish,' said Libby. 'I feel like I'm runnin' round like a headless chicken.' She paused momentarily. 'I hate to ask, but do you know if anyone found any money? Only my dad's wallet is empty, and . . .' Seeing the distressed look on his face, she continued hastily, 'I'm not accusin' you, or anyone else, but at the same time . . .'

He rubbed the nape of his neck with the palm of his hand, leaving a dirty smear. 'At the same time, you want to know where it's gone?'

'It's all I have,' said Libby.

He closed his eyes, before looking at her sorrowfully. 'I wish I could tell you that someone had hold of it for safe keepin', but I was with yer parents the whole time, and . . .'

'I know,' said Libby, glumly, 'you've not seen or heard owt.'

'Sorry I can't be of more help.' He glanced towards the rubble. 'Are you sure it isn't in the house?'

She sighed wretchedly. 'He wouldn't have put it anywhere bar his wallet.'

'I wish I could help, I really do, and if I hear anything I shall be sure to let you know. I'll get the fellers to keep an eye out, just in case. It may seem unlikely, but it wouldn't be unheard of for things to end up in peculiar places after a large explosion.'

'I hope that's true, because I don't know what I'll do without it.'

Thanking him for his understanding, she was about to head back to Mrs Fortescue's when she had a change of heart. Striking back in the direction of Petticoat Lane, she made a beeline for her uncle's stall.

Tony had been happily chatting to a customer, but he turned sombre as soon as his eyes fell on Libby. *Maybe it's because he wants to appear respectful*, Libby supposed, *but I don't see what he's got to smile about, considering he's just lost his brother.* As she neared, Tony raised his head in acknowledgement of her presence.

'Libby?'

She gazed over the furniture, which had belonged to her father only the previous day. Surely Tony wouldn't claim to have bought the stock off him before they'd done an itemised list?

She said as much to her uncle, adding, 'I've also been to the funeral parlour, and whilst they had Dad's wallet, yer money wasn't in it.'

He feigned surprise. 'Really? Are you sure?'

Libby continued to stare at him, determined that her eyes shouldn't leave his, in case she missed a flicker of deception. 'Positive. I don't believe for one minute that a family with the reputation of the Roberts brothers would've stolen from my father.'

'Perhaps,' said Tony, 'but what about the folk what found him?'

Libby's eyes bored into his. 'There were too many of them for someone to swipe it without anyone noticing.'

Tony pretended to be deep in thought whilst avoiding her gaze. 'I don't know what to tell you, Lib.'

Hoping to make her uncle sweat, she spoke her thoughts. 'I suppose there's a slim chance it might be in the rubble. The warden did say it might've been blown out of his wallet. If it was, they'll find it as they sift through everything.'

'I should imagine that'll take for ever,' said Tony levelly.

'I've got all the time in the world.'

'Really? Cos I'd've thought the funeral directors would've wanted their dosh toot-sweet.'

Libby decided to make her uncle show his true colours. 'Are you offerin' to pay?'

Holding a hand to his heart he spoke with what Libby considered to be feigned integrity. 'Had I not just spent every penny on buyin' the business off yer father, I'd've done so, quick as a flash. As it is, I'm now potless, so I'm afraid you'll have to look elsewhere.'

Libby wanted to call him a liar right there and then, but how could she without proof? Unwilling to let him think he'd won, she turned away so that he might not see how much he'd riled her. 'In that case, I'd best get busy. I wouldn't want it gettin' into the wrong hands.' She hoped that her uncle was squirming with worry that she would find that there was no money, which would cause more questions to be raised. Because deep down, Libby was more certain than ever that he'd somehow diddled her father out of his business.

*

59

Libby had been lying in bed when she heard the sirens sound. Quickly getting to her feet, she grabbed the dressing gown which Mrs Fortescue had kindly loaned her and hastily pushed her arms through the sleeves. Lashing the cord, she was about to rouse the older woman when Mrs Fortescue flung the bedroom door wide open. Her hair still in rollers, she mumbled something before popping her teeth in and repeating herself. 'I'll not be sorry to see the back of these damned air raids.'

Libby remained silent, her heart aching too much to comment.

Realising that she had been inadvertently insensitive, Mrs Fortescue clasped Libby's hand in hers as they hastened through the front door. 'Sorry, luv, I wasn't thinkin'. I hope I haven't upset you.'

'You haven't,' lied Libby, adding truthfully, 'and you shouldn't apologise for wantin' to be safe. That's all anyone ever wants . . .' She broke off as a figure caught her attention. Whoever it was appeared to be stealthily crawling around on top of the rubble of her parents' former house. She broke free of Mrs Fortescue's hand in order to take a better look. Pointing, she drew the older woman's attention to the person who was now precariously balanced on debris which was shifting beneath their weight. 'What on earth do they think they're doin'?' she said.

'Bein' idiotic,' snapped Mrs Fortescue, 'that's what they're doin', and if you stand there gawpin' at 'em then you're just as bad! C'mon, gel, we need to get a move on!'

Tearing her gaze from the foolhardy figure, Libby followed Mrs Fortescue into the shelter. As the warden closed the door behind them, Libby told him of the person she'd seen clambering around her parents' house.

'Probably out lootin',' tutted the warden. 'That's why some folks don't want to leave their houses for the safety of a shelter. Personally, I'd rather lose the family silver – if I had any – as opposed to my life, but like they say, "there's nowt so queer as folk".'

Libby sat down beside Mrs Fortescue. 'I could understand if it was a buildin' full of treasures, but everyone knows my parents' house is empty. It seems pointless to search through a house that's nowt but rubble. Even if there was anything left, it would've been crushed to smithereens!'

'Sometimes people go back to a house to see if there's anythin' that can be salvaged,' mused the warden, before hurriedly adding, 'I know that's not the case with yer parents' house, but . . .' He paused as he opened the door for a woman and her children as they hurried into the shelter, and waited until they were safely inside before closing the door again. Leaning forward, he lowered his voice so that only Libby and Mrs Fortescue could hear him. 'There is one reason I can think of.'

Libby and Mrs Fortescue exchanged glances. 'Go on,' hissed Libby.

He grimaced. 'The money that was supposed to be in yer father's wallet. They could be lookin' for that, I suppose.'

Libby highly doubted this, and said as much. 'The only people who know are us three, my uncle . . .' She stopped speaking as the truth hit her. 'That thievin' . . .'

'He wouldn't!' gasped Mrs Fortescue, before adding in less incredulous tones, 'Would he?'

Libby rolled her eyes. 'I'm amazed he paid my father in the first place; hearin' that the money was lyin' unguarded would've been like music to his ears. I told him I was goin' to look through the rubble meself.' Seeing the reproving glance on Mrs Fortescue's face, she enlightened her host. 'I wouldn't, of course, because only a fool puts their life in danger for money; I just . . .' She fell silent as she tried to explain to herself why she'd told her uncle she intended to search for the money. At the time she thought she'd said it out of spite, but why? It wouldn't affect Tony if she got the money which he'd so readily handed to her father. As far as he was concerned, he'd got what he'd wanted when her father had signed the business over to him. She turned to the warden and Mrs Fortescue, who were both eyeing her keenly. 'I said it because I wanted my uncle to worry that I'd know he'd got my family business by foul means not fair. I was hopin' he'd panic and say the whole thing was a lie and that he'd never paid me father in the first place.'

'But instead, you told him where he could find the money,' said the warden, 'or so it would seem, because we don't know for certain that it was yer uncle that you saw. Mad as it may sound, it's not unheard of for kids to play on ruined buildings. Granted it's unusual for them to do so durin' an air raid, but some of them treat the whole thing as a big game.'

'Where are their mothers?' snorted Mrs Fortescue. 'That's what I'd like to know.'

The warden gave her a knowing look. 'Probably earnin' a few pennies down Soho.'

Libby eyed him innocently. 'Why Soho?'

He continued without thinking. 'Cos it's easy money for those who're desperate.'

Mrs Fortescue gave a low chuckle. 'And that's where all the sailors go.' Seeing the blank look on Libby's face, she elaborated. 'They're workin' gels,' she said, adding 'prostitutes' for total clarification.

Libby's lips rounded. 'Oh!' She hesitated, eyeing the warden curiously. 'How do you know?'

Much to Mrs Fortescue's amusement, the warden began to flounder like a fish out of water. 'I don't! Well not from personal experience. This is to say, it's common knowledge.'

Libby wrinkled her nose. 'Mum said my uncle was always down Soho. I thought it was because he had business down there, but do you think he might have been with one of them?'

Mrs Fortescue chuckled as she watched the warden's face grow ever redder. 'I'm sure he was doin' his dodgy dealin's down there, and nowt else,' he said, hoping to bring an end to the conversation.

'Makes you think though, doesn't it?' Libby mused.

'I'll certainly think before I speak in future,' muttered the warden.

The raid had been thankfully short, and it wasn't long before the all-clear sounded. Hearing the various exclamations of people as they left the shelter, Libby knew there must be more damage, but it was the warden's reaction that interested her the most.

Making his way back into the shelter, he waylaid Libby and Mrs Fortescue. 'I've just had a quick gander and I'm afraid yer old house is on fire.'

Libby shrugged. 'It's not like it could've got any worse.'

Mrs Fortescue looked bewildered. 'How can it be on fire? I could understand if it was packed to the rafters with furniture, but it was nowt but bricks 'n' mortar last time I seen it.'

'Well, rafters for one,' said the warden. 'They'll go up a treat, but it's not that which concerns me.'

Libby was intrigued. 'Oh?'

'It looks as though the fire was started deliberately.'

'Why on earth would anyone do such a stupid, pointless thing?' gasped Mrs Fortescue.

'It's senseless,' agreed the warden, 'unless you've got summat to hide.'

Libby sank back into her seat. 'If he's got the money, then what is there to hide?'

'That there wasn't any money to begin with!' said Mrs Fortescue, with a triumphant air. 'What better way to hide a lie than to say it went up in flames! You said yerself that you were goin' to search for the money – albeit just to annoy him – but if he thought you meant it, and he knew that there *wasn't* any money, then you'd be on to him.'

'He panicked because he's paranoid about me discovering the truth!' exclaimed Libby. She hesitated. 'But that doesn't do me any good, does it?'

The warden shrugged. 'Only that you've got him bang to rights. You can't prove it, which is unfortunate . . .'

'But at least I know,' said Libby. 'Although, deep down, I always did.'

'You had yer doubts, though,' Mrs Fortescue reminded her.

'Not any more,' said Libby. 'Question now is where do I go from here?'

'The only way you can go,' said Mrs Fortescue kindly. 'Onwards and upwards.'

The warden agreed with her. 'Don't look back, but don't waste yer time hatin' him, because he's not worth it. I'm a firm believer in karma; that what goes around, comes around. Mark my words, yer uncle will end up payin' for what he did to you and yer family.'

'I hope so, because he doesn't deserve to get away with this, and I'm goin' to make sure he doesn't. My parents fought hard to build that business, and I'm not havin' him swipe it out from under their noses.'

Tony had been almost certain that Libby was full of hot air, but there was a tiny part of him which worried she might be telling the truth, probably because he knew himself to be a liar. He didn't know her very well, but she came across as a pretty determined character, and he knew from his brother that she was well educated; considerably more so than he'd ever been. It had been obvious by the way she'd been looking at him down the market that she hadn't believed a word that left his lips. If she were to search through the rubble she'd find no money, and even though he'd deny it to the hilt they would both know that he was lying, and that might open up a whole new can of worms in itself. So he had waited until most decent folk were in bed before setting off. Of course, he'd been unaware that there would be an air raid, not that it would affect the task in hand. He was carrying a rag soaked in petrol which he had siphoned out of a car, and this he held over the hole from which his brother and sister-in-law's bodies had been extracted before setting a match to it and dropping it as fast as he could. Carefully scrambling down the outside of the rubble, he had looked around for a good spot to place the burned five-shilling note he'd torn in two. It had to be somewhere where the wind couldn't carry it off, but where it would be easily spotted by a passer-by. He knew that whoever found it would soon spread the word, and it wouldn't take long for the news to reach Libby. It had grieved him to set fire to his money, but it would be worth it if it meant he got Libby off his back once and for all.

It was the morning after the night of the fire, and Libby was helping Mrs Fortescue to get the house in order.

'It's hard to believe that I was doin' this with my parents just a couple of days ago, when it feels more like weeks,' Libby told her host as they packed the crockery Mrs Fortescue and her late husband had received as a wedding gift.

Mrs Fortescue carefully wrapped a cup in some newspaper. 'A lot has happened in a short amount of time,' she said wisely, 'and you've been up and down like a blue-bummed whatsit. I was the same when my Leslie passed away.'

Libby eyed the older woman shyly. 'May I ask what happened?'

'Our house got hit in the last lot, only I was out,' said Mrs Fortescue. 'That's why my daughter wants me to go and live with her in Scarborough.'

'Because she's scared that history will repeat itself,' said Libby sadly.

'I'm sorry to say it usually does,' said Mrs Fortescue knowledgeably. 'I remember them sayin' that the Great War was the war to end all wars, yet look at us now. Twenty-one years later and we're back where we started. It defies credulity, but here we are.'

Libby twisted the newspaper which she was folding around the teapot. 'Do you really think this will happen again, even if we win?'

Mrs Fortescue breathed a heavy sigh. 'I'd like to say no, I really would, but there's more than one dictator in this world, and them's the one that causes the wars, you only have to look back through history to know that.' She paused thoughtfully, before adding, 'I blame the parents.'

Libby coughed on a chuckle. 'You're blamin' Hitler's parents?'

'They should've tanned his hide when he got out of line, and taught him that no means no!' said Mrs Fortescue firmly. 'Maybe then he'd have had some respect for others and realise that he couldn't throw his weight around just because he wanted to.'

The comment amused Libby. She wasn't at all certain that you could blame the parents of a dictator, but the thought that worried her most was Mrs Fortescue's belief that history had a habit of repeating itself. 'Maybe you're right, and it is the parents to blame. Personally speaking I think the man's an idiot and a tyrant who actually believes the rubbish he spouts.'

'Talking of idiots, have you decided what you're goin' to do about yer Uncle Tony yet?'

'I can't prove anythin',' said Libby, 'but I'll be damned if I'm goin' to stand by and not let him know that I've sussed him out.'

Mrs Fortescue grinned. 'That's my gel, you give him what for. He's nowt but a tea leaf, and he needs to be told that he ain't dealin' with no fool.'

'Oh, I'll let him know all right,' said Libby. 'By the time I've finished with him, he'll be sorry he ever lied to me.'

Mrs Fortescue took the last saucer and wrapped it in paper. 'I know you're too mature to want someone to hold your hand, so I shan't offer to come with you, but you know I'm here if you need me.'

Libby picked up the box she had been packing and placed it to one side. Mrs Fortescue had been marvellous, but there was no escaping the fact that she would be leaving in a couple of days and Libby had yet to find somewhere else to live. No matter how desperate things became she couldn't contemplate the thought of living with her uncle, and with her best friend safely in Ireland she couldn't turn to her either. She supposed she could write to Emma and . . . she stopped suddenly. The address book had been taken along with the rest of the van's contents, so she wouldn't be able to reach Emma. Not only that, but Emma would find herself writing to her at the wrong address. *If I'm ever going to see my best pal again*, Libby thought, *I shall have to ask the landlord at the house in Norwich if he can forward any mail on to me . . . once I find somewhere to live, of course.*

With so much still to do, Libby turned to her host in a determined fashion. 'My uncle will have more respect for me if I go on me own. I'm goin' now, and after I've taken him down a peg or two I shall find somewhere to live,' she said.

Mrs Fortescue visibly relaxed. 'I'm glad you're takin' matters in hand, because time's marchin' on.'

Taking her coat down from its hook, Libby wrapped it tightly around her as she set out into the frosty air. With leaves still thick on the ground, the icy foliage crunched beneath her feet as she strode along the pavement. Taking care not to glance in the shop windows, some of which displayed fully decorated trees as well as snowmen made from cotton wool, she trod determinedly towards the market. Her mother had always looked forward to Christmas, and it had become traditional for them to decorate the tree after the market closed on Christmas Eve. When the decorations were done, Libby would help Orla to make mince pies, and later, each with a hot cup of cocoa, they would sit down as a family and admire the brightly coloured glass baubles, and the paperchains which Libby had made as a little girl.

A tear tracked its way down her cheek as she remembered that she would never see those family favourites again. The baubles and paperchains had been in the van along with the rest of their belongings. *Worthless to anyone else*, Libby thought, *but priceless to me.*

Making her way through the market, Libby bumped into Pete, who ran the stall next to her uncle's. Obviously keen not to talk in front of Tony, he gestured for Libby to come to one side. 'I'm guessin' you've heard?'

'If you're on about the fire at my parents' old house, then yes, I was there at the time. I don't know for certain who started it, but I've a pretty good idea.'

Pete looked astonished. 'They think someone lit it deliberately?'

Libby glanced in the direction of the neighbouring stall. 'They certainly do. If you'll excuse me, I'd like to have a word with my uncle.'

Pete followed her gaze. 'Is everything all right?'

Her eyes narrowed as she watched her uncle looking as though he hadn't a care in the world. 'Far from it,' she muttered before striding towards him.

Unaware of her presence, Tony tossed an apple into the air and caught it in the crook of his elbow before sending it back up and snatching it out of the air with the other hand. Seeing the scowl etched on Libby's face, he spoke cautiously. 'Blimey, who's rattled your cage?'

'Don't go playin' the innocent with me, Tony Gilbert. I know what you done last night, and I think you're despicable.'

His jaw practically hitting the floor, Tony looked at the stallholders on either side of him, making sure he had their full attention. 'What the hell am I supposed to've done now? C'mon, tell me.'

Libby bridled as she pointed an accusing finger. 'Set fire to me mum and dad's house, that's what, and I know why you done it, too.'

'You do?' Tony asked, before adding sarcastically, 'Pray tell. I'm sure we'd all love to hear why you think I'd set fire to a derelict house.'

'So there'd be no proof that you never paid my father for the business,' said Libby, with an air of satisfaction. 'I saw your face, when you thought I was on to you. I *knew* my father would've put the money in his wallet, which is why you came up with the farcical notion that the money had somehow got blown elsewhere.' She cast him a look of pure disdain before continuing. 'You must think I came down with the last shower.'

'I certainly do, if that's your belief,' said Tony, his tone calm despite the accusations. 'And by the way, I never told you the money had been blown from his wallet, the warden did, so you needn't start spreadin' rumours that I was behind it all, because according to you they were his words, not mine. And as for setting fire to yer parents' house, why would I do that, when I *know* I paid them the money? That would be futile as well as stupid, and I'm not stupid, certainly not when it comes to money!'

'Only you know as well as I do that there was no money,' said Libby, 'and that's why you set fire to their house, so that it could never be proved.'

The holder of one of the stalls beside Tony's gave a small cough. 'Aren't you goin' to tell her?'

Libby whipped round sharply. 'Tell me what?' She turned contemptous eyes on her uncle. 'What convoluted cockamamie story are you trying to pull this time?'

Ignoring Libby, Tony looked to the man who'd spoken. 'Why should I, when she's already got her mind made up? Quite frankly, Arthur, I could have the King himself absolve me of all crime, and this 'un would still want to see me swingin' from the nearest lamppost.'

'Because I *know* you're nowt but a big fat liar!' snapped Libby. Fists clenched to her sides, she continued to voice her opinion. 'Mum had you down pat from the very start. I just wish yer brother would've seen you for the toerag you really are.'

Far from looking upset, Tony took out his cigarette pouch. 'Your father was just as eager to help folk what can't afford top whack as me, yet he gets away scot-free whilst I'm accused of all sorts? Hardly seems fair.'

Arthur interrupted. 'It's not reasonable to let her carry on when she ain't got all the facts. Play fair, Tony, she's lost a lot recently; it's no wonder she's got her head in the clouds.'

'*Me*?' Libby's voice was heavy with disbelief. 'You think I've got my head in the clouds?'

'Anyone would have if they'd lost both parents the way you did,' said Arthur reasonably. 'And they found the money at yer father's house after the fire.' He shot Tony a reproving glance before continuing. 'Although why yer uncle didn't see fit to tell you that straight off the bat is anybody's guess.'

The colour had begun to drain from Libby's cheeks. 'Where is it?'

Arthur pulled a rueful face. 'I'm sorry to say it's no good to anyone. Nowt but a pile of burned-up notes.'

Libby rolled her eyes. 'Oh, how convenient. You find a bunch of burned papers and my uncle tells you it must be the money he paid my father. Honestly, Mr Stebbins, I didn't have you down for a fool.'

Arthur's face coloured. 'Do you really think we'd take his word for it without proof? I saw it for meself, two five-bob notes, charred beyond use, but you can still make out what they are!'

Libby gaped at him. 'Are you sure?'

Tony spluttered incredulously. 'You see!' he called out to all who'd listen. 'I *told* you she wouldn't believe me, which is why I never seen the point in tellin' her the facts in the first place.'

Libby swallowed two or three times, before regaining her voice. 'I – I . . .'

Tony mocked her viciously. '*I – I* . . . Typical that you lose yer voice when you need to apologise, but when you've vicious rumours to spread you've got a gob like a foghorn.'

'Mr Gilbert!' Arthur chastised him. 'I'll thank you to remember what this poor young girl's been through.'

'What *she's* been through?' muttered Tony. 'What about me? I've only gone and lost the last member of me family, I've not had a chance to grieve, and this one's accusin' me of diddlin' me own brother, me own flesh and blood, out of her inheritance! Tried and hanged before the jury's gathered.'

Libby's cheeks were burning with embarrassment. 'You can't blame me for thinkin' the things I did. Not with the way things were.'

Tony gawked at her. 'So much for the apology.'

Arthur turned pleading eyes to Libby, but she was resolute. 'I don't care what they found; it doesn't mean to say that it was *his* money.'

Tony scowled at his niece. 'I've had just about enough of your lip.'

Libby wiped a furious tear away with her thumb. 'Don't worry, you won't have to listen to any more of it. I *know* you're a liar, Tony Gilbert, and so do my parents.' With that, she turned her back on him and stalked her way out of the market. Hot tears of frustration splashed onto her cheeks as she dismissed the efforts of those who tried to calm her as she strode by their stalls. *They all believe him,* she thought to herself, *and it isn't goin' to matter what I say or do, I'll never change their minds. Dad thought these people were the salt of the earth, but he's wrong; they're mindless sheep that follow the herd. Everybody knows what Tony's like. I bet they all knew he was strugglin' to come up with the money for the business, yet it's easier to turn a blind eye than call him out as the liar he so clearly is.*

Libby was still crying when she reached Mrs Fortescue's house. Bursting in through the door, she thundered up the stairs and threw herself onto the bed. Mrs Fortescue followed, and knocked on the door to Libby's room. 'Libby?'

'I can't talk, not yet,' said Libby, between sobs. 'He's got away with murder, and I can't bear to think about it.'

There was a pause from the other side of the door before Mrs Fortescue's voice came tentatively through the wood. 'Are you talkin' about yer Uncle Tony, by any chance?'

She heard Libby crossing the room. Opening the door just a crack, Libby peered out. 'Do you believe him and not me?'

Mrs Fortescue spoke softly. 'Try explainin' exactly what you mean, and I'll let you know.'

Libby opened the door fully, sat back down on her bed with a whump and buried her face in her hands. Speaking thickly through her fingers, she told Mrs Fortescue all about her encounter with Tony, as well as the thoughts of Arthur Stebbins.

Mrs Fortescue sank down onto the bed next to Libby and took her hand in hers. 'I don't know your father's brother, but I did know your parents, and by all accounts your mum was no fan of Tony's.'

Libby gave a disapproving snort. 'You can say that again. In fact, I'd go as far as to say that she loathed him, although she never really made it clear as to why.'

Mrs Fortescue shrugged. 'Sometimes in-laws don't get on, and they rub each other up the wrong way. It sounds to me that this could have been the case with your mother and Tony.'

'But to treat me as if I didn't exist? I was my father's child as much as my mother's.'

She shrugged. 'Maybe he's a man's man. Is he married?'

Libby's eyes rounded at the thought of any poor woman having to put up with her uncle. 'God no.'

'There you are then,' said Mrs Fortescue.

Annoyed that her host wasn't taking her mother's opinion seriously, Libby continued on a different tack. 'I've not seen him shed a single tear over his brother's demise. You're not tellin' me that's natural.'

Mrs Fortescue made a clicking noise with her tongue. 'In men? A lot of the time, yes. They don't show their feelings the same way women do; instead they bottle it up and push it down to their boots, like it never happened.' She rolled her eyes. 'Stiff upper lip and all that nonsense.'

'But what about the money? My uncle lives hand to mouth, always has done. He's not got a responsible bone in his body . . .'

'Which is why he blew his money on the horses,' said Mrs Fortescue quietly. 'He's just lucky that everything came up trumps; had it not, you might have been singin' from a different hymn sheet.'

Libby eyed her host incredulously. 'Do you really believe anyone could be that lucky?'

'You've heard of someone having the luck of the devil?'

Libby nodded morosely. 'Sums him up to a tee.'

'I can understand how angry you must be, and how this all seems so unfair, I really can, but sometimes life just doesn't go the way we want it to.' She fiddled with the hem of her skirt, removing a thread which had come free. 'I don't wish to add insult to injury, but have you found anywhere to live yet?'

Libby sank her head into her hands. 'I will, I promise.'

'It's goin' to be Christmas Eve the day after tomorrow. You need to find something a.s.a.p., because I simply can't take you with me, and the next tenants will no doubt object if they find a lodger in their new home.' She paused, bracing herself for the backlash to her next question. 'I don't suppose you've considered approachin' your uncle?'

Libby looked at her aghast. 'No, I have not. What's more, I don't think he'd take me in even if I did. Especially not after the things I've said.'

Mrs Fortescue twisted the thread around her fingers and pulled it tight. 'A "sorry" goes a long way.'

'Do you really think he'll want to listen to a word I say?' Libby stared at the ground beneath her. 'I know folk might say I'm cuttin' me nose off to spite my face, but I just can't bring myself to do it. It almost feels as though I'd be letting me mum and dad down.'

Mrs Fortescue patted Libby's knee. 'Let's forget about Tony for now. Have you spoken to the funeral directors yet?'

Libby brought her legs up to her chest, tucking her knees beneath her chin. 'No, I've been avoidin' them.'

'You need to go and make arrangements,' said Mrs Fortescue as kindly as she could.

'What with?' Libby sniffed, as fresh tears formed. 'I've not got two pennies to rub together. I can't afford to feed myself, let alone pay for a funeral.'

'And they'll understand that,' Mrs Fortescue assured her. 'There's many an unmarked grave . . .'

Tears flashed in Libby's eyes. 'No! I don't care what it takes, they're not goin' to be buried without a headstone.'

Mrs Fortescue stroked the back of Libby's hair in a soothing fashion. 'There's no shame in it, Libby luv – my Leslie's in an unmarked grave.'

Libby cursed herself inwardly before turning apologetically to her host. 'I'm sorry. I didn't mean to imply anything. I just want somewhere to visit, and for people to know that my parents were loved. I know that you loved your husband with all your heart, but I'm all they have left. If I don't do this, it feels as though I'm not showin' them how much I care.'

'Which is completely understandable, but do you know how expensive headstones are? Because I do, and they don't come cheap,' said Mrs Fortescue mildly.

'I'll find the money,' said Libby, adding sarcastically, 'Maybe I should put a bet on the horses.'

Mrs Fortescue wagged a reproving finger. 'I know that you're only jokin', but trust me, gamblin's a mug's game, and you mustn't let the luck of one individual convince you otherwise.'

'I know you all believe him, but I'm afraid it's goin' against the grain for me to follow suit.'

'Then what are you suggestin'? That he set fire to his own money?'

Libby shrugged in a petulant manner. 'I wouldn't put it past him. Especially if it meant he'd get me off his back. Besides, Dad's business was worth more than ten bob, so he still came out on top.'

'Except he didn't have to, did he?' said Mrs Fortescue reasonably. 'Even if you'd searched every piece of mortar and every loose brick, there's hundreds of different explanations as to why that money wasn't in your dad's wallet.'

'But I *know*—' Libby insisted, before being cut off by the older woman.

'Only you can't prove it, even now,' she said. 'You've got to learn to let this go, luv, otherwise it's goin' to eat you up inside, and your parents wouldn't have wanted that for you.'

'So let him get away with it?'

Mrs Fortescue arched a greying eyebrow. 'Do you have any choice?'

Libby sat in silence as she racked her brains for some kind of solution, but it seemed her companion was not just older, but wiser too. 'No,' she said flatly. 'He's won.'

Mrs Fortescue pulled a doubtful face. 'Maybe in your eyes, but I very much doubt your uncle sees it that way, not if he's as guilty as you believe him to be.'

Libby eyed her curiously. 'Why not? He's got the business and he didn't have to pay for it.'

'No, but he's lost his family because of his actions, and he'll realise that family's more important than money over time.'

Libby tutted beneath her breath. 'Only he's not a family man . . .'

'Maybe not now, but when you get old you realise how important family is,' said Mrs Fortescue knowingly. 'Take yours truly as an example. I'm riddled with arthritis, on top of which I'm gettin' forgetful. A few weeks back, I sat down on me chair whilst I waited for the kettle to boil. Before I knew it, I was fast off. By the time I woke up the kettle 'ad a soddin great 'ole in it, which is why we're makin' cups of tea with a saucepan, cos I can't afford a new one. I've loved 'avin' you around cos you've made me feel safer in me own home, and I've slept better as a result. Not only that, but it's someone to chat to – talk about your day, share a slice of cake, silly little things which mean nothin' when you're younger, but a whole heap as you age.'

'Pity Uncle Tony doesn't see things the way you do,' said Libby.

'He will in time,' said Mrs Fortescue. 'You need to forget about revenge and start concentratin' on yourself; that way you can start to move on.'

'Sounds good to me!'

It was Christmas Eve, and Libby was seeing Mrs Fortescue off at the train station. Standing on the crowded platform, the old lady was staring at Libby with grave concern.

'I'll be fine,' said Libby for the umpteenth time. 'I've not found anywhere yet, but I will; trust me.'

'I'm worried you're bein' too complacent. Christmas is one of the busiest times of year, war or no war. You can't seriously expect to find accommodation on Christmas Eve?'

'Joseph did,' said Libby, hoping to inject humour into an otherwise tense conversation.

'He was with a pregnant woman!' Mrs Fortescue reminded her. 'I really don't mean to sound harsh, but homeless young-sters are ten a penny since war broke out. What makes you so different?'

'Because I'm determined,' said Libby. 'I'll find a way; I always do.'

Mrs Fortescue sighed wretchedly as her train came into view. Libby was acting like a typical youngster who believed that everything would come up roses because it was happening to them. As the train drew to a halt, the older woman appeared to make her mind up about something. 'There's nowt else for it: you're goin' to have to come to Scarborough with me. I'll not take no for an answer, cos I'll be damned if I leave you to fend for yourself in London.'

'Sorry, Mrs F., but this isn't your decision to make. I've not buried my parents yet, and I've still got unfinished business here.'

Mrs Fortescue rolled her eyes. 'Not Tony flamin' Gilbert! I've had enough of hearin' you bleat on about that man. You're cuttin' off your nose to spite your face. I'm afraid it's all goin' to go drastically wrong, and with no one else here I see myself as your guardian.'

'Oh, Mrs F., that really is sweet of you,' said Libby, 'but I'm not your responsibility.'

'Please, Libby . . . I'll not sleep a wink.'

Libby held Mrs Fortescue's wrinkled hand. 'I've got your address; if I need you I'll write, and that's a promise.'

'Swear it?'

Libby made the sign of the cross over her chest. 'I swear I'll come to you if need be.'

'You wouldn't be a burden, if that's what you're thinkin',' continued Mrs Fortescue, but Libby was looking past her to the people who were boarding the train.

'If you don't hurry, you'll not get a seat, and I'd never forgive myself if I thought you had to stand all the way to Scarborough. So please, go and get aboard the train.'

Mrs Fortescue took Libby in a warm and loving embrace. 'Take care of yourself, sweetheart. You're more precious than you realise.'

Her lip trembling, Libby waited a second or two before replying. 'Thanks, Mrs F. You're a star, I hope you know that, cos without you I dread to think where I'd be. Say hello to your daughter for me, and tell her that I think she's incredibly lucky to have a mother like you.' She kissed the old lady's soft, wrinkled cheek before pulling back.

Mrs Fortescue unclipped her handbag and pulled out her purse. Taking out a few pennies, she pressed them into Libby's hand.

'That's ever so nice of you, Mrs F., but I'll be fine, honestly I will . . .' Libby began in protest, but Mrs Fortescue wasn't having any of it.

'Think of it as a parting gift,' she said. 'Cheerio, Libby luv, and make sure you let me know how you get on.'

'I will,' Libby promised, adding, 'and thanks for the money. I swear I'll spend it wisely.' She helped Mrs Fortescue onto the train, and waited for her to appear by one of the windows. When she did so, she made the motions of someone writing a letter. Waving her acknowledgement, Libby was momentarily swallowed in the steam which gushed between the wheels of the train, and then the engine driver pulled the whistle, alerting everyone to its imminent departure.

Following Mrs Fortescue along until the platform's end, Libby waved until her friend was out of sight, and then, turning, took the first step in the direction of her new life. Mrs Fortescue had been right when she said that Libby would find it almost impossible to find accommodation on Christmas Eve, but Libby knew that accommodation came with the territory where she was headed, and, from what she'd heard, finding a job would be an absolute breeze. She also knew that if she had told Mrs Fortescue how she planned to get her parents a headstone, the older woman might well have tried to carry her onto the train, so she had kept quiet, something she would do until her dying day, because she wasn't proud of the move she was about to make. With a heavy heart, Libby set off in the direction of London's Soho.

Libby had returned to the funeral parlour to tell them that she would have the money for her parents' headstone in a few days' time, and that they should go ahead and start making arrangements for the burial the following week. The undertaker she'd spoken to a few days earlier was glad to have a decision, but dubious about the date. He had been polite, but as soon as Libby had finished her piece he had been quick to let her know that they would only arrange for the burial and headstone when the money was in place. He had also made it perfectly plain that time was of the essence, and if she didn't come up with the payment quickly they would have no choice but to bury her parents in a pauper's grave.

As Libby made her way through the streets of Soho, she wondered how one went about telling which ones the prostitutes frequented. It was hardly a question you could ask a passer-by. She glanced up at the street signs, then chastised herself for considering that these might give her an indication as to where to head for. She searched her memory for any snippets of information she might have picked up relating to the seedier side of London, but with nothing springing to mind she supposed she would have to keep her eyes peeled for the smallest of clues.

As it turned out, Libby didn't have to look for prostitution, because prostitution came to her, in the form of a smartly dressed man, the sort her mother would've described as a spiv – a bit like her Uncle Tony. When he approached her Libby had expected him to ask if she were lost, or looking for someone, but it seemed the people who trod the darker streets of London wasted no time on such trivialities, but instead cut to the chase.

'Are you lookin' for work, luv?'

Blushing to the roots of her hair, Libby said yes so quietly he could only just hear her. Resting his chin between forefinger and thumb, he eyed her curiously. Then, reaching out with his other hand, he took hold of her jaw and tilted her head as though he were examining a horse for sale. Pulling a small grimace, he spoke gruffly. 'I reckon I can find you summat.'

Feeling oddly pleased that she had passed muster, Libby looked around them. 'What happens now?'

He glanced at her. 'We need to get you bathed and into something less . . .' he rubbed his hand across his mouth as he sought the words he was looking for, 'childlike. Some of the punters might like it, but we don't want the Bluebottles buzzin' round, do we?'

'How soon will I start . . .' She swallowed, unwilling to say the word which was sticking in her throat, until an image of her parents' headstone came into her mind, prompting her to finish quietly, 'work?'

When the man placed his arm around her shoulders, she tried not to flinch. 'Eager to get goin', eh?' he said approvingly. 'You come with me, and we'll get you workin' before night falls.'

Libby followed him up some steps to a dim and drearylooking house. He knocked a brief tattoo in a rhythmic style against the door, and within moments a woman appeared.

Staring disapprovingly at the man, she turned her attention to Libby. 'Aren't you a bit young for this game?'

The man viewed her through narrowing eyes. 'Who am I to turn away someone what's desperate for money?'

Tutting beneath her breath, the woman slid her arm through Libby's. ''Ello, darlin'. My name's Sadie, and you are . . .?'

Libby blushed. Should she give her real name? No. No one would know any different, and she didn't want word getting out as to her real identity. Choosing the most exotic name she could think of, she mumbled: 'Tallulah.'

A smile tweaked Sadie's lips. No one ever used their real name, not even her. 'Well, you come with me, Tallulah, and I'll run you a nice hot bath.'

Following the woman out of the room and up a sombre-looking staircase to the bathroom, Libby felt her stomach churn as though it was trying to perform cartwheels. Wanting to put off the inevitable, she glanced at the large tub standing before an open fire. 'Why do I need a bath?'

'Because we run a clean house,' said Sadie, adding, 'and we don't want the punters thinkin' we've dragged you in off the streets against your will.' Feeling the water against her wrist, she indicated that Libby should undress. 'I had done this bath for meself, but you can get in first.'

Not wanting to take her clothes off in front of a stranger, Libby hesitated. 'I don't mind waitin'. It was your bath after all.'

Kneeling down on the floor, Sadie eyed Libby with open curiosity. 'Do you mind my askin' why you're here? You don't look underfed, and you've got lovely skin, which indicates good hygiene and nutrition. Something's obviously gone wrong, because no one chooses to be a workin' girl unless they're desperate.'

Libby quickly explained the situation which had led her to seek work. 'The warden said women turned to prostitution because it was easy employment for those desperate enough.'

Sadie spoke thoughtfully. 'He's right, but I think you've misinterpreted the word "easy". He meant easy as in you don't need any qualifications or recommendations to do this line of work. Anyone can come in off the streets and sell their bodies for money, young or old, black or white.' She paused before adding, darkly, 'Male or female.'

Libby stared at her aghast. 'Boys?'

Examining her own hair for split ends as she spoke, Sadie said plainly, 'Not all men like women.'

Libby stuttered. 'But – but . . .'

Sadie turned her attention back to Libby. 'But what? Just because you've never 'eard of it don't mean to say that it's not goin' on behind closed doors. You'd be amazed at what happens when no one's lookin', and if you continue down this road you're gonna find out soon enough.' Standing up, she released Libby's hair from its clip, and began to smooth a brush through the ends. 'Prostitution is a dark world. It's not meant for kids what are too naïve to be sellin' their soul.'

'That may be, but I don't have a choice,' said Libby softly.

'We all have a choice, *Tallulah*, so you'd better make sure that this is the right one for you, because once you've crossed the line there ain't no goin' back.'

'There is if I only do it until I've got enough money to cover the funeral,' said Libby.

'What about food in your belly, a roof over your head, and the fact that you'll find it hard to look civilised people in the face again.' Sadie fell silent for a moment or two. 'You said that you'd tell this Mrs Fortescue where you were livin', but do you really think you could tell her that you were livin' in a brothel?'

Tears formed in Libby's eyes. 'I couldn't tell *anyone* that I was living in a brothel.'

'Exactly, but you mark my words, people know.' She hooked a fine gold necklace which hung around her neck with her thumb. 'You've 'eard the way I talk. If you was to meet me in 'arrods, what would you think I'd done to get this fine piece of jewellery?'

Libby's cheeks were burning with embarrassment. 'I s'pose I might think that you'd nicked it?'

'And is a thief better than a prostitute?'

Libby gaped at the older woman's frank approach. 'Probably worse,' she said after a few moments' thought, 'cos at least a prostitute earns her money, rather than takin' what doesn't belong to her.'

'So, they know that I'm either one or the other,' said Sadie, 'cos they know I can't afford stuff like this, not on a normal girl's wage.' Seeing that Libby was thinking hard, she added, 'I didn't buy it, in case you're wonderin'; I was given this by a grateful customer. I'm savin' me pennies to look after myself when I'm old and toothless, because men don't want sex with summat that looks like a haggard old witch.'

Remembering Sadie's account of the types of people who entered prostitution, Libby eyed her dubiously. 'Are you sure?'

Sadie roared with laughter. 'Oh, bless you, darlin' child, cos you've hit the nail on the head, and yes, you're probably right, cos just as there's a lid for every pan, there's a punter for every worker.' She turned Libby to face her. 'Are you *sure* this is what you want?'

Libby thought about it before jutting her chin out in a determined manner. 'It's the only way.'

Sadie eyed her sorrowfully. 'I'll leave you to take your bath, then. There's no rush, so make sure you have a good think whilst you're in there, and remember: it's only too late to change your mind afterwards.'

Sadie slipped out of the room, leaving Libby to get undressed. As she unbuttoned her shirt-waisted frock, she stared into the bubbles which hid the bathwater. Having never so much as kissed a boy, she wondered what it would be like to have sex with one. She supposed people did it because it was a nice thing to do, but if that was the case then why was prostitution so frowned upon? And why was Sadie concerned that Libby might be doing the wrong thing?

She tested the water with the tips of her fingers. It was delightfully warm, and the bubbles were beautifully fragrant. Slipping a foot into the water, she gently lowered the rest of her body beneath the bubbles. The bath was the biggest she had ever been in, and the bubbles a touch of luxury. At home she would have had Pears scented soap, and at Mrs Fortescue's they used the same soap they'd used to wash the dishes and the clothes. This was something special, a real treat. Could prostitution be so bad if you had lovely baths like this to look forward to?

Libby had been soaking for a good five minutes when Sadie knocked on the door before entering. 'I've got you a bath towel and some clean clothes to get changed into.' She placed everything on a chair which stood beside a dressing table. 'Have you thought any more about what I've said?'

'I have. And whilst I appreciate your words of warning, I honestly think I can do this.' She blushed shyly. 'And me name's Libby.'

Sadie chuckled softly. 'I didn't think it was Tallulah. Nice to meet you, Libby.'

Libby rubbed her arm anxiously. 'Can we keep that between the two of us?'

Sadie passed the sign of the cross over her chest. 'I promise not to breathe a word.'

Taking a deep breath, Libby plunged her head under the water. Wriggling her fingers through her hair, she came to the surface. 'Have you any soap to wash my hair with?'

In reply, Sadie came over to the bath with a bar of pink soap. Frothing the bar between her hands, she began to wash Libby's hair in a comforting, methodical fashion. 'You've got beautiful curls,' she noted as she massaged the soap into Libby's scalp. 'Not a split end in sight. You must take very good care of it.'

Libby's lips trembled. 'My mother used to cut it for me.'

Sadie fell silent for a few seconds as she scooped some of the bathwater into a jug. 'I know you think you're doin' the right thing, or rather the only thing you can do, but are you sure your parents would see it that way? Because I don't think they would. It sounds to me as though your parents doted on you, and the last thing they'd want is to see you degrade yourself in their name.'

'You're right, it would be,' replied Libby simply, 'but I'm doing what I think is the right thing, not just for my parents but for me too. I need somewhere to visit, somewhere I can feel as though I'm close to them, and an unmarked grave wouldn't give me that.' She stood up as Sadie held the towel for her. 'I'm only goin' to do this until I make enough money to cover the burial. I'll find summat else after that.'

Sadie took a hand towel and gently rubbed Libby's hair. 'That's easier said than done.'

Libby dried and dressed in the clothes Sadie had brought for her. The dress was reasonable enough with its sweetheart neckline, but the shoes were higher than anything Libby had ever had on her feet, and she found walking in them incredibly different. Tottering the first few steps, she turned to Sadie. 'Do I *have* to wear these?'

'Perhaps it would be best if you only wore them whilst sitting down,' mused Sadie. 'We don't want you breakin' a leg on your first night.'

Removing the shoes, Libby followed Sadie through to a room with a bed in it. Libby couldn't think of it as a bedroom, as it was distinctly lacking in furniture such as a dressing table, a chest of drawers or a wardrobe. There was just the bed, made up with crimson sheets, and a soft light hanging directly above the bed itself. Licking her lips nervously, Libby turned to Sadie. 'What happens now?'

Sadie held Libby's hands in hers. 'If you're ready, there's a punter waitin' outside. But don't worry – if you're not ready he can have one of the other girls.'

Libby had made up her mind. 'I just want to get it over and done with. The more I think about it, the more nervous I'll get. Send him in.' She grabbed Sadie's elbow as the older woman turned to leave. 'Hang on. What am I meant to do? Take my clothes off before he gets in? Or . . .' She felt the tears prick her eyes. Furious at herself for letting her emotions get the better of her, she quickly banished the tears.

'Most men are just eager to have their pound of flesh, then skedaddle before their wife realises they're missing. My advice would be to lie back and think of England or the money, whichever works for you.'

Libby clenched her fists. 'I'm ready.'

As soon as Sadie left the room, Libby walked over to the bed and lay down. Screwing her eyes shut, she heard the door open and close as someone heavy-footed entered the room. Bunching her fists into balls, she heard him undoing his belt and letting it clatter to the floor. Her heart thumping in her chest, she felt a bead of sweat trickle down the side of her temple. When she heard him approaching the bed she opened one eye just a tiny slit, and felt an enormous wave of relief to see that he still had his trousers on. Closing her eyes, her body tensed as she heard the sound of his trousers dropping to his ankles. This time, when she looked from the corner of her eye, she saw that he was naked from the waist down. Her eyes shot open, and she gaped in horror at the rotund figure which stood beside the bed. His half-aroused member bobbed intimidatingly through the thick bush of greying pubic hair, and when she quickly turned her attention to his face, there was no mistaking the look of hunger in his beetle-black eyes.

Sadie's words burst into Libby's head. *'It's only too late afterwards . . .'*

Half falling off the bed, Libby saw the man's wallet lying on the floor next to his trousers. Without pausing to think, she picked it up and ran out of the house.

Pelting along the street, she heard the sound of the air-raid sirens split the frosty night air. Clasping the man's wallet in her hand, she pushed it into the bra Sadie had provided, which was far too large for her. She had no idea where she was running to, but with an impending air raid coming her way she now had two enemies to outrun. Hearing the furious cries of the man who was screaming blue murder behind her, Libby ploughed on – until her bare feet hit a patch of ice and she found herself sliding uncontrollably into the River Thames.

Chapter Three

Libby had begun to think the air raid would never end, but after an hour's torturous silence she sagged with relief as the all-clear sounded. The man whose wallet she had stolen had continued to shoot her dark, suspicious glances the whole time they had been in the shelter, and she was keen for him to leave first so that she might slip out undetected. Her cheeks reddened as she recalled how she'd told Sadie that a thief could be presumed worse than a prostitute. Libby had stolen the man's money and she had no excuse other than desperation. The fact that he wanted to pay her for sex was no justification for robbing him. But how could she return the money now, without admitting she'd stolen it in the first place? Seeing him get to his feet, Libby made up her mind. Looking at Jack she jerked her head in the direction of the shelter door, indicating that she wanted him to follow her. As they made for the exit, Libby threw the wallet at the back of the man's heels. Nudging Jack, she side-stepped so that she was on the other side of him.

Jogging up behind the man, Jack bent down and picked up the wallet. 'Hello, what's this?' Flipping it open, he stared at the wedge of notes inside. 'Blimey! Has anyone lost their wallet?'

The disgruntled man immediately spun round and glared at Jack. 'That's mine!'

Holding the wallet out of his reach, Jack wagged a chiding finger. 'We can all say that, but I need proof.'

'It's got the monogram H S on the outer corner,' the man muttered.

Jack checked the wallet before handing it over. 'Looks like you must've dropped it,' he said, muttering 'Pickpocket indeed' beneath his breath.

The man looked at the wallet in his hand. 'I never dropped this; I saw her pick it up off the floor.'

Jack glared at the man in bewilderment. 'I thought you said she'd nicked it out of yer trouser pocket?'

The man glowered at him, his face thunderous. 'It fell on the floor *after* she swiped it from me pocket.' He glared from Jack to Libby, his eyes narrowing. 'I demand to see what she's wearin'!'

Gordon, who had stopped to wait for his son, strode back to the group. 'I *beg* your pardon?'

'The girl what stole me wallet was wearing a red dress,' said the man defensively. He pointed to Libby. 'And I reckon that were her. Take that bloody blanket off and stop hidin'.'

But Jack had had enough. 'What do you think this is, a bleedin' striptease? I don't know where you lost yer wallet, but I do wonder what it was doin' on the floor, instead of bein' in yer trouser pocket. Or were they on the floor too?'

Turning puce, the man spluttered a protest, claiming that he didn't know what sort of man Jack mistook him for, but he was sorely mistaken if he thought him to be 'that' kind of man. At last, still muttering his grievance, he stalked off, leaving Libby with Jack and his father.

Her face flushed with embarrassment, Libby eyed her rescuers, shamefaced. 'I can explain.'

Gordon held up a hand. 'No need for explanations; any fool can see you're no thief.'

Libby folded the blanket and put it down on the bench nearest the door. 'Thanks ever so for comin' to my rescue and defendin' me, but it's time I was off.'

Jack stared at her. 'You can't go wanderin' around the streets with your dress all tore up. Besides which, if that feller sees what you're wearin', he'll soon put two and two together and he won't be so easily fobbed off when he sees your dress.' His green eyes twinkled kindly at Libby. 'Do you live far from here?'

Libby opened her mouth to answer, but her throat was choked with tears. Eventually finding her voice, she said softly, 'I have no home.'

Jack blew his cheeks out. 'Then you must come with us and have yourself a nice hot mug of cocoa by a warm fire. I'm sure my mother had plenty of old dresses that you could choose from.'

Libby nibbled her bottom lip, somewhat dubiously. 'That's awfully kind of you, but don't you think you should ask your mother before you go offering her clothes to a stranger?'

Jack cast her a sidelong glance. 'That'd be hard to do, considerin' she passed away when I were still a babe in arms.'

Libby cursed herself inwardly. 'I'm so sorry, I didn't realise.'

Jack was waving a dismissive hand. 'Not to worry. I didn't expect you to know.'

She looked down to her dirty, torn dress. 'Are you *sure* you don't mind my borrowing something? I promise to give it back just as soon as I get back on my feet.'

Jack eyed her curiously. 'Do you mind my askin' what happened to you?'

Libby came to a decision. Jack and his father had been so kind, she wasn't about to repay their generosity by lying to them. 'I think it best if I start at the beginning. An explanation is the least you're owed, no matter how humiliating.'

As they walked the short distance to the flat which Jack shared with his father, Libby told them everything, from her parents' anticipated move to Norwich, to Tony's suspected theft of the business, to her determination to pay for her parents' funeral.

'I'm not a thief,' she said, her cheeks hot with embarrassment. 'I truly don't know what came over me when I took his money.'

'Desperation?' suggested Jack. 'You've already said you couldn't see another way to make the money in time. Why the change of heart though, after goin' to all that trouble?'

'It wasn't mine to take,' said Libby simply. 'I may not approve of men like him, but when all's said and done, whether I like it or not, there would be plenty of women in dire straits without men like that to plump up their wages.'

Jack grimaced. 'I wouldn't be a woman for all the tea in China, if that's what you have to do to make ends meet.'

Libby cast her mind back to Sadie's comment that it wasn't just women who prostituted themselves.

'So, what'll you do now?' enquired Gordon, interrupting her thoughts. 'Cos as far as I can see, you're back to square one.'

Libby shrugged. 'I haven't the foggiest. Uncle Tony's already said he hasn't got the money, and that I should look elsewhere, but where?'

Gordon stopped outside a staircase that ran up the side of a building. 'This is us. Mind your step; they can be treacherous in the dark.'

Libby followed Gordon up the steep stone staircase and through a door black with aged paint. As soon as they were inside, Jack nipped over to the windows and drew the blackout blinds before his father lit the lamp. Libby was pleasantly surprised to see that the flat was neat and clean considering two men lived there. They didn't have a great deal of furniture, but when there were only two of you, how much furniture did you need?

Jack hung his coat on the peg beside the door. 'Have you no other relatives you can turn to?'

'Yes, but they're in Liverpool,' said Libby, 'and I've not seen them in years, plus I wouldn't know where to find them.'

'Do they know about your parents?' asked Gordon tentatively.

Libby's lips parted gently as she stared at him. With all the worry and stress, she'd completely forgotten that her mother's side of the family were still unaware that they had lost their daughter. She hung her head in shame. 'I'm embarrassed to say that they don't, but how am I meant to tell them when I don't even know where they live?'

Jack, who had been deep in thought, looked up sharply. 'What about an address book? Surely their names . . .' He stopped speaking.

'Gone in the van, along with everything else.'

He tutted loudly. 'I'd like to get me hands on the geezer that stole your stuff. How can anyone do that, *especially* in times like these?'

Gordon pulled a disapproving face. 'All's fair in love and war. That's the way they see it.'

'And I was nearly one of them,' said Libby sadly. 'Thank God you came along when you did, else I'd be remembered as a thievin' tart what met her end in the river.'

Jack blew his cheeks out. He wanted to disagree, and to tell her that she was wrong, but he knew she was right.

Taking the poker, Gordon stoked the fire back to life. 'I know you don't exactly get on with your uncle, but do you think he might know whereabouts your relatives live?'

Libby wrinkled the side of her nose. 'I suppose it's worth a shot. I know he went to my parents' wedding, which was in Liverpool, so he's bound to have talked to at least some of them.'

Jack rubbed his chin in a thoughtful manner. 'So, he was friendly with your mother at one time?'

'According to my father, yes. He said that everything was fine until he and Mum moved down to London, and it was only then that the problems surfaced.'

'You've said that your uncle likes to sell the odd bit of stuff on the black market; maybe he didn't want yer folks comin' to London because he knew they wouldn't approve,' supposed Jack. 'And you can kind of see why, when you listen to everythin' your mum had to say about his antics.'

'But Dad wasn't exactly whiter than white,' protested Libby.

'Maybe your mother thought your uncle was a bad influence on him? Especially if he played everythin' by the book in Liverpool.' Jack hesitated. 'How come your father lived in Liverpool, but his brother in London?'

'My father's side of the family hailed from Norwich originally, but my father and Uncle Tony moved to London to see if they could make their fortune. My mother met my father when she came to London on a weekend away with her family – Dad reckoned it was love at first sight. With my father's parents being deceased, they decided to have the wedding in Liverpool, so that Mum's sister and parents could attend, and Dad loved Liverpool so much they decided to stay and help my grandparents run their stall on something called Paddy's market.'

'So how come they ended up back in London?' said Jack.

'Mum fell out with her family, although I don't know what over. That's when they moved to London, and got themselves their own stall down Petticoat Lane.'

Jack fetched three mugs from the kitchen sideboard and began to prepare the cocoa. He glanced at Libby over his shoulder.

'Sugar?'

'No thanks.'

'Cos you're sweet enough, eh?' quipped Jack. His cheeks reddened as the words left his lips, much to his father's amusement. Still chuckling, Gordon fetched a loaf of bread and began to cut it into slices.

'Corned beef do you?'

'That would be lovely,' said Libby. 'Do you need a hand?'

'You rest yer trotters,' said Gordon. 'Me and Jack can manage.'

Jack passed the mugs of cocoa round, and nursing hers between her hands, Libby glanced shyly at her hosts. 'Thanks ever so much for lookin' after me. I really do appreciate it.'

Jack's eyes glittered as he sat down next to her. 'You're welcome. We're not the sort of fellers to leave a damsel in distress.'

'Especially not one as pretty as Libby, eh, Jack?' said Gordon.

Blushing to the roots of his hair, Jack rolled his eyes at his father's remark. 'Dad!'

Gordon grinned. 'I'm only teasin', son.' He handed Libby a plate of sandwiches. 'Get your gums round that lot.'

Libby thanked her hosts before tucking into the food, which tasted all the better for her dip in the Thames.

'That's what I like to see,' said Gordon approvingly, 'a girl with a hearty appetite. I can't stand these women that claim they're always on a diet.' He glanced over to a room which stood just off the kitchen. 'You'll have to take a look through my wife's wardrobe after you've finished your sarnies. You're welcome to anything that fits.'

Libby finished her mouthful before asking, 'Are you sure? Only if you've kept them this long . . .'

He shrugged. 'Only because I didn't like the thought of some stranger wearin' them. I don't mind you havin' them, though, and I know Maisie would like them to go to someone who really needed them.'

As soon as she had finished her sandwich, Gordon showed Libby to the bedroom he had shared with his wife. Opening the wardrobe doors, he said, 'Feel free to try stuff on. Whatever you want is yours to keep . . . as long as you don't take 'em for a dip in the Thames, that is.'

Libby grimaced. 'I promise you I won't be doin' anythin' like that ever again.'

'Then they're yours,' said Gordon. 'Take as much or as little as you want.'

Jack, who had followed his father and Libby from the kitchen, stood leaning in the doorway. 'Where to though, Dad? It's no point givin' Libby a suitcase of clothes if she's got nowhere to put 'em.'

'True.' His father scratched his head, before reaching a decision. 'Then she must stay here until she finds somewhere else.' He turned to his son. 'You don't mind bunkin' down with me, do you, Jack?'

'Not in the slightest.'

Libby gazed at the clothes on their hangers for a few more moments before turning back to the men. 'You've done so much for me already. Are you *sure*?'

Jack and Gordon spoke at the same time. 'Positive.'

'Then I shall be delighted to take you up on your kind offer,' said Libby. She selected a blue frock to change into, as well as a nice pair of black brogues. 'Fingers crossed they fit,' she said as Jack and his father left her to get changed.

Five minutes later, she walked through to the main room and looked to Jack, who was eyeing her approvingly. 'A perfect fit. In fact, you remind me of Cinderella and the glass shoe!'

Libby smoothed the blue material down with the palm of her hand. 'If I'm Cinderella, that must make Tony my evil uncle and . . .'

Gordon grinned. 'Lemme guess. Our Jack here's yer Prince Charming, am I right?'

'Dad!'

Giggling at Jack's protests, Libby spoke up for Gordon. 'Your father might be teasin', but I rather think he's hit the nail on the head, because that's exactly who you remind me of. First you pull me out of the river, then you stand up for me despite knowin' that feller was speakin' the truth, if only in part.'

Gordon gave his son a hearty slap on the shoulder. 'That's cos he's been brought up, not dragged up.'

Libby walked over to the sink. 'Never a truer word said.' She poured some of the hot water from the kettle into the bowl. 'If I'm to stay, then you must let me do what I can to earn me keep.'

'I'll not object to a woman's cookin',' said Gordon. 'I've done me best over the years, but I'll never be as good as my Maisie.'

'I can't promise my cookin' will be as good as hers,' said Libby, 'But I'll give it a good go.'

Jack gave an inward sigh of happiness. He didn't know whether Libby had felt a connection, but from the moment he had pulled her out of the Thames. Jack had known that he never wanted to let her go again.

It was Christmas Day, and rather than lie in bed dwelling over what should have been Libby had made sure that she was up betimes. *It's all too easy to wallow in self-pity*, she thought as she busied herself at the sink, *but life will be a lot harder if you don't at least try to move on. They're gone, and they're never comin' back. The sooner you get that through your head the better.*

Filling the kettle with water, she took it over to the stove and placed it on to boil, then checked on the porridge, which was bubbling quietly. She glanced to the clock above the door mantel. It read six-thirty, yet there was no sign of Jack or his father. She knew it would be selfish to not let the men lie in, but she couldn't stand the deathly quiet which was allowing her mind to wander. *The less time I have to think, the better I shall be . . .*

To her relief, Jack appeared in the doorway to his father's room, interrupting her thoughts. Yawning audibly, his nostrils flared as the smell of warm porridge wafted towards him.

'Mornin', Treacle!' As he walked over, he ensured that the cord on his dressing gown was properly lashed. 'And merry Christmas.'

Libby scooped the tea leaves into the pot. 'Mornin', Jack, and merry Christmas to you too. I take it you both like porridge, seein' as you have oats in your store cupboard – I hope you don't mind me helpin' myself to ingredients?'

He stirred the porridge with the large wooden spoon which was resting in the pan. 'Not at all. And I know Dad'll be cock-a-hoop. The last person who cooked porridge for him was my mum. Dad reckoned she'd have the table laid, the tea stewed and thick creamy porridge sitting in bowls before he'd got himself dressed. All he had to do was sit down and eat. By all accounts she treated him like a king.'

'He must miss her dreadfully.'

He pushed his free hand into the pocket of his dressing gown. 'Very much so. Dad said she was the heart of our family, the glue that held everyone together.' He paused briefly as he took a tentative taste of the porridge. Smacking his lips together, he took another spoonful before continuing. 'He misses her summat chronic. I've tried to encourage him to find himself another woman, because he's too young to spend the rest of his life on his own, and when I get married—'

Libby looked up sharply. 'You're gettin' married?'

Jack laughed. 'No. Or at least not yet, but I will one day, and when I do, I'll want a place of me own.' He eyed her shyly. 'I take it you're not courtin'?'

Libby's brows rose. 'Nope.'

Jack gathered the bowls from the cupboard. 'I learned an awful lot about you last night, but I've still no idea how old you are?'

'Sixteen,' said Libby promptly.

Jack gaped at her. 'Sixteen? I thought you were the same age as me – I'm eighteen.'

Gathering three spoons from the cutlery drawer, she held one up and peered at her reflection. 'Do you really think I look eighteen?'

He cast an eye over her before answering. 'I'd say so, but maybe that's because you act mature for your age? There can't be many young women out there who'd fend for themselves the way you have. You did a crackin' job in fobbin' that geezer off last night . . .'

Libby gazed at him. There was one question which had been bugging her all night, and now seemed as good a time as any to get it off her chest. 'Why *did* you defend me? After all, you didn't know me from Adam.'

'If you'd been a thief you wouldn't have allowed me to take you to the shelter, cos air raids are a prime time for lootin'. It was obvious to me and Dad that summat bad had happened to you, for you to react the way you did. No one jumps into the Thames knowin' they can't swim – especially not in winter.'

She began to dole the porridge into bowls. 'Only I didn't jump in, I slipped on some ice. Having said that, I was so scared I was runnin' blind. I hadn't got a clue where I was, or where I was goin', I just knew I had to get away from him.' She hesitated momentarily. 'I'm glad he came to the shelter though, otherwise I'd not have had an opportunity to return his money. I may've been desperate at the time, but just as I knew my parents wouldn't approve of me sellin' my body in order to pay for them to receive a proper burial, I also knew that they'd be furious if they thought I'd stolen money in order to do so.'

'You could've got away with it scot-free,' said Jack, 'cos Dad and I would've been none the wiser had you not produced the money. A real thief sees nothin' wrong with takin' what ain't theirs, and that's the difference. You've got morals, and integrity.'

She gazed into the porridge. 'I wish my Uncle Tony had, cos that way I wouldn't be in this mess.'

'Perhaps he'll see sense with time? I know you think he couldn't give a fig about you or your parents, but maybe that's the shock talkin'. He might be frightened at the prospect of becomin' an overnight parent, as it were. You've said yourself that he's not a family man, and he has no responsibilities, so that could be what's keepin' him at bay.'

'Or maybe he's a rotten uncle who wants everything for himself,' said Libby dully.

'Either or, I suppose,' Jack conceded. 'Summat tells me you aren't goin' to wait for him to come to his senses?'

'I don't think I have that much time,' said Libby. 'If I don't start takin' care of business, Mum and Dad'll be buried in a pauper's grave.'

'Is that porridge I can smell?' said Gordon, as he stepped out from his bedroom, quickly adding, 'Merry Christmas!'

'I feel dreadful that you've been lumbered with me today of all days,' admitted Libby, a shade guiltily. 'I'd forgotten today was Christmas Day until I woke up this mornin'.'

Gordon waved a dismissive hand as he sat down in front of one of the bowls of porridge. 'Don't be daft. The more the merrier, and I can't think of a better present than wakin' up to a hot bowl of porridge.'

'I'd give you more if I could,' she said ruefully. 'It seems like the two of you are the ones who are doin' all the givin' and I'm the one doin' all the takin'.'

Jack laid his hand over hers. 'It's lovely havin' a woman's touch around the house. You're doin' your bit by bein' here.'

Libby glanced around the flat, which was devoid of Christmas decorations, apart from a small rather bedraggled-looking tree, whose baubles were bigger than its branches. 'Do you not celebrate Christmas much?'

Following her gaze, Jack shrugged his shoulders. 'We did when I was younger, but not so much nowadays. I'd like to blame rationin', but neither of us can cook to save our lives, so we don't bother doin' much foodwise.'

'I feel bad for Jack,' said Gordon, 'but who wants chronic indigestion on Christmas Day?'

Libby chuckled softly. 'I'm sure you're not that bad.'

Jack played his spoon across the surface of his porridge. 'What do you think your uncle'll be doin' today?'

'Gawd knows. We don't ever see him at Christmas, so I've no idea what he usually does.'

Gordon dug his spoon into the bowl before him. 'I wonder if he regrets the wasted years, now that his brother's gone?'

Libby pulled a doubtful face. 'He's probably grateful that he doesn't have to make any excuses for his absence; not that he bothered to make any in the past, mind you.'

'Some people don't realise what they've got until it's gone,' mused Gordon. 'You never know; this could be the thing that makes him sit up and think.'

'I hope so, because it would be a great shame if he went to his grave old and lonely, and if he doesn't wake up soon that's exactly what's goin' to happen. Or at least that's what Mrs Fortescue reckons.'

'Wise words indeed,' said Gordon.

She glanced at the two men as they tucked into their breakfasts. How could complete strangers open their home to her, when her own uncle turned his back? She said as much to them, and it was Jack who was the first to answer.

'Some people don't have it in them, and I think your uncle might be one of them.'

She eyed him shrewdly. 'What would you do if you were me? About my uncle, I mean?'

Jack fell into silent thought as he ate the remainder of his porridge. 'Leave it for a couple of days and then go and see him. If he doesn't ask you where or how you've been, you know he only cares about himself, but if he does ask, then use it as a tool to build a bridge. It's better to be late than never, so I'd not turn my back on him completely, but you have to draw a line somewhere in order to move on with your own life. I know you believe he got the business by foul means not fair, but with no proof you're bangin' your head against a brick wall, which is pointless, not to mention painful.'

'I've got to go up north to see my mother's side of the family at some point. With my uncle bein' the only one who could point me in the right direction, maybe that could be my excuse for seein' him?'

Jack gathered the bowls. 'Liverpool's a long way. Have you thought about how you'll get there, or where you'll stay when you do?'

'I've got a few pennies, which I'm hopin' will be enough for my fare. As for where I'll stay, I'm rather hopin' my grandparents will let me stay with them.' She blew her cheeks out. 'But I've not seen them in years, so they may not remember who I am . . .' Libby's voice trailed off as the recollection that she would be passing on the news of her mother's death came to the forefront of her thoughts. 'And I dare say they won't be too pleased to know that I've left it a while before tellin' them about Mum and Dad.'

Eager for Libby not to leave, Jack voiced his own thoughts. 'If Tony gives you their address, could you not just write to them, instead of goin' halfway across the country?'

'I don't think it would be nice to read about your daughter's demise in a letter. Besides which, they're the only family I've got, and as we've already established, family is everything!'

Jack lowered his gaze. He wanted Libby to be happy, but he didn't want her to go to Liverpool in order to achieve that. Especially when there was a good chance that she might meet someone else. He turned his attention from the brown curls which draped around her shoulders to the dark, almond eyes and their thick lashes. As his gaze travelled to her plump, rosy lips, he found himself wondering how they would feel against his own. Hearing a cough, he turned his head to see his father eyeing him in an amused fashion.

'As we've got two days before we get back to work—' Gordon began, before being cut off by Libby.

'Gosh! I can't believe I haven't asked what you do for a livin' yet.'

'Carpenters,' said Gordon proudly. 'As my father was before me and his father before him.'

'A real family business,' said Libby admiringly. 'How lovely.'

Fearing that she would get back on to the subject of Liverpool, Jack quickly intervened.

'I could show you how to make summat, if you'd like?'

'Like what?'

Jack mulled this over before clicking his fingers. 'How about a mouse? They're easy enough to do.'

'I'll give it my best shot,' laughed Libby, 'but I can't promise it'll look anythin' like a mouse.'

He slapped his hands down on the table. 'I'll have a wash and get dressed, then we can nip down to the shed and get some stuff.' He glanced quickly at his father. 'Is that all right with you, Dad?'

'Of course it is.' Gordon watched his son head off to get ready, whilst Libby busied herself at the kitchen sink. He could see why his son was attracted to the girl, but he could also see that Libby would have to move out in order to move on, and he'd put money on her heading off to Liverpool as soon as she found the address of her mother's family. And what would happen to Jack with his first real love hundreds of miles away? He glanced at the photograph of his wife which graced the mantel. *The boy's found himself a belle, Maisie,* he told her, *and just like I was with you, he's fallen head over heels with her at first sight, so I dare say he'll be nursin' a broken heart come a few days' time.* He gave a weary sigh. Why did love always have to be complicated?

Having selected a few appropriate pieces of wood from the shed Jack and Libby had brought them back to the flat, where Jack was now teaching Libby how to whittle.

'Small bits, that's all you want to remove. There's no goin' back if you take off too much, so little by little, and remember to keep checkin' how you're doin'.'

Libby followed his instruction, and after a few hours of careful work she was left with a small mouse-like shape.

Jack held it in his hand as he examined the tool marks. 'Perfect! I reckon you're a natural. All we have to do is smooth all the rough edges. Much the same as whittlin', you have to be gentle, else you'll take off too much.'

'It's very calmin', don't you think?' said Libby, as she smoothed the sandpaper over the mouse. 'It seems as though I've done nothin' but stress since my parents died, yet all that seems to have left me since I started on the mouse.'

'That's because you had to concentrate on the job in hand,' said Gordon.

'It certainly takes more effort than the spam butties I made for our lunch.'

'Not much of a Christmas lunch, I must admit,' said Gordon guiltily. 'If I'd've known we was havin' guests over I'd've done summat a bit more Christmasy.'

'Not to worry,' said Libby. 'I'm not exactly in the Christmas spirit after losin' my folks.'

'Hardly surprisin',' said Jack. 'Out of interest, what would you have had if your folks were still here?'

Libby spoke wistfully. 'Bread sauce, chestnut stuffin', chicken, roasties, and enough sprouts to sink a ship.'

Gordon felt his mouth begin to water. 'What about gravy?'

Libby chuckled softly. 'Aye, lashings of thick, rich gravy.'

Jack's tummy rumbled audibly, causing them all to laugh. 'Certainly sounds better than the chips we're havin',' he said morosely.

'I know we can't have chicken,' said Libby, 'but I see no reason why we can't do the rest of it.'

'You must be extremely talented when it comes to spuds,' said Gordon, 'cos that's all we've got, and there's no shops open on Christmas Day.'

Libby spoke thoughtfully. 'You've got bread and milk, so I can make the bread sauce, and if you've not got an onion, I can get one from Pete – he's the feller what owns the greengrocers next to our old stall. I know Pete wouldn't object to me callin' round on Christmas Day. It's a shame we had the spam for lunch cos I could've fried it . . .'

Gordon held up a finger, stopping her in mid flow. 'I've got a few sausages. Will they do?'

Libby grinned. 'Perfect!' She stood up from her chair and threw her shawl around her shoulders. 'C'mon, Jack, don't just sit there. We've a dinner to make!'

Delighted at the prospect of a near as damn it Christmas dinner, Jack wasted no time in gathering his hat and scarf. As they headed into the bright winter's morning, he eyed Libby curiously. 'I hope you're not doin' this just to please me and Dad, cos we do understand that you must be finding today of all days pretty hard to deal with, and there's no need for a brave face; not around us.'

She thought for a moment before replying. 'This time yesterday, Christmas was the furthest thing from my mind. I wanted to curl up in a ball and wait until it was over, but in doin' so I would've been turnin' my back on my parents' favourite time of year. When we were talkin', I remembered how much they loved Christmas, and that made me happy. My intentions this mornin' was to pretend that Christmas wasn't happenin', but if I did that I'd be missin' out on some wonderful memories, and quite frankly memories are all I have left. If I turn my back on them, I have nothin'.'

Jack brightened. 'That's good to hear, but are you sure it's all right for us to be callin' in on this Pete feller? It is Christmas Day, after all . . .'

Libby was quick to reassure him. 'Pete has a heart of gold, and he'll be pleased to see I'm out makin' the most of things rather than sittin' on me tod. Mrs F. was the same. The day after my mum and dad passed, she didn't rest until I had summat to eat.'

'I can understand that, but you need to be able to grieve.'

A grim smile crossed her lips. 'All in good time.'

It didn't take them long to reach the small terraced house, and when Pete answered the door his face lit up as his eyes met Libby's.

'Merry Christmas, Lib,' he said, standing to one side so that Libby and Jack could pass through. Once they were inside, Pete turned to Jack. 'I don't believe I've had the pleasure?'

Jack introduced himself, whilst shaking Pete's outstretched hand.

'It's a long story,' Libby told Pete. 'Suffice to say, I'm doin' all right, thanks to this one and his father.'

'Any friend of Libby's is a friend of mine,' said Pete, 'so, to what do I owe the honour?'

Libby quickly explained what they were after, and Pete invited them to come through to the back where he kept his stock. 'Take what you want. It'll most probably be goin' off by the time we reopen, and I'd rather you have it than see it go to the pigs.'

'This is what I'm goin' to miss most about not havin' a stall down the market,' Libby informed Jack. 'The comradeship between the stallholders makes us more like family than colleagues.' She paused as her words caught up with her. 'When I say "family", I'm not includin' relatives like my uncle, cos he's about as far away from family as you can get.'

Pete was helping her to sift through the onions, looking for the pick of the bunch. 'All your uncle's interested in is sellin' his knock-off goods, usin' the stall as cover. I reckon he's got more hooky gear than legit. You should see the crockery he's askin' folk to buy. It's either chipped, cracked or got bits missin'. I know there's a war on, but what's the point of a jug without a handle? I told him straight, a jug without a handle is a vase!'

'He's goin' to ruin our reputation,' Libby said bitterly, 'which was what worried Mum. Dad worked so hard to make the business successful, and for what?'

'What I don't get,' said Jack, 'is why he bought the business off your father if he wasn't interested in sellin' good quality stuff? It would've been cheaper for him to set up his own business sellin' summat else.'

'There's loads of people wantin' stalls down Petticoat Lane,' explained Libby, 'so Tony would've had to go to the back of the queue, but by continuin' the same stall, under the same name, he's simply stepped into Dad's shoes, as it were.'

'Sneaky git,' said Jack. 'He definitely knew what he was doin'.'

'I hope he doesn't bring the reputation of the market back to what it used to be,' said Libby. 'The people in Petticoat Lane have worked hard to put that behind them.'

'Unfortunately, he's exactly the sort of geezer who'd run a stall back in the day,' said Pete. 'Trouble is, the customers don't want to see the back of him, when he's supplyin' them with all the stuff they can't buy in the shops.'

'That's not fair on everybody who's playin' by the rules,' said Libby. 'I know Dad did the odd bit, but only for folk that were desperate. Quite frankly, I'm beginnin' to see where Mum was comin' from.'

Pete laid a reassuring hand on her shoulder. '*Everybody* who frequents the market, be they traders or customers, knows that your father has nothin' to do with the stall what's there now. So you needn't worry about Tony defaming your parents' reputation.'

'Good,' Libby began, but she stopped short on seeing Pete's youngest daughter peeping at her through the gap in the door, a rag doll clasped to her chest. Libby indicated the doll. 'That's a nice dolly. Did you get her for Christmas?'

The child nodded shyly. 'Her name's Raggedy Anne.' She turned accusingly to her father. 'I fought you wasn't workin' today, Daddy.'

Pete held his hands up in a placating manner. 'Sorry guv, I promise I won't do it again!'

Libby pulled a guilty grimace. 'Your daddy's been ever so kind, but it's time we were off to leave you to enjoy your Christmas in peace.'

The youngster produced a book which had been firmly clasped under her arm. 'Father Christmas brought me this.'

'*Winnie-the-Pooh*! My father used to read that to me when I was your age!'

The child looked at her in surprise. 'I didn't fink the book was *that* old.'

Laughing, Libby pretended to be affronted. 'How old do you think I am?'

The small child was about to answer when Pete intervened. 'Best not answer that one, Phoebe, considerin' you think anyone over the age of ten is ancient!'

Holding up the bag of veggies, Libby thanked Pete for his generosity. 'Thanks again, Pete. I'll pop by and see you when you're back on the market.'

Pete assured Libby that he was happy to help, and Libby and Jack set off back to the flat.

'I think this is the most fun I've ever had at Christmas,' said Jack as he peered into the string bag containing the various goodies. 'And it's heartwarming to hear how the market community stand shoulder to shoulder when times are tough.'

'A lot of people look down at market traders,' said Libby, 'but in my opinion, you won't find a finer bunch of people.' She glanced up at the sky as gentle flakes of snow began to fall. 'Snow at Christmas was all my mother ever wished for,' she said wistfully. 'She'd be cock-a-hoop to know it was snowin' on her favourite day of the year.'

'I bet she'd be ever so proud to know that you were cookin' a Christmas dinner, and that Pete and the others had stuck by you when the chips were down.'

'Not that I thought that a few days ago,' Libby admitted.

'Oh?'

Libby explained how she thought the stallholders had taken her uncle's side over hers. 'But I realise now that they didn't have much choice,' she said reasonably. 'With no proof, what were they meant to think?'

Jack held out the crook of his elbow, and smiled when Libby placed her arm in his. 'It's a tough row for them to hoe,' he agreed, 'because whilst I dare say they believe you the evidence points the other way.'

As they passed by one of the houses, Libby glanced through the window to a scene reminiscent of Christmases past. 'That's what our house used to look like,' she told Jack wistfully. 'On Christmas Eve there'd be a roaring fire in the grate, much like that one, but we'd have our tree in the window so that everybody could enjoy the twinkling lights as they passed by. Dad would finish up early at the market before heading down to the Hog and Hound to enjoy a swift drink with the other traders. Then when he came home we'd all dress the tree, and Mum would do a supper of cheese and pickles on crackers, with fresh mince pies straight from the oven for afters. Then, when everyone was ready, we'd settle down for the evening. Dad would read the paper, and Mum would continue with whatever she was knitting at the time, whilst I wished for a pony.'

Jack chuckled softly. 'You must've had a bloomin' big stockin'.'

'I knew it wouldn't happen, of course,' said Libby, 'but the idea was nice.'

'And what about Christmas Day?' asked Jack.

'We would get up round the normal time, and breakfast would be kippers for mum and dad and I'd have porridge cos I don't like the bones you get in kippers. After that, we'd open our presents before heading off to church.' She turned to Jack. 'This will be the first Christmas that I haven't gone to church.'

'Do you want to go? We could call in on the way back if you'd like?'

Libby mulled this over for a moment or two. In truth she had never liked the going to church part of Christmas, not on a cold morning, when you would have to sit on icy pews for what felt like hours whilst the vicar droned on in his monotonal voice, but if it made her feel closer to her parents she was all for it, especially knowing that they'd approve of her decision. 'I'd like that. Should we get your father?'

Jack gave a short, derisive laugh. 'Dad doesn't believe in God and all that, not since my mother died.'

Before her own parents' passing, a statement like that would've rocked Libby to her core, but now? 'I can't say that I blame him,' she said grimly. 'What sort of God takes good people at such a young age?'

'I don't mind goin' if it's what you want to do, though,' Jack assured her.

'Only because my parents would like it if I went,' said Libby plainly. 'In fact, they'd be upset if they thought I hadn't gone, and quite frankly, with a funeral to pay for, I need all the help I can get.'

Jack laughed out loud. 'I s'pose that's one way of lookin' at it.'

As they walked to the church, Libby fought the urge to ask Jack what had happened to his mother, mainly because she supposed he would tell her if he wanted to.

With the church looming ahead of them, Libby felt her heart begin to race as they approached the large studded door with its wrought iron hinges. She turned to Jack. 'My heart's goin' ten to the dozen. Why d'you suppose that is?'

Jack shrugged. 'Dunno. Maybe it's bein' here without your folks?'

They slipped quietly into the church, taking their places on the pews at the very back. As she listened to the vicar talk of justice, patience, and the power of forgiveness, Libby gripped Jack's hand in hers. Her heart was beating so loudly, she was convinced that other people must be able to hear it. With her mouth beginning to go dry, she stared at the vicar as he continued to lecture his congregation. 'I need to get out of here,' she whispered to Jack.

Taking care not to draw attention to themselves, they stood up and left the church with as little noise as possible. Only when they were outside did Libby speak again.

Hot, angry tears splashing down her cheeks, she pointed a shaking finger in the direction of the church. 'How dare he stand there and tell us we should forgive those that trespass against us, when my parents who did nothin' wrong are lyin' dead because

112

some stupid man who doesn't even live in the same country as us wants everything for himself!' She wiped her cheeks with the backs of her hands before continuing, 'What sort of God allows that to happen? I swear, if I'd've stayed in that church a moment longer I was goin' to tell the vicar exactly what I thought of him and his so-called God, something at which my mother would've been devastated. And that's why I was nervous about goin' in, because I *knew* I wouldn't be able to keep my mouth shut, but a small part of me hoped he was goin' to be sayin' something different this year. I thought that with everything that's happened he might've changed his sermon to one where people like Hitler go to hell, no matter how sorry they are, and that the rest of us have every right to be angry about it. But oh no, we have to suck it up and pretend nothin's happened because it's ungodly to hold a grudge. Well guess what, Jack? I ain't never goin' to forgive Hitler for what he did to my parents, because he deserves to go to hell, *not* forgiveness.'

Jack wrapped his arms around her. 'You're right, Lib; that's exactly what people like him deserve.'

'I've been turnin' all my anger on Tony, but it's not really him that's makin' me so furious,' she sniffed. 'I know he's no angel, but he's irrelevant when compared to losin' my parents.'

'He did steal your father's business,' Jack reminded her.

'I know, but at least I know that Mum was right, and he really is a piece of dirt. Tony showed his true colours, which is better than me thinkin' Mum had got him wrong.'

Jack cast her a sidelong glance. 'I notice that you're not referrin' to him as your uncle any more.'

Libby tucked her arm into his. 'No point in callin' him one if he doesn't behave like one. In all honesty, he never acted like we were related when me parents were alive, so I don't know why I expected him to be any different once they'd gone.'

'How does that make you feel?'

'As if my head is empty of everything save for one thought. Mum and Dad are never comin' back, and no matter what I say or do nothin's goin' to change that, which is why I wanted to pretend Christmas wasn't happenin' this mornin'.' She gazed up at him blankly. 'I feel so lost.'

Jack removed his arm from hers and placed it around her shoulders, squeezing her close. 'I guess I've always felt a bit empty inside, because I never knew my mum.' He hesitated. 'I've never spoken to Dad about it, because I don't want to upset him, and I can't speak about it to anyone else, because . . .' He fell silent.

Libby felt his arm grow tense, as though he was gathering his strength to speak.

'You don't have to tell me if you don't want to,' said Libby softly.

'I know, but I want to.' He drew a deep breath, and let it go with the words 'My mother took her own life'.

Libby's eyes rounded as she fought the urge to gasp out loud. Drawing to a halt, she gazed up at him as though her heart was breaking for him. 'She must've been in an awful lot of pain to leave such a wonderful family.'

His eyes glassy with unshed tears, Jack spoke so quietly Libby had to strain her ears to hear. 'She was. No one really knows why, but the doctor said she was a prisoner in her own mind, and suicide was the only way she could break free.'

Libby cupped his face in the palms of her hands. 'Jack, you poor, sweet, brave man. I had no idea you were carryin' such a heavy burden.'

He shrugged. 'I was only a babby at the time, but Dad's always been honest with me, and he never tried to pull the wool over my eyes, or fluff the truth. As soon as I was old enough to understand he sat me down and told me everything. He reckoned that havin' me was the happiest day of their lives, and that Mum loved me dearly, but looking back he realised that things hadn't been quite right for some time. And even though hindsight's twenty-twenty, that didn't stop Dad from tyin' himself in knots, wonderin' if he could have said or done somethin' to make a difference. It was only after a lot of soul-searchin' and talkin' to those that know that he came to the conclusion he was powerless to help her.'

Libby studied his face. 'How . . . I mean . . .' She fell silent, before adding, 'Never mind.'

But Jack knew what Libby was trying to ask, so he answered her anyway. 'She threw herself into the Thames, a week after New Year's Day.'

Libby clasped a hand to her heart. 'Oh, Jack, I'm so sorry. What must your poor father have thought yesterday?'

Jack ran his hand over the nape of his neck. 'I think Dad was just grateful I'd managed to save you.'

They continued on their way, and Libby felt a tingle run through her arm as Jack slipped his hand into hers. 'Do you think that's the real reason why you were on my side, even though you didn't really know which one of us was tellin' the truth?' she asked.

'I know enough to know that you've got to be desperate to end up in the drink.'

Libby rolled her eyes. 'I can't believe I put myself into such a compromising position. I know I thought it was my only way out, but deep down I think that was just an excuse to avoid the real issue.'

He looked grim. 'That your parents have gone.'

'Exactly! And that has sod all to do with funeral costs, Tony, the vicar or anyone bar the bastards who gave the order to bomb civilians.' She paused before adding hastily, 'Not that they should be bombin' anyone.'

'I've put my name down for the services,' said Jack.

Stunned by his revelation, Libby fixed her eyes on the flat as they drew closer. It was not up to her to question his choices. 'Are you scared?'

'That I'll get called up?' He continued without waiting for a reply. 'No. Nervous maybe, but not scared.' He glanced at the fallen buildings around him. 'I'm guessin' it's goin' to be a bit like it is here, only you'll have a gun to protect yourself, which is more than I have at the moment.'

Libby mulled this over. 'If you look at it that way, then I suppose it makes sense. How does your dad feel?'

Jack grimaced. 'He didn't speak to me for a couple of hours after he found out what I'd done, but he soon came round to my way of thinking.'

'Which is?'

'This war isn't goin' to end itself. We need people to make that happen, and the longer it goes on, the worse it's goin' to get, so the more people who put themselves forward the quicker we'll bring it to an end.'

But why you, when there're men like Tony who could easily take your place? Libby thought in the privacy of her own mind. Out loud she said: 'I hope you're right.'

'I know I am. You've only got to see what happened when the B.E.F. went over. They soon came back because they were overwhelmed by the might of the German army. Ergo, the more people who sign up, the greater our chances.'

'Have you any idea when you're off, or where you'll be goin'?' She felt her tummy jolt nervously, as she found herself hoping fervently that Jack wasn't going to be sent overseas.

'Not yet. I'm hopin' to get into the RAF, because I've always dreamed of flyin', but I think you've either got to be proper brainy or born with a silver spoon in your mouth if you're to get into a pilot's seat.'

'But isn't bein' a pilot awfully dangerous?'

'I don't think it makes any odds whether you're sittin' in a trench or flyin' in the air; if you're time's up, it's up.'

'Do you really believe that? Because I think some people make their own fate, whether intentionally or not.'

He eyed her curiously. 'How so?'

'If my parents had made the decision to move to Norwich a day earlier, we'd have left a day sooner, and they'd still be alive.'

Jack cut across her without apology. 'How can you be so sure? For all you know you could all have got bombed as soon as you entered Norwich, or even on your way, come to that. Nobody knows what might've happened, because it's pure speculation.'

'Well, I suppose we can't know for certain,' said Libby slowly, 'but only in the same way that you can't prove that your life is ruled by fate.'

'True, but sometimes it's easier to sleep at night if you think you had no hand in changin' the course of someone's life.'

Certain that Jack was referring to his mother's death, Libby backtracked hastily. 'You're right. Neither of us can prove the other wrong, and, just as you say, we could've been hit just as easily in Norwich as we were here.'

'Only worse, because you'd have been with them,' said Jack. 'I'm pretty sure I know which scenario your parents would've opted for.'

'So, what about Tony, then? It seems a bit unfair that fate has left him to—'

Jack was quick to intervene. 'You're deflectin' again. Turnin' your grief for your parents against your uncle.'

Libby was about to deny this was the case when she realised that it was precisely what she had been about to do. 'You're right. Once again, I'm tryin' to take my anger out on the wrong person. When all's said and done, my parents would still be gone, no matter what did or didn't happen with the stall.'

'Exactly. You can't change what was, so you have to look forward to what will be, because that's summat you can control.'

'And I'm goin' to take a leaf out of your book and do just that,' said Libby, with a new air of determination. 'I might not be able to afford a gravestone as yet, but I'm sure my grandparents won't see their only daughter in a pauper's grave. First chance I get, I'm off to Liverpool.'

'But what about the meantime?' said Jack. 'If you don't pay for a plot . . .'

Libby blew her cheeks out. 'I don't know. I'm goin' to have to come up with the money somehow, but how?'

Jack drew a deep breath. 'I know you're adamant that you want a plot closer to the church, but does it really matter, in the grand scheme of things?'

'It does to me,' said Libby slowly. 'I want them to know how much I loved them.'

'And you think that prostituting yourself would've proved that?' Jack rued the words as soon as they left his lips. 'I'm so sorry, Libby. I didn't mean . . .'

Libby patted his hand. 'I know you didn't mean to be so forthright, but you're quite right, which is, of course, why I changed my mind and legged it.'

Relieved that Libby hadn't taken his words out of context, Jack continued, 'A good burial plot could set you back tens of pounds. Do you really think your parents care which part of the cemetery they end up in?'

Libby fell into silent contemplation. Her parents had never stated any preference for their funeral arrangements, or not as far as she was aware. Her father was a staunch believer in equal rights and bringing down the class system . . . She felt her cheeks grow warm. 'Dad would do his nut if he knew I was tryin' to get him in with the nobs,' she said meekly. 'He was massively against the class system, sayin' that it was unfair on those at the bottom, and that money always goes to money – whatever that means.' She gave Jack a small, tentative smile. 'Thanks, Jack. I never thought of it that way before, but you're right. It's ridiculous that people spend such vast amounts on a funeral just so they can show off the wealth their parents left behind. Life isn't about how much money you've got, it's about bein' the best that you can be, and my parents did just that. Dad didn't see the shop in Norwich as goin' up a notch, but a place to get out of the wind and rain. He loved his life down the market, and if that bloomin' Hitler hadn't started this flamin' war he would still be down Petticoat Lane, sellin' his wares.'

'Precisely,' said Jack. 'We've all seen them graves what're grand but forgotten, and they don't look half as fancy when they're covered in ivy, or hidden behind a thicket of nettles and brambles. I think it's sad to see something that was obviously important to someone go to such waste. Not just that, but it's pretty obvious they've been forgotten when nobody tends to their grave any more, though I suppose that's bound to happen given the fullness of time.' He shrugged. 'What's wrong with a simple cross? Summat to mark the spot.'

Libby puffed her cheeks out. 'Nothin', only I can't afford it.'

He winked at her. 'You seem to forget that I'm a carpenter.'

Libby's face brightened as the penny dropped. 'Oh, Jack, that would be wonderful! I promise to pay you as soon—'

But Jack was holding up a hand, in the manner of someone calling for silence. 'No need. We've plenty of wood and a cross is simple to make. If you'd like, you can help me to engrave their names.'

'I'd like that very much. It would feel so personal, so special, and I guess that's what's important. I want them to know how special they were to me, and something carved by my own hand would be perfect.'

Jack beamed, happy in the knowledge that he had made Libby feel better. 'We'll get on to it first thing tomorrow. Dad and I aren't open until the day after, and it shouldn't take more than a morning's graft to get summat extra special ready.'

Libby felt as though Jack had removed an enormous weight from her shoulders. Her parents were going to get the burial she wanted, but with none of the stress. 'I can call in at the funeral directors and let them know to go ahead with the burial,' she said. She drew a deep breath and let it out slowly. 'That pompous git can look down his nose at me all he likes. It's not my fault that my parents died when they did, or that they'd spent every penny on a new life which never came to fruition.'

'Which pompous git is this?' enquired Jack, visibly annoyed.

'The feller at the funeral directors,' said Libby. 'You could tell he wasn't happy when I said he'd have to wait for the money by the way he spoke. Proper patronisin' he was.' She felt her cheeks grow warm once more. 'He was right, though, when you think about it.'

'Makes no bloody odds,' snapped Jack. 'What sort of person – especially an undertaker – makes someone feel bad about their financial circumstances when they've just lost their parents?'

His jaw flinched angrily. 'I've a good mind to come with you on Friday and give him what for!'

Hearing that Jack was eager to give the undertaker a piece of his mind filled Libby with a sense of certainty. Jack had her back, and he wasn't afraid to let everyone know.

She tucked her arm into his. 'Don't you worry, if he says owt I shan't hold back at lettin' him know exactly what I think. No one's goin' to make me feel bad about my circumstances, and if he even tries I shall be sure to let him have it, both barrels.'

Jack gave her a sidelong glance. He was pleased to know that Libby felt at ease in his company, because he felt the same way. He had thought Libby to be a firecracker after hearing about her encounter with the filthy old man, but he knew now that he'd only seen the tip of the iceberg as far as she was concerned, and he was eager to explore the depths of her titanic personality.

As they reached the stairwell to the flat, Jack ushered Libby ahead of him. 'Ladies first!'

Libby giggled. 'Me? A lady!'

'Ladies come in all shapes and sizes,' said Jack as he followed her up. 'You don't need to be born into the gentry to be a lady. Class isn't summat you're born into. I know beggars what've got more class in their little fingers than some of these nobs you see up and down.'

'How can a beggar have class?' asked Libby as they entered the flat. 'Surely you need some money for that?'

Folding his paper on to his lap, Gordon eyed her over the top of his spectacles. 'Class is how you conduct yourself, not how much money you have in the bank, or how much jewellery you wear.'

Libby pulled the vegetables out of the bag and put them down on the chopping board. 'My father said the class system was outdated and needed bringing down so that we're all level pegging.'

'Sounds like your father was a wise man,' said Gordon approvingly, 'but it'll never happen, or not in my lifetime at any rate.'

'That geezer you was runnin' away from?' said Jack. 'I bet some people would have him down as middle or even upper class, because he certainly looked like he had a bob or two, but would they say the same if they knew what he'd been up to that night?'

'God no!' said Libby, with no hesitation. 'They'd put him in the same category as the fellers on the docks, or the sailors off the boats.'

'And that's why I say that class is based on how you behave, not how much money you have in your pocket,' affirmed Gordon. 'I don't call runnin' after a young girl with yer trousers round yer ankles very classy, do you?'

Libby grimaced. 'No I don't!'

'And he knew I'd seen through him, too,' added Jack. 'People like that build their whole lives around their reputation, but one word from someone who *really* knows what they're like could destroy everything they hold dear, which is why he couldn't wait to get away.'

Libby frowned. 'Are you referrin' to their bank account?'

'No. Their standing in society, cos without that there is no bank account.'

Libby began to peel one of the onions. 'Then why risk it?'

'Because deep down they're all the same,' said Jack, 'a bunch of sad, middle-aged men who like to throw their weight about.' He chucked a knob of lard into the pan and placed it on the stove. 'Or, to put it another way, why would any man who has a wife at home want to pay for sex?'

Libby perused this thought. 'Because they can treat the prostitute like dirt; overpower them and knock them around; do all the things they wouldn't dream of doin' to their wives, because they know there's no comeback when you pay for it.' She gave a joyless laugh. 'It's not as if the women can report them to the Bluebottles.'

'Exactly! Those men have no respect for women. They like to put up a perfect front, but it's a different story behind closed doors.'

Libby spoke thoughtfully. 'Do you think they're all like that?'

'I'd say the higher their rankin' the worse they get, because they feel like they're above the rest of us, includin' the law,' said Gordon. He'd wandered over to see what the two of them were up to. 'Blimey, you've done well! There's enough there to feed an army.'

'You can always rely on your fellow traders to pull you out of the mire,' said Libby with pride.

'Salt of the earth,' said Gordon. 'People like that often are.'

'I know they'd have helped out with the funeral if they could,' Libby went on, 'but they can't afford that kind of money, and I wouldn't want them to try.'

Jack filled his father in on Libby's decision to forgo a burial spot on the sunnier side of the cemetery for a pauper's grave, marked with a cross which the two of them intended to make the next day.

'I'm glad you've seen sense,' said Gordon, his nostrils flaring as the sausages sizzled in the pan. 'You'd have been mortified if your parents ended up in a grave next to that foul man what accused you of nickin' his money.'

Libby's eyes popped. 'My father would have my guts for garters if he had to spend eternity next to someone like that. Had I gone through with it, I'd never be able to grieve properly knowing that the man who'd taken my v—' She blushed to the roots of her hair, before quickly changing her words, 'my innocence had paid for their grave.'

'And that's exactly what he would've done,' snarled Jack. 'He knew what he were doin', but you didn't.'

'As long as you're not goin' to try and break your neck sortin' out this funeral, then that's a good thing,' said Gordon. He stared hungrily at the sausages, which were browning nicely. 'Gawd above, those sausages smell good!'

'You wait until we've done the stuffin', mash and gravy to go with them,' said Libby, pleased to change the topic. 'It might not be turkey, or chicken, but it's good honest fare, and it'll leave a pleasant taste in your mouth knowin' you ain't broke the bank to pay for it neither.'

He clapped a hand on her shoulder. 'Never a truer word said.'

When the meal was ready, they sat down to eat, savouring each mouthful before taking the next, and Libby honestly thought that this was as good as any Christmas dinner she'd ever eaten. She even said so to Jack and his father.

'Things always taste better when you've prepared them yourself,' said Gordon. 'That's what my Maisie used to say.'

'You must miss her dreadfully,' said Libby, adding apologetically, 'Jack told me what happened. I must say I feel dreadful for reigniting such painful memories.'

Gordon wiped the gravy from his lips with the tip of his tongue. 'Knowin' you were safe was all that mattered, and I'm proud of Jack for goin' to your rescue. I wish I could've helped Maisie, but in all honesty I don't think anyone could.'

Libby placed her hand over his. 'You're a wonderful man, Gordon Durning, and if love alone could've saved your Maisie . . .'

Gordon finished the sentence for her: 'she would've lived for ever.'

Libby glanced at Jack. 'Jack and I had a good chat about fate or circumstance, and I believe him to be right when he says that fate plays a big part in our lives. I know my mother used to be a big believer in karma.'

Jack looked from his father to Libby. 'What's that when it's at home?'

'It means that what goes around comes around,' Libby explained. 'In other words, if you're mean to someone, expect something bad to happen to you in return.' She hesitated before adding, 'I suppose you could call it getting your comeuppance.'

'So, do you think Tony'll get his karma?'

She wagged a reproving finger. 'He already has, remember?'

Jack raised his cup of tea in acknowledgement. 'Life without family, a fate caused by his own making.'

'Exactly,' agreed Libby. She turned to Gordon. 'The two of you are ever so lucky to have each other. I dare say you're goin' to miss him summat awful when he's off goodness only knows where.'

Gordon was trying to use his tongue to pick an errant piece of sausage from between his teeth. Speaking thickly, he used his finger to dislodge the pesky piece of meat. 'I will indeed, but I know it's what Jack wants to do, so I'll not stand in his way.'

Jack knew that his father was putting on a brave face for his sake, and that the thought of his imminent departure still pained him terribly. He stood up to fetch the teapot. 'More tea, anyone?'

With Jack across the room, Libby leaned closer to Gordon. 'I realise you must be worried; any parent would be. But your Jack's got a sensible head on his shoulders. I don't think he'd do anythin' reckless.'

'But sometimes he cares about others more than he does about himself,' Gordon told her. 'I only hope he takes as much care with his own life as he will of those around him.' His eyes glittered as they met Libby's. 'I rather think he holds a candle for you.'

Libby blushed shyly. 'He's got a heart of gold. I think he'd care for anyone if he thought they were goin' through the mill.'

Gordon shrugged. 'Maybe, but I know my son, and I've never seen him take to a girl the way he has to you.'

She laughed softly. 'Rescued many a woman from the Thames, has he?'

'I see what you're thinkin', but I reckon you're wrong. This isn't about comin' to the aid of a damsel in distress, this is summat more; or at least I reckon it is.'

Libby watched Jack as he poured more water into the teapot. She'd noticed how protective he was towards her, and how readily he'd come to her defence when she'd told him about the undertakers. Was Gordon right? Or was this a case of standing up for those who were vulnerable? She shrugged inwardly. Either way it was neither here nor there, what with Jack leaving for the services and Libby heading for Liverpool. Chances were, their paths would never cross again after they said goodbye in a few days' time.

It was the day after Boxing Day, and Libby was washing the dishes whilst Jack retrieved the post from the bottom of the stairwell. As he came through the door, Libby saw that he was staring intently at a brown envelope in his hands. He glanced at Gordon and Libby as he headed for the dresser, took out a knife and slit the envelope open.

After reading in silence, he looked up. 'They want me to report for duty a week today.' He handed the letter to his father. 'I must admit, I hadn't expected to hear from them so soon.'

His father passed the letter back. 'It goes to show how quickly things are developin'.'

Libby began to dry the dishes. 'How do you feel?'

'Nervous, excited, and a little anxious. Not because I think anythin's goin' to happen to me, but because I've never done owt like this before.' He shrugged. 'What if I'm no good at it?'

His father waved a nonchalant hand. 'The services have many things you can do. If you're not cut out for one thing, they'll find you summat else.'

Libby folded the tea towel and placed it over the rail of the stove. 'Can you swim?'

'Like a fish,' said Jack, his chest swelling with pride. 'Why d'you ask?'

'I should imagine you have to be able to swim in order to join the Navy,' said Libby absently. 'I know you're hopin' for the RAF, but I would wager a lot of men are choosing the RAF because of the grandeur associated with air crew.'

Gordon gave a loud hurrumph before elaborating his displeasure. 'Not very grand when your kite's rustin' at the bottom of the Channel.'

Libby's brows shot up. 'I say, that's a bit strong, isn't it?'

Gordon pulled a rueful face. 'I'm only sayin' it how it is. People tend to glorify war, but there's nowt glorious about death and destruction. If Jack's goin' into battle, I want him to do so with his eyes wide open. You've got to have your wits about you, and I don't want him to be thinkin' he'll be all right because he's one of the lucky ones. Luck doesn't come into it when you're on the battlefield.'

Libby was watching Jack to see his reaction, but his father's words didn't seem to bother him in the slightest. 'I might believe in fate, but that doesn't mean to say that I'm goin' to approach this in a foolhardy manner.'

Libby glanced at the clock. 'Oh heck. I'd better get a move on. I've a whole heap of things to do today.'

Gordon stood up from the table. 'Why don't you take Jack with you?'

Jack pointed in the vague direction of the shed. 'What about work?'

Gordon waved a dismissive hand. 'Forget about work. Gawd only knows when you'll next get any leave. Enjoy yourself whilst you can, cos it'll be all go once your training starts.'

'Thanks, Dad.' He turned to Libby. 'I'm ready when you are. We can pick up the cross we made for your mum and dad en route to the funeral parlour.'

Libby was already pushing her arms into the sleeves of her jacket. 'Two birds one stone . . .' She looked at her blistered thumb, caused by the chisel. She had worked tirelessly under Jack's supervision, making certain that every letter and number was perfectly etched into the wood.

Jack grabbed the keys to the workshop and pushed them into his jacket pocket. 'You comin', Dad?'

In answer, Gordon got to his feet. 'No rest for the wicked.'

With the workshop being close by, it didn't take long to collect the cross, which Gordon admired greatly.

He ran his finger over the intricate lettering, whilst addressing Libby with a sidelong glance. 'Smooth as a baby's bum, exactly how it should be.'

'You approve, then?' Libby asked anxiously.

Gordon passed the cross over. 'I couldn't have done a better job myself.'

Libby hugged the cross to her body. 'I think this is better than any headstone.'

'The personal touch,' said Jack with a wink. 'I take it we're off to the funeral parlour first?'

'Get it over and done with,' confirmed Libby. 'If they can give us a date, we can call by the market to let everyone know on our way home.'

With everyone agreed that this was the best way forward, Jack and Libby bade Gordon goodbye and headed off. Jack held his hand out for the cross. 'Would you like me to carry that?'

Libby politely declined his offer. 'I'm fine, thanks. I know it may sound silly, but this makes me feel close to them.'

'Not silly at all,' Jack assured her. 'Most people have photographs or keepsakes to remember their loved ones, but that's all been taken away from you.'

'Selfish beasts,' said Libby. 'I wish I knew who'd taken the van.'

'You never know your luck. It could well turn up one of these days,' Jack said optimistically.

They stopped speaking as Libby opened the door to the parlour. She waited for one of the undertakers to appear, hoping fervently that it wouldn't be the same one she had asked to search for her father's wallet. Having to admit that he had been right all along was not going to be a pleasant experience, after her insisting that she could find the money. She was about to say as much to Jack when a portly gentleman with kind eyes and a walrus moustache waddled his way from the back room.

'May I help you?' As his gaze fell on the cross, he cleared his throat. 'I'm terribly sorry to hear of your loss, Miss . . . ?'

'Elizabeth Gilbert,' said Libby.

He stared at her in silence before lowering his head. 'Of course, the young lady who lost her parents.' Taking the cross, he eyed it studiously. 'I must say, it's been beautifully crafted.'

'You're very kind,' said Libby. Her bottom lip began to tremble, and she gently gripped it between her teeth. If she were to let her emotions go now, she didn't think she'd be able to stop crying. 'I know it will have to be a pauper's grave, but if you could give me a date, I can let the traders down the market know.'

But to her surprise the undertaker was holding his finger aloft, calling for silence. 'Speaking of market traders, did you know that they'd had a whip-round?'

Libby's lips parted. 'How do you mean?'

His sky-blue eyes twinkled at her as he told her all about it. 'A chap by the name of Pete McKeown came by with a collection towards your parents' funeral on his way home last night. It seems Mr and Mrs Gilbert were well thought of down Petticoat Lane, so they won't be having a pauper's funeral after all.'

The news sent Libby into a torrent of tears. 'I – I had no idea,' she managed to say in between sobs. 'I knew they were popular, of course I did, but I didn't know they were *that* popular.'

Clearing his throat, the older man clasped the cross in his hands. 'The money is sufficient to pay for both hearses and a car, as well as their plot.'

Jack took Libby in his arms as her shoulders began to shake. 'Thank you, Mr er . . .'

'Caldecott,' replied the man, 'and if you're to thank anyone it's the folk from down Petticoat Lane.'

Libby looked up through tear-brimmed eyes. 'We will, straight away.'

'The funeral will be on the thirtieth of December,' said Mr Caldecott. 'Where should the car go to pick you up?'

Jack supplied the address, whilst Libby blotted her tears with a handkerchief. 'I take it you know that my parents' belongings, as well as my own, were stolen the same day they died?'

Mr Caldecott's jaw flinched. 'I certainly do. I very much hope they catch the scoundrels responsible.'

'Me too,' said Libby. 'I've got nothin' to remember my parents by. Is there any chance I could have their wedding rings back?'

'Of course.' He disappeared into the back, to return a few seconds later with a small brown bag containing not only the rings, but her father's wallet, and the locket which her mother wore round her neck.

Looking at the contents of the bag, Libby wiped away fresh tears. 'I may have lost just about everything, but at least I still have the only things that were truly special to my parents.' She handed Jack the bag containing the rings and wallet, then clicked open the locket to reveal a tiny photograph of her father on one side, and another of her parents with Libby as a baby on the other.

'Mum never took it off,' Libby sniffed.

Jack took the rings out of the bag and slipped them onto the chain of the locket. Placing it round Libby's neck, he made sure that the clasp was securely fastened before stepping back.

Libby admired the jewellery. 'I shall never let them out of my sight.' She glanced up at Mr Caldecott. 'Thank you for making my day just that little bit brighter.'

'I'm glad I could be of assistance,' said Mr Caldecott. 'We'll see you on Monday.'

Jack and Libby left the undertakers and headed for the market.

'How on earth am I goin' to thank them?' Libby asked Jack as they strode along the pavement. 'I don't know where to begin. I can't possibly pay them back, or at least not for a long time.'

'I don't think they probably see it as a loan,' said Jack. 'More as a gift to their friends.'

'Such a heart-warming act of kindness,' said Libby, 'and typical of the street market folk. I shall start with Pete, and work my way around every single stall until I've personally thanked every last one of them.' She glanced up at the underneath of Jack's firm jaw. 'And not just market traders. You and your father have gone above and beyond for me. I don't know what I'd have done without you.'

'I'll miss you,' he said quietly. 'I know we only met a few days ago, but it feels as though I've known you all my life.'

Libby shot him a sidelong glance. 'I've been thinking that too. What with me losin' my parents, and you plucking me out of the water, everything seems to have gone at a hundred miles an hour from the moment we clapped eyes on each other. Do you suppose that's it?'

'Maybe,' said Jack. But inside he thought it was much more than that. Ever since he'd pulled Libby out of the river, he'd felt an overwhelming raw, physical and emotional urge to protect and defend the slim chit of a girl. If he were to sum his feelings up in one word, he would have said that they'd bonded. He couldn't really say that he'd been drawn to her beauty when her face had been blue from the cold, and her dark hair plastered to her head by the water of the river. He conjured up an image of Libby in his mind as she had appeared that day. Gazing into her deep brown eyes, he had seen straight into the depths of her soul, and that was all it had taken for him to fall in love.

Libby, too, was remembering the day she had met Jack. Even though she was terrified of being discovered, she had relaxed as soon as she looked into his eyes of emerald green, surrounded by thick, dark lashes. She couldn't explain even to herself what it was about Jack, but she had felt an instant connection, which intensified when he put his arm around her. She knew he was only a couple of years older than herself, but the sense of comfort and safety she had felt with him beside her was like nothing she had ever experienced before. The thought of him going off to war was something she was finding hard to stomach, but Jack had made his decision long before the two of them had met, and she must just respect his wishes and hope that he was one of the lucky ones, whether he and his father believed in luck or not.

Nearing the head of the market, Jack slipped his hand into hers. 'Which one is your uncle's stall?'

She knew he'd only done it to show solidarity, but feeling his hand in hers sent a wave of warm tingles through her fingers.

'He's a bit further on yet,' she said. 'We'll get to Pete's stall before we do Tony's.'

Sliding his fingers between hers, he gave them a comforting squeeze. 'Best foot forward.'

'My father used to say that,' said Libby sadly.

As they passed the stalls, she made a point of thanking the traders for their generosity.

'It wasn't just us,' said Luke, who ran a hardware stall. 'The customers gave generously too. It was all Pete's idea.'

'How on earth am I goin' to thank all these people?' gasped Libby, as she eyed the throng browsing the stalls.

'Don't worry your head about that,' Luke assured her, 'we've already thanked them on your behalf. Reggie and Orla were well loved by traders and customers alike. It's the least any of us could do, given the circumstances. Have you heard owt about the van?'

'I doubt I ever will,' replied Libby, lifting the locket around her neck, 'but at least I've got these to remember them by.'

A rotund trader on the stall next to Luke's burst into tears before rushing over to Libby, nearly knocking Luke's stall over in the process.

'Oh, my sweet darlin' child. Oh, you poor little mite!' she gushed between sobs. 'I hope they string 'em up, them what took your things. Orla and Reggie was the salt of the earth; the salt of the earth, I tell you!'

Looking slightly strangled, Libby tried to catch her breath as the woman continued to squeeze her in a tight embrace. 'Thank you, Mrs Pratchett, you're very kind.'

Mrs Pratchett broke away to dab her eyes, whilst shooting angry glances in the direction of Tony's stall. 'I know your father meant well, but I wish he'd never sold his stall to his brother . . .'

Luke held up an intervening hand. 'Now now, Cynthia, we can't go throwin' accusations around.'

'We bloomin' well can,' snapped Cynthia, 'or I can, at any rate. Tony Gilbert isn't a patch on his brother, never has been and never will be. He hasn't a clue as to what he's doin', and he makes it flamin' obvious that he's up to no good. Cos he don't care, do he? Not when he's already got Filmer in his pocket.'

Libby gaped at her. 'He's what?'

Luke tried to stop his fellow trader, but Cynthia was on a roll. 'He must have! A blind man could see what Tony's up to, but Filmer turns a blind eye, every time. I've known that man – Filmer I mean – for over twenty years, and he's never allowed such goin's on.' She turned to Libby. 'We all know your dad let the odd thing slide, but that was for the greater good . . .'

'If the greater good's your old man . . .' Luke interrupted, only to be silenced by Cynthia's steely gaze.

'But Tony's palmin' stuff off onto the spivs,' Cynthia went on. 'Reggie would *never* have done that, and you know he wouldn't before you start takin' the Michael.'

'Maybe not, but you have to be careful what you say,' said Luke. Lowering his voice to just above a whisper, he continued. 'Tony might be a streak of p—' Catching sight of Libby from the corner of his eye, Luke changed his wording just in time. ' . . . piddle, but the geezers he deals with aren't, and if you don't want them askin' you to keep your gob shut I should keep your opinions between us, and not shout them for everyone to hear!'

Cynthia's cheeks coloured as she glanced nervously around to see if she'd been overheard. Continuing on a sullener note, she cleared her throat before speaking. 'I'm only sayin' what others are thinkin'.'

'And that's why they keep their thoughts to themselves,' said Luke. He turned apologetically to Libby and Jack. 'I'll make sure those that contributed know how grateful you are.'

Libby thanked him before turning to Cynthia. 'You're right about me uncle. He's a slippery customer, so you need to tread carefully around him. He cares for nothing and no one, not even his own brother. I'd wager good money that he never contributed to the funeral?'

Cynthia sucked her teeth in a reproving manner. 'If word on the street is to be believed, but Pete's your best bet for that info.'

Luke rolled his eyes. 'For Gawd's sake, Cynthia, stop stirrin' the pot.'

Libby jumped to Cynthia's defence. 'She's not stirrin' the pot. I know exactly what sort of a man my uncle is, and I don't want to be thankin' him for his contribution if he never gave anythin'.'

Jack slipped his hand back into Libby's. 'You've a lot of people to thank, so maybe it's time we were off.'

Libby thanked Cynthia for being so forthcoming, and Luke for trying to look out for her, before allowing Jack to escort her to Pete's stall. Noting that her uncle's stall was empty, Libby breathed a sigh of relief as she greeted Pete.

'I've heard all about the whip-round you started, and I've come here to thank you personally,' she said. 'I can never repay any of you for your kindness, but I'll never forget what you've done for me and my parents.'

Pete beamed with pride. 'It was the least we could do.' He cast a glance at Tony's unattended stall. 'Seein' as you've not got anyone to step up for you.'

Libby grimaced. 'I heard he never put his hand in his pocket; is that right?'

Pete sighed. 'I'm afraid so.' He glanced back to the stall where Tony should've been. 'He's burned his boats as far as the traders are concerned, but he's got a few customers what keep him busy.'

'The spivs?' suggested Libby.

Pete glanced back the way Libby and Jack had come. 'Have you been speakin' to Cynthia?'

Libby laughed softly. 'How did you guess?'

He rolled his eyes. 'Cos she's got a gob like a foghorn, but yes, she's quite correct: your uncle's been dealin' in all sorts.'

'Mum knew he would. I'm just glad he's not tarnishin' their good name.'

Pete gave her a stern glance. 'No one associates your parents with him. I'm sorry to say it, Libby, but your uncle's a crook.' He hesitated, eyeing her thoughtfully. 'Do you reckon your folks knew what he was really like?'

'I think Mum did. Dad knew his brother was a rum 'un, but he would never have sold him the stall if he knew the sort of crooks Cynthia claims him to be mixing with.'

'I didn't think they'd sell it to him, knowin' the company he keeps,' Pete admitted.

'Not a chance. Dad would've given it away before he did that.' As the words left her lips, she recalled something her father had said about her mother wanting to sell the stall to Hitler before her brother-in-law. *Had* her mother known something her father didn't? She dismissed the thought as soon as it entered her mind. Orla couldn't have known Tony better than his own brother!

Pete was eyeing Jack studiously. 'I recognise you. You're the geezer what come for the veggies on Christmas Day!'

'That's right! They were much appreciated, by the way.'

Pete pushed his chest out. 'Best veggies this side of London.' He looked from Libby to Jack. 'I must admit I'd had a bit too much Christmas cheer that day; remind me again, how did the two of you meet?'

To spare Libby's blushes, Jack jumped in, saying that Libby had gone to the same shelter as him and his father and that they'd got to know each other as they waited for the air raid to pass.

Pete took Jack's hand and shook it warmly. 'It's ever so good of you and your father to take Libby in.'

Jack waved a dismissive hand. 'Anythin' to help a damsel in distress.'

'Especially one as pretty as our Libby, eh?' teased Pete.

Jack gave an embarrassed chuckle, but said nothing to confirm nor deny his inner thoughts. He fervently hoped that Libby didn't think he'd only taken her in because he thought her pretty, because that wasn't the case at all.

Sensing Jack's embarrassment, Libby was quick to change the subject. 'The funeral is at ten o'clock on the thirtieth. I hope you'll be able to make it?' She glanced around at the other market stalls. 'I know Mondays can be one of the busiest days of the week, so I'll understand if not.'

Pete laid a reassuring hand over hers. 'We wouldn't miss it for the world.' Cupping his hands around his mouth, he drew a deep breath before shouting, the date and time of the Gilberts' funeral, advising everyone to pass the word. Watching as several traders began to do just that, Libby turned to Pete.

'Thanks, Pete. I'd hate anyone to miss it, although I wouldn't want them gettin' into trouble with Filmer either, so . . .'

Pete gave a snort of contempt. 'If Filmer says one word, we'll report him to the powers that be. Allowin' traders to run stolen goods is a sackable offence, never mind the trouble he could get in if the law ever found out.'

'You really think it's that bad?' asked Jack.

'I certainly do,' said Pete severely. 'I swear no one buys any actual crockery off of your uncle, and everythin' he does buy or receive is always in brown paper bags which he keeps hidden below the counter.'

'What about the Bluebottles?' queried Libby. 'Surely they must know what's goin' on?'

Pete shrugged. 'He's probably paid them off, or if he hasn't then someone further up the chain has.'

'What about Filmer? Doesn't he say anything?'

'Not a dickie bird,' said Pete. 'It's a sad situation, because you know he had the greatest respect for your parents, but we think your uncle's made him an offer he can't refuse.'

'With a bit of luck Tony will move on to pastures new; either that or they'll bring on a market inspector that can't be bought off.'

Pete pushed his glasses up from the tip of his nose. 'People are desperate for money, so there's not much chance of that happenin'.'

Libby looked at her uncle's stall. 'Where is he?'

'He only comes for a couple of hours a day,' said Pete, 'probably because there's less chance of gettin' caught if he keeps his time here to a minimum. Well, that and the fact he don't need to work as hard as the rest of us when he's takin' backhanders.'

Libby let out a breathy sigh. 'Oh, Pete, I wish my father would've been a bit wiser when it came to his brother. The last thing you need is my uncle draggin' the reputation of the market back down to where it once was.'

Pete winked at her. 'We're a tough lot, so we'll bounce back. Folk like him don't stay around too long. Summat always happens to upset the pot, and next thing you know, they're off lookin' for somewhere to lie low whilst the dust settles.'

Libby glanced at her parents' stall. Once alive with joy and laughter, it was hard for her to see it looking so drab and destitute. 'I've been wonderin' what I'm goin' to do with meself now I'm on my own, and I think I have the answer.'

Jack eyed her inquisitively. 'Oh?'

'After I've been to Liverpool to tell my grandparents what's happened, I'm goin' to come back here and get a stall of me own. I shall call it Reggie and Orla's, and I shall build their reputation up to where it once was. And I shall make sure that people like Tony and his cronies are banished from every market in London!'

Chapter Four

Libby gazed out from the window to the hearses below. Up until now, she thought she'd managed to successfully put the reality of her situation out of her mind. But she couldn't escape the truth when it was right in front of her. She turned to Jack and Gordon, both of whom were dressed in their Sunday best.

'I've been so busy sortin' everythin' out that I'd pushed everythin' to the back of my mind,' she said, her voice barely above a whisper. 'But there's no more distractions to be had; not now.'

Jack walked towards her, his arm outstretched in readiness to take her in a comforting embrace. 'We're goin' to be right beside you. No one expects you to put on a show, not today.'

'Just as well, because I don't think I'm goin' to be up to much.' Slow tears tracked her cheeks. 'I wish it was yesterday, because I really don't think I'm ready for this.'

'That's called puttin' off the inevitable,' said Gordon wisely. 'Perfectly understandable given the circumstances.'

She fielded a tear with the crook of her finger. 'I did hope my uncle might've turned up, you know, to come with us in the car?'

'I'm afraid not,' said Jack, 'and given his behaviour over the past few days, I'd've been more surprised had he turned up. Having said that, maybe he doesn't think he's got the right after the way he's been.'

'I can see why he'd think that, but when all's said and done, he was my father's brother,' said Libby. 'Mrs F. said that men don't show their emotions the same way as women, so maybe buryin' his head in the sand is his way of dealin' with things?'

'Cuttin' himself off from everyone else, and pretendin' like none of it's goin' on?' mused Gordon. 'I know a few geezers that are guilty of that.'

She took her jacket from the hook behind the door. 'I know that I've got the two of you, and even though you're like family, you never knew my parents. I wish he'd have come, because it would've been another member of the family to share the burden of my loss.'

She began to descend the stairs with Jack and Gordon following her. 'I'm sure he'll be at the church,' said Jack, crossing his fingers behind his back. 'Today might be a good day for the two of you to mend some bridges.'

Libby brightened a little. 'I hope so.'

Stepping out into the harsh winter sunlight, she glanced fleetingly at the caskets in the back of the hearse. Swallowing, she quickly averted her gaze to Mr Caldecott, who was coming forward to greet her.

Libby stared at him as he spoke, her eyes welling with fresh tears. She appeared for all the world to be listening, but in her heart she was wishing he would stop talking so that she could take her place in the funeral car, away from the hearses. When he had finished with his condolences, he opened the door to the car, and Libby took her place, followed closely by Jack and Gordon.

'Not long now, gel,' said Gordon as he took his place beside Jack.

Her heart hammering in her chest, she looked fearfully to Jack, who shifted forward in his seat. 'Do you need to take a minute? I can ask them to hang on whilst I go and get you a glass of water?' He slid his hand in hers. 'We'll do this at your pace, no one else's.'

As Libby felt his skin against hers, her breathing came back under control. 'Thanks, but I'll be okay. I don't know what came over me. It was as if I was finding it hard to breathe.'

Jack gripped her hand. 'If you want to cry, cry; if you want to scream, then scream. There is no right or wrong when you've lost a parent. Be yourself, and don't try and put on a brave face to suit others.'

Libby tightened her fingers around his. 'I don't know how I'd have got through this day without you and your father, I really don't. You're like my knights in shining armour. If it hadn't been for you, Jack, I'd be in one of them hearses myself. I don't know how I'm ever goin' to be able to thank the two of you enough.'

Jack's cheeks warmed. 'Anyone would've done the same in our position.'

She glanced at the people in the street, who'd stopped to remove their caps as the funeral procession drove past. 'I wish I was one of them,' she said, jerking her head towards the people outside.

'I know,' was all Jack could manage.

The journey from the flat to the church was a relatively short one, and as the car slowed to a halt, Libby felt the nervous sensation of butterflies enter her stomach. She turned to Jack, a look of dread clouding her features. 'Oh God, this is it, isn't it?'

'I'm afraid so. Best foot forward,' said Jack. 'I'll be with you every step of the way.'

Her eyes shining with tears, she gripped the car handle in her hand. 'Together?'

He placed his hand over hers. 'Together.'

As Libby got out of the car, she noticed for the first time the tens, if not hundreds of mourners who had come to say good-bye to her parents. Blinking at the mass of people, she felt Jack slip his hand into hers.

'Looks like your parents were well loved,' said Jack. 'And if you're anythin' like them, I can see why.'

Libby gazed at the sea of faces before her. 'Dear God, they must've closed the market . . .' She spied Pete, who ducked his head in acknowledgement.

Gordon stared in wonderment at the crowd who filled the churchyard. 'Are all of these people market traders?'

Libby, too, was staring in awe at the sheer volume of mourn-ers. 'A lot of them are customers too,' she sniffed. 'My mum and dad'd be blown away by this turnout.'

The vicar came forward to greet Libby, first expressing his condolences, and then remarking on the turnout. 'I've not seen this many people at a funeral in I don't know how long,' he said approvingly.

Having recovered from the shock, Libby began to scan the crowd, whilst speaking to the vicar from the corner of her mouth. 'Have you seen Tony Gilbert? He's my father's brother.'

The vicar glanced down at his feet ruefully. 'I'm sure he'll be here any minute.'

But Libby didn't feel as certain. 'I really thought he couldn't sink any lower,' she said, turning to Jack. 'I know this might be his way of copin' with what happened, but he needs to get his head out of the sand and start thinkin' of others. God only knows, I don't want to be here, but I'm doin' it for my parents; because I love them.'

Giving the vicar an awkward grimace, Jack glanced in the direction of the church, and the pallbearers, who were waiting patiently. 'It's time, Lib.'

Libby stared blankly at him for a second or two before remembering where she was. She jutted her chin out in a determined fashion. 'Then we need not waste another second waitin' for someone who hasn't the decency to show his face.' She looked at the vicar. 'I'm ready.'

As they waited for the congregation to file into the church, Gordon turned to Libby. 'They say you can't choose your family, but someone doesn't have to be related in order to be considered as such. Judging by this turnout, you've got the biggest family I've ever seen.'

The whole time Libby was in the church, she half expected her uncle to turn up, mumbling some cock and bull apology, but he never showed. She had let the vicar's words wash over her, and when it came to the graveside committal, Jack had to give her a gentle nudge to let her know that she was being asked to take some dirt from the soil box.

She fell into a trance as the soil trickled from her fingers, and before she knew it she'd buckled at the knees and was halfway to the ground before she felt Jack's arms envelop her. 'Steady on there, gel,' he mumbled as he drew her up to her feet. Feeling his arm firmly around her shoulders, Libby leaned her cheek against his chest, and allowed the tears to flow. Uncaring as to who could see her, or what they might think, she wept unapologetically for the lives which had been so cruelly taken in the name of war.

With Jack, Gordon and Pete as well as many of the other market traders gathering round to comfort her, Libby slowly made her way back to the church. Thanking each of them profusely for the money they'd raised for her parents' funeral, Libby was surprised when Pete made an announcement, telling everyone that there would be a wake down the Hog and Hound.

She had begun to protest before being cut short by Pete. 'But nothin'. This is our way of raisin' a glass to your folks, and we wanted to do it somewhere which meant summat to them.' He winked. 'Especially your father.'

Libby gave a tearful chuckle. 'He certainly liked a swift pint after a hard day's graft.' She pulled a hesitant face. 'My uncle won't be there, will he? I'm not sure I could hold me tongue if I ran into him, and I don't want to cause a scene, not today of all days.'

Pete did his best to reassure her as they made their way to the pub. 'He wasn't at the funeral, so I can hardly see him turnin' up to the wake, can you?'

Libby turned her thoughts to Cynthia's words concerning her uncle's dealings at the stall. 'I can't thank you enough for arrangin' all this, Pete. You're a star.'

'Your parents helped me when I first come to the market.' He made a sweeping motion with his arm, indicating many of the mourners. 'In fact they helped just about every one of us in one way or another.'

'You've gotta have each other's backs, cos it's us against them,' said Libby reminiscently, 'that's what Dad always used to say.'

'Ain't that the truth,' agreed Pete. 'Us market traders are a breed like no other. We're out in all weathers, whether it be rain or shine. Always cheerful and never complainin'. We cater for rich and poor alike, with no discrimination. Everybody's equal in our eyes.'

'That's why I wanted to be a market trader when I left school,' said Libby, 'but Dad always wanted me to do summat that meant I wasn't out in all weathers.'

'I can see his point,' said Gordon. 'Bein' carpenters means that me and Jack work inside.' He cast his son a meaningful glance. 'Although Jack's goin' to have a right old wake-up call when he gets into uniform.'

Pete's brow rose quickly. 'I remember my time in the first lot. Up with reveille, runnin' round the yard in yer undies . . .'

Jack gaped at him. 'Wouldn't they let you get dressed first?'

Gordon chuckled. 'He's havin' you on, son.'

A look of relief swept across Jack's features. 'Thank gawd for that! I know they'll make us exercise from the crack of dawn till dusk, but I draw the line at doin' it in me undies.'

'Imagine if they did that with the women of the WAAF,' mused Libby, much to the amusement of the men around her.

'There'd be no need for conscription,' chortled Pete, 'there'd be a line from here to Parliament Square.'

As they neared the Hog and Hound, Libby's stomach dropped as she caught sight of her uncle's unmanned stall. *He can't even say he had to work*, she told herself. *He has no excuse for his absence.*

Jack followed her gaze. 'At least he didn't turn up for work.'

'I'm glad he's not there,' said Libby stiffly, 'because it would've been a real kick in the teeth to see him actin' like nowt's happened.'

Jack rubbed a soothing hand over her shoulders. 'Like Pete said, we're your family. Forget about him.'

Libby knew that Jack was right, but she'd never forget the fact that her uncle should've been by her side at the committal, if nothing else.

The wake was a mixture of tears and laughter, with people sharing their memories of Reggie and Orla, and the happiness they had brought to the market. Taking a pint and a tub of jellied eels over to the copper table where Libby, Jack and Gordon sat, Pete took a sip of his drink before addressing Libby.

'So, what are your plans now? You do know that we'd be behind you should you want to chance your arm on the market?'

Libby drew a deep breath before letting it out. 'Up until today that was my intention, but after hearing everyone's stories I've come to the realisation that Petticoat Lane isn't for me – not just yet. I need time to heal.'

'Too many memories?'

'Yes! Everywhere I look I see my parents, but I don't see the happiness that they brought, only the misery that their absence brings. I don't want to see the market in that light, especially when it meant so much to them. If I'm to continue in their name, I'll only do so when I can bring the same happiness and enthusiasm to it as they did. Does that make sense?'

'Very much so,' said Jack, 'and you know you'd be welcome to stay with us for as long as need be, so there's no rush.'

She laid a hand on his arm. 'I know, and I'm grateful, truly I am, but I need to find my own way in life. I have a duty to tell my mother's side of the family what's happened, so that's goin' to be my first port of call.'

'You won't go without sayin' goodbye first?' asked Pete.

'Of course not!' Libby assured him, 'but I shall be saying goodbye tomorrow.'

Jack let out an exclamation before wiping the beer from his upper lip. 'Tomorrow? Why tomorrow?'

'Tomorrow is New Year's Eve,' said Libby. 'New year, new start.'

'But it's so soon.'

'You're off yourself in a couple of days,' Libby pointed out.

'I know, but . . .' He fell quiet, before adding, 'I just didn't think you'd leave so quickly.'

Gordon looked concerned. 'Where will you go? You've already said you can't remember where your mother's side of the family are based, and Liverpool's a big city.'

'I shall ask my uncle, and see what he says. Failin' that I'll scour the registry office, see if there's a record of where Mum was born.'

Jack's cheeks coloured as the next question left his lips. 'But what'll you do for money?'

She tapped the side of her nose. 'I shall use my initiative.' Realising how this may sound after her recent escapades, she quickly added, 'I shall wangle a few bob off my uncle.' She held up a hand as they started to object. 'I know you think he wouldn't give me the time of day, let alone any money, but I can only try. Besides, he'll soon cough up if he wants to see the back of me. He's got his fingers in too many pies not to buy my silence. Unlike the rest of the traders, I have nothin' to fear by shoutin' the truth from the rooftops, cos I'll be on the midnight train out of London.'

31ST DECEMBER 1940

Margo Fisher slipped precariously as she pelted along the cobbles towards the market on Petticoat Lane. She hoped fervently that she'd left her father far behind, but having made that mistake once before, she wasn't prepared to rest until she was certain he'd given up. As her boots skidded on the icy cobbles, she prayed that her father might come a cropper, so that she could catch her breath, and get rid of the stitch that had formed in her side.

Still in hot pursuit, her father, Bill, slid on the cobbles, jarring his lower back. 'Thievin' little bitch! You wait till I get my 'ands on you. I'll tan your bleedin' 'ide, so I will!'

Furious that her father was accusing her unfairly, the only thing that stopped her from confronting him was the knowledge that his threats weren't empty. Margo might know that she'd only 'thieved' what was rightfully hers in the first place, but her father didn't see it that way. As far as he was concerned the money Margo earned as a shoeblack was his, and she had no say in how it was spent, because it was his business. This would have been fine with Margo had her father bought food with the money, instead of flittering it away down the dogs, or the horses. She turned her thoughts to the argument they'd had after her first week's work as a shoeblack.

'If you want food, then it's up to you to get some,' her father had said. 'If you get caught that's your lookout.'

'That would be bitin' the hand that feeds me,' she had quite rightly pointed out. 'Most of my regulars use the market, and if any of them were to see me helpin' meself . . .'

'Then make sure they don't,' had come his simple reply.

'But why do I have to nick stuff, when I earn enough to make ends meet?' Margo had begun, but this had only infuriated her father.

'If it weren't for me, you wouldn't 'ave got the job in the first place!' he snapped. 'Who do you suppose pays the rent? The soddin' tooth fairy?'

Margo wanted to point out that her father was often in rent arrears, but what was the point, when it would only end in tears, and a thick ear.

Now, as she continued to wind her way through the stalls, she replayed the moment she had decided to run off with her earnings. It had not been a spur of the moment decision, and it was one she now regretted. She had been standing outside the room she shared with her father in Blendon Row when the argument began. Taking the last of the polish, she had showed it to her father as proof that she needed more, but instead he had insisted that she should make it last.

'It's bad enough you don't buy us anything to eat,' snapped Margo, 'but how am I meant to polish shoes without polish?'

'Make do, that's what them in government keep tellin' us,' snarled Bill. 'If you 'adn't been so careless with the last lot, you'd still 'ave enough. Mebbe this'll teach you a lesson.'

Margo chucked the polish back into the box. 'I ain't goin' to sit there with no polish, askin' folk to pay for a service they ain't goin' to get.'

But her father had remained adamant, so Margo had set off to her usual pitch where she apologised to her customers for her lack of polish, assuring them that she'd put extra effort into getting their boots clean. She felt certain that many of them had only paid because they felt sorry for her. As far as Margo was concerned, this only made matters worse, because she knew her father would crow from the rooftops about how he'd been right, and that Margo needed to be more frugal in her use of the polish.

By the time she had returned home later in the day, she had made her mind up to pocket some of the money and lie to her father, saying that nobody wanted their shoes polished when there was no polish, but Margo wasn't a natural liar. He had fixed her with a steely glare, demanding that she produce the money, but she'd refused. Plunging his hand into her pocket, he'd withdrawn the small number of coins before pushing her to the floor.

He had stared at the coins in his hand before turning his attention back to Margo. 'You little bloody liar! I *knew* you was 'oldin' out on me.'

'I need that for polish!' cried Margo. 'You can't seriously expect me to do a decent job on people's shoes without polish?'

'You done it today!'

'They felt sorry for me,' muttered Margo. Lowering her voice, she added, 'Most probably because they know what a rotten bleeder I have for a father.'

The coins fell from his hand as Bill gripped hold of his daughter's shirt collar. His face turning puce, white spittle formed in the corner of his lips as he pulled her towards him. '*What* did you say?'

Margo pointed to her eye, still yellow from the bruise caused by her father several weeks before. 'Decent fathers don't give their daughters a black eye just because the heavens opened. It weren't my fault people didn't want their shoes shined when it was chuckin' it down.'

'Nothin' ever is!' spat Bill. He pointed to the coins which lay around his feet. 'Pick them up!'

Margo stood firm. 'You threw it, you pick it up.'

Bill began to undo the buckle on his belt. 'You've got one chance. You can either pick them up before or after you've 'ad a beltin'.'

Tears pierced Margo's eyes at the sheer unfairness of it all. Why couldn't her father see things from her point of view? Why did he continue to treat her badly, when all she'd ever done was try to please him? Picking the pennies up, she wondered what he would do to her the following day if she couldn't possibly perform her job. A wave of sickness overcame her as she envisaged his anger when he realised that they had no money to buy polish because he'd gambled it away. Her lids fluttered. She would have no other option than to steal some. Something which she had refused to do in the past, but how could she continue to say no, when it was their only option? Taking the money, Margo did the only thing she could think of. Tucking it into her dungarees pocket, she thrust open the door and fled through the streets of London, with her father in hot pursuit.

Her plan – such as it was – was to get far away from her father and wait for him to tire of searching. She'd then head down the market and buy some polish. He'd be angry, but there'd be nothing he could do about it.

Desperately looking for somewhere to hide, she wasn't paying attention to where she was going, and perhaps inevitably she collided with a woman in front of one of the stalls. Hearing the crash of the stallholder's produce as it hit the floor, Margo mumbled a hasty apology as she scrambled to her feet and ran. Tears streaming down her face as she envisaged her father catching up to her, she was pleased when she heard him yell out behind her. Glancing over her shoulder, she saw to her relief that he was sprawled on the floor near where she'd just fallen. Not wanting to waste a second of her advantage, she ploughed on, determined to get as much distance as she could between them. Having come a cropper would've fuelled his temper and she had no doubt that he would blame her for any injuries he'd incurred as a result.

As she ran past a fruit and veg stall, she grabbed an apple, yelling: 'I'll be back to pay for it later,' at the surprised stallholder, who bellowed in protest.

Stealing what she'd earned was one thing, but Margo knew how hard the market traders worked to earn their living, and she had no intention of diddling someone out of their money, no matter the circumstances. She took a bite out of the apple as she continued to run, and quickly learned that eating whilst running is not a sensible thing to do. Choking on a chunk which had gone down the wrong way, she slapped her chest as she tried to dislodge the offending piece of fruit. With her eyes watering, Margo breathed a sigh of relief as she managed to swallow it. Concerned that her money might've been spilled when she fell, she pushed her hand deep into her pocket and was relieved to feel the coins which she'd earned earlier in the day. Barely enough to buy polish, taking it was hardly the crime of the century, but to Bill, not having money to place on a bet was considered to be the end of the world. She checked behind to make sure there was no sign of him, and slowed her pace.

Margo had often toyed with the idea of talking to her father about his gambling habits, but until now she'd not been brave enough to bring the matter up. She rolled her eyes as a memory of her drunken mother arguing with him over who should have the money came into her mind.

How on earth did I end up with parents like them? Margo asked herself. *More interested in drinkin' and gamblin' than they've ever been in me. It makes me wonder why they ever decided to have a baby . . .* She tutted inwardly. *Because I was a mistake*, she thought, *and Mum being Mum she probably didn't realise she was pregnant until it was too late to do owt about it.* She wondered how embarrassing it must've been for everyone when her mother reeled into the hospital, blind drunk. *I bet Dad was down the dogs when she gave birth*, Margo told herself. *He probably had the shock of his life when she turned up with me.* She tried to imagine how any nurse or midwife worth their salt could have allowed her mother to walk out with a baby whilst obviously intoxicated. As far as Margo was concerned it was a miracle she was still alive. Her mother's reluctance to give up the bottle had resulted in her eventually succumbing to liver disease. With only herself to take care of her mother, Margo had nursed her as best she could through her last few weeks of life. A frown etched her brow as she recalled her father swinging his jacket over his shoulder as he left the house to go to the track. The doctor had already told the family that Betty wouldn't make it until morning, and Margo had presumed that her father wouldn't abandon his wife in her final hours, yet it appeared he couldn't get away fast enough. It had been the final straw for Margo, who couldn't come to terms with her father's total lack of empathy. In the following days they had had many an argument where Margo had chastised her father for his behaviour, but all that did was enrage him further, so she had decided it best to keep her opinions to herself.

I shall never gamble, nor drink alcohol, Margo told herself now, *because I want a proper home and a proper family, and you can't have either of those if you're spendin' all your money on the horses or drink.*

She had asked herself many times why she continued to work, just so that her father could fritter their money away, but the answer always came back the same. *Because without you he's got nothin'. He might be quicker with a punch than a kiss, but that's only frustration. If you're real lucky he might wake up and realise what a complete arse he's been. He might even give up the gamblin', and the two of you could be a proper family.* She had no idea what it would take for that to happen, but she always hoped against hope that one day her father would see the light, and she intended to be there for him should that day ever come.

Yawning audibly, Margo leaned against a wall as she finished her apple. *No wonder I'm tired,* she told herself. *One apple in two days isn't enough to live on.* On the other hand, if she hadn't stolen the apple but stayed with her father, who knows when she'd next have had something to eat?

It's not that he's bein' mean, she thought; *he thinks he's goin' to win big any day now, and when he does we'll have all the food we could wish for. But that won't happen, cos if he ever did win big he'd be convinced it was his lucky day, and he'd continue until he'd bet every last penny, just like he did the one and only time he won a reasonable amount of money.* She tried to think of the days ahead, and the consequences of her defying him. If she didn't buy the polish, they would have no money coming in, and their pitch would be allocated to someone else. No money, no home. *He'll continue until he's lost everything, and he probably won't stop after that. But if I go back and do as he asks, at least we'll still have a roof over our heads.*

When war had been declared, she had been quite surprised that her father hadn't farmed her out to one of the ammunition factories that were springing up left, right and centre. She would certainly earn more in a factory than she would as a shoeblack. *Enough to pay me own rent*, she thought, *and if that were the case I'd not need Dad, or at least that's what he'd think, because in truth, I don't really need him now. It might be his name on the box, but he hasn't the patience to take the time required to polish someone's shoes: he'd skimp the first pair and be straight down the bookies.* She rolled her eyes. *Or he'd try and pick their pockets the same as he did when I first started out.* She recalled the time she'd been busying herself applying polish to a customer's shoes when, to her horror, she saw her father place a finger to his lips as he attempted to dip his hand into the pocket of the man seated in front of her. Terrified that he would realise what her father was up to, Margo faked a violent coughing fit, alarming her father, and bringing the man's attention to him. He hadn't guessed what Bill was about to do, much to Margo's relief, and she waited until they were in the privacy of their home before warning her father that he was never to try doing something like that again.

'If he'd felt you, what then? You're *my* father so they'd think the two of us were in cahoots. I'd be in as much trouble for creatin' a distraction as you, if not more!' she seethed. Nearly at her wits' end, she pressed on. 'We'd have lost our right to earn money, not that we're entitled to do so now, considerin' I ain't even a boy!' She tore the cap from her head, revealing golden locks which cascaded to her shoulders.

'And you know full well that if anyone realises you ain't a boy, we've as good as lost the only money we 'ave comin' in,' snapped Bill.

'You could get a job,' suggested Margo sullenly. 'That way we'd have enough to move somewhere decent.'

Bill gaped at his daughter. 'I ain't workin' some poxy job down the docks for a pittance,' he spluttered, 'not when I could be earnin' good money off of the backs of others.'

'Pickin' pockets ain't earnin' a livin', Dad, it's stealin',' Margo reminded her father, 'and you're goin' to get caught one of these days, you mark my words.'

'Not if I ain't got you chokin' yer guts up every time I spy a pocket, I won't. Besides, if it was good enough for Robin Hood, it's good enough for me!'

Margo's jaw had practically hit the floor. 'What on earth are you talkin' about? Robin Hood wasn't real, and even if he was, he stole from the rich to give to the poor. What you're doin' is totally different.'

Bill shrugged petulantly. 'They're rich, I'm poor, what's the difference?'

'Because they earn their money fair and square,' snapped Margo. 'They're not the tax man, they don't take yer money, they're in the same position as us – or at least they would be if we paid taxes, but we don't even do that!'

'Too right we don't,' bellowed Bill. 'I ain't goin' to give to them, when they don't give me nothin'.'

Margo stared at her father in an exasperated fashion. 'Who on earth do you think is payin' our boys to fight for our country? Not bleedin' you, that's for sure!'

Bill had struck without warning, his fist connecting with her eye before she had a chance to duck. Holding her hand to the abused socket, which was already watering, she cast her father a look of disdain. 'You don't like what I have to say because it's the truth, and you know it is.'

'It's not what you said, it's the way you said it,' snarled Bill. 'Makin' me out to be some kind of villain. Let's see what you have to say when I hit a lucky streak.'

Margo had rolled her eyes. 'You don't really believe that, do you?' She hesitated before answering her own question. 'Of course you do, you'd not be wastin' our money otherwise.'

Bill gawked at her. 'Wastin' our money? Is that what you call it?'

'You spend our money and don't get nothin' back, so yes, I do call it a waste. It'd be different if you had summat to show for the countless hours you spend down the track, but you come back with less than what you left with. No food, no nothin'.' She folded her arms across her chest. 'I thought it might be different once Mum died, but if anythin' you got worse.'

Fed up of hearing his daughter judge him in what he thought to be an unfair manner, Bill took his coat from off its peg and headed out the door. 'You don't know what you're talkin' about.'

'Do I not?' Margo shouted after him. 'I don't need to be a genius to know that you're lousy at gamblin', and nothin's ever goin' to change that!'

Now, Margo decided it would be best all round if she found somewhere to get out of the cold and have herself forty winks. Then, when she woke, she would buy some polish before finding her father and telling him that he needed to change or she would be forced to leave. *I've waited and waited for him to come to his senses*, she thought, *but that that's never goin' to happen whilst I continue givin' him money. He either agrees to change, or I'm off.* With this her uppermost thought, Margo found herself the perfect place to get some respite without fear of being disturbed.

*

157

It was the afternoon of New Year's Eve and Libby was on her way to the market, accompanied by an anxious Jack.

'I wish you'd wait until you had somewhere to stay,' he said as he trotted to keep up with Libby's long strides.

'I won't know where I'm stayin' until I get there,' reasoned Libby, 'but I promise I'll let you know where I am as soon as I do.'

Jack wanted to plead with her to stay, to think things through for a while longer, but as he was leaving himself in a couple of days' time he was hardly in a good position to argue. As all the 'what if's' ran through his mind, he very much wished that he'd never applied for the services. *If I'd met Libby before signin' up*, he told himself now, *then I'd go with her to Liverpool, but I can hardly do that now.* He paused to wonder what would happen if he didn't arrive to do his basic training, but quickly dismissed the idea as a bad one. The services weren't renowned for their compassion regarding people who'd gone AWOL, and he very much feared he'd come under the same rules as those who'd been serving for years.

'I know you worry that I won't be able to look after myself, but I will,' Libby assured him.

'But you're a woman on her own,' objected Jack. 'I know what men can be like. They'll try to take advantage, and you won't have anyone to help fend them off.' He racked his brains as he tried to recall what little he knew about Liverpool. 'They reckon Liverpool's full of dockers, crime and poverty . . .'

'I should fit right in then,' said Libby, 'seein' as I haven't got two pennies to rub together.'

'It's not funny, Lib,' he said sullenly. 'Can you imagine what it'd be like to arrive in London with no money, and no mates?'

Libby was about to say that she could well imagine what that was like, because she'd felt that way when she'd nearly turned to prostitution. 'But I've got family there,' she reminded him, 'so it's not like I'll be on me tod for long. I can't see that it will take me more than a couple of hours to track them down.'

'What if they don't want to know? You could hardly describe them as close when you don't even know where they live. And it's been years since you've seen them.'

'If they turn their backs on me then I shall come back to London. Does that answer your question?'

Jack gave her a grim smile. 'It does, but it won't stop me from worryin'.'

Seeing Tony standing behind his stall, Libby pointed him out to Jack. 'If anyone should be worried, it should be him, not you!' She strode towards her uncle, folding her arms across her chest as she addressed him, loudly enough for people to hear a few stalls away. 'Did you forget that it was your brother's funeral yesterday?'

Watching from the next stall, Pete took the money from the customer he had been serving, and handed them their veg. 'You tell him, gel.'

With Pete's endorsement, and Jack by her side, Libby let her uncle know exactly what she thought of his behaviour. 'I've been turnin' a blind eye to your shenanigans from day one,' she began, but Tony was quick to interrupt.

'You accused me of stealin' the business,' he said evenly. 'I'd hardly call that turnin' a blind eye.'

'I'm your niece, your only livin' relative, yet did you offer me a place to stay?' She glared at him angrily before answering her own question. 'Did you 'eck as like.'

'You was stayin' with that old bat, and quite frankly I'd've thought you'd rather be with her, considerin' you had me down as a tea leaf what'd nick off his own family! You're quick to paint me as the bad one, but I don't remember accusin' you of anythin'.'

'Actions speak louder than words,' said Libby accusingly. 'My father wasn't even cold, yet you'd already set up the stall.'

'In memory of your parents. They'd not thank me for lettin' the business go down the plug 'ole.'

Libby stared at him. 'I'd lost everything! Not just my parents, but all our belongings. What've you done to try and help me find them what took it?'

He held his hands out palms up. 'How do you expect me to find the van when the coppers can't? Be fair!'

'You could've gone with me to the police station,' said Libby, 'or put word out, to see if owt comes back, but you've not lifted a finger to help me at the time I needed you most! You're up to your neck in the underworld, so you've probably got a better chance than anyone else.' Without waiting for a reply, she indicated the people of the market with a sweep of her arm. 'Nigh on everybody here donated a small amount towards the funeral, yet I have it on good authority that you never donated so much as a penny.'

His cheeks flushed. 'Did you?'

Libby gaped at him for a moment or two, until Pete came to her rescue. 'How could she donate anythin' when she knew nowt about it? And how's she meant to make a contribution when she ain't got a job?' Rocking back on his heels, he glanced at the area where Tony hid his goods. 'Whereas you, on the other hand . . .'

Tony kicked what appeared to be a suitcase underneath the stall. 'Is that it? Only I've got a livin' to make.'

Libby shot him a withering glance. 'I'm leavin' London to look for my mother's side of the family. As everythin' includin' the address book got nicked, I was hopin' you might be able to point me in the right direction.'

'Scotland Road,' said Tony, adding nastily, 'You'll not be surprised to hear that it's the roughest part of Liverpool.'

'What's that supposed to mean?'

He fixed her with a steely gaze before looking to Jack, who was eyeing him steadily. 'Nothin',' he said sullenly.

'Well, it obviously means something, cos you'd not have mentioned it otherwise.'

He let out a staggered breath. 'I've told you where they live, so if there's nothin' else?'

Libby leaned forward as she lowered her voice. 'Mum always said you was a wrong 'un, although she never said why, but hearin' the kind of thing you've been gettin' up to I now see that she was right.'

He gave a contemptuous snort. 'Pot, kettle, black.'

Libby's jaw stiffened. 'What do you mean by that?'

'Your mother wasn't exactly holier than thou, far from it. And she had a nerve paintin' me to be blacker than black, when she was no flamin' angel herself.'

Libby's eyes grew round. 'My mother never did anythin' that wasn't totally legit. Dad maybe, but not Mum.'

He gawked at her. 'You haven't got a clue what your mother was really like.'

Jack laid his hand on Libby's elbow. 'C'mon, Lib. You don't need to hear this nonsense from a man who couldn't be bothered goin' to his own brother's funeral.'

'Brother!' spat Tony. 'Don't make me laugh.'

Libby gently pushed Jack's hand away. 'He was more of a brother than you'd ever been! And if you hated him that much, why did you want his business so badly?'

'He took everythin' else of mine,' said Tony sullenly. 'The business was the least he owed me.'

'What on earth did he take of yours?' She cast a sarcastic eye around her as though searching for the alleged items. 'From where I'm standin', you're the one doin' all the takin'.'

He eyed her with an air of incredulity. 'You haven't got a clue; but then why would you? All I'm sayin' is your father's not the man you think him to be.'

Pete tutted irritably. 'Don't listen to him, Lib. We all know your father was the salt of the earth.' He gave Tony a look of sheer disgust. 'It beats me how the two of you are related, cos as far as brothers go you're nothin' alike.'

'You're right there,' snapped Tony. He appeared to calm himself before turning his attention back to Libby. 'Did you never wonder why you were an only child?'

Libby stared at her uncle in bewilderment. She never had, because it hadn't crossed her mind to question it until now. 'No. Why would I?'

He wiped his hand across his mouth, as though he were debating whether he should speak his thoughts, or remain quiet. Appearing to reach a decision, he ducked down behind the stall before standing back up, suitcase in hand.

'You said you were goin' to Liverpool?'

'That's right,' said Libby. She waited to see where he was heading with the sudden change of conversation.

He stuffed his free hand into his pocket and pulled out a series of five-shilling notes. Placing the case back down, he peeled one off, and held it out to Libby, whilst pushing the rest back into his pocket.

Libby eyed the money as though she expected it to explode, or disintegrate before her very eyes. 'What's this for?'

'Whatever you want. Rail fare, bed and board, summat to eat.'

Libby put her hand out to take the money, then hesitated. 'Why give me it me now, when I could've done with it days ago?'

'Because I very much doubt we'll ever see each other again, and . . .' he sighed breathily, as though he had the weight of the world on his shoulders, 'and because it's not your fault that you were born into a web of deceit.'

Libby gave a short, disbelieving laugh. 'What *are* you goin' on about?'

Again, Jack placed his hand on her arm. 'Don't listen to him; he's just bein' spiteful. Tryin' to divert the blame from himself to your parents.'

Tony eyed Jack coolly. 'Oh, I know I'm partly to blame, but I'm not the only one.'

'If you're goin' to start throwin' accusations about, you should at least have the courtesy to tell me what you're accusin' them of,' said Libby stiffly.

Picking the suitcase up, Tony pressed the five-shilling note into her hand. 'Good luck. I hope you find whatever it is you're lookin' for.' Libby opened her mouth to protest, but her uncle was already sieving his way through the crowded market.

She folded her fingers over the money before looking to Pete, then Jack. 'What the hell was all that about?'

Jack shrugged. 'Guilty conscience for not steppin' up when he should've done?'

'One hundred per cent!' said Pete. 'You put 'im on the spot, and exposed all his wrongdoings, so he tried to make your parents out to be summat they weren't in order to make himself look good.'

Libby was about to say that she didn't think that was the case when she was knocked to the ground by a young woman running hell for leather. Gabbling an apology, she sped off before Libby had a chance to react. Before Libby could get to her feet, a man with murder in his eyes ran towards them in hot pursuit, yelling that he was going to break the fugitive's neck. Instinctively, Libby stuck out her foot, sending him sprawling to the floor.

'You stupid bitch!' roared the man as he clutched his knee in agony. 'I think you've broke me knee!'

'That's rich considerin' you were threatenin' to break that young woman's neck! All things considered I think you've got away with things quite lightly, don't you?'

The man was about to lunge at Libby when his path was blocked by Jack and Pete, both of whom were ready for him. Spitting at their feet, he hobbled back in the direction from which he had come.

'That was quick thinkin' on your part, Lib,' Pete said approvingly, beginning to pick up the fruit that had been dislodged from his stall in the collision.

'Instinct,' replied Libby, glancing shyly at Jack. 'There but for the grace of God went I.'

Pete stared at her blankly. 'Eh?'

'Just thinkin' out loud. None of us know the circumstances, but we did know what he said he was going to do.'

'Very true,' said Pete. Snapping a paper bag open he filled it with apples, then handed it to Libby. 'For the journey. I know you've got your uncle's money, but I should only use that if you absolutely have to.'

'Thanks, Pete. It'll tide me over until I know what's what.'

'So, when are you off?'

'Tonight—'

Pete cut her off without apology. 'Today? I knew you'd said you were plannin' on leavin' today, but I thought that was said in the heat of the moment type of thing. Why so soon?'

'That's what I've been sayin',' said Jack.

'New year, new start,' said Libby. She glanced around the market. 'I'm goin' to miss this place, as well as the people in it, but I need to get away for a while so that I can clear my head.'

'The further you get away from your uncle the better,' agreed Pete, 'but we won't half miss you around here.'

'And I'll miss all you too,' said Libby, 'but you've seen what my uncle's like. If I were to stay, I'd not be able to stop myself from badgerin' him for information, and I don't think that would be healthy for either of us, especially if he's goin' to start implyin' all sorts about my parents. Far better that I make a clean break and come back when I'm ready.'

Pete glanced to the stall which used to be run by Libby's parents. 'I reckon you'll get the stall back one of these days.'

'And that's what I want,' said Libby, 'but only when I'm in the right frame of mind. I can't pursue this out of vengeance or hate, because it wouldn't work.'

Jack rubbed the nape of his neck with the palm of his hand. 'Your parents would be chuffed to bits to see how maturely you've handled your uncle, not to mention everything else.'

Libby felt a warm glow of embarrassment invade her neckline. 'I wouldn't say I've handled everythin' brilliantly . . .'

But Jack wasn't having her modesty. 'You realised your mistakes and acted accordingly.'

Pete clapped a hand on Libby's shoulder. 'The lad's right. Reggie and Orla would be proper proud of their gel.'

Feeling overwhelmed by the praise being heaped on her, Libby cradled the bag of apples in her hands. 'Thank you both, and whilst I appreciate your kind words, I think it's time I got goin'.'

'Good luck, Lib,' said Pete. 'You know where we are if you need us.'

Thanking him for the final time, Libby left the market with Jack by her side. 'I know there's a mail train leavin' for Liverpool at midnight,' she told him as they made their way back to the flat. 'If I get on that—'

Jack cut her off mid-sentence. 'Hold on. You can't ride the mail train; it's a passenger train you want.'

'You have to pay on a passenger train,' said Libby, 'and I mean to use Tony's money only in an emergency.'

Jack laughed in disbelief. 'Are you tellin' me that you're plannin' on stowin' away on a train, when you have more than enough money for your fare?'

'If I can get to Liverpool for nothin' then why pay? I'm not hurtin' anybody by cadgin' a ride.'

Jack gave her a lop-sided smile as his eyes twinkled down at her. 'You're one hell of a woman, Libby Gilbert, I'll give you that.'

'I'm goin' to need to be if I'm to tackle life on my own.'

Jack hung his arm loosely around her shoulders. 'I've already told you, you're not on your own. It doesn't matter how far apart we are; I'll always be there for you.'

'That's very kind of you, but you've got enough on your plate without worryin' over me.'

He brought his arm round, pulling her close. 'I'm afraid it's too late for me to not be worryin' about you. I'm already invested!'

Libby wouldn't admit it to Jack, but his caring words made her heart sing. She didn't want to be a burden on anyone, but neither did she relish in the prospect of facing life alone. Hearing that Jack would be there for her if she needed him was music to her ears.

'I wish you could've met Emma,' sighed Libby. 'She would've thought the world of you.'

'Your best mate who's gone to Ireland?'

'Yes. It breaks my heart to think that I might never see her again.'

'Do you think it's worth callin' in at the police station before you go? See if they've heard owt about the van?'

'It can't harm,' supposed Libby, 'and if it's all right with you and your dad, I'd like to give them your father's address should something come up.'

'Of course,' said Jack without hesitation. 'And if you let us know yours just as soon as you're settled, we can pass any info on.'

'Perfect!' She walked in silence as she mulled over her uncle's words. *What on earth did he mean by my bein' born into a web of deceit? Did one of them do somethin' unlawful before I was born? I know Dad wasn't whiter than white, but I can't see him doin' anythin' really bad. As for Mum, she wouldn't dream of doin' summat unless it was above board.* She spoke her thoughts to Jack as they neared the stairs to the flat. 'What do you think Tony meant when he implied that Mum wasn't totally innocent? Do you think he was referrin' to her turnin' a blind eye to Dad's shenanigans, but not his?'

Jack shrugged. 'Hard to say. I suppose it's plausible, especially if your uncle feels like he's bein' judged unfairly, which I suppose he kind of was in a way.'

'That's what I used to say to Dad,' mused Libby. 'I even mentioned it to Mum once. She acted like I didn't know what I was talkin' about, but refused to elaborate, and Dad brushed it off, sayin' that in-laws don't always see eye to eye, and he thought that was the case between his brother and my mother.'

'You've said your mother wouldn't do anythin' illegal, so it's got to be that,' said Jack, 'and maybe he made that comment about your dad not bein' like a proper brother because he thought your father should've stuck up for him more?'

'I don't know what went on in that house before the bomb dropped, but maybe they were havin' cross words because he'd bought the business?'

'And he's regrettin' it now, because he can't take the words back or say sorry,' agreed Jack. 'It must be hard livin' with that kind of guilt, which is why he couldn't face goin' to the funeral. Cos you would feel awful if you'd had harsh words with a loved one moments before they were killed.'

'That must be it,' said Libby as she ascended the stairs to the flat. 'Maybe they had a right old barney.'

'Summat's gone on,' agreed Jack as he closed the door behind them, 'although I doubt you'll ever get to the bottom of it. What with Tony feelin' guilty an' all, he's hardly likely to want to admit what took place.'

Libby looked around for something suitable to carry her belongings in. 'I hate to ask, but I don't suppose you've got an old net bag, or a satchel, that I can put my things in?' She cast her eyes to the ceiling before amending her statement. 'Or rather your mum's things.' She hung her head sadly. 'I feel awful takin' her clothing. I know what your dad said, but are you *sure* he wasn't sayin' it because he felt sorry for me?'

Going through to his father's room, Jack took a satchel from the top of the wardrobe. 'Not at all. Dad always said he wanted Mum's stuff to go to someone in need . . .' he held up a finger to stop Libby from interrupting, 'and even though we'd hardly known you for more than a few hours he knew that Mum would've wanted you to have them. And if it's what Mum would've wanted, it's what we want too.'

'I wish I'd met her,' said Libby softly. 'She sounds like a wonderful woman.'

'She was,' said Jack as he sank onto his father's bed. 'Accordin' to Dad, she was always smilin', and she told the most awful jokes, which made everyone laugh. And that's why it's so hard to see why she did what she did. He said she had her bad days, but she'd soon rally; put on a brave face, and get on with the rest of the day. It's hard to imagine how things could've got so bad for someone who appeared to be so happy.'

'Laughin' on the outside, but cryin' from within,' said Libby softly.

'How do you mean?'

Libby sank onto the bed next to Jack. 'I remember my grandmother on my mum's side sayin' that my mother might be laughin' on the outside, but she was cryin' from within.' She pulled a doubtful face. 'I can't think for the life of me why she said it, but I know I was only little at the time, so I didn't quite understand what she meant.' She shrugged. 'Still don't.'

'Perhaps your mother had had a bad day . . .'

But Libby felt certain that it was more than that, and she said as much. 'We'd been talkin' . . .' She broke off as the penny dropped. '*That's* what Tony meant about me bein' an only child!' She struck her forehead with the palm of her hand, cursing herself for being so forgetful. 'Grandma was sayin' that Mum and Dad had been tryin' to get pregnant for *ages* before they had me, and that Mum would love it if I had a little brother or sister, but Grandma said that would never happen.'

Jack pulled a dubious face. 'Why not? If you've had one child, then surely you can have more?'

'Unless summat goes wrong, and you have to have an op,' supposed Libby. 'I know one of the women who worked the market had to have an emergency hysterectomy after her last child, and she can't have any more kids now.' She blew her cheeks out, adding, 'Although why she'd want any more after havin' ten is beyond me!'

Jack blinked. 'Ten? Blimey, sounds like it's a good job she had a hysterwhatsamajig.'

'Hysterectomy,' supplied Libby. 'That's what the woman's husband said. Maybe summat like that happened to Mum, although' – she was eyeing Jack thoughtfully – 'your mum only had you, so maybe there's another reason?'

Jack hung his head. 'I don't think Mum could've coped with another baby, not after havin' me.'

Libby slid her hand into his. 'It can't have been anythin' you did.'

He shrugged. 'Mum was fine before I came along, everyone said so. Life and soul of the East End accordin' to most.'

Libby felt her heartbeat quicken in her chest. The last thing she'd wanted to do was upset him, and she said as much, adding, 'It's all in the past, which is where it should stay. Summat must have happened that you don't know about.'

'Maybe. It's hard to say when I was too little to understand . . .' He glanced at the things she had put into the satchel. 'Is that all you want?'

She shot him a mischievous grin. 'I can hardly take a suitcase, seein' as I'm goin' to be hunkered down in the back of a mail carriage.'

He laughed. 'I think my mum would've loved you!'

Seeing her laugh along with him, the words 'as do I' entered Jack's thoughts, catching him unawares.

Libby found herself looking into Jack's eyes, the laughter fading from her lips. She felt herself being drawn towards him, in a manner she'd never experienced before. Her heart quickening in her chest, she saw Jack's gaze fall to her lips. Realising that she was about to experience her first kiss, she practically jumped out of her skin when Gordon entered the flat, calling 'I'm home' as he shut the door behind him.

Jack quickly averted his gaze from Libby to the bedroom door. 'We're in here, Dad,' he said, standing up. 'We're sortin' out some of Mum's clothes for Lib.'

Gordon's face appeared around the side of the door, and Libby noticed that his eyes flittered from herself to Jack, finally settling on the bed. Ushering them back into the living area he asked Libby if she'd seen her uncle.

Libby told Gordon of their visit to the market, and all that had ensued as a result, and even though Gordon listened with what appeared to be deep interest, in his mind he was thanking the Lord that he had come home when he had. *They wouldn't be the first to give in to their emotions*, thought Gordon, *but I don't want Jack becomin' a dad when he's not even in his twenties . . . and I don't want poor Libby endin' up like Jack's mother, not after everythin' she's been through.*

Libby had asked him a question to which he hadn't responded, he realised, when she repeated, 'I said is it all right with you if I use your address as contact for the police, should they find the contents of the van – or the people who took it?'

Gordon apologised before giving his consent. 'Sorry, Lib, of course it is. When are you goin' to see them?'

Libby looked to Jack, who glanced at the clock. 'No time like the present? I thought we could get fish and chips for tea as Libby's farewell meal.'

Gordon laughed. 'You'd use any excuse for a fish supper!'

Jack grinned. 'Shan't be long.'

Libby led the way down the stairs with Jack behind her. As they emerged onto the pavement, she glanced at him shyly. 'Was it me, or did your dad look worried?'

Jack coughed on a chuckle. 'That's an understatement. I swear I saw beads of sweat on his brow! I don't know what he thought we were doin' when he came home . . .' He paused before correcting himself, 'Or rather, I *do* know what he thought we were up to, which explains the "rabbit in the headlights" look on his face when he came into the bedroom.'

Libby hung her head. 'Do you think he thought that because of that feller in the shelter? Because I'm really not like that at all.' She blushed to the roots of her hair. 'I've not even kissed a feller, never mind you know what.'

Jack tucked his arm through hers. 'Sixteen years old and never been kissed?'

'Is that a bad thing?'

'Not at all, but a woman as beautiful as you, I'd have thought you'd be fightin' them off with sticks.'

Libby giggled nervously. She was certain that they'd nearly shared an intimate moment in his father's bedroom, but she had no idea how she would feel now if they had.

'Not quite, or rather not at all,' replied Libby truthfully. She glanced up at the sign for the police station. 'Here we are.'

They entered the station, and Libby caught the eye of the constable who she'd seen the day she'd reported her parents' belongings had been stolen. After a quick reminder as to who she was, and why she was there, he pulled a grimace. 'We've found the van, but I'm afraid it was empty.'

'Where?'

'Scotland,' he replied.

'*Scotland!*' echoed Libby. 'What on earth was it doin' up there?'

'I did say at the time that they take the stuff a long way from where they nicked it. Lootin' durin' an air raid is a serious offence, so they do anythin' they can to cover their tracks, first of which bein' to take their spoils where no one will find them. I did get someone to call in at the address you gave, but . . .'

Libby's eyelids fluttered. 'I left Mrs Fortescue's on Christmas Eve. I'm sorry, I forgot to tell you that I'd moved elsewhere.'

His pulled his pad towards him. 'I can take your new address, but without an itemised list I'm afraid we don't realistically stand much chance of recovering anything.'

'I don't see the point,' said Libby plainly. 'The contents of that van are probably sittin' in someone else's home by now.'

The constable agreed, albeit reluctantly. 'I'm afraid so.'

Thanking him for his efforts, Libby and Jack left the station. 'Well, that's the end of that,' said Libby as they headed for the fish and chip shop.

'It certainly looks that way,' said Jack. Seeing the dejection on her face, he pushed open the door to the chippy. 'If I could bring your things back, I'd do it in a heartbeat, because I think that's what hurts the most, am I right?'

'If I could have had just the photos. That would've been something.' She touched the locket which hung around her neck. 'I'm only grateful I've got this.'

'It beggars belief that someone can nick a van full of someone's stuff in broad daylight.'

The woman in the queue ahead of them turned to face them. 'They're like bleedin' rats, lootin' after the raids; durin' them too, from what I've 'eard. Some people 'aven't got the sense they were born with if you ask me.'

'Well, I hope they come a cropper,' said Libby. 'People like that deserve to.'

The woman tutted. 'They never do, though; luck of the devil, that's what they've got.' She paused whilst taking her chips from over the counter. 'Ta-ra, ducks.'

Jack and Libby ordered three fish and two portions of chips which they took back to the flat, much to the delight of Gordon, whose nostrils flared as they walked through the door.

Rubbing his hands together, he scattered salt and vinegar over his portion. 'You two can have them off plates if you like, but I reckon they taste better out of the paper.'

'My dad was the same, but Mum always insisted on having hers off a plate.'

'Don't tell me,' said Gordon, as he licked the salt from off his fingers, 'I bet she used a knife and fork, an' all.'

Libby laughed. 'I can see you've got my mother down pat.'

'A proper lady,' said Gordon, much to Libby's delight.

'She was! Dad said she was a snob, but I reckon he was only teasin'.'

Gordon winked at Libby as she began eating her chips with her fingers. 'I see you take after your old feller.'

Libby grinned. 'I certainly do!'

They spent the evening with Libby relaying stories of her childhood, and Gordon comparing the difference between Jack's childhood and hers.

'I've often wondered whether Jack's upbringing was different from his peers' because he never had a mother figure in his life. I suppose if he'd been born a gel things might've been harder, cos I'm pretty clueless when it comes to frocks and ribbons.'

'I used to spend my days in boots and dungarees,' admitted Libby. 'I was never one for frocks and bows, so you never know, you might've been all right.'

'Boots and dungarees?' chuckled Jack. 'Why does that not surprise me?'

'I was always a bit of a daddy's girl,' admitted Libby. 'I wanted to be just like him, workin' the market from dawn to dusk, come rain or shine. There's no sense in wearin' white cotton when you're out in all weathers.'

'Maybe that's why he wanted what he perceived to be better for you?' supposed Jack.

'Definitely. But I am what I am, and that's a trader to me boots!'

'The move to Norwich would've seen you leave your market days behind,' said Jack thoughtfully. 'Wouldn't that've upset you?'

'I wanted what was best for my parents, and we'd seen other traders suffer with agonisin' rheumatism and arthritis as they got older. Standin' out in all weathers is no good when you're in your sixties and seventies. Runnin' a shop would've kept him tradin' but out of the cold. He'd have had the best of both worlds, only I suppose without the camaraderie that you get with the other traders.'

Jack stoked the fire, causing it to spit and sizzle. 'It sounds as though tradin' was in your father's blood. Did his family run a stall?'

'Not at all. It was Mum's side of the family that worked the market . . .' She fell silent as she tried to recall what her parents had told her about the stall. '. . . I think it was called Paddy's market? Dad helped out on the stall when they lived in Liverpool, and that's where he fell in love with the lifestyle of a trader.'

'I wonder if Paddy's market is anywhere near Scotland Road?' mused Jack.

'What makes you ask that?' said Gordon.

'Libby's uncle said her grandparents lived on Scotland Road,' explained Jack.

'I'm afraid I don't know much about Liverpool,' said Gordon. He glanced at his watch. 'If you want to board the mail train unnoticed, Libby, I suggest you leave here in the next ten minutes. I know they'll not take long loadin' the carriage, and you're goin' to have to be quick pickin' the best moment to sneak aboard without bein' spotted.' A wry smile formed on his lips. 'The excitement of youth, eh?'

'I wish I was goin' off on an adventure,' said Jack.

'But you are!' protested Libby. 'I should imagine bein' in the services will be an adventure in itself. Only you won't have to sneak around, like yours truly. Not only that, but if it goes pear-shaped you won't find yourself up a creek without a paddle, so to speak. Sneakin' around might sound fun, but only if you don't get caught! What do you think they'll do if they discover they've got a stowaway?'

Jack looked to his father, who shrugged. 'Turf you off, most likely, but I suppose it depends on where they find you. If you're already in Liverpool, they'll probably give you a slap on the wrist, but if you're halfway there, who knows? I'd like to think they wouldn't chuck you out in the middle of nowhere, but that'll depend on who finds you. If it's a jobsworth, you might have a long walk ahead of you, but if it's someone with kids they might advise you to keep your head down, although I shouldn't imagine they'll leave you in the same carriage as the mail.'

Libby looked curious. 'Why not?'

Gordon eyed her severely. 'We're at war. There's plenty of people out there that'd want to tamper with the mail, maybe intercept a message, or pass on false information. Thinking about it now, I reckon you might not find a sympathetic ear. You could be a spy for all they know.'

Libby stared at him, her eyes growing wider. 'A *spy*? Why would they think that?' She hesitated before continuing in a concerned tone. 'What will they do to me, if they think I'm a spy?'

'I suppose it might look a bit fishy, you stowin' away when you've got a five bob note in your pocket,' mused Jack. 'As for what they do to spies . . .' He turned to his father, who completed the sentence.

'Perhaps it's best if we don't talk about what they do to spies. I'm sure they'd know you was true blue.'

Libby, however, wasn't so sure. 'It'll be too late to ask questions if they discover me.' She pulled her bottom lip in whilst she pondered her dilemma. 'I'm not goin' to spend my money on a ticket when I can just as easily stow away, so I shall make sure I'm not spotted. And if they do discover me, I shall get the good folk of Petticoat Lane to tell them who I am.'

'You can't get a better testimony than an entire market,' agreed Jack. 'I reckon you'll be fine and dandy.'

Libby clapped her hands together. 'Now that we've covered all options, I say we head off down to the station before I have a change of heart.'

Jack was half out of his chair when he stopped. 'You do know you'd be welcome to stay here, if you wanted? You don't *have* to go to Liverpool.'

'I do know indeed, and the offer is sorely temptin', but a gel's gotta do what a gel's gotta do. I need to tell my grandparents that their daughter has passed away.'

'Then we'd best get this show on the road,' said Jack, deftly swinging his arms into his jacket.

Libby fastened the buttons on her coat, checked that she'd packed her essentials, and pulled the five bob note out of her pocket to tuck it safely into the bottom of her satchel. 'Ready when you are.'

Gordon walked them to the bottom of the stairs before placing his arms around Libby and taking her into a bear hug. 'Look after yourself, Treacle. And don't forget, we're always here should you need us.'

'I know,' said Libby. Her eyelids fluttered as she tried to keep the tears at bay. 'And I know I've already thanked you, but I need to say it again. Thanks for everything, Gordon. I very much doubt I'd be here if it weren't for you and Jack.'

Gordon waved a nonchalant hand. 'Our pleasure. Take care of yourself, luv.'

Waving goodbye, Libby and Jack headed in the direction of the train station. 'I promise to write, just as soon as I get settled,' said Libby, as they strode along the damp cobbled streets.

'I know you can hold your own, because you saw that geezer off the night we found you, but I can't help worryin' that you might be more vulnerable in a strange city.'

'I doubt that,' said Libby. 'Don't forget I only ran into the Thames because I'd lost my bearin's. The way I see it, it doesn't matter where I am, it's how I hold my nerve under pressure that'll see me through. Every city has its fair share of creeps and villains, so I'm not goin' into this like some naïve girl. If anything, my eyes are open all the more for havin' experienced the darker side of city life. I'm a lot wiser than I was a few weeks ago, and I know the sort of thing that really goes on behind closed doors.'

'Heck of a way to find out,' said Jack, 'although maybe it was for the best considerin' you came out reasonably unscathed, and wiser for the experience.'

'As soon as I get into Liverpool, I shall head straight for Scotland Road and start makin' enquiries as to where my grandparents live.' She pushed her bottom lip out in contemplation. 'I suppose there's always a chance I might recognise it as soon as I see it.' She fell silent as she tried to envisage the street where her grandparents lived, but nothing presented itself, so she continued, 'And if I don't manage to find them, I shall go to the local police station and tell them who I am and why I'm there. I'm sure they'll be able to help me.'

Jack looked impressed. 'You've certainly thought this through.'

She gave a mirthless laugh. 'I've thought of practically nowt else since decidin' to head up north. Granted my uncle's money'll make things easier, but I'll still need to be quick off the mark, cos as they say, time is money.'

Jack rolled his tongue around the inside of his cheek before speaking. 'I wish I was goin' with you. It sounds a lot more excitin' than marchin' around some parade ground till your feet hurt.'

She slid her arm through his. 'I haven't a doubt in my mind that you'll make a fantastic soldier, or airman; maybe even a sailor. No matter which of the services takes you on, I know you'll make the most of your time, and if they send you overseas you'll get to see a bit of the world. Think how exciting that will be!' As she spoke the last words, she was hopeful that her voice resonated encouragement and hope, instead of the doubt and fear which she secretly felt. As far as Libby was concerned, you only had to see what the Luftwaffe had done to London to know that life in the services was going to be fraught with danger, but she very much wanted Jack to see it from a different perspective, because the thought of him being miserable so far away from home was more than she could bear.

'I s'pose,' said Jack, eager not to appear ungrateful. He brightened. 'If you let Dad know where you're stayin', I can send you letters, tellin' you where I am. If they send me overseas, I might even be able to say a few words in foreign.'

'Now wouldn't that be somethin',' said Libby, before giggling to herself. 'I'll be able to teach you Scouse. I can't remember much, but I do recall Mum referrin' to the Bluebottles as scuffers.'

Jack eyed her inquisitively. 'Why scuffers?'

'Now there you have me, but if I find out I shall be sure to let you know.'

Jack squeezed her arm in his. He was going to miss Libby's ability to take everything in her stride. No matter what life threw at her, she would take it on the chin, and continue as before. *I wish we had more time together*, he thought, *because I'm almost certain that she's the girl for me.* 'You know how people say they'll keep in contact, but never do?' he said aloud. 'That's not goin' to be us, is it? Because I really do want to keep in touch, not just so that I know you're all right, but because I'd like us to continue our friendship, even when you're settled, wherever that may be.'

Libby looked up at him, her eyes shining in the moonlight. 'Of course I'll keep in touch!' she said, her tone laced with sincerity. 'We've been through a lot together, you and I, and our friendship is very dear to me.'

His eyes twinkled as he gazed down at her. 'Me too.'

They reached Euston Station, and Libby scanned the platform to see whether it was safe for her to board the train which bore the Royal Seal. Seeing a guard leisurely pacing the platform, she looked to Jack. 'He's right outside the only carriage that's open.'

'They must be waiting for more mail, else they'd've closed it by now.' He peered at a van which had just arrived further down the platform. 'We'd better get you inside before they load the rest.'

Libby continued to stare at the guard. 'How? He doesn't look like he's goin' anywhere any time soon, and there's no way I can sneak past without him seein' me.'

'I'll distract him. That way you can climb aboard whilst his back's turned.'

She gazed up at him. 'Thanks, Jack. You're a star.'

He took her in a warm embrace. 'I shall miss you, Libby Gilbert. Take care of yourself.'

Tears pricked her eyes. Whatever danger she might be facing, she felt sure it couldn't be as bad as Jack's venture into the services. The thought of anything happening to the man who'd taken her in, when her uncle had stood idly by, was proving too much for her to bear. She wanted to ask him to abandon the services and travel to Liverpool with her, but she knew that this was the fancy of a young girl smitten with her first love . . . she paused. Is that what Jack was? Was he her first love? *You're gettin' caught in the moment*, she told herself. *Anybody would.*

Jack stepped back, still holding her shoulders. 'It's time you were off. Wait until you see me scratch my head. That'll be my signal for you to nip aboard the train and tuck yourself out of sight.'

'I will, and Jack . . . ?'

He winked at her. 'I'll take care of myself, don't you worry.' He was about to walk away when he made his mind up about something. Turning, he took her in his arms, and kissed her briefly on the lips. Aware that his kiss had been uninvited, he had begun to apologise for being forward when Libby's lips met his. Startled but delighted by her embrace, he kissed her back, and this time he parted his lips ever so slightly, encouraging her mouth to respond. Hesitant at first, Libby soon felt herself being guided by his touch. Her heart racing in her chest, she melted into his arms, carried away by his gentle lips as they caressed hers.

When the kiss ended, his lips brushed over hers. 'Does this mean that you're my belle?'

'Is that what you want?'

'More than anything,' he murmured. He kissed her again, and this time there was no awkwardness. Pulling reluctantly away, he caressed the back of her neck in the palm of his hand. 'Let me know as soon as you're sorted.'

'I will,' Libby promised.

Turning before he could change his mind, Jack hurried over to the guard, whilst Libby looked on, still stunned by the goodbye which had turned into her first ever kiss. And what a kiss it was! Still caught up in the moment, it took her a second or two to remember that she was meant to board the train when she saw Jack scratch his head. Seeing him run his fingers vigorously through his hair, in an overly animated fashion, she immediately sprang to life. Looking towards the mail van, she could see that they were still unloading the sacks, so she ran stealthily towards the train, making sure she kept within the shadows. Her heart in her mouth, she jumped into the open carriage and quickly hid herself amongst the sacks. She lifted her chin ever so slightly to see whether Jack was aware that she was aboard the train, and was relieved to see him wink as their eyes met. Nestling down behind the sacks, Libby kept a keen ear out for the mailmen as they arrived with the last of the sacks, which they dutifully hurled into the carriage before slamming the door shut. Listening to their voices as they walked away, she peeked out from her hiding place to make sure that none of them had decided to travel with the mail, but it was empty save for the sacks. Breathing a sigh of relief, Libby settled down for the journey ahead. It was going to be several hours before they reached Liverpool, and if she could get some sleep between now and then she should be refreshed for the start of her new life. Startled by the sound of the whistle blowing, she felt her tummy jolt as the train's wheels gained traction on the track.

Closing her eyes, Libby let the gentle motion of the train lull her to sleep, an image of Jack at the forefront of her mind's eye, as he stood on the platform. His collarless shirt and dark woollen trousers turned into the smart air force blue, and his flat cap merged into an airman's ordinary side cap, and then to the flying helmet worn by aircrew. His cheerful expression turned into lines of worry, and his eyes looked fearfully to the skies around him. Calling out for him to come back, her heart dropped as she watched him give her a final wave before turning on his heel and heading into the darkness which enveloped him.

Chapter Five

When Libby awoke it was to find herself being jolted from her resting place as the train sped along a rickety part of the track. Wondering what the time was, she saw the bright winter sunshine pierce through the cracks in the door to the carriage. She had no idea how long it took for the train to get from London to Liverpool, but judging by the number of extra sacks, it looked as though they'd made some stops along the way. Yawning, she was about to settle back down when she saw some of the sacks opposite hers moving. At first she supposed it was the motion of the train, but after careful consideration she realised that they were being moved from the bottom up, as if something was underneath them. Ducking down out of sight, she watched fearfully as the first sack toppled to the floor, followed by several more. Surely the guards didn't usually hide amongst their mail? She dismissed this thought as another more alarming one entered her mind. *What if a spy's stowed away in the same carriage as myself, and more to the point, how am I goin' to tell the guard when we get to Liverpool without revealin' myself?'* She froze as she imagined the unknown person erupting from the pile of sacks with a pistol at the ready. Slowly, she cowered down as much as she could, using a tiny gap to spy on the person as they came forth. Libby expected him or her to be wearing a mackintosh – which Libby considered to be standard dress for all spies – and carrying a briefcase which would turn into some kind of wireless device. She was surprised, therefore, to see a young girl of around the same age as herself, with her hair in pigtails, wearing similar dungarees to the ones Libby used to wear. She waited until the girl had fully emerged before gingerly poking her own head above the sacks, and hastily pushed a finger to her lips as the girl let out a scream. 'Shhh! Someone might hear you!' she hissed.

Inching forward, the girl peered up at Libby, who was climbing down from her hiding place. 'You nigh on give me a bleedin' heart attack,' she snapped, eyeing Libby reprovingly. 'You shouldn't sneak up on folk like that – I thought you was me dad.'

'Sorry. I'm Libby, by the way.'

The girl held out her hand. 'Hello, Libby by the way. I'm Margo.' Laughing softly, Libby was about to respond when Margo beat her to it. 'Why've they shut the doors?' She stumbled as the train rocked across the tracks, and turned an alarmed face to Libby. 'Please tell me we're still in Euston?'

Libby's eyes widened. 'I hope not. It was dark when I climbed aboard, and we've picked up a lot more mail since. I'm hopin' we're not far from Liverpool.'

'Liverpool!' cried Margo, before being hastily shushed by Libby. Continuing in quieter tones, she whispered, 'I can't go to Liverpool; me dad'll have me guts for garters! And I never paid for the apple!'

Libby eyed her curiously. 'But if you're not a stowaway, what are you doin' here?'

'I just wanted to get away from me dad,' explained Margo, 'give him a chance to cool down and *then* go home. I wasn't intendin' on stowin' away!'

'Oh dear. It seems as though you've overslept.' Ever since Libby had first clapped eyes on Margo, she had thought there was something familiar about her, but couldn't place her no matter how hard she tried. 'Don't I know you from somewhere?'

'I shouldn't think so, although you might've seen me in passin'.' Margo tucked her pigtails beneath a flat cap which she drew from her dungarees pocket. ''Ello, guvnor, how's about I give yer shoes a nice shine?'

Libby gawped at her. 'You're a shoeblack? But I thought it was only boys that worked as shoeblacks?'

'Me dad makes me pretend to be a boy, so's I can shine people's shoes,' said Margo, 'only he gambles all our money and won't pay for polish, which is why I was hidin' in the train. We'd had a right old barney which ended with him chasin' me down Petticoat Lane.'

Libby clicked her fingers. '*That's* where I recognise you from. You come hurtlin' into me earlier today.'

A slow look of recognition crossed Margo's cheeks. 'That's right! My dad was the one who fell over you.'

'He didn't fall, I stuck me foot out and tripped him up on purpose, so that he couldn't catch you.' She jerked her lip into a downward grimace. 'I trust I did the right thing?'

Margo's eyes grew wide. 'Too right you did. He was spittin' feathers when I run off. He'd've given me a damned good beltin' had he caught me.'

Libby tutted beneath her breath. 'Beast.'

'Still me dad though,' said Margo softly.

'That doesn't give him the right to raise his hand to you,' said Libby. 'My father wouldn't have dreamed of raisin' a hand in anger against me or my mother.'

'Lucky you! Your old man sounds like a decent chap.'

'He was.'

'Was?'

'My mother and father died durin' a bombin' raid. That's why I'm on my way to Liverpool.' She went on to explain everything that had happened from the intended move to Norwich to the moment she got aboard the train.

'Tough luck about your folks,' said Margo. 'That Jack sounds like a lovely feller, though – do you reckon your parents would've approved?'

'Very much so. He's a true gent . . .' Libby's eyes glazed over as she recalled the moment their lips had met, and she had to shake herself awake from her daydream before she concluded, 'and a hard worker.'

'Everything my old feller isn't,' said Margo. She glanced around the carriage, which swayed gently. 'Do you reckon this train'll go back to London, once they've loaded up with return mail?'

'I s'pose so,' said Libby, 'in fact I'm sure it will, but I don't know when, mind you.' She glanced at Margo's toes, which were visible through her boots. 'Do you mind my askin' why you would want to go back? Especially when you know what's waitin' for you?'

'Good question,' sighed Margo. 'I s'pose it's cos I've got no choice.'

'There's always a choice,' said Libby. 'Look at me. I've gone from havin' everything to havin' nothin', but I'm still here. I could've stayed in London with Gordon, but I chose to come to Liverpool in search of my grandparents. If that doesn't work out, I shall go back to London and seek my fortune.'

Margo giggled. 'Seek your fortune? You sound like summat out of *Oliver Twist*.'

'I suppose I am a bit like him,' said Libby, 'no parents, no family to speak of. Only I'm luckier, because I'm not stuck in some God-awful orphanage. Although Jack did say that I reminded him of Cinderella.'

'I thought my life was bad,' admitted Margo, 'but you've been through a lot more than me, all things considered.'

'What about you?' said Libby. 'I've heard about your father, but what about your mother?'

Margo rolled her eyes before explaining the circumstances of her mother's death.

'Flippin' 'eck,' breathed Libby. 'I don't see how you think I've had it worse than you; I reckon it's the other way round.'

Margo contemplated this thought before responding. 'I guess if it's all you're used to, then you don't know any different. Everyone who grew up in Blendon Row had the same kind of upbringin' – if you could call it that.'

'You said you wanted to go back on the next train, but why don't you stay with me in Liverpool, just for a bit, whilst you weigh up your options?'

'I couldn't do that,' said Margo. 'Your uncle give you that money for you to use as you see fit, not for you to squander on any waif or stray that comes your way.'

'First of all, my uncle gave me that money so that he could see the back of me,' said Libby, 'and if I can start a new life in Liverpool, why can't you?'

'But what about me dad?' supposed Margo uncertainly. 'What'll he do?'

Libby gave a derisive snort. 'Do you care?' Seeing by the look on Margo's face that she did indeed care, she tried again. 'I'll put it another way. You workin' all the hours that God sends to support your dad's gamblin' isn't doin' him any favours. Perhaps if you stayed away, it'd be the kick up the jacksie that he needs to get his life in order.'

Margo rolled her eyes. 'I very much doubt it.'

'So, what's the alternative? Cos whilst you may get away with bein' a boy for now, you can't go on like that for ever. Sooner or later people'll twig, and what then?'

Margo shrugged. 'I guess we'll cross that bridge when we come to it.'

'Or maybe the authorities will want to have a word with someone who's been pretendin' to be a boy so they can get work as a shoeblack? That job's only meant for boys that've fallen on hard times, not a young girl with a father who's capable of sup-portin' her, but for his habit.'

Margo eyed Libby thoughtfully. 'You really don't want me to go back, do you?'

Libby shook her head fervently. 'I want you to realise that there's something better out there, and that you don't need to be at your father's beck and call. And before you say that you need to go home for him to survive, think about what I said about feedin' his habit, and how havin' to stand on his own two feet might be the makin' of him.' She paused briefly before adding, 'And besides, you don't owe him a thing. If anything, it's he who owes you a childhood.'

'I suppose a couple of days couldn't hurt,' mused Margo. She glanced down at her dirty dungarees. 'Do you reckon there's a river near Liverpool where I could wash me clothes?'

'I can't remember, but if there isn't I'm sure we can get them washed down one of the laundries.' Libby patted her satchel. 'Jack gave me a few of his mother's clothes, so there's bound to be summat in here that you can borrow in the meantime.'

Margo brightened. 'Looks like we're off on quite the adventure!'

'We most certainly are!' said Libby happily. Sinking back onto the sacks of mail, she handed Margo the satchel. 'Have a look and see what takes your fancy.'

As Margo looked through the clothing, Libby reflected on how fate had dealt a hand in her favour once more. Liverpool might've been a daunting prospect on her own, but with a friend by her side things had just got a lot easier. On top of which, Margo's father reminded Libby of her uncle, and if she could rescue Margo from a man like that it would give her the greatest satisfaction to do so. *Two birds one stone*, she thought; *not only will I have a travelling companion, but if Margo sees how much happier her life is without her father continually breathin' down her neck she might have a rosier future. Certainly, far better than anything she would've had if she'd stayed in London.*

With Margo holding up a frock for size, the girls had agreed that it would be best to keep the clean clothes until they'd managed to have themselves a bath, whether that be in front of a fire or in a river.

'I remember Mum talkin' about the Scaldies,' mused Libby. 'She said all the local kids learned to swim there. Can you swim?'

Margo beamed. 'Course I can. I learned down the Thames, didn't you?'

'Nope! Swimmin's never appealed to me, not after you see some of the stuff what comes out of the water . . . you do know they've pulled bodies out of the river?'

'Beggars can't be choosers. It was the Thames or nothin', and I can't think of a better way to cool down on a hot summer's day than a quick dip in the river.' After a moment Margo went on. 'And it's important to be able to swim in case you ever end up in the river by accident, like you when you was runnin' away from that feller.'

'I can't argue with that,' said Libby. 'If I ever have kids, I'm goin' to make sure they can swim as soon as they learn to walk.'

'I'm surprised your parents didn't insist on you learnin'.'

Libby mulled this over before replying. 'I don't think it ever crossed their minds. We didn't live near the river or the sea, so why bother?'

'But your mother learned to swim in the Scaldies – whatever they are – so don't you think it a bit odd that she didn't teach you?'

'I guess so, but without her here to ask, I suppose I'll never know.'

'Thinkin' about it, now, most parents would worry that their kids might've ended up in the river if they went missin', yet I bet my dad didn't give it a second thought.'

'Do you not think he'll be in the least bit curious, or worried, when you fail to come home?'

'All he'll worry about is where he's goin' to get the money to gamble from,' said Margo distantly, 'because that's all I am to him.'

'I'm sure you're more than that, and he'll realise that once you're not around.'

Margo gave a disbelieving chuckle. 'I very much doubt it. When I think about it, all he's ever done is demand money. He's never asked if I'm all right, or how I'm doin'. It's always "how much did you make" or "you need to work harder".' She sighed miserably. 'I sometimes wonder what I did to deserve the parents I had, which is a terrible thing to say, what with my mother bein' deceased, but she wasn't a proper mum, not like what you had.'

'Why do you think your parents got together in the first place?' mused Libby. 'They must've shared some common ground.'

'Addiction,' said Margo simply. 'Mum would've been drawn to Dad, because he was always boastin' about how he was goin' to win big one of these days.' She gave a snort of contempt. 'He still is. She'll have seen him as someone who could feed her habit, and he'll have seen her as someone as broken as himself. Why on earth they would then throw a kid into the mix is beyond me.' She fell momentarily silent, before adding, 'I guess they wouldn't, or not on purpose at any rate. It seems obvious to me that I was a mistake.'

Libby grimaced in the dark, grateful that Margo couldn't see her expression. 'Or maybe they thought havin' a baby might turn things around? Lots of people do.'

'Maybe . . .' Margo exchanged glances with Libby as the train began to slow. 'Do you think we're in Liverpool?'

Libby gestured for Margo to join her behind the sacks. 'We'll only know for sure if they start takin' the sacks off.'

Margo eyed Libby curiously. 'So, what's the plan for gettin' off unseen?'

'I haven't the foggiest,' Libby confessed. 'I suppose I was hopin' to sneak out with some of the sacks, but . . .' Deep in thought, she punched one of the sacks next to her. 'Some of these sacks aren't altogether full. If we could hide in one, they'd carry us off thinkin' we was part of the mail. What d'you think?'

Margo didn't look at all certain. 'It's a bit of a push, but I don't think we've much choice. It's either that or explain our presence, and I don't fancy bein' sent back to London just yet, or bein' banged up for that matter.'

Libby began to check the sacks over, looking for two of the emptiest. She quickly loosened the top of one of them and encouraged Margo to climb inside before she fastened it again. 'Try not to make a sound when they unload you. I'm goin' to climb into the sack next to yours, so that we'll hopefully be unloaded together. I'll tear a small hole in each of our sacks so that we can have some idea of where we are, and as soon as the coast is clear I'll climb out and come for you.'

'But what if summat goes wrong?' said Margo fearfully. 'What if we get sent to different places? How will I know where to find you?'

'I've looked at these bags and there's nothin' on them to suggest that they're different in any way, so they must all be destined for the same depot.'

Feeling the train slow considerably, Margo pulled a rueful face. She was going to have to make a decision, and fast. Opening the neck of the sack, she climbed into the middle, so that the letters would provide a cushion, should the men throw the sacks into a van or a cart. Libby quickly tied the end of the sack, pushing the cord inside so that Margo might have some control, but the material was too thick to tear. 'I can't make a hole,' she told Margo, 'so to some extent it's goin' to be guesswork. I'll do the same with the top of my sack as I have with yours, only I'll leave a bigger gap in the neck.'

She waited until she heard a muffled 'Righto' from Margo before climbing into her own sack, and had only just managed to tie the cord before the train drew to a complete halt. Keeping her fingers crossed, she waited with bated breath to see what would happen next. *If we can slip out as soon as we're at the sorting office,* she told herself, *we should be able to get away before we're spotted, but if someone does see us, we can always pretend that we're lookin' for jobs.*

She froze as the sound of male voices grew louder and the door to the carriage opened. Praying that Margo wouldn't lose her nerve, she listened intently as the men began to throw the sacks out of the train. Someone commented on the weight of one of them, and she guessed it was the one Margo was in. She crossed her fingers tightly, suspecting that Margo was doing the same.

'Bleedin' 'ell, what're they puttin' in these sacks?' grunted the man as he hefted the sack over to the waiting cart.

'Tryin' to fit in as much as possible,' said a younger voice. 'I reckon we should complain to the union, cos there'll be no compensation should you do yer back in.'

'Pffft,' spluttered the first man, 'you know what the answer'll be.'

'There's a war on,' chorused several of the men in relative unison.

Libby braced herself as she felt the top of her sack being tugged upwards. Breathing out in an effort to make herself as light as possible, she waited for the man to pass comment on her weight, but another man grabbed her bottom of the sack and together they heaved her onto the rest of the sacks with relative ease.

To her relief she heard the engine start, and the vehicle they were on pulled away, but her relief was short-lived when the vehicle came to a halt a few seconds later. Peeking out of the top of her sack, she could see that they were in the back of a van, the doors to which hadn't been properly closed, allowing her to see through the gap. Watching cautiously, she saw that the men had gone back to the carriage where they began to load another van. 'Margo?' she hissed. 'Are you in here?'

Hearing a muffled response, Libby hastily apologised as she fumbled with the cord on the neck of her sack. 'Hang on a mo.' She forced the neck of the sack open and pushed her head through to check on the men, who were engaged in deep conversation. Quickly clambering free, Libby pushed her sack to one side as she hastily looked through the rest for a top which wasn't as securely fastened as the others.

'Margo?'

'Here!' squeaked Margo from underneath another sack.

Pulling the cord through the gap, Libby was quick to open the neck and release her friend. 'C'mon, we can hide at the back.

Once they start the engine we can open the doors and have it away on our toes before we're seen.'

Believing that the plan was foolproof, both girls started as a husky voice spoke from outside the van. 'I'm afraid it's a bit late for that.'

They both hastily ducked out of sight. As Libby peered cautiously between a gap in the sacks she could see the face of a young man, with sandy-coloured hair and deep brown eyes, staring back at her.

He spoke with an air of mirth. 'You do know I can see you?' Without waiting for them to reply, he jerked his head in a backward motion, indicating the men who were still unloading the mail carriage. 'I don't know what a couple of cockney sparras are doin' this far up north, but you're lucky it's me what found you and not one of the other fellers.'

'Please don't tell,' pleaded Margo as she peered at him from behind one of the sacks. 'We didn't mean to stow away. We was only lookin' for somewhere to get our heads down for a bit. Next thing we know, we're in Liverpool.'

The young man eyed her curiously. 'How do you know where you are, if you didn't mean to stow away?'

Worried that Margo might inadvertently make matters worse, Libby was quick to put him straight. 'You mustn't be cross with Margo, cos she truly didn't mean to stow away, but I did.'

Struck by her honesty, he edged closer to the back of the van. 'How come?'

Libby glanced fearfully at the men who were jumping out of the carriage after having loaded the last sack into the van. 'We haven't got time to discuss the whys and wherefores.'

Following her gaze, the young man began to close the door. 'You can tell me when we reach the depot.'

'Can't we get out here?' Margo hissed, as the men drew nearer.

'Not unless you want to get caught. You see, we've been told to keep our eyes peeled for owt suspicious. Trust me, they'd not think twice before turnin' you in. Keep your heads down—' He broke off as one of the men approached.

'You talkin' to yerself again, Tom?' chortled the man.

Tom winked at the girls before slamming the door shut. 'Cussin' these stiff hinges,' he said, slapping the van doors with the palm of his hand. 'It's a good job I noticed it hadn't closed properly, especially the way you drive.'

The older man laughed raucously. 'Yer cheeky sod. I'll 'ave you know my drivin's damned near perfect.'

Tom grinned. 'Mebbe if you're in the Grand Prix.'

'Anyway, we don't get paid to hang about,' said the other man. 'Sooner we get this lot back to the depot, sooner we can get 'ome to us beds.'

The voices faded, and Libby and Margo breathed once more. 'Flippin' Nora, that was too close for comfort,' hissed Margo from beneath the sacks.

'I wonder how far it is to the depot,' Libby mused, 'and how's he plannin' on gettin' us out once we're there.'

Margo sat up on one elbow. ''Ere, you don't suppose he's plannin' on handin' us over, do you? He could've been sayin' all that to keep us from runnin'.'

Libby dismissed this without hesitation. 'Nah. You heard what he said: the other fellers wouldn't hesitate.'

'I s'pose so.' Margo settled down amongst the sacks. 'Pretty good of him to turn a blind eye.'

'It was, wasn't it?' said Libby. She leaned back, using one of the sacks as a cushion. 'Mind you, we don't exactly look like spies, or train robbers, so I s'pose he was only usin' his common sense.'

'Still a crime though, stowin' away,' said Margo. She hesitated briefly. 'Do you think he'd get into trouble if they found out he'd kept shtum about us?'

'I should say so,' said Libby. 'It's called aidin' and abettin', and it's what me mum was always worried about with me dad sellin' hooky gear off the market.'

Margo grinned. 'Because she knew what he was doin'?'

'Mum was paranoid that they'd throw the two of them in jail, leavin' me parentless. I s'pose she had a point when you think about it.'

'What sort of stuff was your dad sellin'?' asked Margo, intrigued.

'Hardly the crown jewels, which is why Dad thought Mum was blowin' things out of proportion. He sold stupid stuff really, like meat or petrol, anythin' that could be hidden inside a vase or summat similar.'

'That sort of stuff might've seemed petty before the war,' said Margo severely, 'but it's pretty serious nowadays.'

'I know, but Dad was never one to see others go short. He'd always help someone who was worse off than him.'

'Big risk to take, though,' said Margo. 'My dad's the opposite; he wouldn't stick his neck out for anyone, not even his own daughter.'

Libby grimaced as the van jolted over a pothole. 'Sounds a bit like my uncle. Me, myself and I, that's his motto.' She gave a mirthless laugh. 'I reckon he'd get on with your dad like a house on fire.'

'Birds of a feather,' agreed Margo. Her face fell as the van slowed to a halt. 'Looks like we're here,' she hissed from her hiding place. 'What now?'

Libby shrugged. 'Sit tight and hope for the best?'

Both girls fell silent as the doors to the van opened and Tom called out to the men behind him, 'I dunno about you lot, but it's been a hard night's work, and I'm keen for me bed. We'll be a lot quicker if I empty this 'un and you lot concentrate on the rest of it, what do you reckon?'

Another voice spoke out. 'Sounds like a plan, and you can oil them hinges when you've finished.'

'Right you are,' said Tom. Addressing the girls in lower tones, he began to unpack the van. 'Once I've got the van unloaded, I'll let you know when the coast is clear, understood?'

'Understood,' hissed Libby.

'We'll push the sacks forward,' said Margo. 'You'll be quicker that way.'

Tom began chucking the sacks onto a trolley with gusto, hoping to have the van empty before anyone could come and give him a hand. At last he closed the doors and heaved the trolley over to the others, and the girls could hear a mumbled conversation as the men took their loads into the office.

After a couple of minutes Libby had begun to wonder whether he'd forgotten about them when she heard him call a farewell to his workmates, adding, 'I'll do these hinges before I go, else I'll forget.' He opened the doors and grinned at them. 'Coast is clear, but if anyone asks, you're my cousins from down south.'

Libby gave him the thumbs up as she and Margo scooted out of the van. 'Thanks ever so much,' gabbled Margo as she brushed her dungarees down. 'Is there a river nearby, only me clothes could do with a wash, as could I.'

He blew his cheeks out. 'You wouldn't wanna go for a swim in the Mersey, not unless you were a heck of a good swimmer.' He caressed his chin between his finger and thumb, before adding, 'It's probably none of my business, but why didn't you sit tight and wait for the train to go back to London?'

Margo glanced at Libby. 'Let's just say I'm learnin' to spread me wings.'

'There's nowt waitin' for her in London, save a clip round the ear,' said Libby, 'so she's agreed to keep me company whilst I try and find my relatives.'

Tom applied oil sparingly to the hinges of the van doors. 'You've family in Liverpool?'

'The O'Connells,' Libby confirmed. 'I don't suppose you know where they live?'

Tom stared at her in disbelief. 'You can't be serious?'

Thinking that Tom must know her family, she looked at him hopefully. 'Do you know them?'

He continued to gape at her. 'Have you any idea how big Liverpool is?'

'I've not been since I was little. They live on Scotland Road, if that's any help?'

He placed the oil can down. 'The Scottie's nigh on a mile long, if not more.'

Libby looked at him blankly. 'I've no idea how long a mile is.'

'It's long,' said Margo, glancing fearfully at Tom. 'I've never been to Liverpool, but if one of the roads is a mile long I'm guessin' it's a big city?'

Tom's eyes widened. 'It's huge! Why, the Mersey's wider than the Thames in places, and as for knowin' someone by the name of O'Connell, then yes, I do, because I'm one, but that's hardly surprisin' considerin' half the population must be Irish.'

Libby leaned against the van. 'I don't suppose you live on the Scottie Road?'

'I'm afraid not.' He pushed his hands into his pockets. 'You seem to be very ill informed concernin' your family's whereabouts and what not. Is there any reason why you don't know much about them?'

Libby told him everything that had happened, from the bomb to their arrival in Liverpool, whilst Tom listened in astonishment. Keen for him not to think badly of her, she left out the part where she had considered turning to prostitution, instead saying that she had run blindly in the wrong direction, ending up in the river. With her tale of woe out in the open, Tom regarded her sympathetically, not only because of the circumstances which had driven her to travel halfway across the country, but because he thought she might have had a wasted journey.

'Liverpool is much bigger than you realised, and your uncle should've explained that to you before you left,' he said stoutly. 'What sort of man lets his niece go off half-cocked?'

'One that doesn't give a monkey's about her,' said Margo sullenly. 'It's more common than you realise down our neck of the woods.'

'It's hardly sunshine and laughter up here either. The workhouse is chocker with unwanted kids, and families that are too poor to put food on the table. If you can't find your grandmother, I'm afraid you might be jumpin' out of the fryin' pan into the fire.'

Libby sighed wretchedly. 'I know it must look as if I've lost the plot, rushin' off the way I did, but the O'Connells are the only family I've got.'

Margo placed a reassuring arm around Libby's shoulders. 'Don't worry. We'll find them, even if it takes us weeks.'

Tom pulled a doubtful face. 'I don't wish to throw a spanner in the works, but how're you intendin' to get by with no money or food?'

Libby brightened. 'I've got some money, remember?'

'Not enough to last you weeks,' said Tom, 'and not if you're havin' to pay for bed and board.'

'We could sleep rough?' Margo suggested.

Tom pulled a reproving face. 'Two young girls out on the streets? Liverpool might be smaller than London, but it's just as dangerous, and there's plenty who'd take advantage of you.'

Libby looked at Margo. 'You should get on the next train back to London. I should never have got you involved.'

'Why? So that me dad can belt me for leavin' him for so long? I was scared of what he'd do to me when I got back, but me dad can't touch me here. I might have a place to lay my head in London, but it's hardly safe with Jerry droppin' bombs left, right and centre, and even if the Luftwaffe don't decide to pay us a call, I've still got me dad to contend with. The more time I spend away from him, the less I want to go back. I feel safe for the first time in a long while, and quite frankly I've nothin' to lose by stayin' here. There's nowt for me in London.' She shrugged. 'Same goes for you.'

Libby was about to protest, to say that her whole life was in London, when it occurred to her that Margo was right. 'I always thought I'd come here to tell the family what had happened to my parents and then return, but you're right. Now I come to think about it, what would I be goin' back to? No job, no home, no family . . .' Her voice trailed off as an image of Jack entered her mind, but Jack wasn't in London any more either, and even though she very much wanted to be by his side she could hardly be that whilst he was away God knew where. Hesitantly, she said, 'I suppose I've got family here, so it's better than nothin'.'

'Only what would you do in Liverpool?' asked Tom.

Libby explained how her father had started off in the market trade by working for her mother's family on their market stall. 'I know the market business inside out,' she went on. 'If there's a pitch goin', or if my family need help on their stall, there's no reason why I can't muck in. Margo too, come to that, cos I bet she's got the gift of the gab after workin' as a shoeblack.'

Margo pretended to doff her cap. 'All right, guvner? How's about I take the grime off of them beautiful leathers of yours? A gent of your stature shouldn't be seen in shoes what's not fit for a king.'

Libby beamed. 'We'll have them eatin' out of the palms of our 'ands.'

'You've got optimism comin' out of your ears,' said Tom, 'but you've got to find your family first.'

'We'll find them,' said Libby, tucking her arm through Margo's, 'and we'll wing it till we do.'

Tom let his bottom lip slide slowly from between his teeth. 'I know we've only just met, but if you need help, just give me a knock.'

'Where do you live?'

'2a Blenheim Street,' said Tom. 'The name's Tom, by the way, although I'm pretty sure you know that already.'

'I'm Libby, and this is Margo, and thanks, Tom. We'll be sure to drop by should we get stuck.'

Margo was peering around the gated entrance to the sorting office. 'How do we get to the Scottie Road from here?'

'It'll take you over an hour from here, so you're best off catchin' a tram . . .' he hesitated, 'although you can't expect someone to change a five-bob note, so . . .' He pushed his hand into his pocket and dug around for a few seconds before producing a few pennies. 'Take these.'

Libby began to protest, but Margo was quick to cut her short. 'Thanks, Tom. We'll pay you back once we've got some change.'

Libby relented slightly. 'Yes, thank you. But we don't know which tram to catch.'

Tom winked at her. 'That's easy. You get the same one as me.'

Libby sagged visibly. 'So you're not far from Scotland Road?'

'A ten-minute walk at most,' confessed Tom, 'so just around the corner really.'

Margo gave a short squeal of delight. 'Thank goodness for that.' She looked at Libby. 'I wish I could be as calm and collected as you, but I'm shakin' like a leaf inside.'

'What's the sense in worryin'? It's not as if we've got anythin' to lose.'

Tom collected his satchel from the front of the van, and swung it over his shoulder. 'Ladies? Follow me!'

Even by tram it took the girls the best part of an hour to complete the journey, but they used the time to find out as much about Liverpool as they could. Tom had explained that he lived in one of the poorer parts of Liverpool, but not in the courts, which sounded to Margo very much like Blendon Row. As they travelled the girls saw first-hand that the River Mersey was far wider than the Thames.

'What about the Scaldies?' asked Libby slowly.

Tom grinned. 'That's where all the lads take a dip in the nuddy.'

Margo's eyes popped. 'I'd sooner take me chances in the Mersey,' she said primly, ignoring the chuckles coming from Tom and Libby.

'The O'Connells will probably have summat you can bathe in,' said Tom, but Margo wasn't looking too keen.

'I'd rather I was a like a shiny pin the first time I meet Libby's folks. I should imagine she feels the same, because they haven't seen her since she was a little gel, and you know what they say about first impressions.'

'I see what you mean,' said Tom, 'but I don't know what to suggest, unless . . .'

'Unless what?' asked Margo suspiciously. 'I'm not goin' into the Scaldies, even if it's with all me clothes on, if there's a load of boys in there with me.'

'I was goin' to say you could have a bath at mine, but my landlord would chuck me out if he thought I was bringin' women round. It'd be different if you was poppin' in for a cup of tea.'

'How would he know if nobody tells him?' asked Margo slowly. 'I know we won't tell, and we promise to be out of your hair in no time.'

Libby folded her arms across her chest. 'I'd love a bath as much as you, but we can't let Tom put his neck on the line for the sake of a wash. We'll just have to meet my folks as we are. I'm sure they'll understand.'

Seeing the look of disappointment etched on Margo's face, Tom made up his mind. 'No. You only have one chance to make a first impression, and you can't come all this way to fall at the first hurdle. We'll tell everyone that you're my cousins, who're passin' through, and that you've stopped off for a cuppa. The landlord won't be too bothered if you're not stayin' overnight, because that's where he'd really draw the line. After all, why get rent off one person if you can charge for three?'

'I feel as if we're really imposin',' said Libby. She watched Tom, who was still looking at Margo, and the penny dropped. Tom was gazing at Margo the same way Jack looked at Libby. She smiled. Who was she to stand in the way of what could prove to be a promising romance? 'I suppose it couldn't hurt as long as we're quick.'

Seeing a broad grin etch his cheeks, Libby gave herself a metaphorical pat on the back for getting it right. Tom was keen on Margo, although judging by the blank expression on Margo's face her new friend hadn't the slightest inkling of it yet.

After they had travelled a few more stops Tom announced that they had arrived at their destination. Descending from the tram, the girls followed him into the house where he rented a room on the lower floor. 'It's not much, but it's home to me,' he said as he ushered the girls inside. 'It'll take a while to heat the water for a bath, and I've no doubt the other tenants will suss summat's up; either that, or they'll think we're drownin' ourselves in tea!'

The girls took it in turns to fill the bath with water, making sure that each kettle was piping hot, so that they could add a large amount of cold water to cool it down.

'I feel guilty,' Libby confessed, 'knowin' that you should be tucked up in bed, tryin' to get some kip so that you're ready for work tomorrow, instead of havin' to help us run a bath.'

He shrugged. 'I'll get some sleep once you leave to look for your folks.' He glanced at the ceiling as something heavy hit the floor above him, followed by a loud argument. He turned to the girls. 'It's not as if I get much sleep anyways.'

Margo fetched a broom which was standing against the wall and thumped it against the ceiling. 'Oi! Keep the noise down. Some of us are tryin' to get some kip down here!'

Hearing the argument come to an abrupt halt, Tom waited for his neighbour to come thundering down the stairs, but it seemed Margo's words had had the desired effect, much to his surprise. 'That's Arnie Brinkworth and his missus,' he explained. 'They're allus havin' a barney over summat or other.' He grinned at the girls. 'I bet they've stopped to have a good gossip about who I've got in my room.'

Libby placed her hands over her face. 'Especially as Margo told them that she's tryin' to sleep.'

Tom threw his head back and laughed until his belly ached. 'Good God, this should keep the curtains twitchin' for a few weeks, if not months.'

Margo was blushing to the roots of her hair. 'I'm so sorry! I never thought . . .'

Libby arched an eyebrow. 'Why have I got the feelin' I'm goin' to be hearin' you say that a lot?'

A cheesy grin flashed on Margo's lips. 'Because I am what I am, and I can't even try to be anythin' but.'

'There's certainly no hairs on your tongue,' agreed Tom.

'A spade's a spade,' said Margo. 'I only ever tried lyin' to me dad once, and he soon found me out.' She rubbed a hand over her eye as the memory of that day came flooding back. 'He demanded I lie to everyone else, but was taken aback if I did it to him.'

'That's called one rule for him, and another for everyone else,' said Libby. She turned away as the last kettle came to the boil. Taking it off the stove, she poured the water into the small tin bath and tested it with her elbow. 'It's ready.'

Tom hooked his finger through the collar of his coat and swung it over his shoulders. 'I'll be back in what, half an hour?'

Margo and Libby exchanged glances. 'You go first,' said Margo, 'cos I'm black compared to you.'

'I reckon half an hour should do us just fine,' said Libby. 'But what should we do if someone comes knockin'?'

'Ignore them,' said Tom firmly. 'They'll likely only be comin' for a nose, especially when they see me leave.'

'But we were only meant to be stoppin' by for a cuppa,' said Margo doubtfully.

Tom shrugged. 'So, you stopped for a bath? Like I said, the landlord'll only throw a wobbler if he thinks you're livin' here, and as you're not, there shouldn't be a problem.'

'What about your neighbours?' asked Libby cautiously. 'You don't want them gossipin' . . .'

Tom laughed. 'Too late. I bet they're sendin' smoke signals up the chimney as we speak.' Seeing Margo glance out of the window towards the chimney of the house across the street, Tom gazed fondly at her. 'I'd best be off; we don't want the water gettin' cold.'

Libby waited until Tom had left the room before closing the curtains. 'After all, we don't want the neighbours' tongues waggin' too much,' she told Margo.

'Tom's a real breath of fresh air, don't you think?'

'He's certainly taken a shine to you,' said Libby, as she unbuttoned her shirt-waisted frock.

Margo, who had been letting her fingers trail through the beautifully warm water, looked up sharply. 'No he hasn't . . . has he?'

Libby indicated for Margo to turn her back as she slipped out of her undergarments and slid into the water. 'You can turn round now,' she announced as she brought her knees up to her chest, hiding what little she had to show, 'and as for Tom, it's as plain as the nose on your face.'

Margo scooped the water over Libby's hair with her hands. 'How can you tell?'

'It's the way he looks at you,' said Libby. 'He was delighted when you agreed to come back to his, and he's obviously willin' to take one on the chin for you when it comes to his neighbours.'

Margo gently soaped Libby's hair. 'I thought he was just bein' kind.'

Libby chuckled knowingly. 'And do you think he'd have put himself out like this if we'd been a couple of men?'

'It's different with men, though,' Margo reasoned, 'cos they can look after themselves.'

'Maybe,' Libby conceded. 'All I know is, seein' is believin', and I saw the way he looked at you, and it's not the same way he looked at me.'

Margo frowned as she tried to run her fingers through her own hair, which was thick with dirt. 'You sayin' he likes vaga-bonds? Because that's what I must look like!'

Libby roared with laughter before hastily slapping her hand over her mouth as the footsteps above them came to a sudden halt. 'What I'm *tryin'* to say is, he likes you despite the fact you look . . .' she cast an eye over Margo's dishevelled appearance, taking in the naturally blonde locks under the dirt, and the startling blue eyes made brighter by the grime which covered her face, 'beautiful. How you ever passed for a boy is beyond me.'

Margo averted her gaze. 'No one's ever said that to me before. In fact, it always upset me that no one questioned my gender. I s'pose it made me feel ugly.'

'Ugly? You're far from that,' said Libby as she gestured for Margo to pass the towel. Stepping out of the bath whilst taking great care not to expose herself, Libby rubbed herself dry before talking thickly through the towel which she had wrapped loosely around her head. 'Maybe the men whose shoes you shined didn't like to pass comment on your appearance for fear that it might make them look stupid.'

Margo shrugged as she cast her dungarees and shirt to the floor and stepped gingerly into the bath. 'I s'pose so.' She relaxed, allowing the warm water to caress her body. 'Sayin' that, you knew I was a girl straight off the bat.'

Libby shrugged. 'It seemed obvious to me, but then you don't see many fellers with pigtails!' Now fully dressed, Libby returned the favour by washing Margo's hair, gasping at the sheer amount of dirt which flowed from the other girl's blonde tresses as she lathered the soap between her hands. 'I hope you don't mind my askin', but when was the last time you had a bath?'

Margo laughed out loud. 'I don't know whether I've *ever* had a bath. Dad reckoned there was nowt wrong with washin' in the Thames, and that it wasn't the sign of a good shoeblack if they was cleaner than the boots they was cleanin'.'

'A bit like the sayin' you should never trust a skinny cook?'

'Summat like that, but I reckon it was his excuse for not gettin' us somewhere better to live.' Margo felt a warm glow embrace her cheeks. 'When Tom was talkin' about the courts, I felt a bit embarrassed admittin' I lived in Blendon Row.'

'Why? You can't help where you're brought up,' said Libby defensively. 'It's not your fault you had lousy parents . . .' Chastising herself for being too outspoken, she quickly backtracked. 'Sorry, I shouldn't have said that. It's not for me to judge.'

Margo chased the dirt from her arms with the flannel. 'You're not though, are you? After all, you only know what I've told you, and as I've only spoken the truth you're speakin' as you find, as it were.'

'But it was wrong of me, because you must still love your parents, despite everything,' said Libby.

'Of course, I do, but it doesn't mean to say I have to like them.' Margo's locks, previously straight under the dirt, now rose towards her chin in a series of curls. 'The East End's a tough place to live, which is why everyone's desperate to get out, but unless you're lucky enough to've been born with a silver spoon in your mouth – or, much like yourself, you've got the sort of parents what've done all right for themselves – you're doomed to eke out a pitiful existence. Or at least that's what I always thought, until I met you that is.'

'Me?' squeaked Libby as she turned aside for Margo to get out. 'What've I done?'

'Shown me that you're the master of your own destiny,' said Margo frankly as she wrapped the towel around herself. 'You've lost everythin', yet you've not let anythin' stand in your way. I reckon you'll get your parents' stall back, and a shop too, given time, because that's the sort of person you are. You're a fighter, who isn't prepared to quit; and that takes gumption.'

'Do I have a choice?'

'Yes. You could've done what the others do. Pick a pocket, steal your supper and grab some kip in the gutter. There's always a choice, and you made the right one.' As she spoke, Margo dressed in the frock she had picked out on the train.

In Libby's eyes, Margo had metamorphosed from a filthy, yet beautiful street urchin into a breathtaking woman whose golden curls set off her sky-blue eyes. 'Wow!' she gasped as she took in the incredible transformation. 'I can't wait to see Tom's face when he sees you.'

Blushing madly, Margo lowered her gaze from the crisp cotton of the frock to her boots, which were riddled with holes, the laces having long been replaced by old scraps of baling twine knotted with string. 'Oh lawks, will you look at me feet!'

Libby followed her gaze. 'First things first: we'll head to Paddy's market and buy you some shoes. We should be able to get some cheap enough there.'

Margo stared at Libby. 'What with? That money's for emergencies, not shoes!'

'I suppose it depends on what you call an emergency, but we've not gone to all this trouble to have you turn up half dressed, so to speak.'

Margo sighed heavily. 'I'm a bloomin' burden, I really am.'

'No you're not,' said Libby stoutly, 'you're my friend, and you need proper shoes.'

Tom rapped a tattoo on the door before calling out, 'Only me. Are you decent?'

'We certainly are!' confirmed Libby.

The door to the room opened and Tom stood in the aperture gazing at Margo, his mouth dropping slightly open as he took in the full picture. Realising that he was staring, he let out a low whistle. 'Blimey! You look . . . er . . . you don't 'alf scrub up well.'

Margo glanced shyly at her boots. 'I wish the same could be said for me boots.'

'Easily rectified,' Libby assured her. She looked at Tom, who was still gazing at Margo. 'Am I right in thinkin' that we'll be able to buy boots pretty cheap down Paddy's market?'

'You are indeed – in fact I wouldn't recommend you go anywhere else – but surely you should dry your hair by the fire before settin' off? You'll catch your death if you go out there with wet hair.'

'We really don't want to put you out any more than we have already,' said Margo.

But Tom was insistent. 'Ten more minutes won't harm.' He held up a brown paper bag. 'I got us some penny buns from the bakery.'

As Tom withdrew the iced buns, Margo's eyes lit up. 'Is that real icing?'

Tom handed her the sweet treat. 'It certainly is.'

Scooping some of the icing up with her forefinger, Margo placed it in her mouth and closed her eyes as she savoured the sugary delight.

'Have you never had a penny bun before?' Libby asked hesitantly, afraid she might appear condescending.

Margo gawked at her. 'You have to be joking! If you couldn't nick it, you didn't get it. Mum spent her money on drink, and Dad spent his on horses. I'm surprised we ever ate, but when we did it was never as fancy as this.'

Tom was staring at Margo as though he couldn't believe what he was hearing. Looking down at his own bun, he folded the bag and held it out towards her. 'Here, take this. You can share it later.'

Margo thanked him as she licked the icing from her fingers. 'Are you sure?'

'Only if you promise to come out with me for a bite to eat one evening. Fish 'n' chips or summat similar.'

A wide grin graced Margo's cheeks. 'We'd love to, wouldn't we, Lib?'

Libby laughed. 'I think it would be best if it were just you and Tom. Three's company and all that.'

Margo looked to Tom, expecting him to insist Libby join them, but Tom was rubbing the back of his neck with the palm of his hand. 'Oh . . .' She looked at the bag in her hand, as the recollection of Libby's words washed over her. 'That's very nice, thank you, Tom, but I'm not about to leave Libby on her own in a strange city.'

Tom bowed his head politely. 'Of course not. Perhaps when you get settled?' he added hopefully.

Anxious at the thought of going on a date, but not wishing to offend their host, Margo gathered her nerves and replied in the only way she could. 'That would be lovely.'

Libby, having finished her bun, was watching the steam rise off her hair as she knelt before the fire. 'I'm hopin' we'll have some idea of what's goin' on later today,' she said to no one in particular, 'even if it's only for the time being.'

'As I work in the post depot, I could put out a few feelers,' said Tom helpfully, 'ask if any of them have heard of a family by the name of O'Connell, whose daughter Orla moved to London with her husband Reggie Gilbert?'

'It's got to be worth a shot,' Libby agreed. 'We can ask down the market, and see if anyone knows if they're still tradin', although I should imagine they are.'

'It's a shame you can't remember what they used to sell,' mused Margo. 'It might've been easier to trace them that way.'

Libby shrugged. 'Dad never mentioned it, or not that I remember.'

Having joined her friend by the fire, Margo gently pulled at the ringlets which formed as her hair dried out. 'We'll find them, I can feel it in me bones.'

'And in the meantime I'll put the word out to see if anyone's hirin',' said Tom. 'I know they're takin' on down the factories, but that would be the last resort.'

'Beggars can't be choosers,' said Libby. 'If it pays to put a roof over our heads, we won't grumble.'

'I start work at ten o'clock tonight,' said Tom. 'If you're really stuck for somewhere to sleep, I don't see the harm in gettin' your heads down here for a few hours whilst I'm out. I—'

But on this, both girls were adamant. 'There's no point in the three of us bein' homeless,' said Libby, and Margo added, 'If there's one thing me and Libby are good at, it's adaptin' ourselves to our circumstances.'

He laughed softly. 'You are that. But promise me you'll come callin' should you need to? I don't care what my landlord says, I won't see two young girls out on the streets.'

Margo held her hand behind her back so that Tom wouldn't see that she had crossed her fingers. 'We promise.'

Satisfied that he had done all he could to help, Tom stifled a yawn behind the back of his hand. 'I'd best get me some kip, else I'll be good for nothin' when I wake up.'

Taking their cue to leave, Libby was the first to rise, pulling Margo to her feet. 'Our hair's dry enough; we'd best be on our way.'

Tom saw the girls to the door, keeping a keen eye on the curtained windows of his neighbours as he did so. He grinned as an elderly lady across the road came out of her house, supposedly to scrub her step. 'She only done that step yesterday,' said Tom shrewdly. 'I bet her ears are waggin' like an elephant's!'

A giggle escaped Margo's lips as she envisaged the old lady with elephant ears. 'I wish I had the luxury to gossip, rather than havin' to find somewhere to eat and sleep.'

'Too much time on her hands,' said Tom, 'that's what's wrong with people like her.'

'I remember my mum always sayin' that the devil makes work for idle hands,' said Libby.

Standing on tiptoes, Margo kissed Tom's cheek. 'There! That'll give her summat to gossip about.' Tom stifled a laugh as Mrs Wilkinson practically did a headstand trying to see what was going on.

Slipping her arm through Margo's, Libby got directions for the market before calling a cheery goodbye from over her shoulder as they walked away, leaving Tom to duck inside before Mrs Wilkinson – who had abruptly finished scrubbing her step – could reach him.

'I told you he liked you,' said Libby, as she and Margo headed off.

'I don't know about him takin' me out for supper,' said Margo. 'I shan't know what to do.'

'Take it from one who knows, if it's meant to be, it'll come to you naturally, or at least it did for me and Jack.'

'Only you and Jack had known each other a lot longer than me and Tom.'

Libby didn't agree. 'Not that much longer. Granted we went through a lot in a short time, but it was kind of the same when Tom helped us to escape unnoticed.'

'Funny how we've both met fellers in extraordinary circumstances,' said Margo.

'Which is why Jack and Tom are such corkers,' said Libby. 'I think most women dream of being rescued by their knight in shinin' armour, and that's how I see Jack and Tom, minus the armour of course.'

'But what am I meant to do on my evenin' out with Tom?' asked Margo tentatively. 'Do I hold his hand or not?'

Libby tucked her arm through the other girl's. 'You let him take the lead. He comes across as a real gent, so I dare say he won't do anythin' you aren't comfortable with.'

Margo looked at Libby sidelong. 'Do you love Jack?'

'I think so. I know that I'd rather he was here with us than goin' off into the unknown, not just because of the war, but because I feel safe when he's with me.'

'I feel safe when I'm with you,' said Margo, 'but that don't mean to say I love you.'

'True, but I'm talkin' about a different type of safe. Just like you can get different types of love.'

Margo eyed her quizzically. 'Don't be daft. You either love someone or you don't.'

'Only I'm not sure that's true,' said Libby. 'I used to have a girlfriend who I loved dearly – we'd known each other since we was knee high to a grasshopper, and we went everywhere together – but I didn't love her the same way I did my parents.'

'But that's family,' said Margo, 'so it's bound to be different.'

'Still love, though,' said Libby reasonably. 'I don't just feel safe when I'm with Jack, I feel secure too. Like nothing and no one can ever harm me, which is ridiculous considerin' we've only known each other for a week.'

'He did rescue you from the river, as well as from that man.'

'That's the trouble. Because he rescued me, I don't know whether my feelings are based on those of a damsel in distress, or true love. What do you think?'

'Time,' said Margo simply. 'If you've no connection other than the rescue, your "love" for each other will begin to wane over time.'

'Golly, I'm glad I've got you to talk to.'

'That's what friends are for.'

Libby eyed her curiously. 'Who did you used to talk to, before you left London?'

Margo rolled her eyes. 'No one. Mainly because they weren't interested in my issues, not when they had similar ones themselves.'

'But surely that would've brought you closer?'

Margo gave a joyless laugh. 'They all hated me because Dad dressed me like a boy, and they said that I was takin' the job off of a real shoeblack.'

'Why didn't they report you, if they felt that strongly about it?'

Margo's eyes grew wide. 'Grass me up? Not on your nelly!'

'But that's silly.'

'Bein' a grass is the worst thing you can be, worse than a murderer even,' said Margo severely.

'So, because they don't want to grass each other up, I'll never find my parents' belongings,' muttered Libby, 'and they think that makes them better people?'

'It's wrong, I know, but it's the honour amongst thieves thing,' said Margo. 'They'd be considered worse than me if they tattle-taled.'

'I suppose that's why the market inspector doesn't say owt about my uncle. Well, that and because he's givin' him a backhander.'

'Paid to turn the other cheek,' said Margo reprovingly. 'That sounds about right.'

'What a world we live in,' said Libby. She fell silent as she spotted a few stalls a little further up the road. 'Looks like we've found the market!'

Margo followed her gaze. 'I hope we find your family as we're walkin' through.'

'Me too,' said Libby. 'Fingers crossed!'

Gordon interrupted Jack, who was in the process of turning a piece of wood. 'Steady on! You're meant to be makin' a stool, not matchsticks.'

Jolting himself back into the now, Jack gave a small grimace as he removed the wood and blew off the dust. 'Sorry, Dad. I was a million miles away.'

'Liverpool's not quite that far.'

Jack wore a glum expression. 'How did you know?'

Taking the wood from his son's grasp, Gordon admired the fillet between the beads. 'It's as plain as the nose on your face. I could see it in your eyes from the first moment I seen the two of you together down the shelter.'

Jack laughed in disbelieving tones. 'Come off it. I didn't even know her name back then.'

'You were lookin' at Libby the same way I used to look at your mother when we first met,' said Gordon matter-of-factly. 'Love at first sight.'

'That's the stuff of fairy tales,' said Jack. 'No one *actually* falls in love at first sight.'

'I think I know how I felt about your mother,' said Gordon bluntly.

'But it was different with you and Mum,' said Jack. 'You met on the dance floor, when Mum was looking at her best, *not* like a drowned rat.'

'What's that got to do with the price of fish?'

'Pulling a woman out of the dirty water of the Thames is hardly the setting for romance.'

'Love doesn't judge on looks, or circumstance,' said Gordon. 'Besides which, does it make any difference whether you fell in love with her straight off the bat, or a day or so later? Point is, you can't stop thinkin' about her.'

Jack gaped at his father. 'Of course I'm thinkin' about her. Blimey, Dad, she's on her own in a strange city – and that's if she even got there, because for all we know she might've been discovered en route, and if that's the case she could be anywhere!'

Gordon picked up a piece of wood and peered along its length. 'And do you really think that a girl like Libby can't take care of herself?'

'Yes, I do!' snapped Jack irritably. 'Libby's wingin' it, Dad, leapin' from one disaster to the next. It's only through the grace of God that she hasn't come a cropper, but her luck mightn't hold for ever, and what then?'

'There's been a bit of luck involved, I'll grant you, but some folk make their own luck, and I believe that Libby's one of them. She's not as naïve as you believe her to be.'

'I'm not denyin' that she's intelligent,' said Jack, 'but she's not savvy when it comes to the streets. You only have to look at the pickle she got herself into the night we met.'

'So, what do you propose you do? It's not as though you can follow her round Britain.'

'I'm hopin' to get posted somewhere close to Liverpool,' Jack began, but Gordon was wagging his head.

'The services are renowned for sendin' folk in the opposite direction from where they want to be. The chances of you endin' up near Libby are slim to none, to say the least. Pinnin' your hopes on summat you have no control over is the equivalent of settin' yourself up for a fall.'

'Then what am I meant to do? Cos the *thought* of bein' so far away is . . .' He fell silent, fixing his father with a look of incredulity. 'This is ridiculous. I've barely known her more than five minutes, yet I can't get her out of my mind.'

'Ridiculous it may be,' said Gordon, 'but it sounds very much like love to me.'

'I thought love was supposed to be the best feelin' in the world,' said Jack sullenly, 'but this doesn't feel at all good.'

'Love is very much like a bunch of roses,' mused Gordon, 'beautiful to look at; a wonder to behold, but with bloomin' sharp thorns that prick you when you least expect it.'

'That explains the pain,' said Jack quietly.

Gordon leaned against the bench. 'Bein' in love is wonderful, but it's no easy ride . . . just look at me and your mother.'

Jack stared at the tools. 'That's why I can't understand why she did what she did. Libby doesn't have much control over her life, but Mum had everything: a lovin' husband, a nice home in the heart of the city, and a bonny baby.' He viewed his father from the corner of his eye, not quite daring to make contact. 'Most women would give their right arm for what Mum had, and you said yourself that I was meant to be the icin' on the cake, so . . .'

Gordon stopped him before he could continue. 'It was nothin' to do with you, son.'

'But how do you know that, if nobody knows why she took her own life?'

Gordon drew a deep, staggered breath. 'Because you were only a baby. It couldn't have been you.'

'If not, then what? Because by all accounts she was tickety-boo before I came along.'

Gordon flexed his jaw before answering. 'Your mother loved you – us – with all her heart.'

'Then if that's what love is, you can keep it,' muttered Jack sullenly.

'Why your mother did what she did had nothin' to do with love. It was summat that just happened to her, but I *promise* you, she didn't want it be that way. She just couldn't cope any more.'

'Could that happen to me, when I have kids?' asked Jack, somewhat anxiously.

Gordon rubbed his hand across his face. 'No. Your mother might've been the life and soul of the party, but there were times – even prior to your bein' born – when her mood was really, really low. It was as though she'd fallen into a pit of misery from which she couldn't escape. She'd come out of it all right in the end, but I suppose the signs were there all along, when I think back. And that's why I'm sure it won't happen to you, because you're not like that.'

'But I am at the moment,' Jack said ruefully.

'It's understandable with you, though,' said Gordon. 'Your mother didn't appear to have a reason for feelin' the way she did.'

Jack blew out his cheeks. 'It must've been dreadful to live with such torment.'

'Which is why she chose a way out,' said Gordon, 'but like I say, that's *never* goin' to happen to you, so stop your worryin' and give that stool a third leg!'

'Thanks, Dad.' Jack took a fresh piece of wood and continued with his work.

Turning away from his son, Gordon returned to his own bench, deep in thought. While he had been truthful regarding his wife's depression prior to Jack's birth, there was no escaping the fact that it had got a lot worse after his arrival, and he couldn't help but feel that the two were connected – not that he would say that to Jack, of course. Jack had been a bonny baby who rarely cried, and as such had won the hearts of all who saw him, yet his own mother had made any excuse she could for someone else to spend time with him whilst she remained in her bed. At first, the doctors had said that she was exhausted by the effort of giving birth, but as time passed, and Maisie regained her strength, she still kept her distance from Jack. He remembered the morning of her death as if it was only yesterday. Gordon had woken early, to find his wife's side of the bed empty. Encouraged by the thought that she might have gone through to tend to her son, he had stayed where he was, thinking he was giving his wife and son some much needed time together. But when Jack's cries resonated around the small flat minutes later with no sign of letting up, Gordon had got up to see if he could help. Expecting to find his wife distraught at not being able to quell Jack's crying, he was surprised to find that she was nowhere to be seen. Assuming that she must've popped out to do some shopping, Gordon had tended to his son before getting his own breakfast. When Maisie failed to return, Gordon had no choice but to take Jack to work. Swaddling him in a blanket, he had left the house, only to see a couple of stern-faced policemen heading in his direction.

Now, with the memory sweeping over him, Gordon closed his eyes as he recalled their words. From that moment on he had vowed to look after his son, and he'd done just that, raising a strapping young man who was already a master carpenter, despite his young age. *Maisie would be proud of him*, Gordon told himself. *If she hadn't been fighting inner demons, he'd have been the apple of her eye, just as he is mine!*

Chapter Six

Libby and Margo perused the market stalls, with Libby making a point of asking each trader if they knew of anyone by the name of O'Connell working the market. It hadn't taken long for her to realise that Tom had been correct in saying that O'Connell was a common name.

'Bleedin' hell, that's like askin' if there's any Chinamen in Chinatown,' laughed one woman in particular. 'You might find them quicker if you told us what trade they was in.'

'I wish I knew,' said Libby dully, 'but all I know for sure is that they're living on the Scotland Road, and their name is O'Connell.'

'And their daughter moved to London, not long after having a baby,' supplied Margo, 'which would've been around 19 . . . ?' She looked to Libby for the answer.

'1924,' said Libby, adding, 'My mother was Orla O'Connell and she was married to Reggie Gilbert; he used to help them run the stall, if that's any help?'

'Sorry, luv, but none of it rings a bell. I'll ask around for you, though.'

Libby and Margo continued their search, asking the same questions each time. When they stopped to buy Margo a pair of second-hand boots, Margo peered down at her new footwear, wriggling her toes experimentally. 'They fit like a glove.

I ain't never had boots what are in as good nick as this before. Thanks, Libby, I really appreciate it. I promise I'll pay you back as soon as I can.'

Libby handed the money over to the stallholder, who passed back her change. 'What do you want me to do with these?' asked the trader, holding up Margo's old boots.

'Whatever you like,' said Margo. 'They ain't no good to me.'

The girls' cockney accent had caused much curiosity among the traders, who were keen to know what two young girls were doing so far away from home, but once they heard the awful truth their curiosity turned into dread.

'We've 'eard about the bombin's,' said a man on one of the stalls. 'I've even seen them in the cinema reels, but it's hard to get a sense when you're so far away. Is it really as bad as all that?'

'Worse,' said Margo flatly. 'There ain't no wonderin' if it's a false alarm – not any more.'

'How do you manage?' enquired a curious woman, her hair rollers partly hidden beneath her headscarf. 'If it's as bad as you say it is.'

Margo shrugged. 'What choice do we have? We run for cover and hope for the best.'

'Unless you're unlucky like my parents, of course,' said Libby. She glanced at the man who she felt had questioned the truth of their statements. 'And it is as bad as we say it is.' She looked around her. 'I've not seen all of Liverpool yet, but you should count yourself lucky, because you've not been hit any-where near as bad as them down south.'

Another stallholder glowered at the man who'd dared to question Margo's words. 'C'mon, Mr Peterson, you only have to sit in the cinema for five minutes to know these girls aren't exaggeratin'.'

'He just wishes they were,' remarked a woman who was standing close by. 'None of us want to believe the worst, and it would be a great relief to hear that things aren't as bad as they seem.'

'It was the whole reason why my folks were moving to Norwich,' said Libby, noticing as she did so that several of the people nearby drew the sign of the cross over their chests.

A small child, who had been listening quietly, spoke the thought uppermost in everyone's mind. 'Will they do that to us?'

'You're too far north,' said Margo quickly. 'They'll not come here when they can concentrate on the capital.'

'The docks . . .' began another, but they were quickly hushed by those who didn't wish the youngster to have nightmares.

A man who had been at the stall where they'd bought Margo's boots spoke up, whilst appearing to be inspecting the fruit with a keen interest. 'You said you were here lookin' for your relatives, but what are you goin' to do if you can't find them? It seems a long way to have come on a whim.' He was eying them intently from under the brim of his fedora.

'I don't know whether I'd call it a whim,' said Libby defensively, 'more like a necessity. I'm sure my mother's family would want to know of her passing, and this is the only way I could think of to let them know.'

The man pressed on. 'So back to my original question, what are you plannin' on doin' if you can't find them?'

She had no idea why he was so interested in her affairs, but he seemed to think that everything was going to go pear-shaped, something which she found most annoying. 'Keep lookin' until I do,' she replied defiantly, adding waspishly, 'Why, have you a problem with that?'

The man held his hands up in a placating manner. 'Not at all.'

'Just ignore Oisin,' said the woman minding the stall, 'he's just bein' nosey.'

'Miserable bugger,' muttered Margo as they walked to the next stall. 'What's it to 'im?'

'Search me,' said Libby. 'Some people don't like a happy endin'; maybe he's one of them.'

Unbeknown to the girls, the man to whom they were referring was hastening towards the seedier part of the city, keen on imparting the information he had just gleaned from the two young girls. Reaching his destination, he hurried up the far end of the court and knocked on a wooden door, warped with age, the bottom half of which had been coloured by the dirt and grime from the street.

A sharp-looking woman answered the door. Her dark curly hair was piled up into a loose bun, and she immediately leaned across the threshold, blocking the entrance.

'Hello, Jo,' said the man, before peering past her as though looking for someone else. 'Where's Donny?'

'Out. Why?' came the short reply. If Oisin wanted Donny, she'd be bound he was up to no good. She viewed him through narrowing eyes. 'You'd better not be tryin' to get him into bother, Oisin Murphy. He's gettin' too bleedin' old for your foolish capers.'

She folded her arms defensively. Oisin was always coming up with hare-brained schemes, the like of which would most likely see him in jail one of these days. Whatever news he had to impart, she wouldn't be jumping in feet first.

Oisin flashed her a smile full of feigned charm, revealing a gold tooth. 'Far from it. But I do think I have news which would be of interest to him – you too, come to that.'

'Oh aye,' retorted the dark-haired beauty, her thick Scouse accent heavy with suspicion, 'and what's that then?'

'I just seen Orla's kid down the market, askin' if anyone knew the whereabouts of her grandparents.'

She leaned up from the doorframe, inadvertently allowing him to enter. 'No! Are you sure?' she asked, closing the door behind him.

'As eggs is eggs,' said Oisin as he squeezed along the hall-way, which was narrowed by the cardboard boxes which flanked either side.

She took a pre-rolled cigarette from its case and placed it between her lips. 'What on earth is she doin' up here, after all this time? I trust she isn't with her mother?'

Oisin raised his brows in the manner of someone who was about to reveal prized information. 'I very much doubt it, considerin' she's dead.'

Stunned by his revelation, it took her a moment or so to speak. 'Are you sure?'

Oisin explained that Libby had come in search of her grand-parents so that she could impart the news of their daughter's death.

Jo listened in deathly silence as his words swam over her. 'Well, she ain't goin' to find her grandparents.'

'I know, but that's not why I'm here.'

Jo deftly smoothed the top down on one of the boxes to prevent Oisin from seeing the contents. 'How much does she know, do you think?'

'Nothin'. Orla would've done her best to keep her in the dark.'

'Which is why she never came back,' said Jo. 'I bet she'd be turnin' in her grave if she knew Libby was in Liverpool.'

'Spinnin' more like.'

Jo walked through to the parlour, flicking her cigarette ash into a discarded mug as she passed. 'So why are you here?'

'Libby was buyin' a pair of boots for her friend with a five-bob note.'

Jo tutted beneath her breath. She had better things to do with her time than listen to Oisin's theories. 'And?'

'How can a kid of her age afford to splash the cash when there's a war on?'

'Don't know, nor do I care.' Jo gazed at Oisin, who was practically hopping from one foot to the other in excitement. There was only one thing that could've got him so agitated, and that was money. 'You think she's had some kind of inheritance, don't you?'

'How else could she afford to throw her money around like that?'

Jo cast her eyes around the poorly lit room with its mould-riddled walls and moth-eaten curtains. 'You think she has money to burn?'

'It would appear that way!' He placed his arm around her waist. 'It's a good job she has her Auntie Jo and Uncle Donny to look out for her.'

Jo sidestepped out of his embrace, grimacing at the feel of his touch. Oisin's schemes always fell flat at some point, and she had no doubt that this one would be the same as all the others. 'Oh no! I'm not havin' her here. You know full well Donny can't stand kids . . .'

He gaped at her. 'Blow Donny! Besides, what've you got to lose?'

Even though it went against the grain for her to agree with anything Oisin said, if he was correct in thinking that Libby had come into a large inheritance it might be just what she and Donny needed to get out of the courts. She eyed him narrowly. 'What about that snake in the grass, Tony? Have you taken him into consideration?'

She scowled when Oisin laughed in her face. 'Can you really see Tony wantin' to play happy families?'

'Probably not, but you never know, when there's money involved, and one word from him would be all it'd take . . .'

'He's not goin' to say owt,' snorted Oisin. 'I'd bet money on it.'

She stubbed her cigarette out on the inside rim of the mug. 'I s'pose it can't harm to go and say hello, see how the land lies. Where is she now?'

Oisin grinned. 'Down the market. If you leave now, you should be able to catch her.'

She gathered her heaviest shawl from a coat peg by the door, addressing him from over her shoulder. 'You'd better be right about this, Oisin Murphy. Donny won't be happy if he finds out she ain't got two pennies to rub together.'

'Don't worry, I know what I seen *and* heard,' Oisin assured her.

The pair hastened towards the market, with Jo warning Oisin that she'd have his guts for garters should he be taking her on a wild goose chase.

Forging their way through the stalls, Oisin kept a keen eye out for the girls as he led Jo through the crowds. 'Whatever happens, they mustn't see us together,' he told her, 'because I feigned ignorance regarding—' He stopped short as Libby came into view. 'There they are!' he hissed. 'Do you see them?'

Jo narrowed her eyes as she peered over to the group of people by the stall. 'As I live and breathe, she's the spit of Orla.'

'Where's Donny? I'll tip him the wink before he gets home.'

'Down the Albert Dock doin' a bit of business,' said Jo. She shot him a reproving glance. 'Tread carefully. The folk he's doin' business with don't take kindly to strangers bargin' in, and I know what you can be like.'

Oisin knew precisely the sort of folk she was referring to, and they weren't prone to asking questions, favouring the more physical form of communication, which often end with a permanent appointment at the bottom of the Mersey. 'Noted,' was all he said before scurrying off in the direction of the docks.

Jo slipped past the girls, heading for a stall a little further on. Making sure she wasn't known to the trader, she tweaked her headscarf so that it hid most of her face whilst she kept an eye on Libby.

Margo and Libby had begun to grow weary of repeating the same question only to receive the same replies, and had decided to take a stall each in order to quicken the process.

'Are you *sure* they had a stall here, and not another market?' asked Margo as she passed Libby by.

'I dunno. I'm beginnin' to think I've got halves of two different stories and stuck 'em together,' confessed Libby. 'Do you think we'd be better off trawlin' the Scottie?'

Margo placed her hands on her hips as she looked down the line of stalls. 'I reckon we finish this row off; then if there's no joy we move on to the Scottie.'

Libby gave her the thumbs up, adding, 'We'll meet at the end of this row, agreed?'

'Agreed.'

A couple of stalls down from where the girls had been talking, Jo busied herself by pretending to be deeply interested in an old kiss clasp purse. Hoping that Libby might overhear, she began to talk to the stallholder in exaggerated tones.

'My parents used to run a stall very much like this one,' she said, watching Libby through her peripheral vision. 'I miss my days on the market, but what can you do?' Pretending to notice Libby for the first time, Jo went to step to one side, before scrutinising Libby keenly. 'Good God, you don't 'alf remind me of my sister! I haven't seen her in *years*, but you're the spit of her, only younger, of course.' She eyed Libby quizzically. 'If I didn't know for a fact that they was livin' in London, I'd swear you must be her daughter Libby.'

Scarcely able to believe her good fortune, Libby felt tears forming in her eyes as she gazed at the woman who had spoken the words she most wanted to hear. Patting her chest rapidly with the palm of her hand, Libby gasped, 'That's me. I'm Libby!'

Easier than shootin' fish in a barrel, thought Jo as she clasped a hand to her mouth. Leading Libby away from the prying eyes of the stallholder, she stared at her round-eyed. 'What on earth are you doin' here?' Standing on tiptoe, she scoured the crowds around them. 'Where's your mam?'

Libby drew a deep breath. 'Can we go somewhere a little quieter?'

'Of course!' She paused before adding, 'Why don't you come back to mine and we can have a catch-up over a nice cup of tea?'

Libby looked over to Margo, who was deep in conversation with a stallholder. 'Margo!' She waved in an exaggerated fashion in order to gain her friend's attention.

Looking back to the stallholder, Margo made her excuses and moved away to join Libby and Jo. 'I've just been chattin'—' she began, only to have Libby cut her short.

'This is my auntie. We met on one of the stalls! What are the chances?'

'Oh!' said Margo. Looking slightly perplexed, she shrugged off the conversation she had been having with the stallholder. 'That's wonderful. Pleased to meet you . . .' She waited for Jo to supply her name.

'Jo Murphy.' She glanced from Margo to the stallholder the girl had been talking to, who was looking over with interest. Keen to get away from the prying eyes of those who ran the market, she tucked one arm through Libby's and the other through Margo's, and turned them in the direction of home. Chatting animatedly about how good it was to see Libby again, Jo raised her original question. 'Where did you say your mam was?'

'That's why I'm here,' said Libby. She stopped walking, so that she could have her aunt's full attention. 'I was on the market when it happened . . .'

Pretending that Orla's death was news to her, Jo covered her face with her hands. 'Oh, my good God, how awful. You must be devastated.'

Libby's cheeks bloomed guiltily. 'I would've told you sooner, only I didn't know your address.'

Drying her non-existent tears, Jo was careful to keep her eyelids lowered. 'And you came all this way to find us? You really are a good kid, cos I dare say we'd never have known otherwise.'

'I thought you deserved to know,' said Libby, 'same as Gramma and Gramps.'

'They're dead,' said Jo. Seeing the look of shocked disbelief etched on Libby's face she continued hastily, 'Sorry, I forgot you wouldn't know . . .'

'I'm afraid not,' said Libby. Deciding to address the elephant in the room, she spoke openly. 'I'm aware that my mother didn't see eye to eye with her parents, but even so . . .' She shook her head sorrowfully.

'Sad, isn't it?' said Jo. 'To think you're my niece and I haven't seen you in years! I'm surprised I even recognised you.'

Libby felt her face grow warm. She had nothing to do with the family fall-out, but that didn't stop her from feeling embarrassed that things had been allowed to go so ridiculously far. 'It's a cryin' shame that they never managed to mend their bridges,' she said. 'Family's so important.'

'It certainly is,' Jo agreed. 'But as is often the case, it sometimes takes a tragedy to bring people together.' Adding, in the privacy of her own mind, *Or inheritance.*

'Indeed,' Libby nodded. 'Not that it made any difference between me and my Uncle Tony – my father's brother. He's just as aloof as ever he was, if not worse.'

Jo snorted reprovingly. 'That doesn't surprise me.'

'Sounds like you've got the measure of him. Did you know him well?'

Jo's eyes widened. 'Enough to know that he's no good. Quite frankly it doesn't surprise me to hear that he's steerin' well clear. I'd wager he kept his distance whilst you were growin' up.'

'Nail, hammer, head.'

'Does he know you're here?'

'I went to see him just before I left. In fact, it was he who told me that you lived on the Scottie.' She looked at her aunt. 'Do you still live there?'

Jo lowered her gaze. 'We moved to Back Bond Street not long after Mum and Dad passed.'

'Was that after you came back from Ireland?' asked Margo, out of the blue. 'Only the trader I was talkin' to said the whole family had moved to Ireland a while back.'

'That's right. My parents wanted to live by the sea so we went back to Dublin, which is where they lived before movin' to Liverpool.'

Margo thought back to what Tom had told them about the River Mersey being wide because it was so close to the sea. 'But you're not far from the sea here. Why go all the way to Ireland?'

Jo glared at Margo. 'What's wrong with Ireland?' she asked accusingly.

'Nothin',' said Margo hastily, 'it just seems a bit far when Tom said . . .'

'And who's this Tom when he's at home?' snapped Jo irritably.

'Our friend,' said Margo meekly. 'He lives on Blenheim Street.'

'Oh aye, and what does Tom know about our family?' queried Jo, her brow rising. 'Nothin', that's what.'

Eager that they should not upset her aunt, Libby spoke in haste. 'I'm sure Margo didn't mean anythin' by it. She was just curious, that's all.'

Assuming that she had touched a raw nerve for some reason she had yet to discover, Margo spoke timidly. 'Sorry if I offended you. I was only wonderin'.'

'Well don't,' said Jo icily.

As they continued to walk Libby shot Margo an apologetic glance over her aunt's shoulder. If the rest of the family were as fiery as Jo, then she could understand why her mother had chosen to keep her distance.

They walked up a narrow alley with houses either side, and Libby wrinkled her nose as a dreadful odour penetrated her nostrils. *We must be in one of them courts that Tom told us about*, she thought. *I expect it's all she can afford now she hasn't got a stall down the market*. She saw a solitary water-closet which she assumed served every house, and to her dismay her aunt made for a door directly opposite. Unable to bear the stench, Libby found herself surreptitiously placing her hand over her nose. Whilst she didn't wish to appear rude, neither did she want the iced bun she had eaten earlier to put in a second appearance. Following her aunt into the tiny terraced property, Libby hoped that it would be different once they got inside, but the odour was as strong indoors as it was out, and Libby wasn't surprised to see that the interior was filthy. In the hallway they passed several cardboard boxes, and Libby noticed that her aunt deftly smoothed the flaps down, as if she didn't want the girls seeing what was inside.

'You won't remember meetin' your Uncle Donny,' said Jo as they entered what Libby presumed to be the kitchen, given the small gas ring and kettle which stood on top of a table cluttered with all kinds of paraphernalia.

'No,' replied Libby, adding truthfully, 'Mum didn't really talk much about her side of the family.'

Jo didn't seem too surprised, or indeed bothered, as she picked her away across the floor which was strewn with everything from old beer bottles to elaborate vases. 'Who'd like a cuppa?' Both girls took her up on her offer, but only because they were too polite to decline. With their host busying herself collecting mugs from around the living area, Margo found herself hoping fervently that Libby's aunt would see fit to at least rinse the mugs before handing them to her guests.

The mugs collected, Jo picked up the kettle. 'I shan't be a mo,' she said, as she swept past the girls, 'I'm just goin' to the pump to give these a rinse.'

As soon as they heard the front door click shut behind her, Libby turned anxiously to Margo. 'I'm sorry if my aunt upset you. I've no idea why she was bein' so defensive. I know they say the Irish are a proud lot, but I honestly couldn't see anything wrong with what you were sayin'.'

'Me neither,' said Margo. 'Maybe it has summat to do with why your mother distanced herself from the family?'

'It certainly seemed like you touched a raw nerve,' agreed Libby. 'I'll understand if you'd rather not stay.'

'I'm not goin' to leave you here on your own,' said Margo. 'I never knew your mother, but I'd wager she was nothin' like her sister.'

'God no! You'd not think they were from the same family,' hissed Libby. 'But there again, my dad's nothin' like his brother, so maybe that's the norm?'

'Black sheep, that's what they say,' said Margo. 'Your uncle is the black sheep in his family, and I reckon your aunt is the black sheep in hers.'

'Unfortunately not,' said Libby sadly. 'That was definitely my mother.' She looked at the ancient wallpaper, which was covered in thick mould. 'Perhaps the death of my grandparents had a bad effect on her?'

Margo glanced at a glass chandelier which lay on the floor. She had no idea where it had come from, but it definitely didn't go with the rest of the décor. 'People deal with grief in different ways, so I suppose that could be one reason.'

Libby asked the question uppermost in her thoughts. 'Was Blendon Row like this?'

'It was no palace,' said Margo, 'and keepin' on top of the mould was a never-ending battle, but I did my best, and it certainly didn't look anywhere near as bad as this. Having said that, without me around I dare say this is exactly what Blendon Row would look like.'

'I don't fancy sleepin' here, do you?' hissed Libby, fearful that her aunt might walk in at any moment.

'I'd sooner sleep in the mail carriage,' admitted Margo. 'I know your plan was for a new start in Liverpool, but with your aunt comin' across more like your uncle, it seems to me as though you could be jumpin' out of the fryin' pan into the fire. Quite frankly, I think you'd be better off without family, if they're as bad as they seem.'

'Like you and your dad, you mean?'

'That's exactly what I mean. I don't have to live with my father *just* because he's my father,' said Margo, 'and you don't have to stay with your aunt just because she's all you've got. I reckon if the two of us stick together we could actually make a decent go of things; certainly more than we would if we stayed with our so-called families.'

Libby sighed ruefully. 'You're right. I'm chasin' rainbows because I'm desperate to be part of a family, but this . . .' she glanced around the miserable-looking room, 'is not what I was expectin' – far from it. We'll go as soon as we've drunk our tea. I only came here to tell them of my parents' death, so they probably aren't expectin' us to stay, and wouldn't want us to, for that matter.'

As the last words left her lips, they heard the front door close and Jo entered the room, a broad beam etched upon her cheeks.

'It's goin' to be grand lookin' after my niece,' she cooed, as she placed the kettle on the ring. 'I know me and your mam had our differences, but I'm sure she'd go to her grave a happier woman knowin' that her daughter was livin' under the same roof as her aunt.'

Libby felt her cheeks redden with guilt. 'I – I . . .' she stammered, before turning pleading eyes to Margo, who stepped in.

'That's ever so kind of you,' she said, 'but we've already found somewhere to stay. Besides, we wouldn't want to impose.'

Jo cocked an eyebrow. 'How can you be an imposition on family?' She glanced at the wallpaper, which was parting company with the wall due to the damp. 'I know it ain't the best, and I dare say your mam and dad had a much nicer house before the Luftwaffe came callin', but it's home to us, and with a little TLC I'm sure the four of us could soon have it lookin' like a palace.' She turned pleading eyes to the girls. 'I know I've let things slide since me mam and dad passed, but just seein' you meks me feel like I'm part of a family once more. I'm sure I can get everything back on track now I have my niece to look after. In fact, I reckon you're just what the doctor ordered!'

Libby looked to Margo, who nodded in a resigned fashion, and turned back to her aunt. 'If you insist, then how can we refuse?'

Margo stared at Jo in a thoughtful manner. No matter how much she tried, she couldn't help but feel that Libby's family weren't to be trusted, even though she couldn't put her finger on why. *If Libby's aunt ain't a bad egg, then I'm the Queen of Sheba!* Margo told herself. *I hope I'm wrong, but I very much doubt it, cos summat about this just doesn't add up. It's almost as if she knew what Libby wanted to hear.*

Having finished their tea, Libby and Margo offered to go and fetch something for their supper from the chippy, leaving Jo to sort out the spare room, such as it was.

'What a bloomin' mess,' said Libby as she and Margo drew clear of the courts. 'But when she started talkin' about how my mother would rest easy in her grave knowin' I was staying with her, I just couldn't bring myself to speak the truth.'

'What? That you'd sooner sleep in the mail carriage than her spare room?' said Margo.

'I reckon we buy a bottle of bleach whilst we're out,' Libby said, scratching the back of her head absentmindedly. 'Do you reckon bleach kills fleas? Cos I swear that mattress she showed us was practically hoppin' its way across the room.'

Margo grimaced. 'The whole lot wants settin' fire to, but if it's all they can afford, what can you do?'

'I dunno, but we can't sleep on that thing.' She slid her arm through Margo's. 'I felt so sorry for her, when she was talkin' about her parents dyin', because I've been through the same thing. Nobody's turned their back on me – apart from my uncle, of course – and I'd hate to be the first one to do that to her.' She squeezed Margo's arm in hers. 'Which is why I've decided to take it on the chin, but you mustn't feel obliged to do the same. My uncle gave me enough money to get a room for a few nights, and I want you to take the money and do just that.'

'There ain't a chance in hell that I'm goin' to leave you sleepin' there whilst I'm living somewhere habitable. We do it together, or not at all. To be honest, Lib, I can understand your aunt wantin' to take you in, but would it really be wise? I know she's family, but she doesn't know us, and there's every chance we could rub each other up the wrong way, especially livin' in cramped conditions like that.'

'But how can I tell her I've changed my mind without hurtin' her feelings?'

'We've already told her we have somewhere lined up,' said Margo reasonably. 'Why don't we pretend we'd paid a week's B&B in advance, and can't get our money back? I'm sure she'd understand if she thought we were wastin' money.'

Libby looked sceptical. 'You mean we should lie?'

'Not lie exactly,' said Margo slowly, 'more bend the truth. Especially if we really do have somewhere to stay. I'm sure it wouldn't take more than a few minutes to make some enquiries.'

'I think it's a brilliant idea,' said Libby, relieved that she wouldn't have to sleep on the aforementioned mattress, 'and it's only a little white lie.'

'A week should be enough time for us to find employment, as well as something more permanent,' said Margo, 'like maybe a flat?'

'You still want to stay in Liverpool?' asked Libby, sounding surprised.

'It's where my dad isn't, so yeah,' said Margo plainly. 'Most people would be frightened of startin' from scratch because they've got summat to lose, but not me. I've only got summat to gain.'

'I thought meetin' my auntie might've put you off,' said Libby.

Margo waved a dismissive hand. 'It's not like we'll be livin' with her. If we can find a flat somewhere like where Tom lives, as well as decent jobs, who knows what our future holds?'

'There's a reason why you ran onto the same mail carriage as me,' said Libby. 'Whether it be fate, or a guidin' spirit, it don't make no difference, cos I couldn't have done this without you.'

Jo turned as Donny called from the bottom of the stairs. 'Hello?'

'Up here,' came the reply. 'Don't worry about the girls, they've gone out to get summat for us suppers.'

Taking the stairs two at a time, Donny quickly arrived in the bedroom which Jo was clearing. 'What the hell are you doin'?' he scowled. 'They ain't stayin' 'ere, if that's what you're thinkin'.'

'Oh yes they are!' snapped Jo. 'That bleedin' Margo's already askin' too many questions for my likin', and if we cast them out onto the streets she'll have every reason, which is why I've sent them out to buy some supper. Meanwhile, I'm goin' to clean this place up so they don't have an excuse to leave.'

'Why? What's wrong with where we live?' He added sharply, 'Have they said summat?''

'Not to my face, no,' admitted Jo, 'but I could tell that Margo was bustin' to say summat to Libby, so I pretended to go out to fill the kettle with water, so that I could hear exactly what she had to say. After all, I can't fix the problem if I don't know what it is.'

'I'm not 'avin' anyone stay under my roof what thinks they're too good for us,' snarled Donny. 'If they wanna go then let 'em. For all we know they could've robbed that five-bob note that Oisin seen them with.'

'No,' said Jo dismissively, 'they're definitely not the type to steal. Which is part of the reason as to why they're not keen on stayin'.' She jerked her head in the direction of the stairs. 'They already think we're up to no good—'

'Which we are,' chortled Donny.

'But we have to prove we're trustworthy,' said Jo, 'which is why I want them to stay. We'll never get our hands on that inheritance if Libby don't trust us.'

He rubbed his hands together in a greedy fashion. 'I wonder how much they left her.'

'Dunno, but they were never short of a bob or two, that's for certain.' She glanced once again in the direction of the stairs. 'What are we gonna do with that lot? I can't risk the girls – or rather that Margo – takin' a sneaky peek as soon as our backs are turned.'

'Never mind that,' said Donny. 'Come nightfall, this house is gonna be a hive of activity, and they'd have to be deaf to not know what was goin' on. If they put two and two together, they'll be off before we can get a sniff of the money.'

'We'll cross that bridge when we come to it,' said Jo. 'For now, it's one step at a time.'

'Softly, softly, catchee monkey,' agreed Donny. 'I just hope it's worth the effort!'

The girls found a suitable B&B just down the road from their new friend Tom, and Libby handed over a week's bed and board, keeping a little back for other expenses. Their landlady had advised them that there were jobs aplenty for two respectable girls, provided they were old enough, of course.

Having agreed to pretend they were sisters, Margo had taken the lead. 'We can't prove our age, cos our documents went up in the fire.'

The landlady, who'd introduced herself as Mrs Brixton, tutted beneath her breath. 'That bloomin' Hitler's got a lot to answer for.' Twisting her lips to one side, she eyed the girls thoughtfully. 'I know there's a couple of jobs goin' down the Chinese laundry. They don't care about papers or how old you are, as long as you're willin' to work hard.'

'We'll do whatever it takes,' said Libby. 'D'you think it's worth us callin' in on our way back to our aunt's?'

'I don't see why not.' She pushed the money into her apron pocket. 'Mr Soo might even know somewhere where the rent's cheap.'

The girls had gone straight to the laundry and sought out the owner. When they had assured him that they weren't runaways hiding from the law, Mr Soo had agreed to take them on, and even pointed them in the direction of a room going for hire just around the corner from Scotland Road. Thanking him profusely, the girls had visited the landlord, who was sceptical until he heard their tale.

'First sign of trouble and you're out,' he warned, 'so I hope you're tellin' the truth.'

'We are,' insisted Margo, crossing her fingers behind her back. They had agreed a sum, with the girls moving in at the end of the week.

'My aunt's goin' to think we've legged it,' said Libby as they headed back up the alley. 'We was only meant to be nippin' to the chippy.' She knocked a swift tattoo on the door.

'Who is it?' trilled Jo from the hall.

'Libby and Margo,' said Libby.

Jo grinned at Donny, who had hastened over to welcome the girls. 'Come on in, ladies. We don't leave family out on the step, not in this house.' He nodded approvingly at the wrapped chips in Libby's hands. 'They smell good.'

Margo stared at the back of the man's balding head. In her opinion he didn't look as though he'd shaved in a fortnight or washed in weeks. Libby caught her eye and grimaced in agreement as she and Margo followed him and Jo into the kitchen.

Indicating two chairs with an outstretched hand, Donny quickly picked some newspapers up off one and dusted the other with the palm of his hand whilst speaking in an exaggerated fashion.

'Talk about a turn up for the books!' he said, still grinning broadly at the girls. 'We were only talkin' about Orla the other day, weren't we, queen?'

'We were indeed,' said Jo. She gazed affectionately at Libby. 'I reckon it's no coincidence you comin' here, only days after we spoke of your mam and dad.'

Margo, who had been watching the pair keenly, thought, *He's got beady, shifty-lookin' eyes. I've seen hundreds of men like him in London – heck, my father's one of them. His whole stance projects excitement at receiving his unexpected guests, yet his eyes read differently. I don't reckon he wants us here, but Jo does.* Continuing to view him critically, she listened whilst Libby gave each of them a parcel of chips, explaining as she did so that they had been back to their B&B but the landlady had refused to give them a refund, so they had decided not to take up Jo's kind offer after all, and she hoped they hadn't offended her aunt and uncle in any way.

'Oh, that's a shame,' said Donny. 'We was lookin' forward to havin' some young 'uns around the house, what with us not bein' blessed with any kiddies of our own. We thought it would be nice, but you have to stay where you see fit, and if it's easier for you to live nearer to your place of work, then who are we to argue?'

He's pretendin' to be disappointed, thought Margo, *but I still maintain that his eyes speak differently. Like he was relieved to hear that we wouldn't be stayin'.* She turned her gaze away as Donny turned to look at her. His gaze intensified as it met hers, and the smirk instantly fell from his cheeks, but only fleetingly, as if he'd caught himself lowering his guard. He turned his attention back to Libby, and Margo desperately hoped that her friend had seen the way her uncle's expression had changed, but Libby was still telling her aunt about their new job, and what was expected of them. *She knows they're bad news*, thought Margo, *but I've got a dreadful feelin' that they're far worse than she imagines, cos I've only ever seen one other feller look at me the way her uncle just did, and that was me dad, right before he give me a damned good beltin'.*

Determined not to sit quietly but to show she wasn't afraid of him, Margo joined the conversation. 'It's good to know that Libby's family are lookin' out for her,' she said in what she hoped was an upbeat manner. 'I know we have our friend Tom to fall back on, but it's not the same as family, is it?'

Much to Margo's delight, the comment appeared to have completely caught Donny off guard. Staring blankly at the girls, he addressed Jo almost accusingly.

'You never told me about this friend?'

Without missing a beat, Jo turned to Libby. 'Your uncle's very protective, and I must say, I can't blame him. You've not been in Liverpool long, so how did you meet this "friend" of yours?'

'We met him off the train,' said Margo, quickly intervening before Libby told the truth about them stowing away. 'We didn't know where we were goin', and as he was walkin' the same way as us it seemed only sensible that we went with him. He showed us where he lived, and gave us a cup of tea and a penny bun before we headed into the market. He says we can call by any time we want. It's lovely to have someone you can trust livin' close by, don't you think?'

'How close?' asked Jo suspiciously.

'Our room is just down the road from his,' replied Margo, 'so I'm sure we'll be seein' a lot of him, as well as yourselves.'

'Margo definitely will,' said Libby absently, 'because I think Tom's rather keen on her. He's even asked her out on a date.'

'Oh, so he's more Margo's friend,' said Jo. Shooting Margo a reproving glance, she added, 'Or should I say boyfriend?'

Donny eyed Margo as though he thought her to be loose. 'Bit risqué, isn't it? Meeting some feller off the train and goin' to his house. He could be anyone for all you know.'

Margo fought back the urge to point out that Donny and Jo were also strangers, and were far less trustworthy in her eyes than Tom. Instead, she said, 'He's not my boyfriend, he's a friend who's asked me out for dinner, that's all.' Seeing the withering look on Donny's face, she continued, 'Not like Libby's Jack.'

Jo gave Libby an enquiring glance. 'Jack?'

'He's a friend of mine from London,' said Libby. 'He's the one who helped me when I lost my parents – well, him and Mrs Fortescue, of course, and Gordon, he's Jack's father; they were all brilliant.'

'They all thought the world of you,' said Margo firmly, 'especially Jack. I reckon he'd climb a mountain for Libby. Which reminds me . . .' she switched her attention to Jo, 'do you have a pencil and paper which Libby could use to let Jack know where she's stayin'? Only he was insistent on knowin', what with her bein' in a different city an' all.'

Donny got to his feet. 'I've got some. Wait here and I'll fetch it for you.' He disappeared for a moment before returning with a grubby-looking scrap of paper, an envelope, and a pencil. 'There you go.'

Libby took the paper and wrote their new address on it, as well as a quick note to let Jack know that everything was all right, before sealing it in the envelope and writing his address on the front.

Donny held his hand out for the envelope. 'I'm goin' to the post office first thing tomorrer, so I can stick a stamp on it for you then.'

Libby made to pass him the envelope before drawing it back. 'It's all right, I can do it on my way to work.'

Margo could've crowed with delight. *If Libby's wantin' to post that letter herself, it's because she doesn't trust him to do it, which can only mean one thing. I'm not the only one who smells a rat.*

Libby also had reason to be cautious when it came to her aunt and uncle, but only because they reminded her of her father's brother. *Tony's only interested in one thing*, thought Libby, *and that's money. Whilst I don't wish to believe ill of my aunt and uncle, I need to be sure that they genuinely want to mend bridges. After all, they didn't speak to my mother for a long time, so it seems odd that they're welcoming me into their lives with open arms now she's gone. On the other hand, maybe that's why? But either way, there's only one way to be sure.* She cleared her throat. 'You've been so kind offering to put us up, but it's important that I learn to stand on my own two feet, because it's unfair to rely on handouts.'

Donny waved this off as inconsequential. 'You're family. There's no such thing as handouts when you're family.'

'It's very kind of you to say so, but I know my parents wouldn't want me to sponge off you, and neither do I, which is why we got ourselves jobs sharpish. I've not got much left of the five bob that my uncle gave me, and once that's gone I really will be up the creek without a paddle.' Seeing a slight flicker cross her uncle's face, Libby went on to explain how the van had been stolen from outside her parents' house, finishing with: 'Whoever stole that van took everything. All I have is the clothes I stand up in.'

Donny was eyeing Libby doubtfully. 'And you say Tony gave you the money?'

'It seems as though he was really keen to see the back of me,' said Libby.

Margo braced herself for Jo and Donny's reaction as they exchanged glances. *If I'm right, and they're up to no good, then they'll chuck her out on her ear without so much as a backward glance,* thought Margo, but to her surprise Jo appeared to empathise with her niece.

'Poor love,' she cooed. 'Well, you won't get that reaction from me or your Uncle Donny, will she, love?'

Donny, who hadn't taken his eyes off Jo until that moment, looked at Libby. 'She's family now, warts an' all.'

Flooded with relief that she had got hold of the wrong end of the stick, Libby felt her cheeks colour at having mistrusted them. *Just because they remind me of Uncle Tony, doesn't mean to say they're bad people. I shouldn't have jumped to conclusions.*

They spent the next hour or so discussing the war, and the tragedies it had brought, and Margo thought that this was the first time she had seen Donny speak openly.

'The lot of 'em want bleedin' shootin',' he snarled, 'comin' over here with their bombs, targetin' innocent folk.'

'You've not seen much of it in Liverpool though?' asked Libby hesitantly.

'Not like your lot down south,' said Donny, 'but I dare say it's only a matter of time, what with Liverpool bein' such a busy port an' all.'

Margo looked dubious. 'Do you really think they'll come this far?'

'Of course!' scoffed Donny. 'He won't stop until he wins.'

Fearing that their pot of gold might go up in flames, Jo asked, 'Do you know where the nearest shelter is to your new place?'

'Mrs Brixton told us, just in case she was in bed when we got back.' Looking out of the window, Libby got to her feet. 'Speakin' of bed, we'd best make a move before it gets too dark.'

Donny and Jo bade the girls goodnight, with Donny offering to walk them home, but only after being nudged by Jo, Margo noticed.

'It's all right,' said Libby. 'It won't take us long to get back.' Bidding them goodbye, the girls set out into the chilly night.

'I know we said we'd be all right,' said Margo, 'but it looks a lot different in the dark. Are you sure you can find your way?'

'Positive. Besides, I don't know what I'd have said to him, had it just been the three of us, do you?'

'Not really,' admitted Margo, 'more because I don't think your relatives like me very much.'

'I think they don't trust you as much as you don't trust them,' said Libby evenly, 'and I must admit I had my own doubts for a while, which is why I wanted them to know that there was no inheritance.'

'I thought as much, and I must say I don't blame you,' said Margo.

'It didn't seem to deter them any,' said Libby, 'so I can only assume that they're genuine, and that they really do want to make a go of things.'

'Why do you think it is they don't like me?' asked Margo curiously. 'I know I'm not exactly crazy about them either, but I've got good reason to be suspicious.'

'I think it's because they don't know you,' said Libby slowly. 'I know they don't know me either, but I'm their niece, so I s'pose that makes it okay.'

'They didn't like the idea of Tom and Jack either,' said Margo. 'Your uncle more or less called me a scarlet woman when you said I had a boyfriend.'

'A bit prudish, perhaps?' suggested Libby. 'And I hate to admit it, but they were right in sayin' that we shouldn't have gone to the house of someone we hardly knew.'

'But you can see that Tom's genuine from a mile away,' insisted Margo, adding in the privacy of her own mind, *not like them*.

Libby continued to walk in silent contemplation. Why was it that total strangers such as Tom and Jack appeared more trustworthy than her own relatives? Was she judging them purely on their living conditions, or was she right to feel ill at ease with her seemingly doting aunt and uncle? *Things would be a lot easier if I knew why Mum distanced herself from the O'Connells in the first place*, thought Libby, *because I can't imagine what could be so bad that they didn't want to see their own grandchild*. She turned to Margo. 'My grandparents died, yet my aunt didn't see fit to tell her sister.'

Margo followed Libby up the steps to the B&B. 'I wonder what your mother's reaction would've been had the shoe been on the other foot?'

Libby turned the key in the lock and the girls entered the warmth of the guest house. 'Obviously I can't say for certain,' she said as she drew the scarf from around her neck, 'but I always felt as though it was them who didn't want anything to do with my mother, and not the other way round.'

'If your mother wore her heart on her sleeve then they probably realised that she didn't approve of the way they lived,' Margo suggested, 'and in response they kept her at arm's length, rather than be judged?'

'But she can't have thought that badly of them,' reasoned Libby, ''cos they all lived together under the same roof when my dad came up to Liverpool.'

Not wanting to back Libby's aunt, but at the same time wanting to be fair, Margo spoke her mind. 'Thinking back, your aunt did say that she'd let things slide since losin' her parents. Which makes it sound as though she used to be different?'

Libby led the way up the stairs to the room they were sharing at the back of the house. 'Hard to say when I never knew what she was like before they died.'

'It's still early days,' said Margo. 'Once we get to know them better we might change our tune. Besides, it's not as if you've got anythin' to lose.'

Apart from a family, thought Libby, *because if they do turn out to be wrong 'uns, then I'm no better off here than I was in London.*

Back in the court, Donny addressed Jo, who was staring out of the window. 'Do you think she was speakin' the truth? Or do you think she were testin' the waters, cos personally I believe the latter.'

'She was certainly speakin' true about the van,' conceded Jo, 'but I don't believe for a minute that she's not got a penny to her name. Cos if that was the case she'd have stayed put.'

'Maybe. But what if she is tellin' the truth, and she really hasn't got a pot to pee in?'

'If Tony could afford to buy her father's business, then what happened to the money? I bet Reggie wasn't stupid enough to keep that in the back of the van.'

Removing a tobacco pouch from his pocket, Donny proceeded to roll himself a cigarette. 'So, you think she's bein' cautious?'

'Too bloomin' right I do. Why else d'you think that Margo's stuck to her side? You mark my words, those two know each other better than they're lettin' on.'

Donny lit the tapered edge of his cigarette as he thought this through. 'So, where do we go from here?'

'That's easy. We bide our time and gain her trust. If Reggie Gilbert had enough money to move his family halfway across the country, forkin' out on rent for a house as well as a shop, then Libby's got more than a five-bob note.'

He glanced at the boxes in the hallway. Having the girls calling by any time they liked could prove to be more of an inconvenience than it was worth. 'What's wrong with the money we earn now?'

'It keeps us livin' in squalor,' said Jo, adding vehemently, 'plus I'm sick an' tired of waitin' for the scuffers to come knockin' on me door. Quite frankly, I'm gettin' too old for this crap, especially when there's an easier way of earnin' some proper dough!'

FEBRUARY 1941

The girls had been in Liverpool for a couple of months, and their life was panning out just as Libby had hoped it would. Mr Soo had proved an excellent employer, as long as they were prepared to work hard, and boy oh boy, did the girls earn their keep. From stoking the coke fire beneath the large cauldron to ironing the stiff collars with the heavy flat irons, they worked from dawn to late in the evening, sometimes not finishing until eight or nine o'clock at night, but the pay of £2.50 a week kept a roof over their heads and food in their bellies. Libby had worried at first that she and Margo might bump heads, once they got to know each other better, but their friendship only deepened and Libby found Margo to be great company. No longer fearing her father's wrath, Margo was rarely seen without a smile on her face.

'This is the first time I've known what it's like not to live in fear of goin' home,' she had said as the girls made their way back from work late one night. 'No worryin' meself sick that me dad's goin' to throw a wobbler because a horse has thrown a shoe mid-race, or fallen at the first hurdle.'

Libby tucked her arm through Margo's. 'I've said it before, and I'll say it again, it was fate that brought us together. You're not the only one who's benefited from a change of scenery. Not havin' permanent reminders of my parents everywhere I look has come as a real breath of fresh air. And if I hadn't bumped into you, I very much think I'd be livin' with my aunt and uncle.'

'A fate worse than death,' Margo concluded, much to Libby's amusement. 'Well, it would be!' she insisted above Libby's snorts of laughter. 'I don't know what your aunt did with that bottle of bleach we bought, but she sure as hell didn't use it for cleanin'.'

'They must have guts like iron eatin' off them plates,' Libby grimaced. 'I can excuse anybody for not havin' money, but elbow grease is free. As we've gotten to know them better, I do wonder how honest she was about my grandparents' passing bein' the reason for her lack of get up and go.'

'Her get up and go got up and went a long time ago if you ask me,' said Margo. 'I know they're your relatives, Lib, and believe me, they're angels compared to my old man, but I find it increasingly hard to believe you're actually related. Your mother must've been very different to the rest of her family.'

'Chalk and cheese,' said Libby. 'Bit like you and your dad I suppose.'

'Ain't that the truth.'

'How do you feel now that it's been a while since you saw him?'

Margo cocked her head to one side as she mulled this over. When she was living in London her whole life had revolved around trying to keep her father happy. If he was in a good mood he would laugh and joke, perhaps even ruffle the top of her hair with his hand, but with his mood depending on his wins these occurrences were increasingly rare. Aware that

Libby was awaiting her response, she spoke her true thoughts. 'The idea of goin' back to London fills me with dread, because I know what I'd be goin' back to. Even though the city is huge, I'd be forever in fear of bumpin' into him, or someone who knows him, and gawd only knows what he'd do when he got his hands on me. I've tried to imagine scenarios where he'd welcome me with open arms, tellin' me how he's free of his gamblin' habit, and that he's sorry that he ever raised a finger to me, but in truth I can't see how that would ever happen, because he's in debt up to his ears. He can't possibly work his way out of it, so he keeps gamblin', hopin' to win his way out, but that just makes everythin' worse. I had thought about bringin' him up here to live with us at once stage, but you can't teach an old dog new tricks, and I know he'd continue to bet up here, striking up a whole new debt.'

'A leopard never changes its spots,' said Libby, 'but if you really wanted to give it a try, you know I'd have your back.'

'I know you would, but if I'm completely honest I don't want him here. I'm truly happy, Lib, and I don't think I've felt that way in my whole life. The thought of bein' with me dad again makes me want to run and hide. Is that awful for me to say? I know you'd do anything to have your folks back.'

'But my parents weren't like yours,' said Libby. 'If they were then I dare say I'd feel the same as you. So no, you're not bein' awful, you're simply tellin' the truth, and there's nowt wrong with that.'

'Thanks, Lib. I knew I could rely on you to tell me whether I'm doin' the right thing.'

'And what about your date with Tom? Have you thought about that much?'

Margo rolled her eyes. 'I've thought of nowt else – and stop callin' it a date, cos it's just two friends goin' out for a meal.'

'Whatever you say,' chuckled Libby. 'But that aside, what are your thoughts?'

'That you can do my hair, and I'll wear me dungarees . . .' She giggled at the look of shock on Libby's face. 'I'm only teasin'. I'll wear that frock, the one I bought off Paddy's market.' She hesitated, a worried look crossing her face. 'You don't think he'll try and kiss me good night, do you? Only I've never been kissed before, and I wouldn't know what to do.'

'We've already discussed this. Tom's a wonderful chap, and a gentleman to boot,' said Libby assuredly. 'He won't do anything that he doesn't think you'll be comfortable with.'

Margo eyed Libby curiously. 'You've been kissed. What was it like? I've always imagined it to be rather disgusting myself.'

Libby roared with laughter. 'I'm not sure I'm the best person to ask, because it was a spur of the moment thing, and in truth it felt a bit clumsy at first, but . . .' she sighed wistfully as she recalled the feeling of euphoria which swept her body as their kiss deepened, 'heavenly once I relaxed. If I were to pick anyone for you to have your first kiss with, then I'd pick Tom, because I know he'll be kind.'

Margo pushed the key into the lock and opened the door of their flat. Bending down she picked up an envelope which had arrived while they were at work. 'Ooo,' she cooed, 'I bet it's from Jack.'

Libby turned so quickly the two girls collided, causing Margo to laugh. 'Blimey, you're keen.'

'Of course I am. I've not heard from him since I left Liverpool.' Hurrying over to windows, she let out a cry of pain as she stubbed her toe on one of the chairs. 'Flamin' blackout,' she muttered as she hastily drew the blinds. She gave Margo the thumbs up and within moments the small flat was illumined.

Slitting the envelope open with her fingers, Libby sat down to read the letter, which was indeed from Jack.

Dearest Libby,

I can't tell you how glad I am to hear you reached Liverpool safe and sound and that you've already found yourself a job as well as accommodation. I'm just shy of two months into my thirteen-week training, and I'm loving every minute of it, although it would be even better if you were here with me!

I was happy to learn that you found your relatives, but sad to hear that they aren't what you were expecting, although I suppose that's family for you! As for another letter, I've only received one, so I'm guessing the other must have got lost somewhere along the line.

Libby paused in her reading. When they had left her aunt and uncle's on the first night they were in Liverpool, she had forgotten to take the letter she had written to Jack, but when she returned to see them the next day her aunt had assured her that her uncle had sent it, as promised, that very morning. Having waited a couple of weeks for a reply, Libby had decided to send another letter, just in case the last one had got lost in the post. She knew that Margo believed her aunt to be lying and that they'd thrown the letter away, but as she'd said at the time, they could hardly go throwing accusations when they had no proof. She turned her attention back to the letter in her hand.

Hopefully things will be better now that you can write to me at my barracks. I've spoken to my corp, and he said we'll all be due a week's leave as soon as we've finished training. If it's all right with you and Margo, I'd very much like to spend my leave in Liverpool. I'm sure I won't have too much bother finding a B&B near where you're living, and it would be wonderful to see you again.

Libby continued to read the letter, which told of the awful food, the early morning exercise no matter the weather, and the sound of young recruits crying softly in their beds at night. *I think some of them have lied about their age,* wrote Jack, *because you can tell they've never slept away from home a day in their life, making it all the harder when they're hundreds of miles away from everyone they know and love. Me and some of the other lads have taken them under our wing, but we're no replacement for the warmth of a mother's love.* Libby's heart ached at the thought of those poor young boys. She was grateful they had someone like Jack fighting their corner, but she still wished he was here with her in Liverpool. *But he will be soon enough,* Libby told herself, *because I shall write back to him saying yes!*

Having placed the kettle on to boil, Margo was preparing two corned beef sandwiches for their tea. 'Is he all right?' she called from the other side of the room.

Libby fielded a happy tear with her forefinger as she got up from her seat. 'He's wonderful! And what's more, he's comin' to see us as soon as he gets his leave.'

Margo gave a small whoop of delight as she walked towards Libby with the plate of sandwiches. 'I can't wait to meet him. Perhaps we could go on a double date: you, me, Tom and Jack?'

Libby hastily swallowed the mouthful of sandwich she had just taken before replying with glee. 'Sounds good to me, although are you sure it would be a date, and not just friends goin' out for a meal?' she asked teasingly.

'Ah! But Tom and I will have had our meal out by the time Jack arrives, and I should know a lot more by then.'

'How so?'

Margo paused, her sandwich poised before her lips. 'If Tom and I do kiss, then I'll know that we're courtin',' came her simple reply.

Libby took another mouthful of her sandwich and chewed it thoughtfully. She and Jack had kissed, and he had assumed that this meant they were courting. Finishing her mouthful, she said as much to Margo.

'I agree,' replied Margo. 'You only smooch someone if you're courtin'. For example, how many other men have you kissed?

'None!' exclaimed Libby, shocked that Margo should ask. 'I don't go round kissin' people willy-nilly.'

'Exactly!' said Margo. 'And that's why I think it makes you a couple.'

Libby thought back to the kiss, and how when Jack was apologising she had swooped in to seal the deal, as it were. She told Margo, who was grinning.

'Wowzers! Talk about takin' the bull by the horns!'

'I know! I doubt I'd do the same again; I wouldn't have the guts. Come to think, I don't know what I'll do when I see him next.'

'I expect he'd rather like it if you greeted him the same way you said your goodbyes,' chuckled Margo, 'only this time I rather think he'll not be so shy about things.'

'It's lovely havin' someone I can trust, to talk things through with. We go together like a needle and thread, you and me.'

Margo beamed. 'I feel the exact same way. I'm so glad it was you in that train and not some other person.'

'My thoughts exactly,' said Libby. She finished her sandwich and tucked the letter into her pocket before heading over to pour the tea. 'My aunt wants me to go round for supper this Saturday. Do you mind?'

Grimacing, Margo placed her dish in the sink along with Libby's. 'Not if you buy fish and chips and eat them out the wrapper! I don't fancy comin' home after goin' out for a meal with Tom and findin' you locked in the lavvy with a dose of the trots!'

'That's a good idea,' agreed Libby, who didn't particularly want to eat anything which her aunt had prepared. 'I can take a bottle of lemonade with me, so that I don't have to keep makin' excuses when they offer me a cuppa.'

'I'll never forget fishin' that cigarette butt out of my tea,' said Margo, pulling a disgusted face. 'I'm sure your uncle put it in on purpose, cos he doesn't like me goin' round.'

Libby's cheeks bloomed, mainly because she too had wondered whether her uncle had planted the butt. It was either that or her aunt hadn't so much as looked into the cups, let alone washed them. 'I'm surprised you didn't throw up,' she said. 'I think I would've.'

Margo shuddered. 'I was rather surprised myself.' As she spoke, she recalled how Libby's uncle, far from being embarrassed, had looked as though he was trying to stop himself from smirking. Not that she'd ever say so to Libby of course, because even though both girls knew Libby's relatives weren't desirable, they were still family.

Eyeing her friend thoughtfully, Libby made up her mind. 'You know, it mightn't be a bad idea to be on my own with them, because that way I can see if they behave differently when you're not around.'

'You're hopin' they'll show their true colours?'

'Yep. I don't think they've been themselves the whole time we've been in Liverpool. Almost as if they're puttin' on airs and graces.'

Margo choked on a chuckle. 'Airs and graces? I think not.'

'You know what I mean,' said Libby. 'It's like they're actin', but maybe that's because you're with me. Maybe they'll be different when I'm on my own. I've always had this feeling that they want to ask me summat, but won't because you're there, although what they would want to ask is beyond me. I've already told them I've got nothing to offer.'

'Well just you make sure you tell them that I know where you are.'

Libby laughed. 'What do you think they're goin' to do? Bonk me over the head and chuck me in the Mersey?'

'Depends on how you answer the question,' said Margo. She had meant it as a joke, but as soon as the words left her lips both girls fell silent.

'You can't seriously think they're dangerous?' asked Libby slowly, a look of incredulity on her face.

'Every time we go round there's a fresh stack of boxes in the hall,' said Margo, 'and your uncle is forever gettin' up to answer the back door; making sure, I might add, that he closes it behind him, so that we can't hear what's bein' said.'

'But what on earth could any of that have to do with me?'

'I guess you'll find that out come Saturday night!' replied Margo darkly. 'People like that don't like folk askin' questions, so just you tread careful.'

As Libby wiped the tea towel over the plates she tried to think what her aunt and uncle could want from her. *They know you've got no money, cos you've told them*, she thought, *and you'd not be workin' all the hours God sends down at Mr Soo's if you had a sizeable inheritance.* She shook the thought from her mind. Whatever it was her relatives wanted, she would find out on Saturday night, and that was an end to it.

It was the evening of Margo's first meal with Tom, and Libby was fussing over her friend like a mother hen.

'You look beautiful, Margo,' she cooed as she stood back to admire her friend.

A warm glow sweeping her neckline, Margo waved a dismissive hand. 'Anyone looks good if they're in a posh frock instead of boots and dungarees.'

'Only you looked good in them too,' said Libby. 'Tom certainly thought so.'

Margo glanced nervously at the clock. 'Oh gawd, he's goin' to be here in five minutes . . .' She fell silent as Tom rapped his knuckles against the door to their flat.

'Margo? It's me, Tom. I know I'm a bit early, but I must've walked faster than I realised.'

'Cos he's excited to see you!' Libby hissed.

Margo held a hand to her stomach, which was performing cartwheels. 'I think I'm goin' to throw up.'

Libby eyed her friend sympathetically. 'Do you want me to get the door?'

'Would you mind? Only I could really do with the lavvy.'

'That'll be the nerves,' said Libby. 'Get you gone, and I'll see to Tom.'

When Libby opened the door, she was overwhelmed by a strong smell of aftershave. Tom stood in the aperture, a nervous grin plastered on his cheeks. 'Hello, Libby.'

'Hello, Tom. Come on in, Margo won't keep you long.'

Tom ran an anxious finger around the collar of his shirt as he stepped into the flat. 'Am I awfully early?'

'Only five minutes,' said Libby. She glanced at his wrist. 'Isn't your watch workin'?'

'I forgot to wind it,' said Tom ruefully. As he spoke, he was looking around for a clock, which he eventually spied above the mantel. Slipping his watch off his wrist he set the correct time, and wound it sufficiently. 'Is Margo still gettin' ready?'

'A few last-minute necessities,' said Libby, before being interrupted by Margo, who coughed politely, alerting them to her presence. Libby stood to one side, and Margo walked forward shyly.

Tom let out a soft, low whistle as he took in her appearance. 'Wowee!'

Margo's cheeks reddened. 'Will I do?'

'I should say so!' replied Tom, his eyes dancing.

Seeing the way Tom was gazing at Margo was melting Libby's heart. She'd known he liked her, but she hadn't realised how much until this moment. 'Where are you taking her?' she asked, as Margo collected her coat from her room.

'I thought we could go to the Grafton, and then on to Byrom's for our supper. Unless you'd rather do summat else, Margo?'

'That'll be just grand,' replied Margo. 'I've been wantin' to dance at the Grafton for some time.'

He beamed proudly. 'Splendid! I promise I won't have you back too late.'

Libby banished the smirk which was threatening to stretch her cheeks. Margo might have been unsure as to whether she and Tom were going on a date, but there wasn't a doubt in Libby's mind that they were on one. *I'm not sure whether tonight will be Margo's first kiss*, mused Libby, as the pair headed for the door, *because I think this is Tom's first date, judgin' by the sweat beadin' his brow.*

Margo half-turned to give her a small wave goodbye. 'Look after yourself, Lib,' she said, before mouthing silently, 'I'll fill you in later.'

Closing the door behind them, Libby turned her thoughts to how wonderful it was going to be when Jack came to visit. *We shall go to the Grafton every night, and we shall eat fish 'n' chips on the overhead railway whilst lookin' out to sea.*

She gave an inward chuckle as she remembered how Mr Soo's wife had given the two girls dancing lessons. *They have to be the best employers a girl could ask for*, thought Libby. *They know that we arrived in Liverpool in difficult circumstances, and they've made it their duty to treat us like family, teaching us all the things our parents never had the chance to do.* She rolled her eyes. Her own parents would indeed have prepared Libby for life on her own, had they known what was coming, but she very much doubted Margo's parents would have done the same. *They didn't want Margo to be independent, because she'd be able to look after herself,* thought Libby now, *but truth be told, Margo has a better chance of survivin' on her own than with her so-called parents.*

Keeping her fingers crossed that the air-raid siren wouldn't sound during Margo's first date, Libby settled down to read Agatha Christie's *The Murder at the Vicarage*, whilst contemplating whether a book about murder was a good idea after her conversation with Margo a few days previous.

It was much later that same evening and Libby had bought fish and chips for three before heading over to her aunt and uncle's. Worried that they might take offence that she had taken it upon herself to supply the food, she was relieved to learn they were pleased with her decision.

'No Margo?' said Jo, adding sarcastically, 'I thought the two of you were joined at the hip.'

'She's on a date with Tom,' answered Libby, a trifle defensively.

Jo looked to Donny. 'Two's company?'

The two stared at each other intently, before Donny broke away. 'I've got some business to attend to, but thanks for the chips, Libby. I'll take 'em with me, if it's all right with you?'

Relieved that her uncle, who always made her feel uncomfortable, was leaving her and Jo to it, Libby gestured for him to take the food. 'Fine by me. I hope you enjoy them.'

Thanking her again, Donny left, chips in hand.

'Plate?' said Jo. She lifted some boxes aside and began to search for a couple of plates.

'Not for me, thanks. I think they taste better out of the wrapper, plus it saves on the washin' up,' said Libby, adding in the privacy of her own head, *not that you appear to do any.*

Aborting her hunt for dishes, Jo took her portion from Libby and sat down. Indicating for Libby to take the chair opposite, she popped a chip into her mouth. 'Thanks for these. It's rare me and Donny get a treat like this.'

'It's my pleasure,' said Libby. 'It's a shame Donny has to eat his on the go.'

Jo selected a chip. 'I'm glad you've come on your own,' she said. 'It'll give us a chance to get to know one another a bit better.'

Libby eyed her curiously. 'And is that the only reason? Only I've got the impression that you don't seem that fussed on Margo.'

Jo felt her cheeks warm. She'd spoken somewhat frankly when Libby announced that Margo wouldn't be joining them, but it was too late to revoke her words now, so she said the first thing that entered her mind.

'I'm sorry, Lib, but me and Donny don't trust her.'

Having half-expected her aunt to make up some sort of lie, Libby was floored to hear her aunt admit what she had. 'Why on earth not?' she gasped. 'I can't see that Margo's done anythin' to make you feel that way.'

Jo chewed the large mouthful she had taken in order to buy her time to think. It was true that she and Donny didn't trust Margo, but only because they suspected that she was after Libby's money, much the same as themselves. Her mind worked feverishly as she tried to come up with something that didn't give away their own intentions, eventually settling on: 'We can't understand why she didn't get on the next train back to Liverpool. Not if her story is true, and she fell asleep aboard the carriage by accident; something which Donny in particular questions.'

Libby stared at her aunt, a tweak of incredulity etched on her lips. 'You actually think she stowed away on the same train as me, and only pretended to have fallen asleep by accident? What would be the point in her doin' that?'

'I bet a lot of people knew you were movin' to Norwich,' said Jo. 'If Margo got wind of your parents' fate, she might have latched on to you with the sole purpose of gettin' her mitts on your inheritance.'

Libby was astounded by her aunt's misconception. 'That can't possibly be the case, because anyone who knew about my parents also knew about their stuff bein' stolen. I wasn't exactly shy about spreadin' the word, because I rather hoped I might get our things back. If Margo was only befriendin' me for money, then she's been ill informed, to say the least.'

Jo stared at Libby. Was she telling the truth? She could hardly accuse her of lying with no proof, but none of this was adding up. *I reckon it's a cover story because she knows we know the truth, and probably that bloomin' Margo does too.*

They spent the next hour discussing Libby's life since coming to Liverpool and how it compared to London. At last, Libby, using the excuse that she wanted to be home before it got too late, bade her aunt goodbye and headed off into the dark. As she walked, she found her mind wandering back to Jo, and what it was about her body language that seemed so non-genuine. Picturing her aunt, Libby came to the conclusion that it was the glint in her eyes. *It's almost as though she's bustin' at the seams to call me a liar.* She recalled the day her aunt had broken down in tears at hearing the news about Reggie and Orla. *The two don't add up*, thought Libby. *I know she's had a couple of months to come to terms with the news, but I've had longer, and yet not a day goes by without me havin' a good cry. My aunt has lost her sister, and she'll never get the chance to make amends. You'd think that would be hard to live with, yet she doesn't seem to give it a moment's thought, or if she does, she certainly doesn't let it show.*

Libby was getting ready for bed much later that evening, when Margo returned. She only had to take one look at her friend's face to know that she'd had the time of her life.

'I could've danced all night!' sighed Margo as she slipped the scarf from around her neck. 'Tom was the perfect gentleman – just as you said he would be – and an excellent dancer to boot.'

Unable to bear the suspense, Libby asked the question uppermost in her thoughts. 'So, what happened when he bade you goodnight. Did you kiss?'

'A lady never tells!' giggled Margo.

'Pish!' retorted Libby. 'Once you've spilled the beans, I'll tell you about my visit to my aunt's.'

Margo sank down on the chair next to Libby's, eager to hear the news. 'He kissed me good night. Now what happened at your aunt's?'

Libby rolled her eyes. 'You can't tell me that he kissed you without goin' into the nitty gritty.'

Margo fought to keep the amusement from invading her cheeks. 'Tom swept me off my feet! And kissin' him was nothin' like kissin' a sink plunger . . .' she waited for Libby to stop laughing before continuing, 'not that I've ever kissed a sink plunger, mind you. Seriously, it was nothin' short of wonderful! His lips were as soft as a feather, and it wasn't at all wet and sloppy like I feared.'

Libby coddled Margo's hand in hers. 'I'm so pleased for you, Margo; you deserve to have a good man in your life after the rotten childhood you've had.'

Margo's cheeks tinged pink. 'Best thing I ever did, stowin' away on that mail carriage.'

Libby cast her eyes towards the ceiling. 'Don't let my aunt hear you say that, or she'll be more determined than ever that it was all part of your plan to get your hands on my non-existent inheritance.'

Margo stared at her open-mouthed. 'She said that?'

'I'm afraid so. I asked her why she didn't like you, and that was her reply. That she and Donny didn't trust you—'

'That's rich,' snapped Margo, adding more sullenly, 'as well as insultin'.'

'I know; and don't worry, because I put her right.'

'But why would they think I was after your inheritance when they *know* your parents left you with nothin'?'

Libby shot her a shrewd look. 'In short, they didn't believe I'd literally been left with nothin', but that was partly my fault, because I hadn't told them about that so-called fire.'

Margo leaned forward in her seat. 'So, what did she say when you put her right?'

'Not a lot really. I'm not entirely convinced she believed me!'

'Judgin' me by her own standards,' said Margo, 'that's what I reckon.'

'I'm afraid you're probably right, but as you can't get blood from a stone she's goin' to be in for one hell of a disappointment.'

Margo nodded briskly. 'Serves her right.' Standing up, she stretched audibly, covering a yawn with the palm of her hand. 'At least we know why they've been a bit off with me, because I was beginnin' to think there was summat deeper goin' on.'

'I don't believe they care about my mother as much as they first pretended,' agreed Libby, 'although I suppose that's obvious, because if they thought that much of her, they'd have made more of an effort to come and see us.'

Margo spoke from over her shoulder as she put the kettle on to boil. 'So, you think it was more a case of them not wantin' to see your mother, rather than the other way round? Because after meetin' them for the first time, I rather thought it would be the other way round.'

Libby laughed. 'I know what you mean, but I've thought about it long and hard, and Mum never had a bad word to say against her family – which is surprisin', all things considered.'

'Especially when you know how she used to feel about your other uncle, cos from what you've told me she didn't have a good word to say about him, yet he sounds like he's been cut from the same cloth as Jo and Donny.'

Margo poured the tea, telling Libby how she and Tom had danced the night away, and how Mrs Soo's lessons had proved invaluable on the dance floor. Listening with half an ear, Libby found her mind wandering. *There's summat wrong as far as my aunt and uncle are concerned*, she thought. *I can't put my finger on what it is, but when I do, I'm sure that everything will make sense!*

Chapter Seven

Libby stood on the platform at Central Station, waiting for Jack's train to arrive. Looking along the track, she felt her heart leap as an engine came into view. She couldn't wait to see him in his uniform, and to hear everything that the censors had blocked out from his letters. Most of it she could figure out on her own, but some of the things had left her and Margo quite puzzled.

Stamping her feet in order to keep warm, she fiddled with her fingernails as she waited for the carriages to roll by. Nervous that their time apart might have changed things between them, she was relieved to feel her fears melt away as soon as she laid eyes on him waving madly at her from the train window.

He's just as I remembered only better, she thought. *It must be the uniform. He's always been handsome, but the uniform definitely adds a certain something. I should imagine he's not short of female admirers.* Then the train came to a halt, and she felt her heartbeat quicken as Jack descended onto the platform.

He strode towards her, a broad grin gracing his cheeks. 'Hello, Treacle.' Placing his bag on the ground, he picked her up in his arms and swung her around before gently placing her back down. When his lips met hers, Libby felt a tingle run through her body as his hand gently caressed the nape of her neck. Wishing the moment could last for ever, she was disappointed when he broke away.

Gazing at her with deep affection, he cupped her cheek in his hand. 'It's *so* good to see you.'

'You too. I must say you look awfully handsome in your smart blue uniform,' said Libby, her voice dripping with admiration. 'A real bobby-dazzler.'

He grinned, revealing a gleaming set of straight white teeth. 'I'm pleased to hear I pass muster.'

'You do indeed,' said Libby. 'What did your dad say when he saw you? I bet he was proud as punch.'

'He certainly was. I felt bad leavin' him though, cos I know he misses havin' me around.'

'Your poor father.' Libby grimaced guiltily. 'I feel awful now.'

'Don't be daft. He wants me to be happy, and if seein' you makes me happy, then that's fine by him.' He paused momentarily before continuing. 'Plus, I know he's also had some concerns about how you're gettin' on, so my bein' here will help to put his mind at ease.'

'It's lovely of him to care,' said Libby, 'but me and Margo are doin' just fine. I can't wait for you to see the flat.'

Jack picked up his kitbag and swung it over his left shoulder. 'I think you've done marvellously,' he said. 'Are we goin' there first?'

'We can if you want?'

He placed his arm around her waist. 'I'd like that very much. I'll admit I was really worried when you left London with next to nothin' in yer pocket, but you've certainly proved that you can look after yourself!'

'I couldn't have done it without Margo,' said Libby. 'It was a real stroke of luck, her bein' on the same train as me.'

'I must say, I felt happier knowin' you had someone watchin' yer back, because I got the impression your Liverpudlian relatives were akin to your Uncle Tony.'

'Like peas in a pod. It's hard to believe my mother's from the same family. Still, though Jo and Donny might be dodgy, at least they haven't turned their backs on me like *he* did.'

'Do you see much of them?'

'Not really, but that's mainly down to timing. I work from mornin' to dusk, and what with them tending to do most of their business when the sun's gone down we don't get to see much of each other, but that doesn't matter because I know they're there if I need them.'

'And that's what counts,' said Jack. 'How does Margo feel about them now she knows them a little better?'

'She rarely comes with me when I go to visit, not now we know they're not goin' to bonk me over the head.'

'Why on earth would you think they'd do that?' cried Jack.

'Margo worried they might be after my non-existent inheritance,' said Libby plainly. 'Or that my probin' them for answers would make them uneasy.'

'I'm glad she's lookin' out for you.' confessed Jack. 'I can't wait to meet her.'

'Nor she you,' said Libby. 'I reckon the two of you will get on like a house on fire. Same with Tom, Margo's beau.'

'The geezer that rescued you from the train.'

'That's the one. He's a lovely chap, and he positively dotes on Margo.'

He squeezed her waist. 'I'm so glad you've got good friends to lean on. I bet your uncle would be shocked if he knew how well you were doin' for yourself.'

'I doubt he'd care.'

'Did you tell your aunt how badly he treated you?'

'Of course. Not that she seemed at all surprised, mind you. I think they're as wise to him as my mother was.'

Jack looked around him as they strolled along the paved city streets. 'I must say I didn't think Liverpool would be as impressive as this.'

Libby felt her chest swell with pride. 'I love livin' here. Everyone's so friendly, and there's a real feelin' of solidarity amongst the Scousers. As for Mr Soo, well, he's more like a friend than a boss. He and his wife have really looked after us, one way or another.'

'Of course, the dancing lessons,' said Jack. 'We'll have to put them to the test whilst I'm here.'

Libby blushed. 'It will be lovely to go somewhere like the Grafton and dance with someone other than Margo or Mrs Soo.'

He coddled her hip in his hand. 'My nan taught me to dance when I were little. She'd take me to the tea dances and tell everyone that I was her date for the afternoon.'

'You must miss her,' said Libby. 'More so because she was the only female influence in your life.'

'She was very dear to me,' said Jack. 'I hope to do her proud when we trip the light fantastic.'

'I'm sure you will,' Libby told him. 'Just remember to count, cos that's the secret.'

'Ah yes,' he said wisely, 'the old *one* two three, *one* two three. I shall have a little practice before I turn in for the night.'

Libby stopped outside the public house which was en route to the flat. 'This is the B&B where you'll be stayin'. Would you like to drop your bag off first?'

'I don't see why not,' said Jack. 'Saves me havin' to lug it around.' He entered the pub, followed closely by Libby. They headed for the bar, where he made himself known to the landlady, who motioned for him to follow her upstairs. When he reappeared a few minutes later, he found Libby waiting by the bar.

'How was your room?'

'Top notch,' said Jack. 'Clean sheets and a comfy bed, what more could a man ask for?'

She jerked her head in the direction of the kitchen. 'The food smells good. Do you fancy gettin' summat to eat here?'

His nostrils flared. 'You can't beat honest pub grub. How about we have a spot of supper here, followed by a trip to the cinema?'

Libby's heart sang. They weren't even an hour into Jack's stay, and they were already doing the things she hoped they would. 'That sounds wonderful!' she said. 'I should imagine the food here will be a bit different from the stuff they serve up in the RAF.'

Jack laughed. 'A bit different? I'm hopin' it's nothin' like the stuff they give us. I know they have a lot of mouths to feed, and it can't be easy with rationin' and all, but even so.'

'Then we must make sure you make the most of your time in Liverpool,' said Libby. 'We'll go to Lyons, and Blacklers, and Lewis's, and' – she waved her hands theatrically – 'everywhere I can think of that serves a decent bit of grub, and that's most places!'

Jack gazed at her affectionately as he stroked her cheek with the back of his fingers. 'It's lovely to see you out from under the weight you were carryin' in London. It's as though I'm gettin' to see the real Libby.'

Libby felt a warm glow enter her body as his hand travelled from her cheek to her arm. 'I certainly feel more like my old self here, but it helps to not have constant reminders of my parents everywhere I look. That and the fact that I don't have to see my uncle any more. It infuriated me to see him actin' as though nothin' had happened when my world was fallin' apart. I know some folk – particularly men – put on a stiff upper lip, and I suppose to some extent I was guilty of doin' just that, but only because I had no choice. It was either carry on or fall apart, and I couldn't afford to do the latter, because there was only me, and if I didn't look after myself no one else would.'

'I would,' said Jack loyally.

'That's very sweet of you,' said Libby gratefully, 'but it's easier said than done when you're hundreds of miles away in the RAF. I don't mean to sound as though I'm criticisin' you, because I certainly don't mean to. I'm just bein' honest. You're not here to make sure I get out of bed each mornin', or to stop me from wallowin' in my own misery.'

'But I would be if I could,' said Jack earnestly.

'I know you would, but I wouldn't want you to. You've got enough on your plate as it is without worryin' over me. Margo does a grand job, because she's in the same boat as me. Fair enough, her father's still alive, but he may as well be dead for all the use he is. Margo and me keep each other goin', and neither of us expects pity off the other, and that's how I prefer it. Because if I were to start cryin', I sometimes think I might never stop.'

Jack squeezed her fingers gently. 'You're a strong woman, Libby Gilbert. I wish I could tell your parents what a fantastic job they did at bringin' you up.'

'I'm hopin' they know,' said Libby, 'cos I'm sure I've got more than just you and Margo lookin' out for me.'

His eyes twinkled at her affectionately. 'Maybe you're right. It does seem too big a coincidence that Margo fell asleep in the same carriage as you. And I believe it was her need for shoes which prompted your trip to Paddy's market?'

'I would've gone there anyway,' said Libby, 'but I definitely had more confidence with Margo by my side.'

Jack's gaze intensified. 'You stowed away on a train, yet look at you now. A new flat, new job, new life, and all in the midst of a war. You're summat else, Libby Gilbert, I hope you know that.'

'Needs must,' said Libby shyly.

But Jack wasn't having any of it. 'Nah. You could've given up, rolled over and gone down the gutter like your aunt did when her parents passed, but you didn't. You stood up and fought for yerself, and that's admirable in anyone's book.'

Shy from the praise being heaped on her, Libby changed the subject. 'I wish you could stay longer than a few days, I just know the time's goin' to fly by.'

'Which is why we must make the most of every second,' said Jack. 'I don't intend to let you out of my sight for one minute.'

Libby was overjoyed to hear such words. The whole time she'd been away from Jack, she'd questioned whether her feelings for him were born purely from his rescuing her all that time ago, but now, as she sat across the table from him, gazing steadily into his eyes, she knew that it was much more than that. She loved to listen to his velvety tones, speaking slowly and calmly, as if he was fully in control. And when he looked at her, he made her feel as though she were the only woman in the room. If only her parents were still alive, Libby would think herself the luckiest woman in the world.

'Then let's get this show on the road,' she said now. 'I was perusin' the menu whilst you were bein' shown to your room and I think I'd like the scouse, because I'm pretty sure that's what I can smell cookin'.'

'Scouse!' exclaimed Jack. 'Please tell me it's not an actual Scouser!'

'It's meat and vegetable stew,' said Libby, through stifled giggles. 'And blind scouse is stew without the meat.'

He placed his hand on his heart, breathing an exaggerated sigh of relief. 'Thank goodness for that!'

'Fancy givin' it a go?'

'When in Rome,' said Jack, and beckoned to the barmaid.

Having ordered their meals, he bought them a drink each, and they selected a table by the window so that they could watch the people go by. 'So, how's life in the laundry?'

She shrugged. 'Each day is pretty much like the last, but it's warm, of course, and gettin' the sheets bright and crisp is oddly satisfyin'. Margo thinks it's the best job ever, but I imagine I'd feel the same if I'd been a shoeblack prior to this.'

'You'll have to show me where you work, as well as introduce me to your relatives, of course,' said Jack. Seeing the look of despair on Libby's face, he chuckled softly. 'Don't worry, I'm not expectin' much.'

'It's just your dad is so lovely, as is your flat, and . . .'

'As long as they have your best interests at heart, I couldn't give a fig what they're like,' said Jack mildly. 'You should know by now that you're all that matters to me.'

Libby felt herself melt in the warmth of his words. 'That really is lovely of you to say, but I wanted you to get some sense as to what my parents were like, and you can't possibly do that through them.'

Jack gazed at her affectionately. 'I can already see what they were like, through you.' Lifting her hand, he kissed the back of her knuckles whilst holding her gaze. 'They were kind, carin' people who'd give you their last penny should you be in need, just like their daughter.'

She lowered her eyes. 'You're makin' me blush.'

'It's true, though.'

She looked back up. 'Mum would do anything for anyone, and Dad was the same. Which is why I find Uncle Tony so hard to fathom.'

Jack leaned back as the waitress approached with their supper. Setting the plates down on the table, she asked if they wanted any condiments before leaving them to eat their meals in peace.

Libby watched Jack as he took his first bite. He chewed thoughtfully for a moment before giving her the thumbs up.

'It's my favourite,' said Libby as she tucked into the stew. Looking at Jack savouring the food, Libby felt a sense of pride in the city she now called home. *I'm havin' my first date in the city where my mother and father married*, she thought. *I hope our relationship is as good as theirs, because they loved each other dearly. I'd be the happiest girl in the world if I could have what they had.*

By the time they had finished their meals, neither felt they could eat another morsel, so they headed into the city and to Libby's favourite cinema, the Savoy on West Derby Road.

'They're showin' *The Thief of Bagdad*,' she enthused. 'Have you seen it yet?'

'No, but I believe it's meant to be highly entertainin'. It's had rave reviews.'

Libby slid her hand through his offered arm. 'What are the cinemas on base like? I can't imagine they're much like the Savoy.'

'Dark huts is the best way to describe them,' said Jack frankly. 'There're certainly no velvet curtains or plush cinema seats.'

'Part of the cinema experience is the atmosphere of the theatre itself, don't you think?'

'Which is why I don't frequent the ones on camp,' said Jack.

It seemed to take them no time at all to reach the Savoy, mainly because they had chattered the whole way, discussing the war, life in the RAF, and Libby's new life in Liverpool. Settling down onto the back row, she unwound her scarf from around her neck, then leaned her head against Jack's shoulder as the silver lights danced across the screen. *This must be what Margo feels like when she goes to the cinema with Tom*, she thought. *I must say, I do envy her havin' him so close by. It would be the icin' on the cake if Jack were to be posted up here, but I can't see that happenin'.*

As they watched the film, Libby noticed that she and Jack laughed or grimaced in the same places, which she supposed was a sign of their compatibility, not that she needed further proof. She had known that Jack was her knight in shining armour from the moment he had pulled her out of the Thames, and shielded her from the wrath of the old man.

Much as they had feared, the four-day break was quickly over, and it hardly seemed like any time at all before she was standing on the platform to see Jack off.

'I can't believe it's time to say goodbye already,' she sniffed as she nestled her cheek against his chest. 'I'm goin' to miss you dreadfully.'

'I'll come back as soon as I get my next leave,' promised Jack. 'And don't forget, you can always come and see me when I get based somewhere a tad more permanent.'

'I hope it's close to Liverpool,' said Libby, fielding a tear from the corner of her eye. 'We could see each other all the time then.'

Jack wrapped his arms around her. 'I'll ask my sergeant if there's any chance of me bein' posted this way, but I must be sure not to mention you.'

She frowned. 'Why not?'

'They don't like to encourage relationships,' said Jack bluntly. 'I suppose they see it as a distraction.' He gave her a cheesy grin. 'And they'd be right, cos if I was up this neck of the woods, all I'd think of is you!' He hesitated before adding, 'Although havin' said that, you're all I think about anyway, no matter where I am, so it's daft for them to think they're better off stationin' couples well apart.'

She grinned. 'A couple. That's what we are, isn't it?'

He leaned in and brushed her lips against hers. 'We most certainly are.'

As his lips gently encouraged hers to part, Libby prayed for his train to be delayed as they so often were, but hearing the sound of an approaching engine blowing its whistle she felt her heart sink. Still deep in their kiss, Jack didn't break away until he heard the porter shout, 'All aboard!'

Libby felt her tummy churn unpleasantly as he bent down to pick up his kitbag. 'Ask your sergeant as soon as you get back, won't you?' she said, standing on tiptoe to kiss him on the cheek.

'First port of call, don't you worry,' said Jack. Holding her hand in his to the last minute, he turned to give her one final embrace. As she melted into his arms, the silent tears trickled down her face as his lips met hers. At last, he pecked her briefly on the cheek before jumping into the nearest carriage.

The guard closed the door, and Jack lowered the window so that he could continue to chat to her until the last minute. 'Let me know what your sergeant says,' said Libby.

'Will do!' He leaned away from the door, before reappearing. 'And Libby?'

'Yes?'

'I love you!'

She stared at him in stunned silence, her heart filled with joy. Just hearing the words leave his lips was more than she could've hoped for.

'I love you too!' she cried, much to the delight of the people around her.

The train blew its whistle, and Libby jumped. Keeping pace as the train pulled away from the station, she kept Jack in sight, waving madly until the platform came to an end. Jack was waving back, and Libby kept everything crossed that his sergeant would see fit to post her beloved beau to somewhere nearby.

*

Jack knew he'd left it too late for a seat, so he found himself a comfy place to stand and rested his shoulder against the carriage wall. Spending time with his belle had proved to be everything he'd wished for and more besides. His father had been quite right when he said that Jack had fallen in love with Libby the moment he met her, and his biggest fear had been that the time apart had moderated her feelings, until she saw him only as a friend who'd come to her rescue in her hour of greatest need. To have her say the words he'd been longing to hear was like all his dreams come true. He had no memory of his own mother, but he felt sure she would have approved of Libby, just the same as his father.

He turned his thoughts to how much brighter Libby was now that she was no longer in London. It would be easier for him if she were to return, but he wouldn't want her back in London, if it meant she was going to be unhappy. *That bloomin' uncle of hers*, he thought irritably, *if only he'd shown a smidgen of compassion, Libby would've returned to London as soon as she'd informed her mother's family of her parents' death.* He'd only met Jo and Donny once, but as far as he was concerned once was enough. Not that he was being snobbish, but he couldn't help but feel uneasy in their presence. They'd been polite when he'd been introduced, but he could tell by the look in Donny's eyes that he'd rather be elsewhere. If Jack was to give his opinion, her uncle was only there because his wife had forced him to be. *Maybe it's because Jo's Orla's sister*, thought Jack as the train clickety-clacked along the track. *What with him only bein' related to Orla through marriage, he might not really be interested in his wife's niece. Plus, he's probably heard all the stuff that went on between Orla and her family that caused them to fall out in the first place. Not that you'd ever think there'd been a falling out if you were to listen to the way Libby's aunt talks. It's almost as though she thinks it of little relevance. But surely something so inconsequential couldn't have kept them apart for all those years? Which makes you wonder what happened. And is Libby doin' the right thing by befriendin' her? For all she knows she could be dancin' with the devil; but unless someone tells us what went on, we have to take Jo's word for everythin'.*

Careful not to appear judgemental, Jack had spoken candidly to Libby, and had been relieved to hear that she also questioned her mother's relationship with her aunt. They had been on the dance floor of the Grafton when she had passed a remark on how her mother loved to dance, but how her aunt had merely grimaced whenever she suggested she might join them.

'If I've said it once, I've said it a hundred times: you'd never believe the two of them were sisters,' said Libby as Jack guided her around the floor. 'Margo never met my mother, of course, but from what I've told her she thinks the same.'

The small lights from the glitterball skimming across his cheeks, Jack adjusted his arm around her waist, pulling her closer. 'Didn't your mother say *anythin'* regardin' her sister?'

'Not really. She was always very quiet when it came to her side of the family. The only thing she spoke passionately about was her desire *not* to return to Liverpool.'

'I know that families can be odd . . .' said Jack, pausing only briefly as Libby emitted a harrumph of agreement, 'but I find you to be plain-spoken, and I'd have thought your mother would be the same.'

'She was, on every other subject than her family. And my uncle, of course. Dad reckoned Mum and Tony rubbed each other up the wrong way, but after meetin' Mum's side of the family, I reckon her dislike of Tony stems from her feelings towards her own people.'

'But why didn't she feel the same about your father?' wondered Jack, sweeping her effortlessly around the edges of the dance floor.

'They say that love is blind, so perhaps that's the answer?'

'Maybe.' The music came to an end, and Libby and Jack gave the musicians a small round of applause before retiring to the bar and continuing their conversation.

'It's one of the things into which I wish I'd delved deeper,' Libby admitted. 'It wouldn't have been outlandish for me to insist on her takin' me to see the O'Connells; they were my grandparents, after all, but I didn't want to rock the boat or upset Mum, so I kept shtum. And now, when it's important to me to learn the truth, I haven't anyone to ask that I can trust.'

Now, as he steadied himself against the swaying wall of the carriage, he turned his thoughts back to Libby's aunt. *No matter what I think of her she's Libby's only family, and if they make her happy, then I'm happy!*

It was a fortnight after Jack's visit to Liverpool, and Libby smiled as she heard his voice come down the line.

'Hello, Treacle. How's tricks?'

'Much the same, which is fine by me,' said Libby, who craved normality, 'aside from the fact that I don't see much of Margo any more because she spends every spare second with Tom. I've not visited Jo and Donny either, but that's mainly down to my working long hours.'

'You still get some time off, though?' asked Jack hopefully.

'Every Sunday,' said Libby. 'And if I'm goin' somewhere on a Saturday night Mr Soo lets me shoot off early, but I've not done that for ages. Margo and Tom are very thoughtful, and invite me to most places, but no one wants to play gooseberry, so I tend to stay in a lot.'

'We'll soon put a stop to all that with my new postin',' said Jack, barely able to keep the excitement out of his voice.

'New postin'?' asked Libby, hope rising in her chest. 'Please tell me you're comin' to Liverpool.'

'Not quite,' said Jack, 'but I am goin' to RAF West Kirby, which is—'

'Just across the water! Oh, Jack, are you really?'

'I wouldn't say it otherwise. What's more, I didn't have to bribe anyone in order to get sent up to your neck of the woods.'

'What made them decide to send you there? Although I'm glad they did, of course.'

'They wanted someone they could trust to work on their own initiative and they thought I fitted the bill,' said Jack. 'I'm comin' up the last weekend in April.'

Libby gave a small squeal of delight. 'Oh, Jack, that's fantastic news! I know we won't be able to see each other on a daily basis, but with a bit of luck we should be able to meet up at least once a week!'

'My thoughts exactly.'

'Margo'll be thrilled. And so will Jo and Donny.'

'Do you really think they will?' asked Jack, surprised.

'I don't see why not.' Libby hesitated. 'What makes you think they wouldn't be?'

Jack had never intended to share his feelings towards her aunt and uncle, but his comment had inadvertently revealed his true thoughts. 'Ignore me. I guess they're just a little guarded when it comes to their only niece.'

'Have they said something?'

'Not per se,' said Jack; 'it's just a feelin' I got when I met them.'

'You never said owt?'

'I s'pose I didn't like to, what with them bein' your only relatives; or at least the only ones you have anythin' to do with.' He hesitated. 'I haven't upset you, have I?'

'No, but I wish you'd said summat at the time. Margo still doesn't trust them, even though they've not tried to fleece me of my non-existent inheritance, but I do so want them to be kosher.'

Kicking himself for putting doubt in Libby's mind, Jack spoke hurriedly. 'Ignore me, Lib. I'm positive your aunt and uncle have no ulterior motives. They're probably shady by nature, due to the business they're in.'

Libby roared with laughter. 'Now that I'll agree with! Whenever I suggest to Jo that I could call in on my way home from work, she looks like a rabbit caught in the headlights as she tries to find an excuse for me not to call round.'

'She must realise that you know she's up to no good. Or do you really think she's that naïve?'

'I reckon she knows all right, but it's one thing knowin' summat, and another seein' it with your own eyes.'

'Families,' said Jack. 'They certainly liven things up. Have you ever bumped into any of your aunt's associates?'

'Golly no.' A blush swept Libby's cheeks. 'I don't exactly advertise that I'm related to them, Jack. Does that make me sound mean?'

'Not at all. If I were you, I don't think I'd shout it from the rooftops either. I dare say your aunt and uncle have made their fair share of enemies due to their line of business, whatever it is, and anyone . . .' he had been about to say that anyone halfway decent would want to steer well clear of them, but changed it to 'or at least most people would be wary of the Murphys.' He twisted his lips to one side. 'It's odd that no one ever mentioned them bein' shady when you were askin' about them down the market.'

'They were hardly likely to say that when I was referring to them as my relatives,' said Libby reasonably. 'Besides which, no one knew who they were. Which is quite odd when you think about it.' She paused, as something came back to her. 'Actually, one woman told Margo that the O'Connells had moved to Ireland.'

'Did she say anything else?'

Libby screwed her forehead as she thought hard. 'Not that I can remember. Do you think I should ask Margo?'

'I think Margo would've said summat by now if she thought it were worth mentionin', don't you?'

'I suppose you're right, but it would be nice to talk to at least one other person who knew my mother's side of the family.'

'Perhaps you should ask Margo if she remembers the woman. If she does you could seek her out and see if she had anythin' to add. She might even know what led to the break-up of your mother's family.'

'Jack, I could kiss you!'

He grinned. 'Feel free!'

'As soon as you set foot in Liverpool,' promised Libby, adding, 'I shall save all my kisses for you!'

The operator cut across, letting them know their time was up.

'I can't wait,' Libby said quickly. 'We'll have to meet up the first chance we get.'

'Sounds good to me. Ta-ra, Treacle, love you to the moon and back.'

'I love you too, Jack . . .' The operator cut the call, and Libby placed her handset down. She would run Jack's idea past Margo and see what she had to say.

Making her way from the telephone box to the flat, Libby wondered why on earth she hadn't thought of Jack's suggestion sooner. *You're frightened of what you might hear. You're scared to death that someone's goin' to tell you that they're bad apples and that you should run for the hills, which is terrifyin' because you don't want them to be bad people. I know their line of business is questionable to say the least, but I'm certain that their feelin's towards me are genuine. No one can keep up an act like that for this long, especially when they know I haven't a ha'penny to my name.*

Entering the flat, she saw Margo making a cup of tea for herself and Tom, both of whom turned to greet her.

'Did you get through?' asked Margo, fetching another mug from the cupboard.

'I certainly did, and guess what? Jack's being posted to West Kirby! And he came up with the most fabulous suggestion.' She went on to tell them about his idea to contact the woman Margo had spoken to down the market, finishing, 'What do you think?'

Margo appeared uncertain. 'I think it's a fabulous idea if you want to hear the truth warts an' all, but not otherwise. How about you? What do you think?'

'The same as you,' Libby admitted, 'but as I already know they deal in dodgy stuff the only thing she might be able to tell me is the reason why they fell out with my mum, and not knowin' the answer to that is the only thing that's holdin' me back.'

Margo shrugged. 'Looks like we're takin' a trip down the market, then.'

Tom took the mug of tea from Margo and handled it to Libby. 'Come what may, you know we'll always be here for you.'

Libby sighed thankfully. 'I know you will, and you're not the only ones, cos Jack'll be here the last weekend in April.'

Margo clapped her hands together excitedly. 'Oh, Lib, that's wonderful news. You must be thrilled!'

Libby sat down on the chair opposite Tom's. 'I'm over the moon, I really am. It's goin' to be wonderful havin' him close by.

We'll be able to join the two of you on nights out to the cinema and what not.'

'With Jack coming to West Kirby, your life has certainly taken a turn for the better,' said Margo, holding her mug up. 'Cheers!'

Libby and Tom followed suit, and Libby relaxed in the knowledge that her friend was correct. It seemed as if everything was coming up roses.

1ST MAY 1941

Libby and Margo were patrolling the market in search of the woman who Margo had spoken to when they first arrived in Liverpool.

'This is better than sittin' at home twiddlin' me thumbs waitin' for six o'clock to come round,' said Libby as they wandered from one stall to the next.

'You've been like a cat on a hot tin roof these past few days,' said Margo, 'not that I can blame you, with Jack bein' closer to home . . .' She hesitated. Calling Liverpool her home always filled Margo with a sense of warm satisfaction. 'I think arrangin' to meet him and Tom in Lyons is a brilliant way to celebrate his arrival.'

'He really liked Lyons when he was here before,' said Libby, 'so I thought it only appropriate. Start as we mean to go on type of thing.'

Margo glanced at a dress which was hanging on a rail above the trader's stall. 'What are you wearin' tonight?'

'The blue dress I bought here,' said Libby promptly, 'along with my kitten heels.'

'Very nice,' said Margo, 'I'm goin' to wear the frock Tom bought for me.'

'Polka dots!' said Libby. 'I know the one.'

Margo chuckled. 'You make it sound as though I've a wardrobe full of frocks.'

'You've certainly got two more than you had when you were workin' as a shoeblack,' said Libby. She glanced at Margo. 'Lookin' at you now, I find it hard to believe that you got away with posin' as a boy for all them years.'

'That's what Tom says.' She stopped laughing abruptly as her eyes fell on the stallholder they were looking for. 'That's her over there, Lib. I'm sure of it.'

Libby felt her tummy give an unpleasant lurch. Placing her hand in Margo's, she walked forward. 'Here goes nothin'.'

Arriving at the stall, Margo cleared her throat, causing the woman to look up from her wares. 'Can I help you?'

'I chatted to you when I first arrived in Liverpool,' said Margo. 'We were lookin' for my friend's relatives at the time. I don't suppose you remember?'

The woman stared at Margo for a moment or two before saying slowly, 'Wasn't it the O'Connells you were after?'

'That's right. We were wonderin' what you could tell us about them.'

Libby piped up, her voice cracking with nerves. 'We know they're not whiter than white, because we've been to their house . . .'

The woman's brow rose swiftly. 'They're back?'

'Only my friend's aunt and her husband,' said Margo.

The woman pulled a dubious face. 'You do surprise me. I'd have thought we'd have heard summat by now if she was back in town.'

Libby grimaced. 'We realise they must have a bad reputation . . .'

The woman was about to speak when she appeared to have second thoughts, and turned her focus entirely on to Libby. 'If

I remember rightly, your friend here said you were related to Orla O'Connell. Is that right?'

'She was my mother, yes,' said Libby softly, 'until the war took her away from us.'

The woman's face fell instantly. 'Oh, dear. I'm truly sorry to hear that, luvvy.'

'I'm Libby and this is my friend Margo,' said Libby, hoping that the woman would introduce herself as well.

'Pleased to meet you, Libby. I'm Carla.' She hesitated. 'Excuse me for askin', but if you've spoken to your aunt, why are you here talkin' to me?'

'Because I can't ask my aunt certain questions, like why she fell out with my mother in the first place,' said Libby frankly.

Carla pulled a rueful face. 'I'm sorry, luv, but I can't help you there. And what's more, I'd be careful who you ask, cos you know what some folk are like. They love to gossip without findin' out the facts first.'

Relieved to hear nothing negative, Libby couldn't help but feel disappointed that she was no nearer to learning the truth.

'We wondered whether it was because of their dealin's,' said Margo outright.

'I don't know of any dealin's,' said Carla, her face perfectly blank. 'How do you mean?'

Not wishing to get her aunt and uncle into trouble, Libby was about to say that it didn't matter when Margo piped up again.

'We think they're dealin' in hooky gear—'

Carla shrieked with laughter, cutting Margo short. 'Whatever gave you that idea?'

Libby and Margo exchanged glances. 'Call it a hunch?' ventured Libby.

'I'm sorry, luvvy, but the O'Connells would rather cut their own throats than deal in dodgy gear.'

'Sorry,' said Libby softly. 'Probably lettin' my imagination run away with me again.'

Margo started to protest that she was doing no such thing, but Libby spoke across her. 'C'mon, Margo, it's time we were off.' She glanced at the woman. 'Thanks for all your help.'

Guiding Margo away from the stall, Libby lowered her voice. 'My aunt said she'd changed since losin' her parents, and that's what she must've meant. My uncle was probably dodgy from the start, and it was my auntie that kept him in place. Now that she's given in he's got free rein.'

Margo wrinkled her forehead doubtfully. 'Only she doesn't seem worried.' Seeing the look on Libby's face, she continued hastily, 'Sorry, Lib, but your aunt comes across as a strong woman, and she certainly seems to pull the strings when it comes to your uncle. I've seen some of the looks she shoots at him, and what's more he never argues back, but shuts up real quick.'

'So, what are you sayin', then? That they've successfully pulled the wool over everyone's eyes for years?'

Margo felt her cheeks redden. Her intention wasn't to upset Libby, but to help her see things from a truer perspective. 'Not at all. What I am saying is that your aunt might've been on the straight and narrow because her parents ran a tight ship, and now that they're gone she's in charge of the helm.'

Libby felt her heartbeat calm in her chest. 'I could see that,' she said slowly. 'In fact, I'd prefer to think that than anything else.'

Margo frowned. 'Like what?'

'Like we'd got hold of the wrong end of the stick entirely.'

'You've lost me.'

'It doesn't matter,' said Libby. 'I was thinkin' out loud.'

Glancing at the clock above the town hall, Margo quickened her pace. 'I hadn't realised how long we'd been down the market. We'd best get a move on if we want to get changed before we meet the boys.'

'Before we meet the boys,' said Libby. 'How good does that sound?'

'I knew from the moment I set foot in Liverpool that our lives were on the up, but I never thought it would be this good,' said Margo happily.

Entering the flat, Margo placed the kettle on the stove, whilst Libby walked through to the bedroom. 'Me neither,' she called over her shoulder, her voice slightly muffled as she pulled her work clothes over her head.

Margo joined her in the bedroom and picked up her hairbrush, glancing at Libby, who was ravelling her stockings between her fingers. 'I wonder what my old man would say if he could see me now.'

Libby pushed her toes into the first stocking. 'He knows you're alive cos you've written to him. If he wanted to know how you were he could write back, or jump on a train.'

'Which was my initial fear,' Margo admitted. 'But I guess I always knew he wouldn't come after me, because that would mean spendin' money, and there's only one thing he wants to spend money on.'

'He's a fool to himself,' said Libby. 'If he could only see what he was missin' out on—'

Margo interrupted. 'Dad would see a break from gamblin' as missin' out. We have different perspectives.'

'It's a shame some people can't see what's in front of them.'

Margo fetched the kettle and poured the warm water into the bowl for Libby to wash her face and neck. 'You're my family now.'

'Sisters,' said Libby. 'Bit like me and Emma before she went to Ireland. I wish I had her address, so that I could write and tell her what's happening.'

'If I could get my hands on the man that took your parents' belongings—'

Interrupting in her turn, Libby spoke thickly as she rubbed her face with a hand towel. 'You and me both! He didn't just take things; he took my life. Because of him, I'll probably never see Emma again.' She sank down onto her bed. 'She'd be mortified if she knew about Mum and Dad.'

'I hope he gets his comeuppance,' said Margo, dipping her flannel into the water.

'I doubt it,' said Libby. 'Look at my Uncle Tony; he always lands on his flamin' feet.'

Margo tutted under her breath as she pulled her frock over her head. 'He'll come unstuck one of these days, you mark my words. I'm a great believer in karma.'

'I hope you're right.' Libby looked at her reflection in the mirror. The blue frock fitted her top half like a glove, with the skirt fanning out from the waist. Twisting from side to side, she admired the skirt as it swirled around her.

'You look beautiful,' said Margo. Pulling her hair to one side, she waited for Libby to fasten the buttons on her dress. 'Too good to just be goin' to Lyons.'

'Is that a hint?'

Margo waited until Libby had fastened the top button before turning to face her. 'Of course it is! You know how much Tom and I love to dance, especially when you and Jack are with us.'

Libby grinned. 'I don't think Tom particularly cares who else is there, as long as he's with you.'

'Cos I only have eyes for you!' sang Margo. 'That's what Tom always says.'

'And that's the way it should be,' said Libby. She watched her friend clip her hair back from her face, whilst humming the tune beneath her breath. 'I'm so pleased you got to find out what a real relationship's like. Most people follow the pattern their parents set out for them, but not you – thank the Lord.'

Margo took her handbag and checked her purse for money. 'I dread to think what would've happened to me had I stayed in London.' A small shiver ran through her body as she envisaged herself married to a man similar to her father. 'Talk about a fate worse than death.'

Libby turned to face her. 'Ready?'

'I was born ready when it comes to dancin',' said Margo.

As the girls headed out of the flat and across town, Libby glanced at the skies above them. 'Fingers crossed there's no bloomin' air raids. I don't fancy spendin' my first night with Jack down a smelly, overcrowded bunker.'

'Don't you fret; I've got a good feelin' about tonight,' said Margo confidently.

'I hope you're right,' said Libby, 'I've been lookin' forward to Jack's arrival for so long, I'd hate for summat to go wrong at the last minute.'

'At least we aren't in London,' said Margo. 'The way the Krauts are goin' at it, I'm amazed there's anythin' left.'

Libby shot her a sidelong glance. 'Do you ever worry about your dad?'

'Course I do. Cos even though he's never acted like one, he's still my father. But my bein' in London wouldn't make him any safer, so I try to put it to the back of my mind.' She laughed, but without mirth. 'I don't think he worries about me, though, cos he'd have written back if he did.'

'But how do you know that the worst hasn't happened, and that's why he hasn't written back?'

'Because I keep an eye on the news, and I read the papers, and whilst Blendon Row and the bookies are still standin' I know Dad's all right.' She pointed to the cafe. 'I can see them!'

Following her line of sight, Libby felt her tummy flutter excitedly. Hurrying towards the cafe, she could hardly contain her excitement, and once inside a sense of euphoria swept through her body as Jack took her in his arms.

Breaking from their embrace, Jack stood back. Eyeing Libby from the top of her head to the tips of her shoes, he let out a low whistle. 'You look fabulous!'

Libby blushed under his approving gaze. 'You're biased.'

'Maybe, but that doesn't take away from the fact that I'm courtin' a corker!'

'You'd not think she were from the same family as her auntie,' said Margo, as she glanced down the list of items on the menu. 'Chalk and cheese.'

'I'm more like my mother,' said Libby, somewhat thankfully.

'So might your aunt be, if she ever ran a comb through her hair or passed a flannel over her face,' said Margo, pulling a reproving face. 'I know we've said it before, but I'm sayin' it again. It never ceases to amaze me how people born in the same family can be so different.'

A waitress approached, and Libby promptly asked for a cheese and tomato sandwich, with Jack following suit. The orders taken, the waitress left them to their conversation.

'Talkin' of families, my dad said he went down the market the other day, and there was no sign of your Uncle Tony,' said Jack.

Libby rolled her eyes. 'He can't not show up, cos they'll give his pitch away, and that way he'd have bought the business for nothin'.'

'I think he only bought it as a front anyway,' said Jack, 'but he still needs it in order to keep the Bluebottles at bay.'

'If I'd've known he was goin' to let it go down the pan I'd have tried harder to persuade him to sell it back to me,' said Libby. 'I'd have even paid him on the never never if it meant I got it back.'

'Well, I'm jolly glad you didn't,' said Tom emphatically, 'else me and Margo might never have met.'

'You would, though, because Margo didn't wake up until not long before Liverpool.'

Margo disagreed. 'On my own, I'd have either hidden away until the train returned to London, or been arrested for stowin' away. I'd never have thought to hide in the mail sacks the way you did.'

'All good things happen for a reason,' said Jack softly. 'I'd never have met you had you not slid into the Thames, and you'd never have met Margo if I hadn't rescued you.'

Margo beamed. 'We're all here because of you, Libby Gilbert, and aren't I glad we are. My life is a thousand per cent better here than it was in London.'

'There's no such thing as a thousand per cent,' Libby chuckled, 'but I know what you mean. They say that every cloud has a silver linin', and my parents losin' their lives was the biggest, blackest cloud ever. If us all bein' together is because of that, then at least their passin' wasn't for nowt.'

Jack coddled her hand across the table. 'If I could bring your parents back, I'd do it in a heartbeat. I believe that if it's meant to be, love will find a way, and we'd have met up somewhere along the line.'

He leaned back as the waitress arrived with their food. 'Just what the doctor ordered!' exclaimed Tom as he took a bite out of his Spam and pickle sandwich.

'We have to keep our strength up for the Grafton,' said Libby, before being struck by a sudden thought. 'You will have time to go dancin', won't you?'

Jack nodded, stowing his mouthful into his cheek. 'The wagon won't be back to pick us up until around ten, so I've plenty of time.'

Margo's eyes grew round. 'But that's not even four hours!'

'Which is better than nothin',' said Libby. 'Besides, we'll have all the time in the world now that Jack's just across the water.'

'Talkin' of which, when will you be comin' into town next?' enquired Margo.

'Probably not for a few days,' said Jack ruefully, 'but I'm hopin' to get in at least once a week.'

Libby could've jumped for joy. The thought of seeing Jack once a week was heavenly.

With Margo desperate to get to the Grafton, they quickly finished their suppers and caught the tram to the other side of town.

'I forget all about the war when I'm dancin',' Margo told Libby as they handed their coats over to the girl behind the counter. 'It's like I haven't got a care in the world when Tom takes me in his arms.'

Libby slid her arm through her friend's as they walked back towards the boys, who were waiting for them by the bar. 'Aren't we lucky to have two such smashin' fellers?'

'We most certainly are, and it's good that they get on.'

'They do, don't they?' mused Libby. 'I wonder if that has anythin' to do with us bein' so like-minded?'

'Possibly—' Margo broke off, staring fixedly a little further along the bar. 'Is that your uncle?'

Libby followed her gaze. 'What on earth is he doin' in here?'

'I dunno, but I can't see your aunt anywhere.'

Libby watched Donny closely. She didn't know what he was up to, but whatever it was she suspected it would have nothing to do with dancing. Seeing him shake the hand of the man who had approached him and walk away, she spoke to Margo from the corner of her mouth. 'I might've guessed.'

'I wonder what he flogged him?' said Margo, who was standing on her tiptoes in the hope of getting a better look.

'Whatever it was, I'd bet a pound to a penny that it wasn't legal,' said Libby grimly.

At the bar, Margo addressed the boys directly. 'Did you see Libby's uncle?'

Tom and Jack both shook their heads. 'I can't imagine him cuttin' a rug,' said Tom.

'Oh, he definitely isn't here to dance,' said Libby. 'He was doin' business with that feller over there.' As one, both men turned to look down the bar. 'Don't look,' she squeaked.

Turning back, Tom glanced towards the barmaid. 'I wonder if she knows she's got fellers like that doin' business in here.'

'I hope not,' said Margo fervently. 'I've always thought of the Grafton as bein' a decent place.'

'Do you think we should tell her?' asked Libby. 'I'd want to know if I were her, and I bet her bosses would also be keen to know.'

'Unless they're in on the act, whatever it is,' said Jack.

The barmaid, seeing the girls talking to Tom and Jack, came over. 'What can I get you?'

'You see that feller, the one with the greasy hair at the end of the bar?'

'I don't think he's for sale,' quipped the barmaid, adding sarcastically, 'although he'd probably sell you his mother if the price was right.'

Libby arched a single eyebrow. 'So, you know him then?'

'I should think everyone knows Callum Haggarty, whether it be for good or bad reasons.'

Libby grimaced. 'Sounds about right. You know the feller he was with?'

'Donny?'

Libby and Margo exchanged glances. 'I'm sorry to say that he's my uncle,' Libby said.

The barmaid's cheeks instantly flushed. 'Oh. Sorry, I didn't mean to be rude or anything.'

Libby held up a nonchalant hand. 'Don't worry, we know what he's like, we just wondered if you did.'

'Oh, we know all right. If I had my way, they wouldn't be allowed to set foot through the door, but until they do summat other than chat, or give each other money, there's not a lot we can do about either of them.'

'I bet you wish he'd stayed in Ireland,' said Libby miserably.

The woman blinked. 'Don't you mean Blackpool?'

'No, definitely Ireland,' Libby affirmed. 'He moved with my aunt and her family.'

The woman tilted her head to one side. 'When was this?'

Libby shrugged. 'I'm not really sure.'

'Well, it must've been a long time ago, because as far as I'm aware he's only ever lived in either Liverpool or Blackpool.'

Libby stared at her, open-mouthed. 'I think you've made a mistake.'

The barmaid pulled a doubtful face. 'When I first started workin' here, I didn't have a clue who he was until one of the girls told me that the Murphys had only just moved back from Blackpool after gettin' themselves up to their necks in it here. Apparently, things got so bad they had to lie low whilst everything cooled down.'

Jack caught the barmaid's attention. 'Sorry to interrupt, but could I have two pints of mild, please, and two . . .' He looked to Libby, who was staring at Margo.

'Lemonades, please,' said Margo, keeping eye contact with Libby.

The drinks poured, the four of them went to find a table. Sitting between Jack and Margo, Libby stared at the bubbles as they rose up the side of her glass. 'Why on earth would she think that my uncle and aunt had been living in Blackpool?'

'Maybe she got them mixed up with someone else,' suggested Jack. 'Either that or they've lied to her pal about their past. Let's face it, they're hardly beyond tellin' people a few porkies, are they?'

'No,' said Libby slowly, 'but why would they lie about where they'd been?'

'Dodgy dealin's?' suggested Tom.

Libby lifted a single eyebrow. 'I thought the Irish were meant to be God-fearin'?'

'You must've heard of the IRA,' said Margo incredulously.

Libby rubbed her forehead, trying to ease the headache which was beginning to form. 'But why lie? Besides which, I can't really see them gettin' up to much when my grandparents were alive.'

Jack placed his arm around her shoulders. 'This is really botherin' you, isn't it?'

She nodded. 'But only because there's a whole ocean between here and Ireland. It's not as if you can get the two easily mixed up.'

'It's the Irish sea,' said Tom informatively.

'Sea, ocean, whatever it is, it's a vast body of water and the Irish are a different nation.'

Jack got to his feet. 'Shan't be a mo.'

Libby laid a hand on his arm. 'I hope you're not thinkin' of approachin' that man?'

Jack chucked her under her chin. 'I ain't havin' you frettin' all evenin' when the answer could be sittin' a few feet away. Don't worry about me, I know what I'm doin'.' Without waiting for a reply, he marched away.

'What on earth is he goin' to ask him?' hissed Margo.

Tom pushed out his bottom lip. 'I'm guessin' he's tryin' to find out where Libby's uncle's been livin'.'

'But he's goin' to want to know why Jack's showin' an interest,' said Libby, half rising out of her seat. 'I can't imagine he'll be happy that Jack's pokin' his nose into his business.'

Tom made a gesture for Libby to sit back down. 'Jack isn't stupid, Lib. He knows what he's doin'.' Suddenly, Callum roared with laughter. Jack too chuckled, said something else, and walked back to join them.

'See?' said Tom. 'He's comin' back.'

Libby waited for Jack to sit down before leaning forward conspiratorially. 'What on earth did you say that made him laugh so much?'

Jack grinned, and broke into a thick Irish accent. 'I told him that Donny reminded me of a priest I used to know back in Ireland, so he did.'

Clapping her hands together, Libby burst into laughter. 'The thought of him bein' a priest is enough to make anyone laugh.'

'Understandable,' said Tom, 'considerin' Donny's battin' for the other team.'

Libby nearly choked. 'You what?'

Jack laid a reassuring hand on her knee. 'He means that Donny would be workin' for the devil.'

Libby giggled. 'I see!'

'So did you ask him anything else?' asked Margo eagerly.

'I didn't have to. According to Callum, Donny's never set foot in Ireland, never mind a church.'

Libby's face fell. 'So the barmaid was right, which means that they've been lyin' to me all along.'

'I'm afraid it does look that way,' said Jack ruefully, 'although I'll be darned if I can think why.'

'I'm goin' to ask them outright when I see them next.'

Margo looked worried. 'And when will that be?'

'I'll call there after work tomorrow.' Libby tutted irritably. 'You've all said that you thought they were hidin' summat, and that they're up to no good. Why on earth didn't I see it?'

'Because you were desperate to have a family,' said Margo quietly, 'and I think you did see it really, Lib, because I don't reckon you've ever fully trusted them, have you?'

Libby thought back to the times she had had reason to question the intentions of her relatives, and how she had gone out of her way to make them aware of her circumstances. 'But only because I thought they were after my inheritance,' she said. 'Once they knew I was potless, I didn't think twice about their integrity.'

'Are you sayin' that you do now?'

'Yes! Why else would they lie about their whereabouts? It's obvious they weren't in Ireland with my grandparents like they said they were, so why lie?'

'Maybe they had a fallin' out with your grandparents too, just like your mother?'

'Then why not say so? It's not as if I could've judged them, not after my own mother stayin' away all them years,' retorted Libby. 'I haven't a clue why they've told a pile of porkies, but I promise you I will find out.'

'Are you sure that's wise?' Margo hazarded. 'I shouldn't imagine they'll take kindly to bein' called liars.'

Libby rolled her eyes. 'Don't worry, they aren't goin' to bonk me over the head. Whatever the reason, it's nowt to do with me.'

'That's for tomorrow,' said Jack. Taking her by the hand, he led her onto the dance floor. 'Tonight you're mine, and if it's all right with you, I'd rather not spend it talkin' about the likes of them.'

She gazed up at the underside of his strong, clean-shaven chin. 'I promise I won't mention them for the rest of the evening!'

Sliding his arm further around her waist, he pulled her close so that there wasn't a sliver of light between their bodies. 'Good, because I want you all to myself.'

Libby rested her cheek against his chest as he guided her around the floor. She always felt safe when she was with Jack, and she was confident that he would stand by her, no matter what the following day's conversation might unveil.

It seemed to Libby that hardly any time had passed before Jack was telling her that it was time for him to leave. 'They don't like hangin' about,' he told Libby. 'If I'm not there, they'll leave without me.'

'You remind me of Cinderella, havin' to leave the ball before the clock strikes ten,' Libby chuckled. Pushing her arms around his waist, she continued on a more serious level. 'I wish you didn't have to go so soon.'

'Me too, but there's always next weekend,' said Jack. 'And the weekend after that, and the one after that.'

Libby gazed into his eyes, which twinkled down at her. 'I hope you stay in Kirby for the remainder of the war.'

'Me too,' said Jack, 'but nothin's ever certain, not in the RAF, and certainly not in war.'

Margo and Tom appeared by their side, with Margo pushing her arms into the sleeves of her coat. 'Ready when you are.'

'You don't have to leave early just because of me,' said Jack. 'I'll see Libby back to the flat, if that's what you're worried about.'

Margo stood firm. 'We came together, so we leave together.'

Tom offered his elbow to Margo. 'All for one, and one for all.'

Libby looked at the sky as they stepped into the cool night air. 'Not quite a bomber's moon, but clear skies always make me uneasy.'

'At least we're not in London,' said Margo. 'I used to hate seein' the moon when I lived there.'

As they chatted, they began the walk back to St George's Hall, where Jack would be meeting the wagon.

'Now that you're in the RAF, do you have any more idea than us as to what's goin' on with the war?' asked Margo.

Jack gave a brief, mirthless laugh. 'They don't tell us any more than what they tell you. Loose lips an' all that.'

Libby snuggled into the warmth of his body as he slid his arm around her waist. 'Surely it can't go on for much longer?'

'I hope not,' said Tom; 'it does seem to have eased off since Christmas. I'm hopin' Hitler's realised that he's bitten off more than he can chew.'

'You'd not think that if you'd seen London,' said Jack grimly. 'It's a lot worse than when Lib and Margo were there.'

Libby tightened her arm around his waist. 'I wish your dad could move up here. Not just because it would be nice to have us all in the same area, but . . . you know.'

Jack kissed the top of her head. 'I do know, and I have suggested it, but his whole business is in London. Movin' up here would be startin' afresh, and he thinks he's too long in the tooth for that.'

'Nonsense,' said Libby. 'My father was the same age as yours, and he was goin' to up sticks to Norwich.'

'That's what I told him, but he's adamant about stayin' put.'

Margo blew her cheeks out. 'There's no fool like an old fool.'

Libby gasped. 'Margo!'

But Jack was laughing. 'She's right though, Lib.'

'Your dad's lovely,' said Libby, 'and it's different for him to just up and leave when he's all on his own. Especially as you could be moved just about anywhere in the country.'

'I s'pose,' conceded Jack. 'But I'd sooner be in Timbuktu than London, if the likelihood of gettin' bombed was less.'

'Fingers crossed this war ends soon,' Libby sighed.

Jack pointed to a wagon parked up ahead of them. 'That's my ride.'

Libby tutted. 'Trust him to be on time.'

'Her,' corrected Jack.

Libby stared at the lorry open-mouthed. 'A woman drives *that*?'

Jack laughed. 'You'd be amazed at some of the things the Waafs do. I know I was.'

Margo was looking at the wagon admiringly. 'I wish I could drive; it must be wonderful to just take off whenever the fancy takes you.'

'You'd not get far with petrol rationing,' said Tom.

Jack turned to Libby and wrapped his arms around her waist, his lips brushing against hers as he kissed her softly. Hearing the driver honk the horn on her wagon, he broke away. 'I'll let you know when I've next got an evening pass, but it shouldn't be too long.'

She nuzzled her cheek against him. 'Even if it's only once a fortnight, it's much more than we had before.'

Kissing the top of her head, he slipped his hand from hers. 'Cheerio, Treacle.' Libby, Margo and Tom waited until he was aboard the lorry before waving him off and heading for home.

'I have a feelin' that life is goin' to be just perfect from now on,' said Libby happily.

'What about your relatives?' said Margo.

Libby shrugged. 'I've been thinkin' about that, and whatever their reason for lyin', I can't see how it can affect my relationship with them. It's probably a bit of somethin' and nothin'.'

Reaching the door to the flat, they were about to part ways when the air-raid siren sounded.

'You have to be kiddin',' snapped Margo to the world in general as they made for the nearest shelters. 'Don't they know that some of us have work in the mornin'?'

Tom smiled. 'I don't think Hitler's bothered about your work commitments.'

'Oh, ha ha,' said Margo, as she passed through the door into the shelter.

Libby found herself wishing that Jack hadn't had time to board the wagon, and said as much to her friends. 'He'd've had to shelter down here with us then, don't you think? I wonder where they'll go now.'

'Wherever it is, I'm sure they'll be safe,' said Margo reassuringly.

'I hope it's over soon,' said a woman sitting next to Libby. 'I can't remember whether I left the kettle on.'

'I reckon we all have those doubts,' said Libby. 'Luckily for us, we've just come back from the Grafton.'

The woman grinned toothily. 'I love a good dance, I do. The waltz was always my favourite. I could never get the hang of the foxtrot.'

Libby had opened her mouth to speak when an all too familiar sound pricked her ears. She turned round eyes to Margo, her lips parting. 'Oh my God, no.'

Fear dawned in Margo's eyes. 'Not here, surely?'

The woman frowned. 'What are you on about?'

Libby turned hollow eyes to the woman. 'We used to hear that sound regular when we was in London.'

'Bombers,' said Tom flatly, 'and lots of them, by the sound of it.'

The woman eyed them incredulously, certain that the youngsters had got it wrong, or at the very least were being overly dramatic. 'Don't be daft! They won't hit us the same way they do London.'

Libby glanced at Margo, who spoke up quietly. 'I'm sorry, but we were in London durin' the Blitz, and there's not a doubt in my mind—'

She was interrupted by a woman who came flying into the shelter. Her eyes like saucers, she stared wildly around her. 'I never seen nothin' like it,' she gasped, before sinking onto a bench. 'Too many to count . . .'

Margo gave a small whimper. 'Perhaps they're headin' somewhere further up the coast?'

But Libby was looking grim-faced. 'Why would they do that, when the docks are right here?'

Margo swallowed. 'What about Jack? He hadn't long gone when they sounded the alarm.'

'He'll be fine,' said Libby stoically, but the tears which pricked her eyes told a different story.

Tom held out his hands to Libby and Margo, and the three of them sat in silence as they listened to the distant thud of bombs growing ever nearer. Closing her eyes, Libby willed Jack to safety. *Not now*, she thought, *not again*.

It was several hours before the all-clear sounded, and Libby was one of the first out of the door. Blinking in the light of the phosphorus fires, she looked at the devastation around her. 'It's just

303

like London,' she whispered to herself, her heart sinking. She turned in the direction of the flat, only to see that her worst fears had come true. Silent tears tracking their way down her cheeks, she looked to Margo who was also staring at what remained of the flat. 'This is exactly like the day my parents died.'

Margo slipped her hand into Libby's. 'At least you've only lost things this time . . .'

'Jack,' said Libby suddenly. 'I don't know where he is.'

Margo wrung her hands nervously, but Tom stepped in. 'We'll telephone his base; they'll be able to let you know whether he's safe.'

Libby wiped away her tears as they headed for the nearest telephone box. Picking up the receiver she crossed her fingers, hoping that the line wouldn't be dead. When the operator's voice came down the line, she asked to be put through to RAF West Kirby. Staring blindly at the havoc around her, she asked the person who answered the telephone whether they could put her through to Jack, and felt her knees buckle as his voice came down the line.

'Libby! Are you all right?'

Sobbing, Libby spoke through her tears. 'I'm fine. We're all fine.'

She heard Jack give a heartfelt sigh of relief. 'Thank God for that. I've been that worried.' He went on to explain that their driver had stopped in the middle of the Queensway tunnel, thinking that it would be the safest place. 'We couldn't believe it when we come out the other side,' he said. 'It was like bein' in London again.'

'That's what I said,' said Libby. 'You don't suppose they'll come back, do you?'

Jack dearly wanted to assure her that the Luftwaffe wouldn't see fit to pay them a return visit, but he couldn't bring himself to give her false hope. 'I hope not.'

Libby knew it would have been wrong of Jack to give her a direct answer, when no one could possibly know what was around the corner. She pressed on. 'The flat's gone.'

There was an audible silence before Jack spoke, his voice hoarse. 'Thank God you weren't in it. What will you do tonight?'

Libby grimaced. 'See if we can stay at my aunt's, but I haven't told Margo yet.'

He gave a small chuckle. 'Things are bad enough without tellin' her that, eh?' Picturing the Murphys' house, which was a stone's throw away from the docks, he continued on a more serious note. 'They're a bit close to the docks there. Is there nowhere else you could stay?'

'Probably, but there are goin' to be a lot of people what've lost their homes, and they'll all be lookin' for alternative accommodation.'

'So you're probably better off sleepin' at your aunt's, even if it's just for the night,' conceded Jack.

'Unless her house has gone too,' said Libby, before quickly correcting herself. 'What am I sayin'? Things like that never happen to people like them.'

'In that case, you should move in.'

She rubbed her hand across her face. 'I'd better hope Mr Soo's wasn't hit, cos Margo and I are goin' to need money to replace everythin' we lost.'

'Don't worry about buyin' new clothes, cos I'll pay for them.'

'Thanks, Jack, but you've done far too much already,' said Libby. 'I need to stand on my own two feet.'

'You've been doin' that ever since I met you,' said Jack. 'Besides, if I want to buy my gel a new frock, I shall.'

The operator cut across, letting them know their time was up.

'Good luck with everythin', Lib. Let me know how you go, won't you?'

'I will. Ta-ra, Jack, and—'

She heard the call terminate before she had a chance to finish the sentence, and whispered 'I love you' before placing the handset down. As she turned to leave the phone box, she could see that there was a queue already forming.

She went over to Tom and Margo, who were waiting close by. 'I've told Jack that we'll be stayin' at my auntie's until we've found a place of our own,' she said grimly, much to Margo's horror.

'Surely there must be somewhere else?' pleaded Margo.

'You could stay at mine,' said Tom tentatively. 'I know we'd set tongues waggin', but needs must and all that.'

But Margo had already made up her mind. 'It's ever so kind of you to offer, Tom, but I seen what that old neighbour of yours was like when we first called round. Gawd only knows what sort of rumours she'd start if she knew we were sleepin' over.'

'Stuff her,' said Tom loyally. 'You and Libby are the only ones that matter.'

'That's lovely of you to say so, but Margo's right. Not only that, but I wanted to have a word with my auntie, so we may as well kill two birds with one stone.'

He pushed his hands into his pockets. 'The offer's always there. You don't need to ask.'

Libby tucked her arm into Margo's. 'We'd best go and see Mr Soo and explain what's happened.' Bidding Tom goodbye, the girls set off to their place of work.

Margo turned to Libby. 'I hope to God the laundry ain't been bombed. I don't know what we'll do if it has.'

'I know I've had my fair share of bad luck, but I hope that even I'm not that unlucky,' said Libby, crossing her fingers behind her back.

The girls were relieved to see that the laundry was still standing, and after a quick word with Mr Soo they hurried to her aunt's so that they could let them know what was going on.

'Did you see her face?' Libby hissed to Margo as they gingerly settled down for what was left of the night.

'She didn't exactly look thrilled. I'd love to be a fly on the wall when she tells your uncle that we've moved in with them.'

'I have a feelin' that it won't matter what he thinks; it's my auntie what wears the trousers.'

Margo glanced sidelong at her friend. 'I know you intended to confront your aunt over the whole Ireland and Blackpool thing, but do you really think that's wise when we're goin' to be stayin' here?'

'Don't rock the boat, you mean?'

'You must remember how angry she got when I first mentioned the trader sayin' that she'd moved to Ireland?'

'I'd completely forgotten about that,' said Libby. 'But you're right, she wasn't at all happy.'

'Exactly. I don't think they'll appreciate you pointin' out that they're a pair of liars, and as we've nowhere else to stay . . .'

'We haven't tried to find anywhere else,' said Libby, 'and the more I think about it, the more I'm uncomfortable sleepin' under the same roof as them, knowin' that they're untrustworthy.'

Margo stared at Libby. 'But we've always known that they're untrustworthy!'

'Only when it comes to business. I didn't think they'd lie to us. Besides which, I'm just as bad as they are, if I don't tell them I know the truth.'

'Principles are all well and good, but they don't keep you warm at night,' Margo pointed out.

'So what am I meant to do? Keep quiet, when I know we're bein' lied to?'

Margo shrugged. 'They've only lied about where they were livin' prior to comin' back to Liverpool. There could be a really good reason why they did it.' She hesitated momentarily before continuing. 'And whilst I believe the barmaid and that Callum Haggarty chap that Jack spoke to, has it ever occurred to you that your auntie might be tellin' us the truth, but lied to them?'

'But why would they do that?'

'Any number of reasons, especially if they were goin' away until things calmed down. Who knows what sort of trouble they might've got themselves into, livin' in the world they do?'

Libby mulled this over. Margo had a point; what's more, her relatives might not be happy if they knew that she had been snooping around behind their backs. She pulled a grimace. 'Perhaps you're right and it would be better if we gave them the benefit of the doubt.'

'Just because you aren't goin' to say owt doesn't mean to say you have to take your eye off the ball,' said Margo. She tapped the side of her nose. 'You'll learn more by keepin' your eyes peeled and your ear to the ground than you will if you confront them.'

'So, you do think they're up to summat?'

'I believe there's no smoke without fire, but if you confront them they'll clam up, and then you'll never learn the truth, whatever that may be.'

'The sooner we find somewhere else to stay the better,' said Libby, 'cos I don't like lyin' down with wolves.'

Chapter Eight

After several months of living with the Murphys, Libby and Margo had received the welcome news that there was a flat for rent on Walton Road. Wishing to waste no time in moving out, the girls had headed for Paddy's market where they hoped to buy necessities such as cutlery and bedlinen.

'Shall we have a look for some Christmas decs whilst we're here?' Margo suggested. 'I can't wait to have a proper Christmas tree, with lights and baubles.'

'Christmas!' cried Libby. 'It's only September!' Seeing the disappointment on Margo's face, she relented. 'I suppose it wouldn't harm to look, but it'll have to be a small tree. Anythin' too big and there won't be room for us round the table.'

Margo was jigging up and down in her excitement. 'I know we won't have anythin' as fancy as a chicken, but I'm still lookin' forward to me Christmas dinner. All I got when I was livin' at home with me dad was a thick ear for askin' why we wasn't havin' special food.'

'Not this year!' said Libby firmly. 'This year we shall have the boys round for lunch, and we shall sing carols and swap pressies and eat till we pop!'

'Sounds like my kind of Christmas,' said Margo, 'but we're goin' to have to be pretty frugal with our money if we're to buy decorations as well as everyday things – and next time there's an air raid I'm takin' everythin' with me. Losin' your home is one thing, but everythin' in it?' She abruptly stopped speaking as she listened to her own words. 'Oh Gawd, Lib, I'm sorry.'

'Don't worry about it,' said Libby. 'And you're right, it is hard when you lose everything, but if it's any consolation it's easier the second time round, because the stuff doesn't hold as many memories.'

Margo picked up a chipped mug from a crockery stall and inspected it for usability. 'I s'pose it was the first time to me, because I never had owt to call me own when I lived in London.' She held the mug up for Libby's inspection. 'What d'you reckon? I can't see the point in payin' for flawless when we could get hit again, can you?'

'Unfortunately not,' agreed Libby. 'That's what my father would've called throwin' good money after bad.'

Margo inspected the other mugs, selecting one to match the one she already had. She winked at the woman whose stall it was. 'Matchin' mugs with matchin' chips. If anyone asks, we'll tell them it's all the rage.'

Taking the mugs from Margo, the woman placed them in a brown paper bag. 'I like your thinkin'. Perhaps I should put a sign on the front advertisin' designer chipped mugs?'

Libby laughed. 'Whack a huge price tag on, and you'll get all the toffs flockin' to buy 'em.'

As the woman handed Margo her change, she referred back to their previous conversation. 'I heard what you was sayin' about losin' everythin' to the Luftwaffe, but now they've turned on Russia do you really think we'll see the like again?'

Libby pulled a hesitant face. 'Who knows? We moved up here from London, believing you'd never get the pastin' we did down south, but the May blitz showed how wrong we were.'

'It was bad,' agreed Margo, 'but let's face it, Lib, it was nothin' like it is down south.'

The woman paled. 'You see the newsreels, but I guess you never know unless you've lived through it, eh?'

As they spoke, Margo picked up a photo album which was lying next to some notebooks. 'Why on earth do people buy other people's photographs? I think that's plain creepy. Especially the really old ones, when they all looked like ghosts. Some of these look pretty recent, though.' She shivered as a thought entered her mind. 'They don't belong to dead people, do they?' She hastily put the album back on the table, whilst wiping her hands on her skirt. 'The thought of some poor soul havin' their personal possessions sold because the worst has happened sends a shiver down me spine.'

The woman picked the album up. 'A lot of the stuff we get here is house clearance. I agree that buyin' photos isn't for everyone, and I've no idea why some people do, but I guess it's a case of each to their own.' She flipped the book open and looked at the photos inside. 'Maybe they're hopin' to find someone they know.' She fell silent as her eyes flicked from the album to Libby. 'I don't want to put the willies up you or owt, but this girl in here doesn't half look like you.'

Margo wrinkled her nose. 'See? That's what I mean! Plain old creepy.' She paused, before continuing, unable to help herself, 'She's not wearin' clothes from the Victorian period, is she? No one wants to see themselves as a reincarnation.'

Libby chuckled as despite Margo's morbid curiosity she took the album from the woman's outstretched hands. 'My ghost from another life, you mean?' However, her tone soon changed as her eyes fell on the photograph. She cast the woman an accusing glance. 'Where did you get this?'

The woman shrugged. 'Like I said, it will've come from a house clearance. Why d'you ask?'

'Because this photograph is me with my parents,' said Libby, 'and it wasn't from a house clearance. This stuff was stolen from outside my parents' house right after they were bombed by the Luftwaffe.'

Gasping, the woman held a hand to her mouth and spoke thickly through her fingers. 'That's terrible!' She glanced at the rest of the stuff on her stall. 'If there's anythin' else of yours here, take it. I want nowt to do with stolen goods.'

'It needs reportin' to the scuffers,' said Libby stiffly, 'and so do you.'

Seeing the look of utter despair on the woman's face, Margo was quick to come to her rescue. 'I know you're angry, Lib, but this is hardly her fault.'

'It's sellin' stolen property,' said Libby, 'and that's illegal.'

'But I *swear* I didn't know,' pleaded the woman. 'If you saw the warehouse where they take everythin', you'd understand how it's impossible to know where half the stuff comes from. You just have to take people's word for it and hope that they're as honest as you.'

'And this stuff was taken nigh on a year ago,' added Margo. 'It obviously did a few laps of the country passin' from dealer to dealer before windin' up here.'

Having got over the initial shock, Libby relented slightly. 'Sorry for goin' off at the deep end, but the thought of catchin' the evil swine who took my parents' belongings . . .'

'And I can understand that,' said the woman kindly. 'Heck, I'd be the same if I were in your shoes, and I feel sick at the thought. I wish there was some way of tracin' who brought the stuff to the warehouse, but there's little the scuffers can do, especially not nowadays. This war has been like a pot of gold to the criminal fraternity.'

'I know,' said Libby sadly, 'but it's so unfair!'

The woman cast an eye over the notebooks and trinkets that had been next to the album. 'You might want to take a gander through the rest of the stuff. I got this lot in one lump, so there's every chance there might be summat else of your parents here.'

Libby handed Margo the photograph album and began to search through the rest of the items on the stall. Picking up the first notebook, she flicked through the pages, but found that apart from a few shopping lists there wasn't much in it. When she searched through the rest, however, it didn't take her long to find a series of diaries, all of which had been written by her mother.

'How can you be sure they're your mum's?' asked Margo.

Libby turned the diary to face her friend. 'Because she's written her name and our old address in the front of each one.'

The stallholder took a pencil and paper. 'What's your mam's name, luv?'

'Orla Gilbert,' said Libby promptly. 'Why d'you ask?'

'Because I'll put word out amongst the other traders to keep an eye out for anythin' that might have your mam's name on it. I've a memory for faces, so I'll likely as not recognise any photographs that I come across. I'm assumin' that you reported your belongin's stolen when you were in London?'

Libby nodded. 'I'll give the Bluebottles a call to let them know that I've managed to recover some of the stuff.'

'Righto. You do that, and I'll let the scuffers know this end.'

'They told me that everything would be taken far away from London to be sold on,' said Libby, 'and I never dreamt I'd see any of it again.' She hesitated. 'Won't you get into trouble if you report it?'

The woman shrugged. 'I doubt it, because I bought those items fair and square from the warehouse. If anyone should get into trouble it should be them, although it's highly likely they're also none the wiser.'

Libby felt her tummy jolt unpleasantly. The thought of her father's old bric-a-brac stall having stolen property on it had never entered her mind until just now. She said as much to Margo. 'It never occurred to me that the stuff we was sellin' might be stolen. But what if it was?'

Margo shrugged. 'Too late now.'

Libby sifted through the rest of the things on the stall, before placing four diaries and the photo album, along with some loose photographs, into her net bag. As she turned to leave, she gave the stallholder a sympathetic glance. 'Thanks for this, and please don't feel you have to report it. I'd hate to see you get into trouble for something when we all know that it will only come to naught. And I'm sorry about what I said earlier.'

'Thanks, luv, but like I say, I don't want owt to do with stolen gear. The scuffers know me of old, so they know I'm not the type to dabble in stolen goods. And you never know your luck, someone might just know summat that'll lead them to the real culprit!'

Thanking her once again, the girls headed on to the next stall; but Libby was only picking things over with half a mind, because in her bag she had words from her mother, and she couldn't wait to start reading.

Margo glanced meaningfully at the bag in Libby's hand. 'What do you reckon your auntie will say when you tell her?'

'I'm not goin' to,' said Libby, 'not until I've had a chance to look through the stuff myself.'

'But why ever not?'

'Because there could be a lot of answers between these pages, and my auntie might not be keen for me to learn the truth, whatever it is.'

Margo tucked her arm through Libby's. 'C'mon, let's go back. I can see you've lost all interest in shoppin' for the new flat.'

'Sorry, Margo. I can't stop thinkin' about the diaries, and the answers they could hold.'

Margo patted her hand. 'Don't give it another thought. She's not my mum, but I'm chompin' at the bit to take a gander when you're ready.'

The girls walked the short distance back to Jo's, chatting about how good it was going to be when they received the keys to their new flat in a few days' time.

'I understand that we have to pay your aunt some rent for stayin' with her,' said Margo, 'but I'm sure we're payin' the whole thing, plus more besides.'

'It pains me to admit it, but I rather think you're right,' agreed Libby. 'Our flat is much nicer than their house, yet we're only payin' half the rent that they say they do.'

'And we're nowhere near the docks – thank God,' said Margo. She gave an indignant huff. 'I bet the house goes back to rack and ruin in no time at all without us there to do the cleanin'.'

'Not to mention the cookin',' said Libby. 'Families are meant to look out for one another, not fleece each other as soon as the proverbial hits the fan.'

'Families, eh?'

'On one hand I've got an uncle who wants naff all to do with me, and on the other I've got an aunt and uncle who take me in, but only at a cost! Maybe my Uncle Tony wouldn't have been so quick to turn his back on me had I offered to pay his rent and do his dishes!'

'Family, but only at a cost,' mused Margo. 'Sounds a bit like my old man's idea of family, does that.'

'But what can you do, when they're all you've got?' Libby sighed.

'If your aunt and uncle were as bad as my dad, I'd say walk away,' said Margo, 'but at least they don't give you a good hidin' just because they feel like it.'

'That's true,' conceded Libby. 'Besides, I think they're not stupid enough to bite the hand that feeds them.'

'Your uncle looked proper disappointed when you told him we'd found somewhere to live,' Margo chuckled. 'I think he's goin' to miss comin' down to a bowl of porridge.'

'They always say the way to a man's heart is through his stomach,' agreed Libby. She looked down at the bag she was carrying. 'Can you do me a favour and catch their attention whilst I take this lot up to our room? I don't want them askin' what we've got, because I don't want to have to lie, but I don't fancy tellin' them the truth either.'

Margo tipped her forelock in mock salute. 'You can count on me. It's easy to send them scuttlin'. All you have to do is ask them what they're up to.'

Libby coughed on a giggle. 'To most people that's a polite way of sayin' hello, but to people like my aunt and uncle it's an accusation.'

They entered the house, and Libby was relieved to see that Jo and Donny weren't in. Taking the stairs two at a time, she sat down on her bed and pulled out the album. Browsing through the photographs, she was fascinated to see that her parents had seen fit to write the dates next to the photographs – most of which had been taken before she was born. She beckoned Margo over to take a look with her.

'This group are my grandparents, my parents, my Uncle Tony, and some other people I don't know,' she told her.

Margo peered at the photographs. 'I can't see your aunt and uncle in any of these.'

'Nor me. I expect they must have been somewhere else at the time. I'm sure they'll be in some of the others.'

But as they looked through it became quickly apparent that her aunt and uncle were in none of the photos. Scanning through the loose ones, Libby shuffled them into a neat pile and placed them inside the album.

'I'm beginnin' to think that my aunt and uncle had fallen out with my mother's side of the family way before my mother did,' she concluded.

'Unless they're camera shy and don't like havin' their photos taken?' suggested Margo. 'Which is unsurprising when you think of the circle of people they mix with.'

Libby pulled a reproving face. 'You mean they don't want any proof of their existence in case the scuffers come knockin'?'

'Could be. Especially if the photo links them to a time and place.'

Libby rolled her eyes. 'What a ridiculous way to live your life.' She placed the album under her pillow and picked up the diaries. 'I'll read them in date order.' She hesitated. 'Do you think it's all right for me to read them, or would I be delvin' into my mother's private thoughts?'

Margo screwed up one side of her face as she ran through this thought. 'When it's all you have left, and you're in need of answers, I don't see the harm. Perhaps if you start readin' summat you think your mum would rather you didn't, you could skip over that day?'

'Or you could read it first? That way you could warn me if you read summat you thought I shouldn't?'

Margo sighed. 'Only I'm not as good at readin' as you. You'd be better off askin' Tom, or Jack.'

'Jack,' said Libby promptly. 'He knows me inside out, so he'll know what's all right and what's not.'

'As well as bein' a good excuse to see him,' Margo chuckled, 'not that you need one, mind you.'

Libby beamed. 'He really is perfect, don't you think?'

'The two of you go together like fish 'n' chips,' said Margo. 'Bit like me and Tom.'

'If it weren't for the fact that I'd lost my parents, I'd say that my life was idyllic,' said Libby. 'Livin' with my bezzie, and both our boyfriends just a stone's throw away. In some ways I've been very fortunate.'

'Me too,' agreed Margo.

Libby pushed the diaries beneath her pillow along with the album. 'I'm goin' to nip out and call Jack's base to see when would be a good time to meet up; do you wanna come?'

'I'll stay here and wrap the things we've bought, ready for the move.'

Libby picked up her purse before heading for the telephone box at the end of their street with a spring in her step. While she waited for the operator to put her through to Jack's base, she crossed her fingers that he'd be available.

'Libby?'

She grinned. 'Hello, Jack.'

'Is everything all right?'

'Better than all right. I've found some of my mother's old diaries.'

She went on to tell him about their trip to the market and the discovery they had made there.

Jack gave a long, low whistle. 'Talk about a stroke of luck.'

'Wasn't it just? The only trouble bein', I'm worried I might read summat my mother would rather I didn't, so I was wonderin' if you'd read them first?'

Caught out by her suggestion, Jack stuttered, 'Eh?'

'I know it's a big thing to ask, and I don't want you to feel uncomfortable, but Margo's not very good at readin' and there's no way I want my auntie readin' them.'

Jack stepped up, as Libby knew he would. 'Don't worry, luv. If you want me to read them, then I will.'

'Thanks ever so. When are you next comin' into the city?'

'Not until Saturday.'

'I could always bring them to you?' Libby suggested. 'We could meet at the gate, and you could read them at your leisure.'

'I think that's a brilliant idea,' said Jack. 'How many years have I got to go through?'

'Four,' said Libby promptly. 'I've had a quick gander and the first one was around the time she met my father, which is why I'm thinkin' there might be stuff in there she wouldn't want me to see.'

'Gotcher! Bring them over Friday, around . . . what?'

'I finish work at eight, so I could bring them any time after that.'

'I shall look forward to it.'

'Thanks for doin' this,' said Libby.

'Anythin' for you, Lib, you know that,' Jack replied.

The operator cut across their call.

'See you on Friday,' said Libby hastily.

'Ta-ra, Lib. I love you.'

'I love you too—'

The call ended, and Libby replaced the handset before hurrying back to Margo to tell her the good news.

'I knew he would,' said Margo. 'That man would do anythin' for you.'

'Sometimes I think I'm the luckiest girl in the world!' agreed Libby happily.

Donny had mixed feelings as the girls left to go to their new flat. On one hand he was going to miss being waited on hand and foot, but on the other, he'd no longer have to live like a cat on a hot tin roof.

'I ain't goin' to miss jumpin' out of me skin every time one of the fellers starts to speak to you,' he informed Jo as the girls walked out of the court. 'We were damned lucky that none of them slipped up.'

'You worry too much,' said Jo.

'It's not down to me bein' a worrier,' said Donny indignantly, 'it's called sod's law. I'll be relieved when that girl finally admits the truth about the money, although I'm beginnin' to have serious doubts as to whether there *is* any money.'

'They paid our rent and more,' said Jo reasonably. 'How could they afford to do that if they hadn't a pot to dip into?'

'It's not like they looked as though they wasn't bothered about it,' said Donny. 'Far from it! I heard that Margo tuttin' on more than one occasion.'

If Jo was being honest with him, she'd have admitted that she too had begun to wonder whether Libby was telling the truth, but the thought that she had gone to all this trouble for no reason didn't bear thinking about.

'It was bloomin' Oisin what put the idea in my head in the first place, and what's more you agreed with him. If anyone's to blame, it's him.'

Donny rocked on his heels. 'Even if he's wrong, we still have information and that can be more lucrative than any inheritance. The gift that keeps on givin', as it were.'

'And just who are you plannin' on blackmailin'?' snapped Jo. 'In case you'd forgotten, Orla's dead.'

'Maybe, but it teks two to tango,' Donny grinned.

'You can't get blood out of a stone,' said Jo, 'besides which, we don't even know where he lives.'

Donny tapped the side of his nose. 'You can rely on me to sniff him out.'

Jo remained tight-lipped. Blackmail was all well and good in theory, but it was liable to get nasty, and if things didn't work out people could get hurt.

It was Friday evening, and with Libby having telephoned to say that she was on her way, Jack was waiting by the gate to his station. He wasn't in the habit of reading other people's personal information, and had it been anyone but Libby who'd asked, the answer would've been a resounding no. But how could he turn her down when he knew how desperate she was to have answers? Reading the diaries would make Libby feel close to her mother, but not if Orla had put down personal details about her relationship with Libby's father. He pulled a reproving face. *No child wants to read that kind of stuff about their parents*, thought Jack.

Seeing the bus slow down on its approach, he stepped in front of the gate, eager for a glimpse of his belle. Walking steadily towards the rear of the bus, Libby thanked the clippie before descending onto the road. She hurried over to Jack and gave him a quick kiss hello before handing him the bag containing the diaries.

'I've been dyin' to take a peek,' she confessed, 'but I knew I'd not be able to stop myself once I started, so I've been very good!'

'So, obviously you don't want to know the ins and outs of your parents' relationship,' said Jack, 'but is there anything else you want me to avoid?'

321

'Not that I can think of. I need to know why Mum fell out with her side of the family. My Uncle Tony too, if it comes to that.'

'Are you sure you wouldn't be better to leave sleepin' dogs lie? Your mother wrote these a long time ago; she might well've changed her mind since then.'

'Not about them, though,' said Libby reasonably, 'because if she had, they'd have made amends, don't you think?'

'I s'pose so,' Jack agreed. 'And we know she never changed her mind about your uncle.'

Libby gave a short burst of laughter. 'You can say that again!'

He looked up and down the desolate road before pulling her towards him, wiggling his eyebrows suggestively. 'There won't be a bus back for at least ten minutes. What do you propose we do to kill the time?' Libby blushed as she gazed into his eyes, which were dancing delightfully. He brushed his lips over hers. 'I suppose I can think of one thing.'

'Jack!' hissed Libby. 'Not when there're people around!'

Jack glanced back in the direction of the guard, who was feigning great interest in his paperwork. 'Don't worry about Curly. He's no peepin' Tom.'

Still feeling shy, Libby relented. As Jack's lips met hers she responded to his kisses, which were soft at first, but grew in passion as his love for her took over. Breaking away, he gazed tenderly at her. 'I wish we had longer.'

'We've got all day next Saturday,' Libby reminded him.

'I think we should go to the cinema,' Jack began, only to have Libby burst out laughing.

'I don't see why! We never get to see any of the films, cos all you wanna do is smooch.'

He chuckled softly. 'So you *do* see why, then?'

She gave him a playful slap on the bicep. 'Honestly, Jack, you haven't half changed since we first met.'

Tightening his arms around her waist, he cuddled her close. 'No I haven't. I wanted to kiss you the moment I pulled you out of the Thames.'

'You never did, though,' Libby mused.

'Because a gentleman respects a lady,' replied Jack, 'and no matter what it may have looked like, I knew you were a lady.'

She continued to gaze lovingly at him as he leaned in for another kiss. 'I don't know what I did to deserve you, Jack, but I'm really glad I did it.'

Hearing the return bus trundle towards them, Jack let out a soft groan of disappointment. 'Trust it to be early!'

Libby gave him a quick peck on the cheek before trotting towards the road, waving at the driver to stop. 'I'll see you on Saturday!' she called as she stepped onto the platform. Taking a seat by the window, she waved until he was out of sight.

Looking at the bag of diaries, Jack strode back towards his Nissen hut. *You'd better hope and pray there's nowt in here that'll upset Libby*, he thought to himself, *but Orla kept her family at a distance for a reason, and it can't have been a good one.*

Sitting down on his bed, he pulled out the four diaries, and placed them in order. There was far too much to read before he met Libby the following Saturday, so he decided he would skim through each one rather than read it in depth. Crossing his fingers, he prayed to learn no more than what time of day her mother awoke and what she had for breakfast.

It was the Saturday Jack was due to meet Libby, and, in short, he was dreading it. Orla had used the pages of her diary to express her innermost thoughts, as he told his father whilst talking on the phone.

'Honest to God, Dad, I don't understand why people feel the urge to spill the beans to a book what can't give them advice! It seems pointless to me.'

Gordon had laughed this off. 'It's what women like to do, son; men are far more practical. If a man has a diary it's to write reminders, or important dates, but women use theirs to bare their souls.'

'You're tellin' me!' cried Jack. 'I don't wanna know her innermost thoughts regarding Libby's father.'

'Then I should skip over those bits, but make sure you take note where they come so that you can advise Libby to do the same. That's why you're readin' them, after all.'

Jack had taken his father's advice and noted each page which he thought Orla wouldn't want anyone else to read. Had that been where it ended, all would've been well and good, but despite himself he found himself being attracted to the diary as a whole, which was beginning to read very much like a book. His curiosity aroused, he became intrigued with Orla's way of hiding information from anyone who might look between the pages. Jack found himself trying to figure out who 'he' or 'she' was, and that was how he fell into the trap of learning far more about Libby's mother than he had wanted to. But how could he tell Libby about his interpretation of what she had written? If he was wrong Libby might never speak to him again, but the same could be said if he was right. If he pretended to have not read certain passages, simply marking them up as pages Libby should skip, he would run the risk that she might read them one day, which would place him in danger of being accused of withholding secrets from her, or even lying.

Clutching the books beneath his arm, he waved to Libby, who was standing outside the cinema waiting for him. *You're goin' to have to tell her*, he told himself miserably, *cos it's not your secret to keep.*

Libby greeted him with a kiss, eyeing him curiously. 'What's up? You look like you've lost a pound but found a penny.'

He lifted his arm to show her the books. 'Can we go somewhere private?'

Libby's eyes rounded. 'Have you found out why Mum fell out with the others?'

Jack lowered his eyelids. 'I've read stuff which I don't think you should, but at the same time, it's not right that I know summat about your family that you don't.'

Libby nodded slowly as they walked in the direction of St George's Hall. 'We both know my aunt and uncle aren't exactly saints, so . . .'

But Jack cut her short. 'It's nowt to do with your aunt and uncle; in fact they don't seem to come into your mother's diary much, other than in bits like "I went to Blacklers with Jo".' They had reached the grounds of the hall, and Jack led her over to a quiet bench and sat her down.

'Does she mention my grandparents?' said Libby.

He shrugged. 'I'm assumin' so, because there's a few references to Mum and Dad not approving of her actions.'

'Whose actions? Mum's?'

'I think so.' He paused. 'It might be the way I was readin' it, but if I'm right, I think I might know why your mum fell out with the rest of the family.'

Libby gaped at him. 'Was it bad?'

He scratched the back of his head. 'That depends on whether I'm right or not.' As he spoke he withdrew the book from his satchel, and turned to the page which he'd earmarked before handing it to Libby. 'I don't want to be puttin' thoughts in yer head, so I think it best if you read this for yourself.'

Libby read the entry he'd indicated.

I can't believe we've been so stupid. I don't know what we were thinking of, but what's done is done, and it's too late to go back. He's adamant that no one will ever find out, but I know these things have a way of coming back to haunt you. I can barely look Reg in the eye, and it makes me sick to my stomach to think of my betrayal of the man who's always been there for me no matter what. If he knew . . . Libby frowned over the next few words, which were blurred by what she presumed to be tearstains. Unable to make them out, she continued to read. *The truth would kill him, and he'd never speak to me again. I can only hope nothing comes of this, because I don't think I could live with myself if it does.*

Libby looked to Jack, who was looking grim. He passed her another of her mother's diaries. 'This was written around eleven months later, around two months after you were born.' Libby's eyes fell to the words written before her.

Having Libby should've been the happiest day of my life, but instead it turned into the worst. Seeing Reg holding her in his arms, so happy to finally be a father, kills me inside, because I know he'd be devastated if he were to learn the truth. Mam's suspicious, so much so she's practically put two and two together. I've denied it, of course, but she knows I'm lying. In turn Reg is also getting suspicious, asking me what's wrong with Mam, but of course I can't tell him. I've decided to ask Reg if we can move down to London. I know that Mam will realise my true reason for wanting to be away from Liverpool, but what choice do I have? If I stay here, the truth will out, and what then?

She stared up at Jack, tears pricking her eyes. 'Oh my God.'
Jack heaved a sigh. 'I take it you think the same as me?'

'My mother had an affair.'

Jack wanted to reassure Libby that they didn't know that for sure and that it was easy to interpret something incorrectly when you only had one side of a story, but even he couldn't deny her mother's last words.

'It certainly seems that way, but she obviously regretted it very much. Which is why she moved away from Liverpool,' he said softly. 'So that your dad would never find out.'

Libby's eyes filled with unshed tears. 'My *dad*? And just who might that be, d'you think?'

Jack took her hand in his. 'He's the man who brought you up, Lib. I've no idea who the other geezer is in your mum's diaries, but he is *not* your father.'

Libby's face crumpled. 'I hear what you're sayin', but biologically—' She stopped suddenly as another pressing thought entered her mind. 'Do you think my auntie knows?'

'If she does, then your mother didn't seem to realise,' said Jack. He remembered the photograph album which he had yet to see. 'Does the album name any of the people photographed?'

'No,' replied Libby simply, adding, 'I suppose if you know who's in the picture, then why would you feel it necessary to write it down?'

'As a reminder?'

'Maybe.' She stared at the diary. 'Is there anything else I should know about?'

'Not as far as I know, but this is the last one we have, so there could be more out there somewhere.'

She rolled her eyes. 'God, I really hope not.' She gave him a sidelong glance. 'What do you think? Am I my father's?'

'Only your mum can answer that one, and you've read for yourself that even she wasn't sure. I guess the odds might be stacked against her, because as far as we know she didn't fall pregnant again, but that doesn't mean to say that you're not.'

'I wish I knew who the other feller was,' said Libby. 'Do you think he lives in Liverpool?'

'He must've. Because he was certainly around for your mother quite a lot.'

'Bloody snake,' sniffed Libby. 'He knew my mother was vulnerable, so he should've left her be.' She rested her head in her hands. 'Thank God my father never found out.'

'I think we can be sure that he didn't,' said Jack, 'because by all accounts she never saw the other geezer again, or at least not after movin' to London.'

Libby eyed him curiously. 'How do you know?'

'Simple. He's never referred to again.' He hesitated. 'I'm not condonin' what your mother did, Lib, but she must've been in a really dark place to turn to another man. Because there's not a doubt in my mind that she loved your father.'

'No one must ever know,' said Libby. 'Apart from Margo, of course. I'd never keep summat like this from her.'

'You're right. You need someone to talk to; a shoulder to cry on.'

'Margo won't let me dwell too much on what's past. She's always been a big believer in lookin' forward, not back.'

'At least you know why your mother fell out with the rest of her family,' said Jack. 'I suppose your grandparents kept your mother's infidelity close to their chest, which probably means your auntie *doesn't* know.'

Libby stared at Jack. 'Do you think that's why my grandparents moved? To avoid the gossips?'

Jack shrugged. 'Possibly. Although I'd have thought Jo would've wanted some kind of explanation as to why she was bein' moved to Ireland.'

'But she didn't go with them,' Libby reminded him. 'I know she says she did, but we know differently.'

Jack rubbed his fingers across the newly formed stubble that hemmed his chin. 'Unless she does know, and she's keepin' it a secret from you?'

Leaning back, Libby tilted her head to the sky. 'What a flamin' mess.'

'How do you feel? About your mum, I mean?' asked Jack tentatively. It was the one question he'd been fearing, but it was important to him that Libby forgive her mother, as he didn't want her spending the rest of her days twisting herself into knots.

'I don't know how to feel. I'm hopin' it was a one-off, and if my father never knew then I suppose no one got hurt. But I guess it's goin' to take time to sink in.'

'Try not to dwell on it, Lib. It'll only fester, and as you'll never know the truth, I suggest you forget about the diaries.'

Libby entwined her fingers with his. 'I love you, Jack Durning.'

Cupping her cheek into the palm of his hand, he kissed her softly. 'I love you too, Treacle.'

Libby knew that Jack was right, and that she shouldn't dwell on the past, but how could she move on knowing what she knew?

DECEMBER 1941

Hearing the sirens sound the alarm, Libby and Margo headed for the safety of the shelter.

'They ain't havin' me matchin' chipped mugs,' said Margo, holding them close to her chest.

Libby tutted as she followed Margo through the curtained doorway to the shelter. 'Honest to God, Margo, you could've chosen summat more precious than that!'

'I ain't got nothin' more precious,' Margo pointed out. 'What've you brought?'

Libby opened up the bag containing the photographs and her mother's diaries.

Margo stared at the diaries in particular. 'I'm surprised you'd wanna keep them.'

'Jack was surprised too,' said Libby, 'but when it's all you have left, you don't let go. Besides, I might learn summat else should I come across the other diaries, and that could make me see things in a whole new light, so I'll need this lot to refer back to.'

'I s'pose so . . .' Margo fell quiet as they heard the thrum of bombers passing overhead.

'Flippin' 'eck,' said Libby quietly. 'I dunno why, but I assumed it was a false alarm.'

'As did the rest of us,' said a woman close by. 'It's easy to get lulled into a false sense of security when the bombin's eased off.'

'Well, they can't bomb our flat,' said Margo stiffly. 'Lightnin' don't strike in the same place twice.'

Libby cleared her throat. 'Better make that thrice?'

The woman stared at Libby, open-mouthed. 'You poor bugger. Once is bad enough, twice even worse, but three times?'

'We're hopin' not,' interjected Margo, worried that the woman's words might tempt fate.

Everyone in the shelter ducked as the sound of distant explosions reached their ears.

'I keep sayin' it can't go on for much longer,' said Libby, 'but that Hitler's like a dog with a flamin' bone.'

'Surely we stand a better chance now that the Yanks are on our side?' said Margo.

'Aye, but it'll still take time,' said a man on the opposite side of Libby. 'Hitler's dug himself deep into the heart of Europe, and it ain't goin' to be easy to winkle him out.'

'We will, though?' said Margo, her voice full of hope.

''Course we will, queen.'

Reassured by his words, Margo leaned back on her bench. 'We've just got to sit tight and hope for the best,' she said to the room in general. 'As long as we don't give in, we'll be victorious, I know we will.'

It wasn't long before the all-clear sounded, and Margo and Libby were pleased to see that their flat remained unscathed. However, when they made towards it, they found their way barred by an ARP warden.

'Sorry, ladies, but you can't go any further. The whole of the street's been shut due to a gas leak.'

'The whole street?' cried Margo. 'But we only work up the road!'

He pulled an apologetic grimace. 'Sorry, but them's the rules.'

'How long for?' asked Libby.

'As long as it takes, but I can't see them lettin' you back in any time this week.'

Libby rolled her eyes. 'What are we meant to do until then? No money, no home?'

He shrugged. 'You could go to Hollybank Farm. They take people in what's lost their homes and jobs.'

'A *farm*?' said Margo, in withering tones. 'Great! From boot polish to poo.'

Libby shrugged her indifference. 'I'm easy. We can go to the farm, or stay with my aunt and uncle.'

Margo baulked at the very thought. 'The farm it is!'

'Life is an adventure,' said Libby, 'and I can't think of a bigger adventure than workin' on a farm.'

'It'll certainly be summat different,' agreed Margo, 'but we'll have to let Tom and Jack know where we are.'

'We can go and tell Tom before we . . .' she hesitated, then looked back to the warden. 'What do we do? Just turn up?'

'Certainly. There's always room at the farm.'

'Probably have us sleepin' with the pigs,' muttered Margo as they set off.

'You know the alternative.'

Margo weighed this up, before replying. 'At least we won't have to worry about the scuffers comin' round to cart us off.'

Libby chuckled darkly. 'Where's your sense of adventure? Go on – you tell Tom, and I'll phone Jack.'

Margo soon found Tom, who had been making his way home from work. When she told him of their change of address, he approved wholeheartedly. 'I wish you could stay there for the duration of the war. You'll be far safer on a farm than you will in the city.'

But Margo shook her head determinedly. 'I'm a city girl, Tom. Animals don't come natural to me, which is why I almost considered stayin' with Libby's auntie.'

'What do you think they're goin' to do, eat you?' Tom chortled.

She shrugged. 'From what I know, *all* animals kick, bite and do their business anywhere and everywhere.' She grinned. 'They remind me of my dad in a way.'

Tom roared with laughter. 'No wonder you were keen to get away!'

Down the road, Libby stood in the queue for the phone box, patiently waiting her turn. The phones were always busy after an air raid with people eager to reassure their loved ones that they were all right, and to check that everyone at the other end was safe and sound.

When it came to her turn, Jack's voice soon came down the line.

'Hello, Treacle. How's things your end?'

Libby explained the situation, ending, 'So, it looks like we're goin' to be farmhands, even if it's only for a little while.'

'Stay there as long as you can,' said Jack. 'The country is far safer than the city, which is why so many people make the journey night after night. Believe me, sleepin' in a stable is preferable to sleepin' under a hedge.'

Libby's jaw dropped. 'Is that what people are doin'?'

'It's safer under a hedge than under a tiled roof, although I dare say I don't need to tell you that.' He hesitated. 'Where did you think they were stayin'?'

'I don't think I ever thought about it,' confessed Libby, 'or at least not seriously.'

'I take it you're goin' today?'

'As soon as possible. Why d'you ask?'

'I've got the use of my friend's car, if I want it. I could run you to the farm if you like?'

Libby gave a small whoop of joy. 'Oh, Jack, that would be fabulous! Are you sure, though? I haven't got a clue where it is.'

'I'll have a look at the map. It can't be too far if they're takin' people in from the city.'

'How long will it take you to get to us? We could wait for you at Tom's.'

'Perfect. I'll be with you in half an hour, give or take.'

The operator cut across them to let them know their time was up, but Libby didn't need telling. 'See you soon, Jack, and take care. It's quite treacherous out there, what with broken gas pipes and what not.'

'Will do. Ta-ra, Lib.'

She replaced the handset and hurried round to Tom's, where she found Margo waiting for her. 'Jack's goin' to give us a lift! I didn't even know he could drive, but I suppose he has to, bein' a mechanic an' all.'

'I hope the car's big enough for all of us,' said Margo, 'cos I'd love it if Tom could come too.'

'I'm sure it will be,' said Libby. She stopped as a sudden thought came to her. 'I've only just realised – we're goin' to be spendin' Christmas on a farm!'

Margo burst out giggling. 'Do you think there'll be a donkey and a manger?'

Libby's face softened. 'I'd love there to be a donkey!'

'Why? They'll be as bad as all the other animals.'

'How do you know? You've said it yourself: you've never been near one.'

'Common knowledge,' said Margo. 'Ain't that right, Tom?'

Tom shrugged. 'I know as much about donkeys as I do about cows, which is nothin', save that one gives you milk and you can ride the other.'

'Well, I'm lookin' forward to it,' said Libby. 'It'll do us good to get out in the fresh air.'

'In winter?' said Margo doubtfully.

'It'll make comin' into the warm even cosier,' retorted Libby optimistically.

'You're really lookin' forward to this, aren't you?' said Margo, tilting her head to one side.

Libby nodded happily. 'I think it'll do us the world of good to have a change of scenery.'

'And what about your aunt and uncle? Have you told them where you're goin'?'

Libby clapped a hand to her mouth. 'I completely forgot.' She tutted audibly. 'I'm goin' to have to tell them, else they'll only worry.'

'Worry that they're missin' out on us slavin' over them,' said Margo.

Libby wagged a reproving finger. 'I'm sure that we mean more to them than that. And besides, they're the only members of my mother's side of the family who didn't know what was goin' on.'

'Doesn't make them decent,' said Margo. 'Sorry, Lib, but it doesn't.'

'I know.' She sighed. 'But back to my dilemma. If I tell my aunt where we're goin', she might try and persuade us to stay with her, and I really don't want to. On top of which, we can't afford to pay her with no money comin' in, so it might prove to be awkward.'

'You can tell her once we're settled,' said Margo, 'when it's too late.'

'Sounds good to me,' said Libby. 'And we don't have much of a choice if we're to get to the farm before dark.'

When Jack arrived a short while later, even Margo had begun to look forward to their new venture. 'Libby's been fillin' my head with stories of ridin' white horses, and feedin' baby lambs,' she said as she and Tom climbed into the back of the Daimler.

Jack chuckled. 'Aren't lambs born in spring?'

'It's nearly spring,' said Libby, determined not to put a damper on Margo's new-found enthusiasm. 'Do you know the way, Jack?'

'I took a look at the map, and it's relatively easy to get to.'

As they left the city, Libby admired the glorious countryside. 'I had no idea this was on our doorstep.'

'You should see it from the air,' Jack told her.

Margo leaned forward in her seat. 'Are you tellin' us that you've been in a plane?'

'The skipper of the Lancaster I service took me up so that we could try to identify a problem with one of the engines.'

Libby frowned. 'Isn't it safer to do that *before* takin' off?'

Jack laughed. 'Don't worry, it was perfectly safe, but I can understand it wouldn't sound that way to someone who doesn't know anything about aerodynamics.'

'I'd love to go up one day,' said Margo, her voice dreamy. 'Only not when there's a war on.'

'I take my hat off to the aircrew, I really do,' said Jack. 'It takes a lot of guts to fly one of them things on a normal day, so imagine when there's people firing bullets at you!' He blew his cheeks out. 'Bugger that for a game of soldiers.'

'I've often wondered what I'd do if I joined the services,' mused Margo, from the back seat.

Jack gave a short, mirthless laugh. 'The services decide what they want you to do, not the other way round. Unless you're rich, of course, and then you're straight in as an officer or summat similar.'

'And that's meant to be a privilege?' asked Libby. 'I think I'd rather be poor and keep both feet firmly on the ground than be shoved into a pilot's seat just because I'm loaded.'

Jack slowed, before turning the car up a long stony driveway. 'Here we are. Welcome to Hollybank Farm!'

At the top of the drive he pulled into the courtyard and parked near a small white cottage opposite a far more impressive farmhouse. He peered around him before asking Libby the question uppermost in all their thoughts. 'What now?'

Getting out of the front seat, Libby looked to the small stone cottage. 'The ARP said to report to Rose Cottage.' She walked smartly up to the front door and rapped a short tattoo on the knocker. After a moment, a woman of around her own age answered. 'May I help you?'

Libby explained who they were and what had happened, and the woman closed the door behind her while Margo, Jack and Tom got out of the car to greet her.

'I'm Adele, one of the land girls. If you come with me, I'll take you for a quick tour of the farm before taking you to the barn where you girls will be sleeping.' Seeing the look of dismay on Margo's face, she was quick to reassure her. 'Don't worry, it's not as bad as it sounds. It's dry, warm, and people have donated proper beds for you to sleep in. All we ask is that those that are capable help around the farm in return for bed and board. We've plenty of spare wellies, so you'll be all right for footwear, and we've also got plenty of dungarees for you to try on.'

Margo let out a low groan. 'Back to dungarees. I thought I'd seen the last of them when we left London.'

'You're welcome to wear your own clothes, but you'll soon wish you hadn't when you muck out the pigs,' said Adele with a bright smile.

They followed Adele around the farm whilst she pointed out the various livestock, with Margo's eyes growing wider with each pen they passed. 'It's like a flippin' zoo,' she hissed to Libby as they came to the last stable.

'I think it's wonderful,' sighed Libby. She stroked the muzzle of the large horse Adele had introduced as Goliath. 'I wonder if we could apply to be full-time land girls with proper wages?'

Adele overheard, and drew to a halt. 'You most certainly can! Hollybank's cryin' out for land girls.'

Margo wrinkled her nose uncertainly. 'Don't you think we should give it a go before jumpin' in with both feet?'

Adele waved a nonchalant hand. 'Don't worry, you don't have to sign up right away. There'll be plenty of time for you to do that if you decide it's right for you. To be frank, we don't want workers who don't want to work, so you'll only get in if it's what you really want to do.'

Jack walked over to join Libby. 'I must say, Adele, I think you're ever so lucky to be workin' here. It must be marvellous to work with colleagues that don't answer back.'

Adele burst out laughing. 'I suppose that's true, although they can be quite demanding when it comes to feedin' time.'

Margo heaved a sigh. 'I'm willin' to give it a go, as long as someone shows me what to do.'

'Don't worry, there're three permanent land girls here, not to mention Bernie the farmer's son, as well as his parents, so there're plenty of folk to show you what's what.'

Tom wrinkled his brow. 'Sounds as though you've got enough people already. Are you sure you need more?'

Adele looked to the farm behind her. 'Hollybank is huge. I've not shown you the fields and pastures because it would take too long.'

Jack placed his arm round Libby's shoulders. 'Are we all right to come and visit?'

'Of course you are, especially if you're willin' to lend a hand whilst you're here.'

'Count me in!' said Jack.

Libby was beaming. 'I think this might be the icin' on the cake.'

'I'll leave you to have a wander round,' said Adele. 'Come and see me when you're ready to get started.'

Bidding her goodbye, the two couples wandered from stable to stable, peering in at the various occupants. 'I can't think of anywhere I'd rather you were than here,' Jack concluded as they watched the ducks waddle across the yard. 'Safe from the Luftwaffe, but close enough for us to be able to see each other.'

Margo flinched as a bird flew out through one of the stable doors, narrowly missing her head. 'I think it's goin' to take some

338

gettin' used to, but I can definitely see the appeal of not havin' to worry about whether you've somewhere to come home to or not. And I've never lived in a place as big as that barn!'

'Quite a few of these beds looked slept in,' noted Libby, who had already placed her satchel down on one of them, 'so we shan't be on our own.'

Jack jerked his head, indicating that he'd like to talk to her away from the others. Slipping his hand into hers, he led her back towards Goliath's stable.

'I'm hopin' this new start will take yer mind off them diaries.'

'I don't think anythin' could do that,' said Libby ruefully.

Worried that the diaries could end up taking over Libby's life, he spoke his thoughts. 'But what's the point in worryin' about it when you'll never know the answers?'

'Only I reckon I might have a way of findin' out the truth,' said Libby. She glanced up at Jack. 'I've often questioned my Uncle Tony's reasons for not likin' my mother, but now I believe I have the answer.'

Jack stopped in his tracks. 'You think he knows about the affair, don't you?'

She nodded sadly. 'It would explain why he was off with her, and me, but fine with my dad.'

Jack blew his cheeks out. 'I'm sorry to say I agree with you, because it's the only thing that makes sense.'

'I bet Tony promised to keep quiet to save my dad from gettin' hurt,' said Libby. 'But he probably drew the line at playin' happy families, which I can understand.'

'So, what are you goin' to do?'

She drew a deep breath. 'I shall go to London and ask him if he knows who my mother was havin' an affair with.'

'But what if we're wrong, Lib? Cos we don't know for certain, and your honesty could let the cat out of the bag.'

Libby began ticking the list off on her fingers. 'Tony never used to spend Christmas with us, nor birthdays, but he was always happy to see me dad. Not only that, but if you remember, Tony said my father wasn't who I thought he was, and asked me why I thought I was an only child.'

Jack held a hand to his forehead. 'Oh, my Gawd.'

'And when I told him how me mum had been right about him, he said I didn't have a clue what my mother was really like.' She shook her head. 'Knowin' what he knew would be enough to get anyone's goat. You could tell at the time that he was itchin' to say summat, and he nearly did. I reckon he only held back out of respect for me dad. It also explains why he didn't want me to stay with him, and why he didn't include me in the business. The way he sees it, if Dad's not my father, I have no right to the business *or* the family name.'

'If you're right, then what makes you think Tony will tell you who your father *could* be? Cos I'm guessin' Tony ain't his number one fan, whoever he is.'

'I never thought I'd say this, but I want to apologise to Tony on my mother's behalf and to let him know that I understand why he is the way he is. It must've been awful knowin' the truth but not sayin' owt, and this will be his chance to get everythin' off his chest.'

He placed his arm around her shoulders. 'Bleedin' hell, Lib, as if you haven't been through enough. And there was me worryin' about rushin' things.'

'Rushin' things?' she echoed.

He squeezed her shoulders. 'I know it's not even been a year since your folks passed, which is why I've been tryin' my best to keep a lid on my feelin's, but each time there's an air raid I worry that you're not goin' to be lucky this time.'

'You mean I've been lucky before?' asked Libby in disbelief.

'You're alive, Lib. Stuff the buildin's; they're just brick and mortar. You're what counts.'

She felt a warm glow as his hands slipped around her waist. 'I honestly don't think you'll have to worry now that we're here,' she said.

'That's if Margo stays,' said Jack. 'What will you do if she wants to leave?'

Libby pulled a rueful face. 'Go with her. I'd not see Margo on her own in the city.'

'Exactly.'

She gazed at him affectionately. 'You said summat about not rushin' things. What did you mean by that?'

Jack licked his lips before plunging his hand into his pocket and drawing out a small jewellery box. 'This was my mum's engagement ring, and I'd like it to be yours.'

Libby stared at the ring, her eyes rounding. 'What are you sayin'?'

'I'm askin' you to marry me,' said Jack.

Libby stared at the man who had pulled her from the jaws of death. The man who fell on his sword to defend her honour, even though he barely knew her. The man that followed her halfway across the country so that he could make sure she came to no harm, and who broke the news of her mother's infidelity so calmly she didn't hate her mother for it. Libby might be young, but her circumstances had made her grow wise beyond her years. She didn't have to think about the answer.

'Yes!' she cried.

Giving a small whoop of joy, Jack pushed the ring onto her finger, and the two gazed down at the circle of gold which fitted her like a glove. 'We're meant to be,' said Jack softly. 'It's no coincidence that my mother's engagement ring fits you perfectly.'

'When I think of all the things that brought us together, it's hard not to believe I have someone watchin' over me.'

Jack smiled before kissing her softly. 'I think we both do. And if you want to learn the truth about your father, then I shall be with you every step of the way.'

She hugged him close. 'Together?'

'Always!'

Dear Reader,

This year has simply flown by and I can't believe Christmas is upon us and that you're holding my latest novel, *Winter's Orphan*, in your hands.

The idea for Libby's story came about on one of my many trips to London. I've always been fascinated with the city's rich history and iconic settings, and so decided to set my latest novel in the infamous street market known as Petticoat Lane, so called because rumour had it the people would steal your petticoat down one end of the market and sell it back to you at the other! Indeed, it was a place where police officers feared to tread, but with hard work and determination, the stallholders turned the reputation of the market around, and it became a fashionable place for folk to do their shopping.

As I was writing *A Family Secret*, the last book in this trilogy, I had to marvel at Libby's ability to cope with whatever life throws her way. Always overcoming the many hurdles in her path, she really is a shining example of how strong women can be when facing life's adversities!

I loved writing this book, and I hope you enjoy it just as much!

Warmest wishes,

Holly Flynn xx

Read on for an
exclusive extract of

A FAMILY
SECRET

AVAILABLE TO
PRE-ORDER NOW

CHAPTER ONE

Despite their restless night, Libby and Margo were up betimes the following morning to milk the cows and put them out to pasture, before continuing with the rest of their chores.

'I'm sure the pigs would prefer it if we left the muck be,' said Libby as she transferred the dirty straw from her fork to the wheelbarrow. 'Why else would they say "happy as a pig in muck"?'

Margo had opened her mouth to agree with her friend, when Adele came racing into the stable. Hastily checking to make sure that she wasn't being followed, she closed the door before turning to the girls, wide-eyed.

'You're not going to believe what I've just heard!'

Libby's face lit up expectantly. 'Have we won the war?' she asked, her fingers crossed.

Adele grimaced apologetically. 'I'm afraid not. I'm talking about Suzie and Bernie having a blazing row in the milking shed just now. He was calling her all sorts, saying that she was an evil little bitch, and a backstabber, and that he should chuck her out on her ear.'

Libby was shocked to hear that Bernie had behaved in such an ungentlemanly way, and said as much to Adele, adding, 'What on earth has Suzie done to make him act in such a manner? I know she can have a bit of an attitude with some of the girls, but I thought she and Bernie got on like a house on fire.'

'They do – or rather, she did,' corrected Adele, 'and it's because of her attitude with the land girls – or Roz in particular – that everything's gone pear-shaped.'

'Why Roz?' asked Margo curiously. 'She seems nice enough to me.'

'Me too,' agreed Libby.

'That's because she is,' said Adele. 'Suzie's angry at Roz because she thinks Roz is in cahoots with her mum.'

'Has this got summat to do with Suzie thinkin' her mum was dead before she came to Hollybank? Cos that's hardly Roz's fault,' said Margo as she peered through the top half of the stable door.

'It's more complicated than that,' said Adele. 'You see, Suzie's father – Callum – is a right nasty piece of work, and when Joyce disappeared, the whole community – including Suzie and her gran – thought that he'd thrown one punch too many and got rid of the evidence, as it were.'

'He obviously hadn't though,' Margo pointed out. 'As she's alive and well, and here at Hollybank!'

'Only because Joyce ran away before he had the chance,' said Adele.

'I don't blame her,' said Libby, moving the wheelbarrow to the far side of the stable. 'Better that than a one-way trip to the bottom of the Mersey.'

Adele agreed before continuing in hushed tones. 'Did you know that Suzie's gran died during the bombings?'

'Joyce said summat about it when we first arrived at the farm,' confirmed Libby.

'Well, from what I've just overheard, Callum was the one responsible for the gran's death . . .'

Margo gasped out loud, but Libby was sceptical.

'You can hardly accuse Callum of foul play if it's the Luftwaffe that took her out,' she said fairly.

'Under normal circumstances I'd agree with you, but Suzie reckons her dad forced her gran to stay behind in case someone tried to rob his loot while they were sheltering from the air raid.'

Libby stared at her aghast. 'Well, that's a different kettle of fish entirely. If it's true then Suzie's right: he as good as murdered his own mother.'

'Evil – there's no other word for it,' breathed Margo, 'and, considerin' what her father's like, I don't see why Suzie's angry with her mother for runnin' away.'

'She probably felt abandoned, and I can't say as I blame her,' said Libby. 'But these things are rarely black and white, and I'm sure there's a perfectly good explanation for Joyce leaving her behind.'

'I suppose she must've been desperate,' said Margo, adding

curiously, 'What I don't understand is why Suzie singled out Roz in particular.'

'That's a much bigger story, which is best told from the beginning,' said Adele. She went on to tell the girls how she had met Roz and Felix whilst waiting to board the ferry which would take them from Holland to England.

'I didn't know you were a Jewish refugee!' Margo cut in abruptly. 'You don't sound in the least bit German to me.'

'That's because I'm not; I'm English born and bred. My father was sick of not having permanent employment so he moved us out to Germany, where he was promised regular work. I hated it at first because I missed my friends, but I soon made new ones and, given time, I grew to love my new life. Indeed, everything was perfect until *he* came to power. I was too young to understand why our neighbours were concerned about the new leader, especially given my parents' optimism that things couldn't be as bad as they seemed. But when people began smashing the windows of Jewish shopkeepers, it became clear that we were in real danger. My parents were desperate to get me back to England but reluctant to travel as a family for fear that the Nazis might accuse them of being spies – the soldiers would use any excuse to cart you off to one of their camps – so they agreed to travel when it was safe to do so.'

Libby stared at Adele, horror-struck. 'So where are your parents now?'

Adele shrugged. 'As far as I know they're still in Germany, but I try not to think about it too much, because I don't like to get my hopes up, or imagine the worst.' Her features darkened as she fell momentarily silent before pressing on. 'Where was I? Oh yes, the ferry! I began chatting with Roz and Felix and that's when I learned that Roz wasn't meant to be on the Kindertransport.'

'How come?'

'Her parents had visas to get out of the country legally, but they were involved in a car crash on the way to the station, and when Roz came to, she found herself on board a train with no knowledge of her parents' whereabouts.'

Libby leaned against the fork handle. 'Poor Roz, she must've been terrified.'

'She was, but she's made of stern stuff – she'd have to be to put up with Suzie's family.'

Margo rubbed her brow with the back of her hand. 'How on earth did she end up with them?'

'Slave labour,' said Adele simply. 'The Haggartys saw the refugees as a good way of making money for nothing.'

'That man really is the lowest of the low,' snapped Libby. 'How could anyone prey on innocent children like that?'

'It's more common than you'd think; there were many taken in like Roz – Felix and I were the lucky few.'

'If Roz was livin' with the Haggartys, how come she wound up as a land girl?' asked Libby curiously.

'Luckily for Roz, Callum chucked her out.'

'How come?'

'She's no idea, but she's just glad he did, because it gave her an opportunity to join the land army with her friend Mabel. They started off working at Glasfryn Farm high up in the Welsh mountains, where Mabel still works, but with Hollybank being desperately short on land girls, Roz came to us.' She arched a single eyebrow. 'Bernie fell for Roz as soon as she arrived, but Roz was in love with Felix, and that was the end of that – until Suzie arrived.'

'What's Suzie got to do with the price of fish?'

'As you can imagine, it came as a huge shock to find that her mother was still alive, but when she saw that Roz was also at the farm, she got it into her head that they were laughing at her behind her back.' She heaved a sigh. 'The silly girl stormed off, vowing never to return, leaving Joyce in bits.'

'What made her come back?' said Libby.

'She had nowhere else to go,' said Adele simply. 'Which is why she came to Hollybank in the first place.'

'It must've been a bitter pill to swallow, comin' back when she'd made such a dramatic statement,' supposed Margo.

'She certainly didn't want anything to do with any of us,' said Adele, 'which is why she insisted that Bernie be the one who showed her the ropes, or she really would leave for good.'

'But that's ridiculous!' cried Margo. 'In fact, I'm surprised he agreed.'

'Ah, but Bernie only agreed because Roz persuaded him to and Roz only did that because Joyce couldn't bear to lose her daughter after only just getting her back.'

'Good job he was sweet on Roz,' said Margo. 'I bet he wouldn't have agreed otherwise.'

'And therein the trouble lies,' said Adele ruefully. 'You see, Bernie thought that by doing this favour for Roz, he and she might be in with a chance of forming a relationship.'

'Even though he knew Roz was in love with Felix?' asked Libby somewhat disapprovingly.

'I'm afraid it's not as straightforward as that,' said Adele. 'You see, there did come a time when it looked as though Roz and Felix's relationship was on the rocks, something which Bernie knew about – and I rather think he hoped things might swing in his favour if he and Roz spent some time alone.'

'Unfortunate,' conceded Libby, 'but that was hardly Suzie's fault.'

'Only it was – because Suzie knew how keen Bernie was on Roz, and she was the one who led him to believe that he could win her heart if he headed her off at the station this morning.'

'But isn't Roz going to spend Christmas with her pal Mabel?' said Libby, a line creasing her forehead.

'Along with Felix,' said Adele, nodding darkly.

Margo's jaw dropped as the realisation dawned. 'She set him up!'

'Hook, line and sinker.'

'Poor Bernie! No wonder he's angry. He must've felt a real fool.'

'So that's why he threatened to chuck her out on her ear,' said Margo.

'Yes, but that was before he heard everything that Suzie had been through,' said Adele.

'It's Roz I feel sorry for,' said Libby. 'She was only tryin' to do the right thing.'

'Exactly what I was thinkin',' agreed Margo. 'Why be so spiteful to Roz?'

'Jealousy, simple as.'

'Of what?' cried Libby

'Roz!' said Adele. 'She might have lost everything when she

came to this country, but in Suzie's eyes, Roz had everything she didn't.'

'Like what?' asked Libby, who could hardly believe that anyone could be jealous of a refugee.

'She had loving parents who had moved heaven and earth to get her to safety, and good friends who stuck by her through thick and thin, which was a lot more than Suzie had.'

'I s'pose if you put it that way,' said Margo, adding, 'Where's Suzie now?'

'She's gone to the station to see if she can patch things up between Roz and Felix.' Adele breathed out a staggered sigh. 'I hope she's successful cos Roz and Felix have been through too much to risk losing it all over some petty act of jealousy.'

Libby glanced fleetingly at Margo. 'And you thought livin' on a farm was goin' to be borin'!'

'We'll certainly have a lot to tell the boys when they pick us up later this evenin'. Talkin' of which, we'd best get a move on if we're to finish on time.'

'And I'd better get back to work if I don't want people to think that I'm standing round gossiping! Even though I am . . .' said Adele. 'See you later, girls.'

The girls bade her goodbye before returning to the task at hand.

'We never had owt as excitin' as this happen when we were workin' down the laundry,' said Libby. 'The closest we came to a scandal was when we found that pair of gentleman's undergarments in the widow Thompson's washin'.'

Margo grinned. 'Poor mare blushed to the roots of her hair when I asked if she knew whose they were.'

'It didn't help matters that you couldn't keep a straight face,' said Libby, adding, 'and we never did find out who they belonged to.'

'Rumours and gossip are only excitin' if you're not the one who's bein' talked about,' said Margo. 'I bet Suzie doesn't find any of this in the least bit excitin'.'

Libby put the last of the muck into the barrow and rested the fork on top. 'Probably not. Mind you, it does explain her petulant attitude when it comes to her mum and the rest of the girls. I know she's rushed off to see if she can fix things between Roz and Felix, but

do you think she only did that in order to smooth things over with Bernie?'

'It does seem a tad fishy to have had such a big change of heart in a relatively short space of time,' agreed Margo.

'Or maybe hearin' a few home truths has made her realise how unreasonable she was bein'.'

'Possibly,' said Margo as she closed the stable door behind them. 'Funny thing is, if someone were to ask which one I thought to be the refugee between Roz and Suzie, I'd have picked Suzie every time.'

'Because she walks around lookin' like she's found a penny but lost a pound,' said Libby as they began to walk toward the muckheap.

'Exactly! Which doesn't make sense considerin' she found her mother to be alive and well, whereas Roz has no idea if her parents are dead or alive.'

Libby pushed the barrow up the plank and tipped the contents onto the top of the muckheap. 'If you look at things from her point of view, it's easy to see how she could feel as though Joyce had deserted her, made a fool of her even. And seein' Roz with her mum probably exacerbated the situation.'

'Roz had everythin', includin' Suzie's mum,' said Margo. 'I suppose that does make sense.'

'Believin' yer mother to be dead for all them years must've been dreadful, especially if you think your own flesh and blood was the one that done her in. Seein' her years later, not only alive and well, but livin' a lovely life on a farm in the heart of the country must've been a real kick in the teeth.'

'Only that wouldn't have been how it was for Joyce at all,' said Margo. 'It must've been heart-wrenchin' for her to leave Suzie behind.'

Libby wheeled the barrow back down and they headed towards the rest of the stables. 'I hope Suzie forgives her mum, cos she's not the one Suzie should be angry with.'

'From what Joyce said, it sounds as though their relationship is well on the road to recovery,' said Margo. She jerked her head in the direction of the barn. 'C'mon, let's have some lunch before we start on the afternoon chores.'

WET NELLY

This traditional Liverpudlian treat is somewhere between
a bread pudding and a Nelson cake (Lancashire fruit cake)
but is moister than either. The recipe was sent to me
by Katie Flynn reader, Megan Ratcliffe.

INGREDIENTS

- Loaf of white bread (day-old bread is fine)

- 100g butter

- 140g brown sugar

- 3/4 litre warm milk

- 2 tsp mixed spice

- 3 medium eggs

- 500g mixed fruit

METHOD

1. Cut the crusts off the bread and slice into chunky squares.
Soak bread in milk for at least 4 hours or overnight.

2. When fully soaked, add all other ingredients, mix together well
and pour into a greased deep-sided roasting tin.

3. Bake at 180°C (160°C fan/gas mark 4) for approximately
1 hour–1 hour 15 minutes, until soft but springy to touch.

4. Serve hot with custard or cold with a cup of tea.

KATIE FLYNN

If you want to continue to hear from the
Flynn family, and to receive the latest news about
new Katie Flynn books and competitions,
sign up to the Katie Flynn newsletter.

Join today by visiting
www.penguin.co.uk/katieflynnnewsletter

Find Katie Flynn on Facebook
www.facebook.com/katieflynn458